WHEN THE SAINTS

WHEN
THE
SAINTS

DAVE DUNCAN

TOR®

A TOM DOHERTY ASSOCIATES BOOK
NEW YORK

This is a work of fiction. All of the characters, organizations, and events portrayed in this novel are either products of the author's imagination or are used fictitiously.

WHEN THE SAINTS

Copyright © 2011 by Dave Duncan

Edited by Liz Gorinsky

A Tor Book
Published by Tom Doherty Associates, LLC
175 Fifth Avenue
New York, NY 10010

www.tor-forge.com

Tor® is a registered trademark of Tom Doherty Associates, LLC.

Library of Congress Cataloging-in-Publication Data

Duncan, Dave, 1933–
    When the saints / Dave Duncan.—1st ed.
        p. cm.
    "A Tom Doherty Associates book."
    ISBN 978-0-7653-2348-4
    1. Magic—Fiction.   2. Imaginary wars and battles—Fiction.   I. Title.
PR9199.3.D847W47 2011
813'.54—dc22

                                                                    2011021617

First Edition: November 2011

Printed in the United States of America

0 9 8 7 6 5 4 3 2 1

To Editors

I have lost count of all the editors who have worked on my books over the last quarter century.

I have cursed them, slandered them, and upbraided them, but secretly I have always appreciated their efforts. My books have always been improved by them. To them I offer apologies for my intemperance and thanks for their invaluable contributions.

I dread to think what the books of the future will look like if computers make editors obsolete.

PRINCIPAL CHARACTERS INTRODUCED IN BOOK ONE OF THE BROTHERS MAGNUS SERIES

OTTOKAR MAGNUS: Thirteenth Baron Magnus of Dobkov, former warrior, eldest of the brothers and thus head of the Magnus family

VLADISLAV MAGNUS: Knight, a warrior recently ransomed from captivity in Bavaria

MAREK MAGNUS: (Now deceased.) Was a monk in the Benedictine monastery at Koupel, and a Speaker

ANTON MAGNUS: Newly created Count Magnus of Cardice, keeper of Castle Gallant, lord of the march, companion in the order of St. Vaclav

WULFGANG MAGNUS: Youngest of the brothers, a Speaker

MADLENKA BUKOVANY: Daughter of the late Count Bukovany, now handfasted to Anton Magnus

UGNE: Bishop of Cardice

HAVEL VRANOV: Count of Pelrelm, known as the Hound of the Hills, lord of the northern marches, thought to be a traitor in league with the Wends

VILHELMAS, FATHER: (Now deceased.) A priest of the Orthodox Church, a Speaker, distant cousin of Havel Vranov

AZUOLAS, FATHER: (Now deceased.) A priest and Dominican friar, a Speaker

KONRAD V: King of Jorgary, an invalid

WARTISLAW: Duke of Pomerania, leader of the Wends

ZDENEK, CARDINAL: King Konrad's first minister, head of government, known as the Scarlet Spider

WHEN THE SAINTS

CHAPTER 1

It is a truth universally acknowledged that agreements negotiated in the dead of night rarely last as long as those signed in daylight.

The hour was late, but candles still burned in the royal palace in Mauvnik. After a long day, the king's first minister was still in his office. Cardinal Zdenek's working hours were legendary, even now, but age was weighing on him at last, and tonight he truly felt his years.

He had just opened critical negotiations with a wily and dangerous opponent. She went by the name of Lady Umbral. She was grandly attired in a gown of white samite, shot through with silk thread; her jewels would have ransomed a minor king. From her lofty steeple hat trailed a gossamer veil that hid her features. When Zdenek had met her eighteen years ago, she had seemed older than he; but now his hands were gnarled and obscenely marred by age spots, while hers, which were all that he could clearly see of her, were creamy and smooth. She might not even be the same woman. "Umbral" was just a title, like "pope."

"Some wine, my lady?"

She declined, as he had expected. To drink she would

have had to lift her veil, and she had not even done that when she kissed his cardinal's ring.

Brother Daniel, Zdenek's secretary, sat dutifully at his desk behind the door, a gangling, scrawny young man, anonymous and unimportant in his Franciscan gray robe and leather eye patch. Several Brother Daniels took turns attending the cardinal; not all were genuine friars, but all were Speakers. The two companions the lady had brought with her sat side by side near the curtained windows, counting rosaries. They were dressed as senior servants, silent and anonymous, their faces concealed by the protruding brims and lappets of their bonnets. One of them would be a Speaker, too.

"I am honored that you came in person, my lady," he said.

"My pleasure. It is far too long since we crossed swords. Besides, I happened to be in the area." That might mean anywhere south of Sweden or west of Cathay.

"I know you travel widely. How is Christendom?"

"Boiling with war and vice, plague and hunger, as usual." Her voice was low-pitched and her accent intriguingly unidentifiable. They were, of course, conversing in Latin. "And how is Jorgary? Your king is still breathing sometimes, I understand. Quite a feat, that. Your crown prince continues to wallow in what all young men long to wallow in and rich ones actually do."

"And the old condemn, forgetting their own past."

"And yourself?" she purred. "Jorgary suffered a shattering defeat in the War of the Boundary Stone two years ago. Many bets were laid that your long reign had come to an end at last."

"It was not on my recommendation that His Majesty decided to invade Bavaria." Konrad had been talked into it by the meddlesome crown prince, who saw himself as Jorgary's answer to Alexander the Great. The army had seen to it that the brat never got anywhere near the fighting, but the Bavarians had won hands down anyway.

"You got blamed for it," Umbral said with a chuckle. "Life is so unfair, isn't it? I suspect that the outcry still echoes, or you would not have called out to me for help. How can I assist, Your Eminence?"

Eighteen years ago, soon after Zdenek had been appointed King Konrad's first minister, the woman had come to him, asking that a certain convicted rapist be spared the noose. The case had been odious, and Zdenek had been very reluctant to grant her wish. On the other hand, he had heard of her power and was not inclined to make an enemy of her. He set an impossible price on his cooperation by demanding a cardinal's hat—a price to which Lady Umbral had quietly agreed.

So he arranged the royal pardon she sought, and within a month the pope had summoned him to Rome to be ordained a deacon and inducted into the College of Cardinals. That was true power! King Konrad had been so impressed that he had let Zdenek run the country for him ever since.

In all those years, Zdenek had communicated with Lady Umbral rarely, and always indirectly. This was only their second meeting, and the fact that she had come in person suggested that she might need something from him as much as he needed help from her.

"Duke Wartislaw of Pomerania has invaded Jorgarian territory," he said.

She nodded impatiently.

"Specifically, he is moving a monster bombard, known as the Dragon, down the gorge of the Ruzena River to lay siege to Castle Gallant."

"Brave of him to launch such a venture so late in the year," she murmured. "He's a cunning young rogue, Wartislaw, yet inclined to be foolhardy. Of course, Castle Gallant stands athwart the Silver Road, and has been regarded as impregnable for centuries. Alas, those days are over and done with. It will blow away like a cloud of feathers if the Wends attack it with firearms. So you must stop the gun being emplaced. You need troops, Your Eminence, not a frail little woman like me."

"Describing you as frail, my lady, would be like calling the Danube seepage. I need troops because Wartislaw is in league with the devil."

"Ah!" She breathed the word seductively. Satanism changed matters. Satanism was her business. "You are sure of that?"

"Very. You have heard of Havel Vranov, Count Pelrelm, lord of the march?"

"The Hound of the Hills?"

"That one. All his life he has fought the Wends like a rabid hellcat, and now he has changed sides and is engaging in treason against Jorgary. He has also apostatized, gone over to the Greek Orthodox Church. His priest is a Speaker. Of that I am confident, if not quite certain. But that priest, Father Vilhelmas, who has repeatedly been seen in Havel's company, was leading the vanguard of the Pomeranian army the day before yesterday. They were well inside Jorgarian territory."

Umbral laughed. "If you are aware of what happened in one of your northern marches just two days ago, Your Eminence, then I question your moral right to censure the duke for dabbling in Satanism."

He smiled tolerantly. "Two weeks ago, Count Bukovany and his son were struck down by Satanism. That news took eight days to reach me. Our minister of the army told me that it would be a month or more before he could assemble a force and deliver it to Cardice. Meanwhile, of course, Castle Gallant and the entire county were leaderless and vulnerable."

"How tragic for you!" Lady Umbral said with a crocodile chuckle. "You faced a second disaster in less than two years. Your life flashed before your eyes, ending with the flash of the headsman's ax. The crown prince called in his hatter and began trying on crowns? Meanwhile, your entire team of Speakers is fully occupied keeping the old king alive and guarding you!"

Again Zdenek refused to rise to her bait. "I sent a new Speaker. He is young and inexperienced, but so far he has done a wonderful job. However, the Wends are unlikely to have limited themselves to one such helper—Hannibal took more than one elephant when he crossed the Alps. In short, my man needs to be reinforced." And Speakers moved much faster than conventional troops.

The woman lowered her head and touched a fingertip to her lips to indicate that she was thinking. "I need to know more. Where did you find a spare falcon[1] around?"

"I like to keep a few in reserve."

"So do we all, and only the pope can ever afford to. The Saints currently supply you with five hirelings, two of whom are growing old—as we all are—and all of whom must be currently occupied." She glanced around briefly at Brother Daniel, but if she offered a smile, her veil hid it.

---

[1] Please see the Glossary section on page 331.

"The Church has five or six Speakers in Jorgary, possibly seven. So where did you find another? I won't help unless you give me all the facts."

Zdenek never lost his temper. "It so happened that I had become aware of a new Speaker just the previous day." He was proud of his speedy reaction to an unexpected opportunity—the old warhorse's mettle had not rusted yet. "A young esquire recently came to Mauvnik to enlist in His Majesty's Light Hussars. Twenty years old, the sort of arrogant whippersnapper who breaks ladies' hearts and men's heads with equal abandon. A week ago, he pulled off an incredible demonstration of horsemanship before half the court, at a hunt in the royal forest."

"My, my! How convenient. A *miraculous* feat?"

"At least spectacular," Zdenek said complacently. "He was mostly trying to impress the women, of course. But he is sprung of a notable baronial family, so, with His Majesty's permission, I sent for the lad and appointed him Count Magnus of Cardice."

She laughed aloud. "A count at twenty? Did he pinch himself very hard?"

"No, he seemed to regard it as more or less his right. He certainly did not question his own suitability for the post. I also passed on His Majesty's command that he marry the late count's daughter, Madlenka Bukovany, a fabled beauty of seventeen. That seemed only fitting."

She laughed again. "I expect he thought so."

"I even explained that his odds of surviving to enjoy her or any of the rest of it were very slight, but by then there was no holding him. He was out of here like a ferret down a coney hole."

"A Speaker as count?" the lady mused. "An interesting ploy." Speakers usually operated out of the public eye. They could be instantly identified by other Speakers, and public miracles would expose them to the wrath of the Church, which was tolerant enough of its own Speakers, but condemned occult "talent" in the laity as Satanism.

"No," the cardinal admitted. "The Speaker was his younger brother, who was attending him as his varlet, Wulfgang by name."

"Ah! And how old is he?"

"Eighteen."

For a moment she did not speak, and he sensed a very shrewd mind at work behind her veil. "So his talent should be fully developed. It is curious that the Saints have not heard of him and the Church has not enlisted him. Who trained him?"

"I did not inquire."

"You don't mean he's a haggard? You sent a *haggard* into a war?"

"Whether haggard or trained, he has done extremely well. He moved himself and his brother safely to Cardice. His brother proclaimed himself count and promptly showed that he meant business by hanging the constable of Castle Gallant for treason. A couple of days later he received a surely fatal wound when he blundered into the Wends' vanguard near the border. Wulfgang healed him. After all that, the boy went home to report to the head of the family."

"He must have nerves of iron and an incredible resistance to pain."

"Quite so," Zdenek said impatiently. Magnus males were all human bulls. The boy had shown he could cope and would cooperate—at what cost to himself was irrelevant.

"And the new count—Anton?—is his cadger?"

"Possibly. These matters were not mentioned when I spoke with the Magnus boy." But they had both known that sorcery would be required to get the lad to Castle Gallant in the time available. "Yesterday, the baron himself—their brother—came to call on me. He pointed out that one Speaker is not enough to counter an entire army. It is a reasonable point."

"Mm. . . . Speakers are in very short supply just now." Lady Umbral turned to her two companions. "Justina?"

The taller of the two looked up from her rosary. "My lady?"

"Would you enjoy a few days' vacation in fabled Castle Gallant, freezing in those ghastly mountains, defending it from ravening hordes of Wends?"

"Among droves of handsome young men-at-arms, my lady? Singing romantic ballads to me under my window?" No mere servant spoke so, or in such polished Latin.

"More likely an insufferable raunchy rabble of diseased, flea-ridden drunks."

"Life as usual, then. A few days would make a pleasant change from dusting."

Lady Umbral turned back to the cardinal. "I believe I could spare one Speaker, but for a limited time only."

"Not enough," he said flatly. "Not nearly enough."

"No?" Her voice hardened. "Then there would seem to be no purpose in continuing this conversation. I am not merely staking out a bargaining position, Your Eminence. One is all I can possibly spare at this time. When winter is over, perhaps more. Have you asked Archbishop Svaty to lend you one of his? The Church has plenty."

Svaty would help if he could, because the Wends followed the Orthodox heresy, but his price would certainly include Wulfgang Magnus himself, and Zdenek had his own plans for the boy.

"What can one more Speaker achieve against an army?" he demanded.

Lady Umbral had the French knack of shrugging graciously. "Against the bombard, you mean. The gun is critical to your problem, is it not? Wartislaw has little time to take the fortress before the weather drives him back home. Pomerania needs the tolls it levies on the merchant caravans just as much as Jorgary does, and he cannot afford to keep the Silver Road closed for long. That explains why he launched his campaign so late in the year: he waited until the great fall trading fairs were over. Spike the gun or roll it into a lake and you will have won."

"True," Zdenek admitted. "And I am confident that the boy could achieve that. But the Wends will certainly have posted their own Speakers to guard it, so he needs protection while he does it."

"What do you offer in return?"

"What do you ask?"

"The hand of a princess." Now there was no mistaking the smile behind her voice. "Jorgary's delectable Laima, of course. Sweet sixteen and beautiful by any standard, not just as the usual courtesy compliment awarded to royalty."

No! No!! No!!! Zdenek had been urgently matchmaking all over Christendom for months, frantic to see a betrothal contract signed and sealed before the old king died and his grandson appointed a new first minister. Princess Laima was not only a beauty, she would be heir presumptive, and her brother showed no signs of fathering an heir. The bidding was spirited, and the cream that Zdenek expected to skim off this one contract might exceed all the graft that had flowed his way in the last twenty years. Now he knew why this hag had answered his call so promptly . . . but if she thought she was going to sup one spoonful of that deal, she was hugely mistaken.

"There have been negotiations," he admitted. "Which suitor are you backing?"

"A very suitable young man, with a distant claim to the crown of France."

Louis of Rouen! Zdenek registered polite regret. "This is not yet public knowledge, but in fact a marriage contract has been initialed and will be finalized within a week. So the princess is not available. Name a second choice."

The lady remained silent for at least a minute, which was always a good debating technique. He remained silent also, and eventually she spoke. "A piece of the Wulfgang boy. About half would be fair, I think."

"Oh, no! 'Finders keepers!' That's the rule we all play by."

She shook her head vigorously. "The Church doesn't, and in this case I won't. Blue-blood Speakers are rare and therefore precious. Besides, if Gallant falls, he may well die with it, so his life is worth very little at the moment. Your back is to the wall, Your Eminence. Obviously Duke Wartislaw blindsided you. Another military disaster like the Bavarian campaign and you will have nowhere to put that red hat of yours. I can spare Justina for a week, maybe two, which should be plenty. Take it or leave it."

"A quarter."

Again she paused, leaving him staring at that faceless veil. Finally she said, "How about a third? My final offer."

Zdenek mentally shuffled papers into heaps, which was his way of weighing decisions. The boy could not possibly save Castle Gallant single-handedly if the Wends had arrayed more than one Speaker against him—the *yes* pile. If Gallant fell, then both the boy and Zdenek himself were likely to go down with it—*yes* again. Archbishop Svaty might be willing to assign two or three of the Church's Speakers to keep the Orthodox Wends from taking a Catholic fortress—the *no* pile. But Svaty's price would certainly include the boy himself, and probably much else—*yes*. Lady Umbral was a trader in magic that the Church publicly condemned as Satanism, whatever it really believed, and thus her dealings must always be secret, and her reputation for honesty was vital to her continued success, but no one would ever dare denounce her if she cheated. Now that she knew about the boy, she must be bound by some sort of agreement, or she might feel free to grab him for her own purposes, leaving the castle, Zdenek, and Jorgary to fall together—*yes, certainly*.

He sighed and nodded. "Your Justina must serve until the Wends withdraw, though. As you said, it cannot be very long."

"Until the Wends withdraw or the castle falls."

"If the castle and the boy survive, then you get one-third of him." There might still be opportunities to renege on that part of the agreement. The Magnus family had a long tradition of patriotism and service to their king.

"Agreed."

"The password is 'Greenwood'."

"How do we arrange the travel?"

"Brother Daniel has met Count Anton. Brother?"

The friar nodded. "But the hour is late to go calling on a fortress under siege, Your Eminence. Men-at-arms in dangerous situations often strike first and ask questions later. Too late." He removed his eye patch to let the visitors have a clear look at his face. "If you will come calling on me tomorrow morning at, say, terce, my lady, I shall be happy to conduct you to Cardice."

"I'm no 'lady,'" the Speaker said. "Just Justina. I will see you then, Brother."

The women rose as one.

"A pleasure doing business with you, Eminence," Lady Umbral said.

A gap seemed to open in the air itself. All three stepped through it and vanished, leaving the cardinal with his hand out, offering his ring to empty air.

CHAPTER 2

"Can't you even pretend to enjoy it?" Anton raged.

A week ago he had been Lancer Magnus, most junior recruit in the king of Jorgary's Light Hussars, living on gruel in a repulsive attic and forced to share a bed with Wulfgang. Now he was Count Magnus of Cardice, Companion in the Order of St. Vaclav, lord of the march, keeper of Castle Gallant, one of the premier noblemen of the realm. So life felt good, with a few exceptions. One of which was his current problem.

"Pretend how, my lord?" she said. Her voice was muffled, because they were both deep in a feather mattress and buried under a mountain of down quilts. She was underneath.

He was on top, which he always preferred, and also inside, but not making much progress. He must have swived two dozen young girls in the seven years or so since he became capable, but none had been so unresponsive. Older women— there had been even more of those—had always agreed that he was a good lover, delivering as much pleasure as he took. But Madlenka had been bewitched, and there was only one man around Castle Gallant who could use witchcraft.

Meanwhile, she was still waiting for instructions, although

all he could do was repeat what he had told her a dozen times in the last three days. "Moan, thrash around. Bounce. Shriek. Bite and scratch. Above all, in the name of the Almighty, don't just lie there and *weep* like that!"

A week ago he had been stalking the bawds of the court, hoping to work his way into the bed, if not affections, of some rich lady who might expand his income and advance his career. Now he was married—or at least handfasted, which was as good as married—to the daughter of the previous count. Only men who admired flattish chests and sinewy legs would regard her as a beauty. Anton's taste ran to the voluptuous. He liked buttocks he could sink his fingers into and breasts like melons, great twin pillows where a man could bury his head; not these pale, pink-tipped pears. Her ivory skin, moonlight hair, and sapphire eyes were bloodless. She looked like an ice maiden and acted like one.

Madlenka sniffed. "I am not weeping, my lord."

"You have tears in your eyes!"

"It hurts!"

Anton made an exasperated noise. What he might have said then remained unsaid, because another man spoke right behind him.

"Anton! Are you awake?"

Anton withdrew, rolled off, and peered out from under the quilt to make sure the bed curtains were safely closed.

"Otto?" He would tell anyone else to go to hell and stay there for at least two hours. "What the devil—"

"It's urgent. Very bad news. Put some clothes on and come out here, to the fire."

The door thumped shut.

Cursing, Count Magnus struggled out of the mattress and the curtains. Shivering as if he had fallen into icy water, he quickly covered his goose-flesh with the garments he had dropped on the floor last night, which were all just as cold.

He paused at the mirror to drag on his hat, dab some wax on his mustache, and twirl up the ends. He scowled at the bruise on his jaw and winced as he poked a loose tooth with his tongue. Anger, as much as cold, made his breath smoke. The windows overlooked the bailey and showed a thin slice of milky blue sky above the battlements on the far side. Up here in the mountains, September mornings felt like November back home at Dobkov.

The count's quarters in Castle Gallant were shabby and ancient. As soon as he had driven off the Wends and settled into his demesne, he would have them redecorated in the Italian style; more like, say, the bedroom of Baroness Nadezda Radovan in Mauvnik. Now, there was a woman who understood the finer points of copulation! As she should, having been at it for thirty years. He strode out into Madlenka's dressing room and shut the door behind him, ready to face whatever disaster the new day had brought.

Even a brother should not invade the count's private quarters uninvited. But it wasn't just Otto: three of them were out there, waiting for him. They must have brought a firepot, for the wood on the hearth was blazing merrily already. And they all stood up to honor the count, their host.

At thirty-six, Ottokar Baron Magnus of Dobkov was the senior brother and head of the family. He had arrived in Gallant yesterday on what was intended to be a brief celebratory visit, but now he dared not go home again lest he carry pestilence with him. Although Anton would not admit it, he was more than happy to have his oldest brother here to lean on in the present crisis. Otto was big, solid, and battle-hardened, but those qualities mattered much less than his level head, steady nerves, and experience. Whenever there was a dispute, Otto's opinion would always be the soundest and the safest to accept.

The giant hiding behind the huge and very unfashionable black beard was second brother Sir Vladislav, even bigger than Otto, and a renowned warrior. He had come to Gallant to advise on how to fight off the Pomeranian army that was poised to attack the north gate. All through Anton's childhood, Vlad had been a bullying pest, dispensing bruises on the training ground or mocking all lesser men with his cruel, hobnailed humor. But Vlad would still be languishing in captivity, a hostage in some godforsaken castle in Bavaria, had Anton not come up with his ransom, so Vlad owed him a gigantic favor and was having to behave himself at last.

And the youngest, Wulfgang. He looked small and babyish alongside the other two, but was neither. He was a superb horseman and packed a punch to fell oxen, as Anton's sore jaw and loose tooth reminded him. No longer the amiable varlet who had tended his brother's boots and clothes and tack without complaint last week, he was now a killer, as dangerous as a lightning bolt. Furthermore, he lusted after the Ice Maiden, and she craved him too, although she staunchly denied it. Shining like gold sequins, his pale eyes stared fixedly at Anton; his face was unreadable and almost frightening.

The absence of middle brother Marek meant that this was a military emergency that did not concern a renegade monk.

"Please sit!" Still shivering, Anton squatted before the fire to hog the heat. The others were all well swathed in furs and hats. Otto took the stool by the dressing board, Vlad and Wulf folded down atop clothes chests.

"You picked the worst possible time to interrupt," Anton grumbled, carefully not looking at Wulf. Let him yearn!

"Oh, did we?" Vlad growled. "Well, let me tell you, *Count*, that while you've been sarding your brains out, we three have been doing your work for you. None of us has been to bed even to sleep, let alone getting any of what seems to be your only interest in life." Always the soul of tact, was Vlad.

"Sorry," Anton said airily, not meaning it. "Didn't know that. Explain." Outranking his two most senior brothers, so that they must report to him, was a pleasant novelty. In three centuries, no Magnus had ever risen to the rank of count.

"It's like this," Otto said. "The rain stopped in the night, although later we had snow. The pickets on watch saw fires down at High Meadows. They woke Dali Notivova and he came and told Vlad. We doubled the guard and began reinforcing the south gate, stockpiling weapons and arrows, and so on. Didn't think you'd want your married life interrupted."

"Who is it?" Anton demanded, although he could guess.

"Havel Vranov."

"Sure?"

"At first light I went and looked," Wulf said quietly. His boots were muddy and had blades of grass stuck to them.

"I gave orders," Anton barked, "strict orders, that the gates were to remain shut until I said otherwise. You have no authority to overrule me."

"I didn't."

"Oh!"

"Arrghem!" Only Vlad could clear his throat and make it sound so much like mockery. "He says they're flying the Hound's pennants."

The Hound of the Hills, Havel Vranov, lord of the Pelrelm march, and thus a neighbor—but now a traitor to his king.

"How many?"

"Didn't try an exact count," Wulf said, his face still wooden. "Many hundreds. At least twenty knights' pavilions. They have closed the road, of course, which is why no one got through to warn us."

So now Castle Gallant was truly under siege. There were only two ways in and out. The Wends held the road to the north gate, and now their lackey Havel was at the south. Not that any Magnus in history had ever dreamed of running away from danger.

Anton turned back to Vlad. "You're the expert, Brother. What happens now?"

The big man laughed. "We have unlimited water, unless the enemy breaks in and takes the Quarantine Road, and even then we can lower buckets to the river. So far I've tracked down two weeks' rations, which could be spread out to four or five weeks, but only four days' fodder for the horses, so we'd better start eating them while they're plump. We can get by until mid-November, more or less. By then the Wends are going to be freezing their pretty little butts, sitting out there in the hills while the lake ices over behind them."

"But what do we *do*?"

Vlad leered through his wilderness of beard. "You're giving me overall command?"

Anton restrained his temper, never an easy feat early in the morning. Vlad was notoriously prone to speak his mind, but having to accept orders from a younger brother who had been promoted to the giddy rank of count while he was still a mere knight must be straining every fiber of his self-control.

"Vlad, I am trying to apply your renowned expertise in warfare and siegecraft. I already appointed Dalibor Notivova constable. To reverse that decision after two days would not help the men's opinion of their new count."

"Dalibor Notivova doesn't know a halberd from an arquebus."

"He lacks your experience, yes, but he's a local, the men like him, and obviously he's been deferring to you already. What more do you need?"

"Dali's a good man," Wulf said softly.

Vlad glared down at him as if about to ask how a boy knew what a good man was, and then, surprisingly, agreed. "Yes, he is. We can expect the Wends to appear at the north barbican any minute. You need to issue a proclamation that we're under siege and all able-bodied men are to report for defense."

"Do it," Anton said. "Sound the tocsin. Tell Dalibor that you speak with my voice. He won't argue."

For a moment Vlad looked mutinous again, but Otto said quietly, "That sounds like a fair compromise."

A satisfied leer parted the big man's beard. He nodded but did not rise. "I need weeks and we may not have an hour. We've got a few pathetic old firearms but almost no powder. There are emplacements on the roofs of the barbicans to anchor trebuchets, but we need timber and ammunition. I'll have to tear down houses."

"Many people fled town," Anton said. "Take their homes."

Showing his teeth in a ferocious grin, Vlad rose to his full, enormous height and marched out, leaving the door ajar. Wulf went and closed it, then returned to his seat on the chest.

"Is that all?" Anton said. "Can I go back to what I was doing?" That was a second jab, but again he did not look at Wulf as he said it.

"No," Otto said, frowning. "More bad news. Marek has been taken from us. He was murdered last night, just after you went off to bed."

Dead? Marek? No! It was too early in the morning to deal with that. Anton whispered an Ave and crossed himself. Marek, Marek! Marek had always been the brother who mattered. Their mother had died bearing Wulf, and in Anton's earliest memories, Otto and Vlad were already adolescents in weapons training. But Marek, just three years older than he, had been a brother to love and follow and look up to—though not literally, for even as a child Anton had been the taller. Five years ago Marek had been taken away and locked up in a monastery. Only yesterday he had come back into Anton's life, arriving here in Castle Gallant, his smiling little self again. . . . They had barely had time to exchange a dozen words. A long chat with Marek, getting to know each other again, had been the top item on today's agenda. *Murdered?*

"By whom?" Anton had already hanged one man in his fiefdom, and he would certainly hang this one.

"I'll let Wulf tell you," Otto said.

Oh, it was like that, was it? A cold shiver of fear prickled down Anton's back as he turned to meet Wulf's wolfish yellow eyes. He still had not adjusted to the dramatic transformation of his dreamy younger brother. An affable, soft-spoken youth had become a sinister presence; everybody's friend, a minion of the devil. He killed men in cold blood.

But now he was strangely downcast. "Last night, when I went over to Long Valley to kill Havel's in-house Speaker, Marek not only insisted on coming with me, he begged me to let him pull the trigger. He wanted to prove to us that he was still a true Magnus, I think. So I opened the gate through limbo for him, and Marek shot the bolt into Father Vilhelmas. It was Marek the witnesses saw. And it turned out that Havel had another Speaker there with him. A short while later, after you left us drinking in the solar, that one turned the tables. He appeared in our midst and cursed Marek for killing Vilhelmas. And then Marek fell back in his chair, dead."

"*Who* appeared?"

"Leonas."

"The half-wit?" Anton exclaimed. "You're telling me that weedy moronic brat is a Speaker, like you?"

"Leonas is Havel's son. Vilhelmas was a cousin. Ours is not the only family with the curse. Or gift, if you prefer," Wulf added wryly.

"Leonas's not like Wulf," Otto said tactfully. "We think the lad doesn't really know what he's doing. His father must have put him up to it, and very likely put him up to cursing Count Bukovany and his son, too. Havel uses him as a weapon, a miracle machine."

"Miracles?" Wulf's face tightened. "Would a saint strike Marek dead? Or are you implying that it's witchcraft? The Voices I heard claimed to be the voices of saints, but now I'm starting to think the Church is right, and they were demons. Remember how Marek warned us when we went to visit him at Koupel that their aid would always turn to evil? And if I have sold my soul to Satan, Brothers, then you may all be damned too, for accepting my help."

"I refuse to believe that," Otto snapped.

"Or I," Anton said. To be told that Wulf's miracles had twice saved his life so that he could fulfill some Satanic purpose was unacceptable.

"I don't want to, either," Wulf said, "but Vilhelmas is dead, the Dominican Azuolas is dead, and now Marek is dead, and . . ." He shrugged and looked down at the floor. Had he been about to add that the woman he loved was married to the wrong man?

"Where is he? Marek, I mean. I must go and see him."

"You can't."

Otto the peacemaker intervened again. "We decided. . . . We didn't know how we were going to explain his death, and both town and castle are jumpy enough after Havel's performance last night. . . . Wulf took him back to Koupel, so the monks could give him Christian burial."

"I left him in the church," Wulf muttered, "between matins and lauds. It seemed kindest."

"We must endow prayers for his soul," Otto said.

"Is that all?" Anton demanded. "We are beset by enemies on both sides and Marek has been murdered. Anything more to brighten my day?"

Wulf stood up. "Not so far. If you mean has anyone else died of pestilence, then such has not been reported."

"Don't even speak of that!" Anton snapped. "Whatever that trollop died of, it was not plague!"

The Speaker looked him over coldly. "That bruise suits you, but I suppose I'd better cure it, just to preserve your confounded dignity as lord of the march. Did I improve your teeth at all?"

"This one's loose." Anton pulled down a lip.

The pain disappeared. Wulf turned on his heel and stalked out, shutting the heavy door with a bang.

Otto stood up also. "He's taking Marek's death very badly."

"It's tough on all of us."

"You're not blaming yourself, and he is. He's starting to doubt his Voices."

Then Anton realized. . . . "He didn't Speak to anyone! He cured my lip and my tooth, but he didn't say anything. He used to pray aloud to his saints." Or Satan.

Otto shrugged. "He doesn't do that anymore." He took two steps toward the door and stopped. "He's in terrible danger, you know. The Wends will be after him, and so will the Church. I've been trying to talk him into going away, somewhere very far away. He refuses."

Of course he refused. He wanted Madlenka.

"I hope," Otto continued, "that we can win this war without having to ask for any more aid from him."

"If it comes from the devil, yes."

"I'm going to go and help Vlad. You should come and be seen making an inspection. Put your sword on."

Anton reluctantly grunted agreement and went back into the bedroom. The bed-curtains were open and Madlenka's face was just visible between quilt and pillow. Her smile of welcome failed to convince.

"Just came for my sword," he said. "Havel Vranov is laying siege to the south gate. I'll ring for your maid." He hauled on the bell rope and went out to join Otto. He would rather have waited until the maid arrived, because Wulf might pop up the moment his back was turned. Although his earldom came directly from the king, not from his marriage to the late count's daughter, he would be the laughingstock of the kingdom if his wife ran off with his younger brother.

CHAPTER 3

Marching along the dim, cold corridors of the keep at Anton's elbow, Sir Ottokar, thirteenth Baron Magnus of Dobkov, recalled with ironic amusement that he had decided to visit on a mere whim. Normally the journey here and back would have required about three weeks on horseback, but when he had a Speaker in the family both willing and eager to transport him anywhere in the blink of an eye, why not take advantage? True, the Church might thunder that he was imperiling his mortal soul by dealing with the devil, but he found it hard to take that seriously when the reward being offered was so trivial. More important, Otto had known he was the only person who could hope to keep peace in the family. Anton had barely had time to find the latrines in his new castle and was well out of his depth trying to defend it against predatory foes like Duke Wartislaw of Pomerania. Sir Vladislav was a superb warrior, but he had the tact and grace of a hungry bear.

Another smoldering fuse, even more worrisome, was the head-over-heels infatuation between Wulfgang and Madlenka, which they considered love but others might see as first-time adolescent infatuation. Very likely the girl would soon cave in to social and religious pressure and start being properly respectful of her husband. Very few heiresses could choose who they married any more than a sheet of parchment could dictate the terms of an agreement written on it. Men had choice and men could fight for what they wanted. Men fought over women more than they did over anything else except honor—ever since Troy, and probably before that. All Magnuses were stubborn, but since infancy Wulf had set new standards in pigheadedness. Where Anton was the ultimate lecher, Wulf was virtuous and highly disciplined. Love for him, as for his namesake the wolf, would be a lifetime matter, as it was for Otto himself.

Just in case Otto might be tempted to throw up his hands and go home, Anton had admitted that the German mercenaries had fled the town because they believed there was plague there. Otto dared not return to his beloved Branka and the children before he was sure that the rumor was false. If it was.

Anton had already learned his way around his labyrinthine castle. He strode past a staircase without hesitation and brought Otto to a gateway on the same level. The porch was guarded by two men-at-arms, whose breath smoked and whose surcoats were white with frost. They saluted the count, and Otto noticed that Anton remembered to smile in acknowledgment as their father had taught his sons. From there a high drawbridge led across a street to the battlements of the curtain wall that surrounded the town.

Castle Gallant stood on a rocky platform that occupied half the width of the valley. Snow had fallen in the night, so the snow line that had been a third of the way up the mountains yesterday was now down to the tussocky moorland of the valley floor. Steep slopes or cliffs closed off the valley on three sides, with the peaks of the Vysoky Range as a backdrop and the Ruzena River emerging from a gorge about half a mile north of the castle. When Otto leaned through a crenel to peer down the outer face of the wall, he could see it frothing and foaming on its way south to the plains. But between wall and river was a cliff, two hundred feet high.

"It's an incredible site," he said. "If we can't hold it, we deserve to see our heads on pikes." He shivered. "Does the wind always howl like this?"

"It hasn't stopped in the five days I've been here. Come and see this, though." Anton headed southward along the parapet until they were clear of the keep and had a view of the town. "We'll have to tear down houses to make firebreaks."

Like any walled city, Gallant was a warren of roofs and alleys without a square inch of unused space. The keep towered over it at the eastern edge, with the cathedral nearby and three lesser spires spaced around. One taller building might be the bishop's palace.

"Stone walls," Otto said. "What are the roofs made of?" They were white at the moment, with black patches where the snow had already slid off. Chimneys smoked in the sunlight.

"Slate, all of them."

"Then you don't need firebreaks. Fire arrows won't do much damage on stone and slate, especially with all this snow around. And if the enemy breaks in, you want to make them fight door-to-door. That's the worst sort of fighting there is. I saw a little of it when the French took Bordeaux. How good is your water supply?"

"Excellent. Never fails, so I'm told."

"Then forget fire arrows. Set the women and children to topping up water buckets. Order all window shutters to be kept closed, maybe. Not yet, though. Sounds like Vlad's got them busy already. Let's go and see."

They carried on along the top of the wall, urged forward by the spiteful wind and heading for the sounds of hammering. When they moved around to the south side of town, Anton pointed out High Meadows, which was summer pasture, normally abandoned in winter. The Hound's camp was there now, west of the river, an array of bright tents and pavilions, with colored pennants thrashing in the wind. Only part of it was visible, though, the rest being hidden by a spur of the Hogback.

"Five or six hundred men-at-arms," Otto said confidently, "at least. There could be thousands more we can't see. Better them than me at this time of year." But cold weather meant less chance of dysentery, which took more lives than fighting ever did. "How many have you got?"

Anton shrugged. "About five hundred. I called in the levy, but less than half of them have arrived, and now of course they can't. Given time, Havel can probably muster four or five times that many. Our civilian workforce must number two or three thousand. That's including women and boys."

So the odds were bad, and if the departed *landsknecht* mercenaries had gone over to Havel, they widened even further. Heaven alone knew how many thousand Wends Wartislaw might have brought.

Beyond High Meadows the valley widened and descended to merge with the forested Jorgarian Plain. High Meadows was a staging post on the Silver Road, one of the great highways of Christendom, a major trading route between the Adriatic and the Baltic. It climbed the side of the Hogback to the south barbican of Castle Gallant, and the work that had gone into its construction must have rivaled the building of the castle itself. In many places it had been chiseled out of near-vertical cliff, and it spanned gaps with high trestle bridges.

"I should have taken out those bridges," Anton grumbled. So he should have, but it was unlike him to accept blame, even when he'd earned it. He and Wulf were both learning that good intentions were not enough. Welcome to adulthood.

"Tearing up the Silver Road in peacetime would be going a bit far," Otto said reassuringly.

Putting guards on it would have been a smart idea, though. Anton had blundered badly in not foreseeing an attack from the Pelrelm side. Pickets stationed down at High Meadows could have warned the castle of approaching danger; they could have made a fighting withdrawal while destroying the bridges behind them.

"All is not lost," Otto said as the brothers drew closer to the barbican tower. "Even if the Hound's guns open a dozen breaches in the wall, they'll do him no good at the top of these cliffs. He must attack along the road and break in where the gate is, which means he has to put his guns *there*, right there, where we can get at them."

He pointed to a spot little more than a hundred yards away, where the road disappeared around a spur of the cliff. The next section visible from the barbican was at least half a mile farther down the hill, and much lower. A good bombard could throw a ball from there, but its aim would be erratic and its impacts lessened by the angle of flight.

Of course Vlad had worked that out, and was planning to hold the bend as his first line of defense. About thirty Cardician men were already building a breastwork across the road there, with more men jogging up and down the hill, ferrying supplies on their shoulders or in handcarts.

Wagons would be impractical, because there were few places on the road where they could pass.

Vlad had another team working on the top of the barbican tower, evidently building the trebuchets he had mentioned. Sounds of shouting and banging also came from below, where no doubt the main gate was being reinforced or walled up completely. A demolition team in the town was dismantling a building. Another gang was hauling its rafters and beams up on pulleys to the barbican roof to build trebuchets; its stones would supply their counterweights and ammunition.

"I should have started this work days ago," Anton said angrily, having to raise his voice over the din.

"Perhaps, but your predecessor was more at fault. He'd been warned about both the Wends and the Hound, and he had months to prepare for an attack. He should have acquired guns. Cardinal Zdenek was caught napping too, and he knows it. Nobody's blaming you." Not yet, and if the castle fell Anton would likely die and be hailed as a dead hero.

The barbican was a four-story tower, L-shaped in plan. Otto and Anton, going in through the big double doors on the parapet level, found themselves in the machine room, largely taken up by the gears and treadmills that raised the gates. As Otto had seen yesterday, there were two gates, inner and outer, both massive timber portcullises. Enemies breaking in through one then faced the second, and might soon find themselves trapped between them, being attacked through the many murder holes whose hatch covers showed all over the machine room floor. Even if the attackers managed to break though both those gates, they would still have reached only as far as the Quarantine Road, not the town itself. It was an ancient system, but still effective and deadly. A hundred years ago, or even fifty, Castle Gallant could have thumbed its nose at both Count Pelrelm and Duke Wartislaw while it waited for the arrival of winter and the Jorgarian army. Not anymore. The monster gun they called the Dragon would open a breach in a few hours.

"We should find Vlad," Anton said.

"Let's inspect the north gate first. Then we'll know where we can be the most help."

"Shortcut. No need to go all the way back around." Anton led him along the other arm of the L, a smaller chamber that held machinery to raise the third gate, which led from the Quarantine Road into the town. A door at the far end led out to the wall that flanked the town along its western side.

Here the battlements faced the beetling cliffs of the Hogback across a narrow and gloomy canyon. Ancient moss grew down in the shadows. No one would want to live too close to the precipice, which wept moisture and must shed rocks from time to time, but obviously the way was kept clear for transportation.

The brothers headed along the wall. "It's a clever system. Questionable visitors can be let in here and sent on through without coming into contact with the good townsfolk. There are three gates across it, so that big caravans can be divided into sections. I think it was designed to make sure nobody sneaks by without paying his tolls."

"And to stop smuggling!" Otto suggested. "Never forget that your precious castle is basically a glorified toll gate."

The brothers had not walked far when they came in sight of a cataract, spraying down a notch in the cliff. The water was caught at about their height and diverted across the Quarantine Road on a narrow arch, well above the filth of the roadway. This aqueduct fed it through the wall, into the city.

"Four of these," Anton said proudly. "Good water, too."

A few minutes later they passed a heavily built gateway, capable of closing off the Quarantine Road. It also supported another aqueduct. Small wonder the castle was famed as invincible: if both barbicans, north and south, came under attack, the defenders could readily shift forces back and forth as needed. Of course, the dark side of that invincibility was that, if the Wends did manage to seize the fortress, then Pomerania would hold it for evermore. Which is why Cardinal Zdenek had been worried enough to grasp at any faint hope that might save Castle Gallant and his own neck, even an untried Speaker.

The wind was gusty, eddying off the cliff, and the sky ahead was as black as iron. There would be more snow before long, praise the Lord. *Freeze, Wartislaw, freeze!*

Guided by loud hammering noises, they found Vlad on the roof of the north barbican, a mirror image of its southerly twin. The roof was flat and sheathed in lead, with its western side abutting the cliff face, and the other three crenelated. Some irregular blocks protruding from the lead would have puzzled Otto had Vlad not earlier mentioned foundations for trebuchets. That was what the big man was working on now, directing four carpenters in assembling something that might well grow up to be a monster-sized catapult. Other gangs were hauling up more balks of timber, obviously precut to fit together. Anton stopped and questioned a pimply apprentice, learning that somebody's grandfather had remembered that a great pile of oak beams stored in the top story of the north barbican were the missing trebuchets. The boy did not know whether there would be enough to supply the south gate also. Anton thanked him and sent him on his way. Meanwhile a nearby house was being demolished for its stones.

Staying clear of the bustle, Otto took shelter from the gale behind a merlon. He had experience with firearms in battle, especially at the Battle of Brusthem, but he knew almost nothing about trebuchets. Vlad's military career had been longer and more varied.

In a few minutes Anton joined him and pointed out the northward extension of the Silver Road, shouting over a wind that was either growing stronger or was just more noticeable up there. Again the trail had been hacked out of the cliff, but here more of it was clearly in view, gradually ascending. After half a mile or so, it turned a corner and disappeared into the gorge of the Ruzena.

"You haven't tried to build a redoubt up there?" Otto asked.

"Course I did! We were too late. The Wends were there yesterday already. See them?"

At that distance any figures would tend to merge into the rock, but Otto peered with wind-watered eyes and eventually made out a couple of lookouts sitting at the side of the road, inconspicuous against the cliff. A company of archers or arquebusiers would be on standby, sheltering around the corner, and any sortie from Gallant would be mowed down before it arrived.

"If we could hold that bend, their damned bombard would be useless junk. Can we risk a night attack?"

"I'll leave that up to Vlad," Anton said. So now he was ready to admit who was in charge of the defense, and that was good. "About five or six

35 ⇥

miles upstream, the gorge widens into Long Valley, where we have our border post, and where they almost killed me. The Pomeranian ferry dock is on the lake, a mile or so farther on."

"Wulf thinks he saw the Dragon at Long Valley last night, with at least one Speaker guarding it."

Anton shivered, as if that news was even colder than the wind. "Then it should arrive here today or tomorrow. Even if they need to reinforce bridges, I can't see them needing more than two days."

"Less if they have Speakers to speed things along." Otto blew through his fists to warm them. "If that bombard is as big as they say it is, then I don't like this situation at all. The range is too great for bows, especially firing uphill and into the wind. Arquebuses might reach, although they would be hopelessly inaccurate."

"We only have three, with very little powder and shot. I expect Vlad will save them for the main assault."

But the Wend's bombard was going to have both wind and elevation working for it. Properly dug in, it would put a stone ball on target every time. Even if it only fired six or seven times a day, in two days the barbican would be a rock pile. The defenders had nothing to oppose it except some hope of future trebuchets to throw rocks at it. Flying rocks might not hurt the gun itself, but they ought to delay its emplacement and flatten a few gunners.

Realistically, all that a conventional defense would do now was delay the inevitable end for a few days. Gallant's chances of survival depended on Wulf. Ever since Father's illness had called him home from his youthful days of battle, Otto had assumed that he would eventfully die in his bed at home. Now he saw that this little junket to Cardice County might be the death of him. He might never return to Dobkov.

"*You!*" Vlad came striding over like an enraged Goliath of Gath, with the wind rippling his beard and his nose flaming red with cold. "You two prissy nobles come here to dance to entertain the men, or did you plan to be useful?"

"I was about to ask how we could help," Otto said mildly.

"Half this junk," the big man boomed, waving a meaty hand at the spread of timber that was threatening to pave the entire roof, "is rotten with woodworm and useless. Go downstairs and get those drunken whoresons to pick out the good stuff and sort it into types, so if I need a left rear upright I can send for it. Also have them come up and clear the crap wood out of our way. Then burn it and all the rest like it."

This hardly seemed like a job requiring a count and a baron, but Otto dutifully led the way to the stairs. The attic below was a noisy, very dusty cavern, low-ceilinged and lit only by loopholes; he and Anton could barely stand erect in it. A dozen men were heaving timbers around, and several of them were shouting orders. As soon as the count himself arrived, though, he was able to seize everyone's attention and impose silence. Before he could start issuing orders, Otto tugged at Anton's cloak. "The light in here isn't good enough to sort out the bad wood."

Anton nodded and amended Vlad's orders accordingly. Who was in charge here? No one. How many were master carpenters? Two were. He appointed one of them gaffer. First, six men were to go back up and stack the bad pieces that Vlad had already discarded; they would do as ammunition. The rest were to start sorting all the timber into types, making a pile of each shape. When they had done that, they were to choose the worst pieces from each pile and take those away to be copied so that new trebuchets could be built to their model. And whenever they winched a piece up to the roof, they were to inspect it in good light and bring it back again if it was no good.

Any questions? Then get to work. Yes, my lord.

Every man ran to obey. In peace or war, men worked better when they had orders directly from a nobleman. No one argued with gentry. The big man upstairs with the beard was a knight, but a count was much higher in the eyes of God or man. Counts were very special.

Noble blood or not, the dust was making Otto sneeze, so he gratefully followed Anton as he ran down another flight to the machine room. Count and baron shared the same dream of escape to somewhere where they could be more useful.

"I'm going to the armory next," Anton said, heading out the archway to the parapet walk. "Our supply of arrows—"

"My lord?"

He spun around to frown at the woman who had spoken. Tall but bent, she was swathed in a laced-up cloak of coarse cloth with her shoes and a few inches of black dress visible below it; from the front of it protruded a wind-reddened hand clutching a distaff like a bizarre scepter. A black felt bonnet hid her hair and ears, revealing only a face from which wrinkles and weathering had driven any trace of beauty. Her age might be anywhere between forty and seventy, depending on how many children she had borne. Undoubtedly she was a servant, almost certainly a widow, and hundreds of her like could be found in the streets anywhere. Women of her station did not normally address counts, and certainly did not stand in wait outside doorways to ambush them.

"I am Count Magnus."

She smiled, nodding as if she knew that. "And I am Greenwood."

"Who?"

"Greenwood!" Otto said joyfully. "Then you are welcome, goodwife. I am Baron Magnus of Dobkov."

"And who else would you be?" She bobbed a curtsey that seemed to be intended equally for both of them.

Anton remembered now. "A mutual friend sent you?"

"Doubt that anyone calls him friend, my lord, but he is widely known and not without repute." She simpered. "My name for today is Justina."

"You are not quite the sort of helper I was expecting."

"And what sort of helper was that, my lord? Someone like that great hairy giant up there on the tower?"

"That is my brother, Sir Vladislav."

"Oh, by the angels, my terrible tongue has run away with me again! Tongue, you will be getting me birched, I do swear."

Anton drew a deep breath, but before he could use it Otto coughed a warning. "I suspect that Justina's innocuous demeanor is designed to confound more our adversaries than ourselves, Brother." Anton had a limited sense of humor.

"Save us. Those are precious big words to be using on a humble drudge like me, your lordship."

"Are they truly?" Otto said with a chuckle. "Now, I assume that the first thing you want to do is meet our other brother, Wulfgang?"

"Heaven be my witness, my lord, that will be the second thing. The first will be to have a trusty gentleman, such as your noble self, my lord, be warning him that I have come to aid and mean him no harm."

Otto recalled Wulf telling him that Speakers could recognize one another at a glance. "Is that your usual way of working, or have you been warned about his hair-trigger temper?"

Justina rolled her eyes in mock terror. "By Our Lady, a fearful combination you are naming. Yet it be vital that I speak with him."

"All very well," said Anton. "But where is he? I don't remember him saying where he was going, do you?"

Otto shook his head while racking his brain. It had been an hour since they parted; Wulf could be literally anywhere in the world by now. As a love-smitten swain, he might have doubled back to speak with Madlenka, which he had done the night before during Anton's absence. But he would not endanger her reputation, and Anton would be making sure that she was never alone for more than a few seconds.

"He was in low spirits," Otto said. "I think the best place to start would be a church."

"A church?" Justina cried. "A church you say? Terrible things can happen in churches! Quickly, quickly, let us find him."

CHAPTER 4

Downcast by lack of sleep and the nightmare of Marek's death, Wulf had indeed gone in search of peace and solitude. Avoiding the cathedral, where he might run into that nosy, pompous bishop, he went in search of the other spires he had seen in the town. The first church he found turned out to belong to St. Sebastijan, which seemed a good omen, for he was the patron saint of soldiers. It was tiny and very bare, the air laden with old incense, murals hidden under layers of candle grease. Wulf wanted no other worshipers around, and especially did not want a priest. It was hard enough to imagine confessing to committing a couple of murders, but to admit to having dealings with the devil was unthinkable. He was cut off from the Church and hope of salvation. He was Faust, and had sold his soul to the devil to make Anton a count.

Staying well away from the altar and the Host, he knelt in a gloomy corner at the back to pray. Prayer to the Virgin was what he had tried as a youth when the Voices spoke. He still had calluses on his knees from the hours he had spent in the castle chapel.

He was determined not to swear more oaths. His journey from Koupel to Gallant had levied such a price in pain that he had vowed never to call on his Voices again. But two days later he had been forced to break his word in order to save Anton's life a second time. That had seemed a worthy use of Speaking—Jesus had healed, so how could healing be evil? And yet evil had followed. Three men had died, all servants of God. Where had he gone so terribly wrong?

Despite his resolution not to use his Satanic powers, he could not help trying to see what was happening on the battlements. First he stole a Look through Vlad's eyes: *Vlad was up on the roof of the north barbican, directing the construction of one of the trebuchets he had promised.* But his attention never wandered to the north, so Wulf could not tell what the Wends were up to, if anything.

Madlenka was being bathed by her maids, under the direction of Giedre, her best friend and chief lady-in-waiting. Then it became impossible not to steal a Look from Giedre's point of view, and. . . . *Stop it!* He must not even think about Madlenka, let alone spy on her naked. But he found the temptation almost irresistible and hated himself for letting it distract him from his prayers.

He had received no answers and found no comfort before he heard the church door creak. Annoying boots came tapping over the flagstones in his direction. Standing over him, Otto said, "I almost didn't see you there. It's lucky your hair is so bright."

"Go away, I'm busy."

"There's a woman outside needs to speak with you. Cardinal Zdenek sent her. She knew the password: Greenwood."

Wulf was tempted to refuse. If Speaking was Satanism, then another Speaker was the last person to ask for help. Yet he desperately needed to talk with someone who could explain who the Voices were, and why they had chosen him for their favors. He also needed to let Cardinal Zdenek know that he was being unfair, making Wulf do all the work and giving Anton all the rewards. Shouldn't Madlenka be allowed a say in which brother she married? And just to talk for a few minutes with another Speaker might save him from going crazy. If he was already damned, he had nothing in all eternity left to lose.

He sprang up and squeezed his face into a smile. "Is she beautiful?"

Otto led the way to the door. "No, but she has a wicked sense of humor. She started plucking Anton's feathers in no time."

"A lady after my own heart."

"She doesn't admit to being a lady. You wait here and I'll send her in."

Wulf stood back. An old woman entered, carrying a distaff, and Otto closed the door from the outside. She was garbed as a servant, but the nimbus around her head blazed very bright in the dim church, so Wulf bowed to her as he would to a countess.

"I am Wulfgang Magnus, my lady, an esquire in my brother's service."

She curtseyed with surprising agility. "Justina be my name today, squire."

"And is your social status equally protean?"

She smiled. "Ah, a poor woman must beware young gentlemen seeking to beguile her with fine words. You haven't been swearing any oaths in here, I ween?"

"No."

She seemed relieved. "Sooth, it is a drab, cold place. Will you come with me to one more pleasant, where we may talk undisturbed?"

He had already accepted that he had nothing to lose. "*Omnia audere,*" he said. That was the family motto, *I dare all.*

"Ha! You're not risking a whit or tittle, boy. Your Voices will bring you back here anytime you want. Speak you Greek as well?"

"A few words."

"Then we'll go to Avlona and peradventure teach you a few more."

A gate through limbo opened in front of them, a gap in the air admitting a blaze of golden light and a rush of warm, scented air. He followed Justina through and found himself not in Heaven, as he half expected, but in a tiny vineyard, about twenty yards square, enclosed by stone walls draped with creepers. The light that had seemed blinding in St. Sebastijan's holy gloom was just sun-dappled shade below the ceiling of vines on trellises. The color came from their fall-tinted leaves; the grapes had all been harvested. Humid, cloying air told him that summer still lingered here, far from Cardice.

"Now, you come this way, young squire." Justina headed along a path paved with red tiles, flanked by vines and trellis posts, and he saw that what he had taken for just another wall was the side of a low farmhouse of white walls and red roof, its windows masked by weathered wooden shutters.

She was already untying the laces on her cloak, which seemed like a good idea, so when they arrived at a lichen-blotched stone table flanked by stone benches, he tossed his down beside hers, to be joined by a distaff, a saber, and Justina's felt hat. Her black skirt and white blouse were of finer quality than her outer garments. Although he could not identify any difference other than the clothing, she looked less a servant now, more a rich merchant's wife, and much less ancient.

He sat opposite her and gazed around in wonder. The tiny paved area was littered with old presses, broken furniture, and cart wheels; even a rusty anvil. The house had been inhabited a very long time. A few straggly flowers grew in giant pots, but he could see no great distance in any direction except straight up, to a sky enameled in cobalt blue.

"Where is this, my lady?"

"Justina. Suffer me to play servant, lest you forget and misspeak when another is present." She spoke more like a chatelaine lecturing a scullery wench than a servant addressing a noble.

"Tell me where this is, Justina."

"Near Avlona, in Greece."

If she worked for Cardinal Zdenek, why bring him to Greece? She read the question in his face before he could ask it.

"It is a safe place for Speakers. The Orthodox Church is less bloodthirsty than that rabid pack of cardinals in the Vatican, and their Islamic overlords won't let them roast people anyway."

He distrusted that gibe at Rome. "What do the Turks do to witches?"

"Stone them."

"Much better." He smiled a peace offering. "May I ask where your loyalty lies?"

"I am doing a favor for the Scarlet Spider. I am to hold your coat while you belabor the Pomeranians."

Help at last! "But normally you work for Archbishop Svaty?"

"God's blood! Will you waste your whole life in useless gossip, young sir? War itself is too stupid to spoil a fine day on. Question to some purpose."

"Do your Voices, and mine, come from God or the devil?"

She nodded, amused. "Yes, that is the nub. Would you have me admit to being in league with Satan? Do I look such a fool? Are you in state of grace, Squire Wulfgang?"

He hesitated. "I do not know. That is what I must learn."

"And any princely cardinal or pauper priest will tell you that you can never know, not in this life. None of us ever can, so they say. So now you just do whatever you think is right, lad, and we'll tend to the state of your soul later. I can direct you to an understanding confessor. Your brother was bemoaning things that went awry yesterday. There were deaths, he said."

Wulf stole a quick Look at his brothers. However far Avlona was from Cardice, distance seemed not to matter to his spying magic. *Otto was in a large, dim storeroom, probably in the barbican, helping to supervise work gangs; Vlad still up on the roof. Anton, though, was striding through the narrow streets, probably going back to the keep.*

"Three deaths. Father Azuolas, Father Vilhelmas, and Brother Marek—a Dominican friar and priest, an Orthodox priest, and a monk posing as a friar. Marek was also my brother, the middle one of the five of us."

"Three?" Justina pulled a face. "Best you start explaining."

"I went to fetch a crossbow from the armory. When I came back, I found Marek being assaulted by a Dominican friar and a Benedictine monk. They both had nimbuses, and I wasn't going to risk attacking Speakers with my fists. I had spanned the bow to try it out, so I just dropped a bolt in the notch and loosed. I hit the friar, Azuolas. The monk, Brother Ludovic, attacked me."

"Hardly surprising, I'd say."

"I could see the friar was dying. I kept shouting at Ludovic to stop so we could join forces to heal him, but he wouldn't. He overpowered me, but then Marek hit him with the poker. By that time Azuolas was dead. I told Ludovic to go back to Koupel and take the body with him."

Justina pursed her lips and drummed fingers in silent disapproval on the weathered stone of the table. "Mother of Heaven! And won't the Church be setting its hounds baying after you now? Well, that's one death. There's more?"

"Havel's Orthodox priest, Father Vilhelmas, a Speaker. I opened a gate through limbo to where he was and Marek shot him with the crossbow."

The old woman stared at Wulf in horrified disbelief. "That's murder! Assassination!"

"Maybe. I was very sure that Vilhelmas had killed the old count and his son—although now I'm not so certain—but Anton found him leading Pomeranian troops inside Jorgarian territory. They had attacked the garrison at Long Valley without warning, which is a clear breach of the Church's rules of war, and massacred them. What sort of priestly behavior was that? I'm a warrior, Justina. I come of warrior stock and I was trained to fight. Even Marek was. He had to beg me to let him do the killing, because it was my idea and I wanted to do it. I still think Vilhelmas deserved it."

Justina shivered and clasped herself as if the morning had just turned cold.

"The third death was Marek himself," Wulf said. "Vilhelmas was a distant cousin of Havel Vranov's, but Havel also has an imbecile son, Leonas. Leonas turned out to be a Speaker, too, although he has no halo and doesn't seem to know what he's doing. He came to Gallant and cursed Marek for killing his friend. Marek died right away."

After a moment Justina whispered, "Had we known about this . . ."

"You would have refused to help me?" he asked bitterly.

"Not I, but another. . . . Have you never heard of the first commandment?"

"I am the Lord your God—"

"Not that one! Lord a'mercy! For Speakers, any Speakers, there are three laws, three commandments. The first is: *Talent must be used in secret.* You never let workadays see you using power! Nor the Church neither, if you know what's good for you. Any people may panic if they see you using talent. Only the Wise—that's the folk who already know about talent: the Speakers and a very few workadays, like yon brothers of yours—can be allowed to see it."

"Marek said as much."

"But he was willing to step out of limbo to kill a priest before witnesses?"

Wulf sighed. "My brother saved a boy's life once, and for that he was shut up in jail for five years. He was tired of playing by the Church's rules." Marek was no longer around to defend himself; someone must. "Besides, we had just seen Havel Vranov and three other men vanish from a crowded banquet hall. Havel's not a Speaker, but he cursed Anton and Castle Gallant like Thyestes cursing Atreus, then he and his companions disappeared. What was that, if not a deliberate display of Satanism? Two hundred people saw it. A mob tried to flee out the doorway and at least a dozen people were hurt."

Justina rolled her eyes, clearly furious at this news. "It is rank insanity, that is what it is! You'll have all Jorgary packed with cardinals and awash in holy water. And quite apart from secrecy, whether you like it or not, you are a Speaker, not a warrior, so you must not resort to violence to solve problems. You have no cadger?"

Wulf wondered if the woman was mocking him, as Otto said she'd done to Anton. "Justina, I am a mere esquire, a youngest son. I don't own a horse, let alone a mews."

She smiled. "You don't know what a cadger is?"

"Of course I do. My brother Ottokar employs four cadgers to carry the birds when he goes hawking."

"Not what I meant. Who was your handler?" She stared at his puzzled expression. "Who trained you, boy?"

"No one trained me."

"Then you are what we call a haggard."

"Thank you," he said icily. A haggard was either a wild hawk captured as an adult, or an unkempt savage person living in the woods. He fancied himself as neither. "When you talk about a cadger you mean a trainer?"

"No. Tell me of this Leonas, who slew your brother."

"He's a simpleton. Fourteen or fifteen, tall as a pike, but not shaving yet. He has the mind of a small child, yet he's a Speaker. His father uses him as a weapon, but I'm sure Leonas doesn't understand what he's doing."

Justina nodded, looking grim. "Madness and Speaking are not so rare a mix as you might think. The likes of him is dangerous. We must do something about him."

"Kill him?" Wulf said, and it was his turn to feel revulsion.

She shook her head. "No. But trim his talons. Now I've told you the first commandment. Tell me what you do know about Speaking."

"Almost nothing. Teach me, I beg you!"

"Beg all you want, but that I won't do." She countered his frown with a satisfied, cat-licking-cream smirk. "There is a very fine reason why

Speakers do not speak about the talent, and I won't be telling you what that reason is, even. But you tell me what you have learned, and I will warn you when you talk sewage. Sybilla! Why aren't you with your father?"

The girl who had sauntered into view from somewhere behind Wulf's back was nut-brown, or at least her face, lower legs, and arms were. She was barefoot, clad in a dress of costly white silk that clung to her like skin. Her hair hung long and thick, black and shiny, her eyes shone like obsidian, and her lips were redder than pomegranates. She had a nimbus.

She pouted. "I got bored. Father has no time for me just now. He's too busy preparing for the conclave."

Justina rolled her eyes like martyred mothers everywhere. "May the saints preserve us! Yes, child, my guest here is what is commonly called a young man. I believe he would enjoy some wine. And even were he bonnier than Apollo, he could not possibly enjoy the way you are looking at him. Move, you brazen little trollop!"

With a heartrending sigh, the girl tore her gaze away from a lingering inspection of Wulf and retraced her steps. Wulf stared after her, wondering if other women could make their hips do that when they walked. He was horribly afraid that his cheeks were a brighter red than her lips. He hadn't shaved that morning.

"And change your clothes!" Justina shouted after her. "Pardon her, good squire."

He swallowed a few times. "Yes, my . . . Justina. Your daughter? She is very beautif . . . How old is . . ."

"Lady preserve me, not my daughter! You flatter me. A distant relative—not distant enough, I sometimes think. Talent runs in my family, like yours. She's fifteen. Women Speakers are usually fledged at sixteen. Girls are older than boys of the same age, and being a Speaker makes a girl different."

"What sort of different?"

"Different in that she doesn't have to fear men."

"Fear men?" Father Czcibor had always taught that men had to fear women, who were agents of the devil, always tempting men into sin. Wulf had never quite believed that, although Sybilla had just opened his eyes a little wider than usual. Madlenka had shown no signs of being frightened of him.

Justina shook her head pityingly. "And why wouldn't women fear men, squire? Men are stronger than us, love violence as we do not, and trap us with honeyed words so they can sow their seed in our furrows. Then they leave us to reap the crop. Tell me what that lanky brother of yours is up to."

Startled, Wulf stole another Look through Anton's eyes and saw a curtain wall to his left and sheer rock to his right. "He is hurrying along the Quarantine Road, going to the south gate." *With his long legs, Anton was moving like a starving foal, moving so fast that the dancing image made Wulf feel giddy. He was staring fixedly ahead, so Wulf could not tell if he had any companions with him, but there seemed to be many men-at-arms running in the opposite direction, hastily saluting the count as they passed him. Alarm bells were ringing, bugles sounding.*

"It would seem he has had an urgent summons," Justina remarked. "An angel whispered in his ear, perhaps. We must finish our talk. Sit down. You can be there when it happens, whatever it is."

Yet Otto and Vlad had stayed at the north barbican. They were both on the roof parapet, staring out between the merlons at a column of men-at-arms marching down the Silver Road. Hundreds of them were coming around the bend at the mouth of the gorge, with the end of the column not yet in sight.

"The Wend assault has started!"

"Sit down, I said!" Justina snapped. "This matters more. Wherever you are, you can get there faster than they can. Here comes the wine. Best close your eyes."

That was not at all necessary, or even advisable. The seductive Sybilla had returned with a flask and two crystal goblets. If she had changed her clothes, it was to make them even more provocative, with a lower neckline and higher hem. The only women Wulf had seen exposed like that in his entire life had been the street wenches in Mauvnik, and he had stayed well away from those. She slunk up to the table; he dared a small smile. She tossed her head as if he'd farted a bugle call. She thumped the flask down on the table, then spoiled the effect by setting the delicate goblets down gently. She flounced around and stalked away.

Madlenka had never scared him the way that chit did. He watched her disappear around the corner of the house.

"What did I do wrong?"

"You noticed her," Justina said with a sigh.

"What was I supposed to do?"

"Notice her. She's just practicing, pay her no heed. Are you as ignorant about Speaking as you are about poop-noddy?"

"About what?"

"Poop-noddy. Jig-jig. Shagging. Sarding."

Oh, that. Anton had explained fornication many times, but it was not relevant to today's discussion. "More ignorant. Marek told me what little he had been taught in the monastery, but it wasn't much. And nothing to do with poop-noddy."

"It wouldn't be. You do understand that a nimbus is the sign of a qualified, fledged Speaker, a sort of ordination? And other Speakers can see it, whether or not they have nimbuses of their own yet?"

He nodded. Marek had never developed a nimbus. Wulf filled the goblets. The wine was a pale gold and had a foreign tang, strange but not unpleasant.

"Marek said there were at least seven steps. He called them sins, though. The first sin was hearing the Voices to begin with."

Justina said, "Which is rare, but those who are destined to do so start at about thirteen."

"The second sin is learning to understand what they are saying. My Voices claimed to be St. Helena and St. Victorinus. Of course, the Church would say that they were demons of hell." He paused a moment for a reaction, hoping she would deny that bit about demons, but she said nothing. "The third step is starting to talk back and pray for little favors." Like making a sour apple taste sweeter, he recalled. "The fourth was asking for real miracles—or witchery, if you prefer."

Justina just shrugged and waited.

"And that really hurt!" he said. "The trip to Cardice—why did it hurt me?"

"That I won't tell you. Can't. Mustn't. I will say that not all Speakers have to climb the same ladder. A handler could have eased your path. Go on."

"Fifth is refusing the pain and getting the miracles without having to pay that price." This time he earned a nod. "And the sixth step seems to be the nimbus."

"Harken to him! He'll be bragging he can read and write next. That's good. Excellent! Of course, you had Marek to help and you were dropped into very deep waters, where the secrets lie, but you've done very well, even so."

Vlad was bellowing at the carpenters and porters rushing to complete the first trebuchet. Archers were taking their posts at the merlons on the roof. Otto was down in the machine room, organizing more archers at the loopholes. Neither happened to be looking at the Wends, so the undetected spy could not. Anton was still heading in the opposite direction. It would make sense for the traitor Havel to attack the south gate at the same time as his Pomeranian allies attacked the north. Or perhaps they were in a race to see who could take Castle Gallant first. And Madlenka . . . Madlenka was dressing in frantic haste, with Giedre and the maids all trying to help and all getting in one another's way. Whatever the news was, it had reached the keep also.

Wulf discovered that he was starting to twitch, staying on his bench only with great effort. Yet he could not deny what Justina said, that he was doing more good here—learning how to use his talent, as she called it—than anything he could achieve at Gallant as a novice warrior with sword or bow. She was waiting for him, eyebrows raised. Even if the Scarlet Spider had sent her, how trustworthy was she?

"So what comes next?" she asked impatiently. "Seven stages, you said."

"Last night, after five years, my Voices deserted me. Today they still do not answer." He waited for a comment, but she just sipped her wine, watching him over the glass. "But I found that I could travel through limbo without having to ask them. Until then I had always had to Speak aloud, and now I just . . . just decide what I need and they seem to know. I discovered, too, that I could see things at a distance, Looking out of other people's eyes."

"Only people you have met," she said, volunteering information for the first time. "Just as you can only go to people or places you know. Is that all? Just seven stages?"

"I ask you that. And I ask why my Voices no longer speak to me."

She tossed her head, much as the girl had done. "I answer only that there is one higher stage, but I won't be saying what it is or what it brings; all I tell you is that your Voices do not answer now because you don't need them now. How long since that hunt where you first used your talent?"

"Friday. Exactly one week ago." It felt like years, a different life.

"Lord be praised! I never did hear of a haggard climbing so high so fast."

Unable to resist his sense of urgency any longer, Wulf drained his goblet. It was time to return to Gallant and join the battle. "Was Joan of Arc a Speaker?"

Justina showed surprise, and perhaps approval. "Indeed she was. For fourteen years the French lost every battle with the English. After she appeared, they never lost. You think any workaday chit of a girl could have managed that?"

Wulf wondered why she had not thereby broken the first commandment that Justina had described, but he had more urgent questions to ask about Joan.

"Then how were the English able to catch her and put her to death? Did they do to her what you said you would do to Leonas: 'trim his talons'?"

"I won't tell you that."

Annoyed, he tried another ploy. "My brother Otto says that the Church fears Speakers."

"Of course it does! A miracle worker will be hailed as a saint, and saints are a threat to the pope's authority. They might disagree with him and the bishops. They might start a new church of their own. So Speakers must be denounced as agents of the devil."

"The Church confines them and trains them to obedience?"

Justina clicked her mouth shut stubbornly. "That's enough for today."

"Does Bishop Ugne know about the Church's use of Speakers?"

Justina dismissed Bishop Ugne with a snort. "Cardinal Zdenek is one of the Wise. Abbot Bohdan of Koupel is. Archbishop Svaty may be. Offhand, I can't think of anyone else in Jorgary except the Speakers themselves, their cadgers, and their close family, if anyone, who knows. It may be that even the king on his throne doesn't."

Being privy to a secret that one's king might not know was a mind-bending thought. The Hound of the Hills knew, but the Vranovs were as talented as the Magnuses.

"Can a Speaker cure pestilence?"

Justina drew in her breath sharply, then studied him carefully to see if he was serious. Finally she nodded. "One case or two. But not an epidemic! If you broke the first commandment on that scale, you'd be hailed as the Second Coming of Our Lord. Why do you ask?"

He rose. "I must go back and help my brothers."

She made no move. "Sit down. I don't want to do this, but you are a babe in arms. I haven't told you the other two commandments."

Wulf sat down.

Justina stared around for a moment—at the broken wheels, the vines— but she did not seem to be seeing them. He wondered if she was Looking elsewhere, or even consulting someone.

Madlenka and her mother were in the great hall of the keep, shouting orders to a mass of servants, mostly female, but some male, all running to and fro with burdens of cloth or furniture. Obviously they were organizing the great hall as an infirmary for the wounded, with baskets of bandages, buckets of water, and pallets laid out in rows. Nursing was traditionally a women's duty, and tradition would be strong in a border castle like Gallant.

Justina raised her dark eyes to stare right at him. "The first, I told you, is to keep your talent secret! All Speakers are shy as field mice and now you know why. Never forget it! The second commandment is: *Thou shalt not tweak!*"

"Tweak?"

"Tweak. Tweaking is using talent to change a person's mind— workadays' minds, of course; it won't work on Speakers. It's a crime and it's dangerous, because you can drive people insane. Havel would have brought a Speaker with him to the banquet to protect him from being tweaked. But why they made such a display when they left, I cannot imagine." She scowled. "Certain, the pope himself will hear of that."

"And the third law?"

"It's not so much a law as a warning: *Two's company, three's dangerous.* I honestly did not know Sybilla was here. I was not laying a trap for you, I swear. But when she appeared with her nimbus, you should have left.

Instantly! Your precious Cardinal Zdenek employs Speakers. He has one in attendance at all times."

To detect other Speakers, of course. Wulf nodded impatiently to show that he understood that much.

"One Speaker is defense," Justina continued. "Two are aggression. Always, unless you've agreed beforehand. Two Speakers can almost always overpower one. Remember that. Morally, you were right to go to your brother's aid last night. By sending two Speakers after him the Church was being aggressive. It should have just sent one, or else waited until you were present also. It will never admit that, of course. If a monk has second thoughts about his vows, he should speak to his confessor, his abbot, the archbishop, even the pope. He can ask to be released. No Speaker will ever be released, but the abbot should have sent a brother monk to reason with him—one Speaker, not two! So Marek was being assaulted, and law everywhere recognizes a man's right to defend members of his family, his brothers not least. You were in the right, morally and legally. But never will the Church admit that. It will claim that you assaulted and murdered a priest, and it is going to hunt you to the ends of the earth for it."

"And Count Pelrelm, the Hound of the Hills? Two but never one?"

She laughed. "You are a hound, too, lad! I've known bloodhounds slower to pick up a scent than you. Yes, Havel brought a Speaker to Gallant, his Father Vilhelmas. He knew by then that Anton must have a Speaker, who had healed him of his mortal wound. So he was entitled by the rules to bring a Speaker of his own. But you tell me he also brought the moron Leonas, who has no nimbus. So that was cheating. Two's company, three's dangerous!"

Wulf thought of that disastrous banquet and smiled to himself. "But Anton had two also, because I was there and so was Marek, who did not have a nimbus either. There were four of us: two journeyman Speakers and two apprentices!"

"Not 'journeyman' and not 'apprentice.' We talk about 'fledged' Speakers and 'branchers' instead of 'apprentices.' 'Handlers' instead of 'teachers' or 'masters.'"

"Why?"

She waved a hand dismissively. "Half of all Speakers are women. You ever heard of a female apprentice?"

"No," Wulf admitted. A brancher was a bird that had left the nest but not yet the tree. He suspected his current teacher-handler was trying to distract him. "So what did Havel want? Why did he come?"

"I know not. He was given no chance to say, as you told me."

"To kill me?"

Marek had suggested that, but Justina shook her head vigorously. "Speakers do *not* go around killing Speakers! Likely he just wanted to speak with your brother, the new count, and he expected there to be a guardian Speaker present, so he brought his own to make sure the discussion was fair."

Like having a lawyer present. Speakers could detect the use of talent. Wulf realized that he was nodding. At last things were starting to make sense. Above all, he no longer felt all alone. "How much do Speakers earn?"

Justina frowned as if he had asked a stupid question. "Their lives."

"Oh."

"Work it out. I think you had better get to work, warrior. I'll stay here. War is not a woman's place. It is not a place for Speakers at all. Come with me." She heaved herself to her feet, leaning on the table, and walked stiffly to the corner. Wulf took up his cloak and sword and followed, listening as she continued her lecture.

"If you glimpse another nimbus, stay and keep them honest. Be prepared to talk. If you see two or more, come back here *instantly*, you hear? You're not ready for a fight. And come back here and ask my advice before you use any major power. Don't worry if I'm not alone, just come."

She paused at the door to the cottage. "Take a look."

He looked. It was obviously a kitchen, and a well-equipped one, with a big table in the center and shelves around the walls laden with crocks and pots.

"I'll be here in Avlona, outdoors or indoors. Don't come to me if I'm anywhere else. If there's anyone with me here, come to the other side of the wall and enter like a workaday. And on no account murder any more priests or clerics! Come at dusk, in any case, and we'll think what we can do about that bombard."

"I thank you for your help," he said, not meaning to be ironic. She had told him very little, but she had hinted at much. It had been his first proper discussion with another Speaker, and already he felt like less of a freak—there were other people out there like him! She had taught him more than Marek had learned in five years at Koupel. That wall of silence was itself informative. He slung his cloak over his shoulders. "I look forward to many more lessons, Justina."

"We'll see. You're in very great danger. Not just the castle, you personally. I was sent to help you, but if my superiors . . . To be honest, I can't see that I'll be allowed to continue helping when this news gets out."

So the helping hand was being withdrawn and the prison gates were closing. He did not feel surprised. The sense of doom that had come with Marek's death returned stronger than ever. Father had always told him his temper would kill him one day.

He bowed. "Thank you for what you have done already. I don't want to cause you any trouble, so if you'd rather I just dissolved into thin air, I'll—"

"Wait!" she said. "That horrible gallows contrivance your hairy brother was building . . . Now, I am no warrior, only a simple serving wench, but I do hope they call in the bishop to bless it."

Wulf paused in buckling on his sword. "The wood may be unsound?"

She nodded. "It's old."

"A blessing is a sort of curse in reverse?"

She nodded again, eyes twinkling.

"How close must a Speaker be to bless?"

"The closer the better. Laying a hand on it would be best."

"Thank you, Justina."

"And hereafter, mind well what you bless or curse or what oaths you swear! You may do more than you intend."

"Thank you again!" About to open a gate through limbo, he realized that the castle and town would be a whirlwind of activity, people every-where. "Um . . . how do I find a safe place to return unobserved?"

She shrugged, seeming amused at his naïveté. "You don't want to be seen stepping out of thin air."

"No, I certainly do not."

"So you want not to?"

"Yes." What was she hinting?

"You think your Voices don't know that?"

Not wanting to seem stupid, he nodded. "Thank you. God be with you, Justina."

He went back to Gallant.

CHAPTER 5

Wulf stepped out of limbo in the corner behind one of the outdoor stone staircases that lined the streets of the town. Even if his Voices no longer spoke to him, they must still be looking after his well-being, because nobody noticed. A band of women was hurrying away from him, but no one was coming in his direction, and he saw no faces peering out of windows. The north barbican tower loomed over the road ahead, so he took off at a run, shouting at the women to get out of his way. They cleared a path at once for a man dressed as a noble.

There was no direct access to the barbican from the town at ground level, so he ran out through the big gate to the Quarantine Road. He found himself in a human anthill, with men and horses bringing in tools, timber, and bales of arrows from the town. Dalibor Notivova, the constable, was shouting himself hoarse in the tumult. There had been no time to erect derricks and pulleys, so men on the roof were hauling the supplies up on ropes, hand over hand. Every few minutes one would lose his grip and screams of warning would announce a load coming down much faster than it had been going up.

Wulf silently cursed the late Count Bukovany, who had

done nothing to put his castle on a war footing. But Anton had been keeper for five days now and done no better. He had not even stocked the two barbican towers with ammunition. *Anton had still not reached the south barbican.* That was a dizzying reminder that the world of ordinary, er, workadays moved at a snail's pace compared with the Speakers'.

Deciding that he could do no good there, Wulf ran back into the town. He was trying to find a way into his first battle with no orders, no specific duty, and no armor. He wielded the most potent weapon imaginable, but had not been trained in its use. About all he was sure of was that he was not Jove, who could have smitten that advancing column of Pomeranians with thunderbolts. And if he were, that would be a breach of the first commandment.

The nearest house was being demolished by men up at roof level, who were prying it apart stone by stone. Porters below were waiting until they saw a safe moment to dive forward and grab a block from the rising heaps. These they would then carry up the stairs flanking the curtain wall. Wulf needed to go up those stairs. Pride would not let him go empty-handed, so he joined the carrying line and was amused by the astonished expressions, the hasty bows and salutes. Only noblemen wore swords, so they stood aside to let him go next, and of course pride made him choose one of the largest stones he could see. Bent backward by its weight, he staggered over to join the line of sweating, half-naked men on the staircase.

Building stones were usually cut to a size one man could conveniently move, but even so they could conveniently crush feet when dropped. He could probably use his talent to make his burden lighter, but then he would despise himself for cheating. Climbing stairs with such a load was especially tricky, for the steps were high and made him waddle. The countercurrent of men hurrying down to fetch more stones was going by on the outside, and to jostle one of them might send him plunging down to death or injury. All in all, it was a challenging experience, and he could not let his attention wander to spy on what was happening elsewhere.

He could hear the sounds of war coming over the curtain wall, though: shouts, screams, bugles, the constant rat-tat of crossbows, the even louder cracks of firearms. He could smell powder smoke, although he could not see any. Several dead or badly wounded men had fallen from the curtain wall to the street, and once he had to wait while a body lying on the steps was removed. With so few men to defend the city, Vlad might fail to hold it even against a conventional attack. And while the defenders were occupied with this assault, gunners would be preparing a nest for the Dragon at the mouth of the gorge.

Just as he thought his arms would be dragged out of their sockets, he arrived at the top of the stairs, level with the walk along the wall. The porters ahead of him went hurrying into the shelter of the barbican, but he needed to see what was going on. He stepped across to the parapet, which was about waist high, and heaved the stone up on it. Then he vaulted up beside it, staying down at a crouch to avoid becoming a target, and trying not to get in the way of the archers stationed there. The dozen or so crenels nearest the barbican were manned by two archers apiece—crenels farther away from the barbican would be too far from the road for accurate shooting. The men took turns shooting through the gap and then retreating to the shelter of the merlons to crank up their bows again. Crossbows were much handier for this battlement work than longbows, but sometimes an archer was not quick enough, and a bolt from an attacker would hiss past him, or thud into him. Half a dozen dead or wounded lay in full view.

Madlenka was hurrying along the battlements in this direction, but keeping her gaze straight ahead. Giedre was sure to be somewhere close, so he switched his point of view to her, and discovered that she was bringing up the rear of a parade of at least a dozen boys, women, and older men, coming from the keep, bringing stretchers and bandages. Madlenka was out in front, of course.

Wulf waited until the nearest crenel was vacant, then stood up to peer through it. At least a thousand Wends were approaching down the Silver Road at a slow, deliberate pace like a funeral march, obviously trying to keep their formation, and still far enough from the gate that the defenders could not yet drop rocks on them. The front three ranks and the file on their left, which was the open side of the road, carried large shields as protection against archery, but the defenders were taking a fearsome toll on them. The men on the right of the column were protected by the cliff. Those at the rear, roughly half of the troop, were archers, shooting over the heads of the rest. They must outnumber the castle's archers by five or six to one, but they were handicapped by having to keep moving. They would stop to span their bows, run forward to the rear of the main force, then load and shoot. Then repeat. Of course they were shooting almost blind, aiming at loopholes and crenels, while presenting childishly easy targets to the defenders. So what were the rest of the men planning, those carrying neither bows nor shields? If they did not do whatever it was soon, their whole force was going to be obliterated.

Yes, more men were busily doing something in the distance, at the mouth of the gorge. Digging a trench to hold the Dragon, most likely.

"Boy!" roared an archer, grabbing Wulf's shoulder and yanking him out of the crenel. A bolt clanged off the side of the merlon and twanged away into the town. "You trying to get yourself killed?"

"Seems I almost did," Wulf admitted sheepishly. "Thanks."

Idiot! Even a Speaker would be no help if he had a quarrel sticking out of his chest. Steadying his sword, Wulf jumped down off the parapet. He succeeded in lifting the building stone without damage to toes or fingers and then inserted himself in the line of porters heading into the barbican, where progress slowed to a crawl.

Now he could let his mind roam to the south barbican. *Anton was standing just inside the sally port, talking with Arturas, the herald. A few men-at-arms were lurking nearby and nobody seemed to be unduly alarmed.*

". . . cardinal warned me that I might find myself between the dogs and the wolves."

Arturas laughed and the eavesdroppers exchanged proud smiles.

Of course they would be impressed to hear that their count was on joking terms with the king's first minister, which was what Anton had intended. The story would be all over town by nightfall. Arturas was a short, nondescript, clerical sort of man in his late twenties, rarely seen without a diffident smile. Today he was wearing a formal herald's tabard, which meant that Anton's sudden summons to the south gate had been a call to a parley. Count Pelrelm must have sent up a flag of truce, as required by the Church's laws of war. Anton was not as experienced in wrangling as Otto or even Vlad, but he was glib of tongue and fast of wit. He had thrown Havel out of the cathedral on Sunday and the great hall yesterday, and would not be easily fooled. If Havel wanted to talk now, it was probably because his bishop had insisted. The Church always tried to arrange a negotiated settlement before a battle. And one would get you ten that the present delay was because the Cardicians were waiting on Bishop Ugne to complete their team.

"One Speaker is defense," Justina had said. Havel would certainly have brought a Speaker along to defend him against tweaking, assuming he had found one to replace Vilhelmas. The boy Leonas lacked the wits to undertake that sort of task. So Wulf's place was at his brother's side. He must quickly do whatever he could at the north gate and get to the parley before the dirty work began.

Madlenka and her helpers were almost at the battle scene. She would be exposed to stray arrows out there on the wall, but she would insist on doing her duty as she saw it. He could do nothing to stop her, short of transporting her to Portugal, Outremer, or the land of Prester John, and she would never forgive him if he did that.

The machine room was less dangerous, with the defenders there enjoying better protection behind the narrow loopholes than the men exposed on the wall. The trickle of bolts that came whistling in through the loopholes had a low trajectory, so that more of them struck the far wall than the ceiling—a real threat, but also a welcome source of replacement ammunition.

Now Wulf realized with dismay that the stone he carried was destined to go all the way to the roof of the tower, so he could not leave yet. He still had more stairs to climb: spiral staircases, narrow and steep, and the up traffic was waiting its turn. He directed his attention to Vlad, who was still up there, supervising the fitting of ropes to the first trebuchet. He was ignoring the Wends, so Wulf could not Look to see what mischief they were up to, but an effort to burn down or undermine the gate was the most likely guess. *Their archers were concentrating their shots on the tower roof, dropping a steady barrage of bolts on it. There were a lot of bodies lying there, some with more than one arrow stuck in them. Men were stripping off the lead sheeting, exposing the timber roof below. . . .* Why?

The waiting line lurched forward and Wulf began to walk again, aware that his hands and shoulders were cramping with the strain. No, he would *not* use his talent to cheat. Almost all of the other men were much older than he was, and most of them were smaller. He was not big as Magnuses went, but he had eaten well all his life, and few commoners enjoyed that luxury.

The staircases from the machine room to the attic, and the attic to the roof, were too narrow for teams to pass safely, so they were sent up in relays. That meant they were expected to go faster. Wulf was streaming sweat and gasping when he emerged into the icy wind, blinking at the sunlight. He had expected that the stone he had brought would contribute to the trebuchet counterweight, but he was directed to add it to a pile beside a merlon. There were other piles beside other merlons, apparently intended to be dropped on the attackers when they came close enough.

As he stepped back, a crossbow quarrel slammed into the lead of the floor right at his feet, making him jump. All in all, the defense had already lost two or three dozen men, more than it could afford, and four injured men sat curled up small beside the stair, waiting for help. Crossbow quarrels stuck up everywhere like hairs on a wart.

"You!" roared a sergeant-at-arms. "Back down!" He waved for Wulf to go to the stairs.

Wulf waved back politely and instead trotted over to the trebuchet, where Vlad and half a dozen men were loading rolled sheets of roofing lead into the counterweight cradle. Another four men were attempting to hold shields over them and also themselves, but Wulf doubted very much that a limewood shield would stop a bolt dropping from a great height. Vlad noticed his arrival and straightened up, angrily pushing two shields aside. "What do you want?"

Wondering if his brothers were starting to doubt his loyalty, Wulf said, "Victory for His Majesty and obliteration of the ungodly. You've done a fine job here, Big Man." He patted the nearest upright. *May your timbers stay strong and your ropes endure. May your aim be true and your blows decisive.*

A bolt cracked into the wood not a finger length from his hand.

"Crazy young idiot!" Vlad bellowed. "This is no place for boys. Get yourself downstairs and do something useful."

"I'll go roast an ox for the victory feast," Wulf said. He went off to the top of the stair, where the collection of wounded had already increased to six. Men lining up to go down were loading them on their backs.

At that moment Wend bugles blew and everyone's attention went to the battle. The massed attackers dropped their shields and revealed their attack: not battering rams or kegs of gunpowder, but ladders, two of them. Made of two tree trunks apiece, they were not only enormously long and heavy, they were rigged with ropes to raise them. The slow and deliberate approach had been designed to keep those ropes from becoming entangled. In an impressive display of training, the men divided into three groups. A center group steadied the base of the ladders, a group behind pushed them up with pikes and poles, and the group in front, by far the largest, ran forward with the ropes. Meanwhile the archers at the back worked their crossbows in a frenzy.

"Rocks!" Vlad roared. Men rushed to the battlements and began throwing out the building stones. Most of them fell short of their targets, and the supply would obviously run out in minutes. Wulf again silently cursed the late Count Bukovany.

Gradually the far ends of the ladders rose and the attackers' main problem became the need to keep the bases from slipping. They had as many men attending to that as they had pulling on the ropes, and the defenders poured arrows into them. Higher yet, and now the haulers by the gate were clearly winning as the angle improved. First one ladder, then the other, reached the vertical and began to topple toward the barbican. As soon as that happened, would-be heroes began scrambling aboard.

The rain of rocks had stopped for lack of ammunition. There was still plenty of discarded timber lying around the roof, though. Full of rot or worms those balks might be, but every one of them was heavy enough to kill or maim the men it landed on. Wulf found himself swept up in a gang manhandling one of the largest to the edge and raising it to go over the crenels, which was no mean task. They were just in time. As it vanished towards the ground, the top of the first ladder came rushing down to the battlements. The second followed moments later. The tower trembled at the impact.

The Wends' planning had been excellent. They had judged the length of the ladders and their distance from the gate perfectly, for they were neither too long nor too short, overtopping the coping stones by a useful three or four feet. Defenders jumped to try and push them aside with hands or pikes, but already Wends were swarming up the rungs, weighing them down. Other attackers were holding the ropes as guylines to keep them vertical.

Wulf clawed his way to the front and managed to scramble up over the massed men-at-arms until his fingers could touch the rough wood of a ladder. —*Break! You were damaged in the impact. There is a weakness near the third rung from the bottom. When the men reach the top you will be overloaded.*

A sword flashed, swinging at his hand, and he fell back, lost his footing, tipped off the parapet, and sprawled headlong on the deck below, narrowly avoiding impaling himself on a couple of the embedded bolts. He was dazed for a moment, but a rattle of crossbows snapped him awake. The defender archers were lined up, shooting at Wends mounting the ladders. So he had failed. The rungs were full, and the rails were holding their weight. His curse had not prevailed against whatever blessing the Wends' Speakers had used. Archery stopped as the defenders ran out of ammunition, leaving them only swords and pikes to repel the assault.

Then came a great roar from a thousand throats, part wailing, part cheering. The ladder he had cursed began to slide sideways. One leg had failed, as he had commanded. The top caught in a crenel, so the whole structure twisted and slammed into the other. Both ladders went then, with their human cargoes shrieking in terror and despair. Some who were low enough would fall to the road and crush other men, but most would be hurled over the edge, down to the banks of the Ruzena far below.

Madlenka and her helpers were on the wall near the barbican, loading a wounded man on a stretcher for transport back to the keep. There they had been within range of arrows, but there would not be many arrows coming now. At the south barbican, Anton was just stepping out the sally port, following Bishop Ugne.

Everybody on the roof was up on the parapet, peering through merlons and even over crenels, cheering and jeering as they watched the Wends crash to destruction. No one was watching Wulf. The battle at the north gate was won for today. It was time to go and attend to the other foe. Busy morning.

Wulf unbuckled his belt, dropped it, sword and all, and went to attend the parley.

CHAPTER 6

He did not break the first commandment, because he emerged from limbo directly behind Anton just as the sally port thumped shut at his back. The door itself would have hidden his mysterious materialization from the men inside, and the slight overhang of the arch from any watchers on the walls.

The new outpost Vlad had ordered, a hundred yards down the road at the first bend, comprised a timber breastwork and some blindings to conceal his archers while they reloaded. Those would also prevent the enemy from knowing how many men opposed them, which at present was no more than a dozen. The outpost, in short, was a sham, but the Jorgarian flag flew above it, beside the pennant of the new count of Cardice. If Havel Vranov tried to force his way past, he would be making war on his king. He must not be allowed to see behind the blindings, so the parley would have to take place on the far side of it, in no-man's-land. Bearing a white flag, Arturas led the way down the slushy trail, with count and bishop following, and the gate-crashing Speaker in the rear.

Wulf poked Anton in the back, under his corselet.

Anton warped around and gave him a what-are-you-doing-here glare.

Wulf returned a knowing, you-need-me smirk. After eighteen years' practice in dealing with each other in war and peace, the brothers needed few words to communicate. Anton pulled a face and returned to attendance on the bishop.

Ugne was not an especially short man, but he appeared so next to Anton. His conspicuous belly and flat-footed waddle made his legs seem short, though, and perhaps they were. He had a very prominent curved nose. Madlenka said that he looked like a parrot, but today he was enveloped in a robe of snowy ermine with a red miter. Wulf decided he was more of a cockatoo.

"Bishop Starsi is a most holy man," he proclaimed. "His health has been causing concern of late and it is a measure of his dedicated service to the Prince of Peace that he has made the arduous journey over these hills to participate in this holy discourse."

"I am not yet familiar with the limits of my own fief, my lord bishop," Anton said. "I do not even know how far away Pelrelm is."

"Oh, a day's ride or less to the border. But Pelrelm is much larger than Cardice, and mountainous. The bishop's see is in Woda, three days' hard riding away from here in summer, and more in these conditions."

They should let the holy man make an early start on his homeward journey, Wulf thought. But this was Friday, and on Sunday Anton had arrived in his new domain and thrown the conspiring Havel Vranov out on his ear. There should not have been time since then for him to ride home to Woda and rout the bishop out of bed to come and negotiate a parley. Havel himself certainly dabbled in Satanism, but was his bishop one of the Wise?

The garrison on the redoubt saluted as the dignitaries arrived. They had already opened a gap in the breastwork, so Arturas led the way through and the others followed. Wulf grinned at a couple of faces he recognized from the banquet and took note of them as people whose eyes he might want to borrow in the near future—especially Master Sergeant Jachym, who was currently in command of this suicide squad.

Less traveled, the snow beyond the outpost was less slushy. A few more yards of it brought Wulf to his first view of what lay around the bend. The road descended more steeply down the side of a V notch in the cliff, which it crossed on a trestle bridge. If Anton had shown some foresight, he could have stripped the deck off of it days ago and given himself a better first line of defense.

Havel's armed escort of at least two hundred mounted men-at-arms and archers was already on the Castle Gallant side of the bridge, drawn up in rows. The Hound and four companions were closer, still on horseback. Apart from the count himself, there was a portly herald in a tabard, a crozier-carrying bishop in miter and vestments, a man in armor, and a boy on a pony. They now began to dismount, with the herald and the man-at-arms assisting the bishop, and the boy taking charge of the horses.

The groups met halfway. The heralds proclaimed a parley. The two bishops exchanged the kiss of peace and blessed the proceedings. The wind was damned cold. *Madlenka was up on the roof of the north barbican, bandaging a wounded boy. Idiot woman! A few Wend arrows were still falling.*

Starsi was elderly, with the spare, parchment face of an invalid. He was taller than the tubby Ugne, but sorely bent; the bony hand clutching his crozier trembled constantly. He ought to be home in bed, not out here on a mountain trail in winter.

Ugne presented Count Magnus. Anton kissed Starsi's ring.

Unnecessarily, Starsi introduced Havel Vranov to Ugne. Wulf had not previously set eyes—his own eyes—on the notorious Hound, but he had stolen Looks at him through others'. He was a heavyset man of middle years, wearing a salt-and-pepper beard that made him seem older than he probably was. His nose was generous and aquiline, although not on the same Alpine scale as Ugne's, and he had a slight limp.

That should have been that for introductions, for attendants did not matter. The man-at-arms was a squire, taller than anyone else there, other than Anton, of course. Although his helmet obscured most of his face, it revealed enough of his chin to show that he was still quite young, not yet fully matured into his height. His nimbus reflected beautifully in his highly polished helmet and cuirass.

Anton could not see that, but he glanced from Wulf to the youth and back again and guessed what was happening. He begged leave to present his brother and squire, Wulfgang Magnus. Wulf dipped a knee in the snow to kiss the bishop's ring.

Havel Vranov went through much the same procedure to introduce "My nephew and squire, Alojz Zauber."

Alojz was probably wearing leathers under his armor, so he would not get his knee wet. He might rust, though. He and Wulf exchanged stares, appraising each other. Possibly there should have been smiles and nods to acknowledge their common talent, but two Speakers had died last night, like an exchange of chessmen, so there could be no trust now. They were there to protect their respective principals and keep each other in line. They and the two counts knew the real rules of the game. The bishops and heralds probably did not.

The six conferees had automatically grouped themselves in a circle, each facing his counterpart.

"Havel," quavered Bishop Starsi, in an ancient, moss-encrusted voice, "is most anxious to do his duty by our sovereign lord, King Konrad the Fifth, beloved of his people and anointed by God. He believes that the schismatic Wends under that dog turd Wartislaw are planning to attack Castle Gallant and wishes to offer his aid. Yet he tells me that Count Magnus has twice refused it."

"As he should!" Bishop Ugne declaimed. "Your precious count invaded Castle Gallant last night in the company of Satanists. Four of them came in all. I saw their foul witchcraft with my own eyes. They vanished in the plain sight of all. He is a tool of the devil and should be dealt with accordingly."

The aged Starsi bleated nervously, "Is this true, my son?"

Havel was showing fangs like a charging bear. "Not a word of it! I was helping my men pitch camp on High Meadows last night and can produce innumerable witnesses. Alojz, for one, will support me in that, won't you, lad? Whatever you think you saw, my lord bishop, can only have been a foul sending, an apparition raised by evil Wend witchcraft. It has been no secret for years that Wartislaw is in league with Satan. No doubt his purpose was to divide Count Magnus and myself so that we are misled by distrust and fail to unite against him."

"That is the truth," Alojz said.

Fires of hell! That had been a flash! Wulf had let his thoughts wander to Madlenka again and had failed to keep an eagle's gaze on Squire Alojz. Glaring at him now, he was awarded a small smirk of triumph, hidden from anyone else by the Pelrelmian's helmet.

"It . . . it could have been a sending, I suppose," Ugne mumbled uncertainly. He looked to Anton, who did not speak.

Alojz had tweaked at least one of the bishops, perhaps both, and Wulf had no idea what he could do about it.

Old Starsi was clearly relieved. "I would believe anything of those schismatics, those children of Satan. Did you seek to exorcize the apparition, Brother? Did you banish it back to the nether regions?"

Ugne made an effort to square shoulders that were not made for squaring. "I tried," he boomed, "but the sending was too strong for an impromptu invocation. It did not depart until it had left an offering in the shape of a young dog—which, I hasten to add, we ritually burned as we purified the hall where this phantasma had appeared . . ."

And so on. But a story of four bodily intruders had now become one of a mirage. Alojz had changed Ugne's mind for him in that flash of talent. Yesterday Wulf had seen Marek do the same thing when the Castle Gallant guards refused him admission, and even Marek had glowed for a moment. Justina would call that obscene abuse of power a crime, but the ability to change people's memories explained how talent could be kept so secret. Now Bishop Ugne's report to the archbishop would describe an apparition, and the other clergy would follow his lead when preaching to their flocks, no matter what he had said previously. Wulf was aware of Anton looking sideways at him, either outraged by this absurd volte-face, or perhaps himself uncertain if he had caught a side-splash of miracle.

Tweaking was forbidden by the second commandment, but what was Wulf supposed to do about it? Reverse it? Counter-tweak? How did he defend Anton against that sort of mental aggression? No doubt "brancher" Alojz had been trained by "handler" Vilhelmas and knew all the answers. A week ago Wulf had been thrown all alone into deep water with no help but an anchor, and he was still sinking.

"Can we now discuss the forthcoming attack by the schismatic Wends?" Ugne demanded. His face, always ruddy, was glowing brighter than ever in the icy wind. "What is Havel proposing?"

"I am begging on my knees that I be allowed to fulfill my vows and perform the duty I swore to King Konrad, may God preserve His Majesty!" Havel said. "Count Magnus and I are both lords of the northern marches. Our lands march together. We are bound by fealty and custom to come to each other's aid when hazard looms, as our respective predecessors have done oftentimes. I know how poorly the late Count Bukovany, may Christ cherish his soul, prepared for this emergency, even after he had been warned of Wartislaw's intentions. I know that his successor is young and understandably headstrong, but now he and his fief stand in deadly peril. Almost his first act on his accession was to dismiss the *landsknecht* mercenaries his predecessor had hired and whom he now so sorely needs."

He paused for breath. Wulf kept his eyes firmly fixed on Alojz, who returned his attention with the amused contempt of one who is ahead on points and need only keep his opponent from scoring in order to win the match.

"You mean," Anton said sarcastically, "that, having foxes yapping at my north gate, I should now open the south one to wolves? Cardinal Zdenek himself warned me not to make that mistake."

Alojz rolled his eyes. Wulf did not lower his guard. If he saw the least flicker in the Pelrelmian's nimbus, he was going rip the kid's ear off—inside his helmet where no one else would notice.

"I hope you laugh at your folly when your head is mounted on a spike, my lord." Havel looked to Ugne. "My lord bishop, can you not make this popinjay countling see reason? Can't you explain to him that my life and lands are as much at risk as his are? If Wartislaw takes Cardice, he will have forced open the front door to Pelrelm also. I have fought the Wends all my life, and to accuse me of treason now is ludicrous!"

"How much did you pay the *landsknechte* to desert?" Anton asked.

Havel reached for his dagger. The bishops and heralds all wailed that this was a parley.

"You cannot defend this castle without my help!" the Hound yelled.

"I have the help of my brother," Anton drawled, deliberately provoking the older man. "No, not this one, although he keeps our spirits up with an endless flow of droll stories. I refer to Sir Vladislav Magnus, a knight banneret famed throughout Christendom, who is now supervising our defenses and has assured me that there is no cause for alarm. He can hold off the Wends until it's so cold their pissers freeze. Which is what the wind is about to do to me, so we should discontinue this meaningless blithering and save your venerable bishop from further distress. Or are you about to threaten to blast your way into my castle and steal it before the Wends do?"

Nobody spoke. Wulf wanted to look at their faces, but dared not take his attention off Alojz.

"That is your last word?" Havel growled at last.

"Almost. If you truly wish to help us," Anton conceded, "I will admit that we are short of crossbow bolts. So if you care to deliver a wagonload or two to our outpost, I shall happily pay for them at standard rates. The same goes for rent or purchase of any bombards or other firearms you are not using, and of course suitable powder and shot. In short, your help with matériel will be welcome and gratefully acknowledged to His Majesty, but none of your men will set foot inside my gates, and that is final."

Nicely done. A true patriot should be willing to negotiate on that basis. Wulf raised an eyebrow to invite Alojz's approval of Anton's verbal dexterity, but the youth just sneered.

And Havel turned his back. "Come, my lord bishop," he said. "The boy is mad and we must leave him to God's mercy."

"Anton, my son, is this wise?" Ugne muttered.

"My lord bishop," Anton declared, loud enough for all to hear, "I have knowledge sure as Holy Writ that Havel Vranov is in league with the Pomeranians." He knew that because Wulf had seen the Hound drinking with the Wends at Long Valley last night; but Wulf could never testify to that in a court of law. "He has taken their silver on the promise of delivering Castle Gallant into their hands. His head will fall in good time to the headsman's ax, and his soul will writhe in Satan's furnace for eternity. Take your rabble out of my domain, Hound. You are an irrelevant nuisance."

Anton took Bishop Ugne's arm and turned him around. Arturas looked sadly at the opposing herald and both shrugged. The meeting broke up. The workadays went their separate ways, but Alojz Zauber lingered, probably checking that Wulf did not try anything as soon as his back was turned. Wulf also waited.

"How many of you Magnuses are there?" the Pelrelmian demanded. "You must breed like rats."

"Enough of us to handle the Wends and the Hound without working up a sweat. You're filling in for Father Vilhelmas, are you?"

The boy bared his teeth. "Assassins!"

"Are we? Ask the late Count Bukovany and his son."

"Ask your brother the friar."

"That murder was really stupid," Wulf said. "For three hundred years, killing Magnuses has been a swift form of suicide. Go home and talk to your confessor before it's too late, boy."

A life-and-death parley had degenerated into a child's slanging match. Assuming that Anton was now safely out of range, Wulf turned on his heel and strode away.

CHAPTER 7

Although there had been no attack on Castle Gallant in Madlenka's lifetime, nor in her father's either, her mother had lived through the siege of Castle Zamek before her marriage and knew exactly what had to be done, or thought she did. Quick as Madlenka usually was to find fault with Dowager Countess Edita, she had to admit that the old scold did a fine job in this instance. In no time, she had collected bedding, bandages, and priests, and transformed the hall into an infirmary. Every barber-surgeon in town had been ordered to attend and bring his implements. Boys and able old men were lined up as stretcher bearers. Even before the first Pomeranian quarrel rattled against the barbican wall, the infirmary was open for business.

Madlenka herself took charge of the stretcher-bearing teams, partly because she thought her authority would get help to the wounded faster, partly because she dreaded the horrors of blood and pain that would unfold in the hall. In a way, she was being cowardly in choosing the danger of the battlements, and she remembered Father telling Petr that courage usually sprang from fear of being thought a coward.

Halfway to the barbican she realized that her mother had blundered when she set up the infirmary in the keep, for it was too far from the north gate. She should have consulted one of the Magnus brothers, any of whom would probably have advised her to requisition St. Sebastijan's church, which was much closer. And as soon as this skirmish was over, they must organize another hospital near the south gate, probably in St. Petr's. People forget how to fight wars after too many years of peace.

When she arrived at the fighting, Madlenka had no trouble sweeping up the casualties on the curtain wall, but collecting them from the roof of the barbican was a challenge that required every glint of aristocratic arrogance she could summon. Carrying loaded stretchers down a spiral staircase would be both slow and dangerous, so she moved her first-aid station into the machine room and issued orders that the porters taking materials up must not come down empty-handed. Soon screaming wounded were arriving piggyback, or over shoulders. The bolts had been falling at very steep angles, so the wounds were mostly in shoulders and feet. More than one man had been temporarily nailed to the floor, though, and one even had his helmet spiked to his skull; he died on the stretcher.

If anyone had asked her yesterday, she would have said that such gruesome sights would throw her straight into hysteria, yet in the heat of battle she found herself so caught up by the urgency of moving these suffering men to relief as fast as possible that she never lost her nerve for a moment. Neither the blood on her hands and clothes nor the crossbow bolts going *zang!* off the stonework distracted her.

She was only dimly aware of what was going on outside, but she knew that the Wends must either climb over the battlements above or force the main gate below, and in either case the fighting would head for the machine room. The thick stone walls muffled the noise, the shouted orders, the cheers and groans, the clamor of firearms and crossbows. But she registered the roar when the ladders fell.

Jubilation reigned. The defenders screamed their lungs out in triumph. The emergency was over for the day, and soon the Wends withdrew, leaving hundreds of dead behind them. Most of the defenders were allowed to stand down, and promptly rushed away in search of beer, song, and other means of celebration. The last of the wounded in the machine room were carried off to the infirmary, and Madlenka breathed for the first time in too long.

She wiped her forehead with the back of her wrist and smiled at Giedre, who looked a freak. Her hair hung in a tangle, as if her head covering had gone for bandages. Her clothes and hands were filthy and bloodstained. Madlenka could be in no better shape, although at least she had retained her turban. They had survived their first battle. Please God that it be their last!

"That seems to be all, my lady," Giedre said, probably the first time anyone had used Madlenka's title in . . . how long? An hour? Two?

"We'd better check." She headed for the spiral staircase, just as Dali emerged from it. He carried his sallet under his arm, but he seemed to be unwounded, and was grinning as widely as any human being ever could, rattail hair plastered over sweat-streaked face. Forget transient visitors like Sir Vladislav Magnus. Officially Dalibor Notivova was in charge of the defenses of Castle Gallant and had just repulsed a major assault. One more for the history books, and perhaps the greatest moment in his entire life.

"Well done, constable!" she said. "Or are you Sir Dalibor now?"

"Not yet, my lady." Incredibly his grin grew even wider. "But Sir Vlad has promised to dub me—tonight in the hall!"

Not too many years ago, when she was a child and he was a married man, she would have given him a hug over news much less grand than knighthood, but now it could not be. She congratulated him. So did Giedre. Was that a slight blush under her grime and bloodstains? Why did Dali abruptly put his sallet on, hiding his face? Madlenka had not suspected . . . but she had been too drowned in her own troubles. And why shouldn't they? Dali needed a stepmother for his children, and Giedre could no longer count on accompanying Madlenka to some far-off land when she married some distant noble. Madlenka was going to be staying right here till the day she died.

Dali thanked them both for caring for the wounded.

"Any left up there?" Madlenka asked.

"Two or three still linger, but can't be moved. The rest are beyond your help, ma'am."

Corpses were men's business.

Madlenka sent Giedre off to the keep, with orders to turn back any stretcher parties she met coming this way. She ran up to the roof to check on those wounded who were not to be moved, and see if Wulf was there. He wasn't, and had certainly not been among the wounded carried off to the infirmary, so he was probably with Anton, wherever that was.

At least a score of bodies lay around the roof with their faces covered, to show that they were indeed dead and had received the proper rites. Surely Dali or Vlad would arrange to have the corpses removed as soon as possible? There was no sign of the biggest Magnus. Beside the unfinished trebuchet, though, a priest was administering extreme unction to a casualty, and Baron Ottokar was kneeling beside him, bareheaded. As she drew nearer, she saw that he was holding the dying man's hand, which seemed an oddly touching gesture from so hard a man.

The victim was little older than she; she knew him by sight but not by name. He must have tripped or been knocked down by a previous hit, for he had obviously been prone when an arrow had dropped from the sky and nailed him to the floor. She knelt down on his other side just as the priest reached the final blessing. She and the baron crossed themselves. The man himself was obviously unconscious. The priest rose.

"I believe that's all, Father," Ottokar said, glancing around. "No, there's one more over there, see?" He pointed to where someone was urgently beckoning, and the priest, having frowned disapprovingly at Madlenka, swished off to attend to another casualty.

Madlenka looked suspiciously at the unconscious man before her. She took his other hand and felt for a pulse. "I think he's dead," she said.

Ottokar nodded and laid the man's arms gently on his chest. "You don't happen to have a cloth on you, do you?"

She did, a spare bandage already badly bloodstained. She gave it to him and he covered the corpse's face. Then he rose, and she did too. "How long has he been dead?" she asked.

The baron was very big, although not as huge as Vladislav. He was almost as tall as Anton, but much wider, and he had a broad, stony face, with very cold, dark eyes. On her first sight of him yesterday she had decided that he was both clever and potentially dangerous, and she saw no reason to change her mind now. But his eyes were red-rimmed and his face stubbled, reminding her of Father, the time he had been up all night directing a fire-fighting operation in the town.

"I have no idea," he said softly. "He might have been dead when I got here."

"You lied to the priest?"

He shrugged. "But now the holy man can in good faith tell the boy's family that he died in a state of grace."

She realized that a small smile was twisting the edges of His Lordship's mouth. If it was mockery, it seemed to be directed less at her than at his own sentimentality. So there was a gentle side to this man after all? She had failed to find it at the banquet last night, when they had been seated next to each other.

"This is the worst part of battle," he said, starting to stroll across the deck toward the northern battlements. "Counting the bodies, I mean. But thanks to you and your team, there may not be as many bodies as there might have been. I was watching. I congratulate you on a fine job."

"Thank you." She had only done what was needed.

"First aid is the best part of a siege. Sieges are the nastiest sort of war, you know, but at least the defenders receive decent medical care and aren't left lying all night in the mud, waiting to have their throats slit in the morning."

That did not sound like a hard man talking, nor even like a warrior.

"And I congratulate you on a successful defense."

He glanced down at her, sideways, and this time there was no doubt about the smile. "I don't deserve any credit. That was a very dramatic end to the assault, wasn't it?" He leaned into a merlon to peer down at the shambles in front of the gate. "No, don't look," he said, straightening up. "The plunderers are at work already."

"The Wends took a bad beating!"

He leaned back against a crenel and folded his arms, regarding her quizzically. "Yes and no. They lost at least ten times as many men as we did."

"That's good, isn't it?"

"Ye-e-e-s." He dragged the word out. He might have been mocking her, but his smile seemed genuine enough. "But if they had more than ten times as many men to start with—twenty times, forty times as many?

DAVE DUNCAN

Most people would say that Wartislaw can afford to lose ten times as many men as Anton can."

"But you don't?"

"Not necessarily. Armies are funny things. . . . The Cardician men are fighting for their families, their homes. They'll go on to the last drop of blood, and their sons and wives and daughters beside them. The Wends are fighting for money, mostly. A couple of bad maulings like this one and they're apt to start recalling things they forgot to do before they left home. Their best leaders will have died or been wounded. I've seen armies lose faith and just melt away, even mercenary armies."

"But they won't make the same mistake again, will they?"

He shrugged. "If they knew how little ammunition we have left . . . You're not planning to go out there and minister to injured Wends, are you?"

The thought had not even occurred to her. "Is that normal?"

"I've never heard of it. If their flag of truce gets here before the scavengers deal with them, they can rescue their own. They'd better hurry, though."

His manner to her was somehow fatherly but not patronizing, confiding but not gossipy. He was certainly not talking down to her; in fact he was almost speaking in riddles, encouraging her to question more deeply. "Have you ever seen ladders fail like that?"

His eyes twinkled. "No. Oh, I've seen ladders break, but never with such dramatic results. But then, I've never seen an assault attempted against a wall so high in such a narrow space. Rash, it was; asking for trouble. They knew that road was a killing ground; they knew the castle's history."

"The ladders' collapse was unusual, though?"

He shrugged. "I think so, but I won't go around talking about it."

He was talking with her about it. Why? If it had been Wulf's magic that broke the first ladder, how many men's deaths must he now have on his conscience? But how many defenders' lives had he saved by preventing a sack?

If it had been Wulf's doing.

"We're all very stubborn, us Magnuses," Baron Magnus remarked, turning his head to stare across the valley at the snowy mass of Mount

Naproti. "Notoriously so. I expect Vlad and I were holy terrors when we were children. Don't remember. Marek never was. Marek was always owlish, bookish; didn't give a spit about weapons or training or even horses, much."

Madlenka hadn't seen Marek around all morning. She wondered where he was. A man in holy orders couldn't fight, but he should have been helping in the infirmary.

"Anton was," his brother said thoughtfully. "A holy terror, I mean. Drove the castle staff crazy. And Father. Even Vlad and me."

So the abrupt change of subject was a lead-in to a litany of Anton's virtues and pending sainthood, was it? She thought she already knew quite as much about her husband as she ever needed to.

"We were all," the baron said. "Or almost all, glad when he discovered puberty. At least that channeled his villainy along predictable lines. But Wulf . . ." Ottokar sighed.

It was not to be a lecture about Anton. She waited.

"Until he was about seven, Wulf was a bull; a small bull, but deadly. When he charged, you couldn't stop him. You just had to get out of his way, although sometimes you could distract him by waving a red flag, or a honey cake, in his case." Otto turned to peer up innocently at the bulk of the Hogback, rising almost vertically to the clouds above them.

"And after he reached seven? A little young for puberty, surely?"

"I'm not at all sure he's reached puberty even yet."

"I am."

"Well, he's growing up fast," the baron told the sky. "After he reached seven, he was more like a bull*dog* than a bull. Once he got his teeth into something, there was never any way to get them out again." Otto sighed and then smiled at her. "No way at all."

So what was he hinting? Was this a warning or encouragement?

"We must all be very grateful to him for what he did today," she said. "If he did it, I mean."

"If he did it," the baron agreed.

"And he cured Anton's injuries on Tuesday."

This time it was the baron who remained silent.

Was he hinting that Anton ought to step aside and let Wulf marry Madlenka, or was she just reading too much into an offer of friendship and perhaps support? Something, almost certainly this morning's victory, had changed Otto's attitude since last night, when he had plainly disapproved of Wulf's intrusion into the Anton-Madlenka match.

"Gratitude becomes a man," Madlenka said. "But it's too late, isn't it?" A handfasting was as binding as a marriage. "Would even gratitude help now?"

"I don't know," Otto said sadly. "I just don't know."

CHAPTER 8

Satisfied that there were no more casualties in need of transportation, Madlenka headed home along the wall walk, smiling to all the happy people she passed, listening to the laughter echoing up from the streets.

She was effectively alone! Since her handfasting three days ago, Anton had made sure that never happened—except for one precious moment last night, when she had exchanged a few words with Wulf. But otherwise she had always been escorted by her maids or Giedre or Noemi or Ivana or Mother or some combination. And now, just by chance, there was nobody watching over her. Except possibly Wulf? When she came to Fishermen's Bartizan, the temptation was much too strong to resist. She turned aside and ran up the steps.

Because the curtain wall that enclosed both town and castle stood atop high cliffs, it could not be assaulted, and so had few watchtowers. Fishermen's was about midway between the north gate and the keep, roughly at the northeast corner, and was so named because the drop below it was very nearly sheer. In theory you could lower a fishing line to the Ruzena River, although in practice the resident wind would never let it reach the water. When Petr and she had been young, they had tried dangling bait, in the hope of catching eagles. All they had accomplished was to get themselves thoroughly soiled with bird droppings and forbidden to go in there again—an edict they would conveniently forget in a month or so.

As always, the bartizan was deserted, just a small stone cage suspended from the lip of the wall. A drifting of snow hid the filth on the floor and the swallows had fled their nests in search of winter quarters. There was nowhere to sit, but she stood for a few minutes relishing her solitude. To the north she could see the mouth of the gorge. The Wends were building their gun emplacement there. The last ragtag survivors of the assault force were still slinking homeward, tails between legs.

If they did not quickly return under a flag of truce to collect their dead and wounded, there would not be any wounded. Already the Gallant scavengers were out on the road, stripping armor and weapons, slitting throats and purses. Undoubtedly some Wends must have ridden the ladders over the cliff, down to the riverbank. There was a small patch of forest there, an inaccessible corner between the base of the cliffs and the river. Ancient stories told of other assailants ending down there and long-ago bishops consecrating it as a Christian graveyard.

The wind was making her shiver. Mother would notice her absence and raise a hue and cry. Still she lingered, wondering, hoping. . . . If she knew the names of Wulf's Voices, she would pray to them to tell him that she was alone, so if he could spare a minute from important men's work in this hazardous time. . . . But she didn't know the names. Dreams, only dreams.

She turned to go and he was standing in the doorway, gazing at her.

They collided into each other's arms in a rib-cracking embrace. Anton had taught her what a man expected from a kiss. Wulf did not know the details, but he proved to be a very fast learner. It was a wonderful, passionate, soul-consuming, never-ending kiss.

Yet nothing in the world lasts forever. They broke it off eventually and just hugged, chins on shoulders, cheek against stubbled cheek. She was as tall as Wulf was—too tall, really, but the right height for Anton. Nothing else was right about Anton.

"Oh, God!" he whispered. "I love you! I have never wanted anyone or anything as much as I want you."

"Me the same." If he asked her to go away with him, she would, and damn the consequences, terrible though those must be. But he knew that already, and for either of them to say so now would trigger disaster for both.

"Now I know why lust is such a popular sin."

"Love, not lust! You think I kiss every man like that?"

Grunt.

"If your brother gave kisses like that, you think I'd be here with you?"

Wulf pulled back just enough to put them eye-to-eye, much too close to focus. "You mean you like my kissing better than Anton's?"

"His are just slobber. Yours are heaven."

"Lady, my experience of kisses can be counted on the thumbs of one hand."

She gave him another one for practice. Not quite so intense, perhaps, but even better, more deliberate, even longer. When it was over—

"Don't let go," she murmured. "I'll fall down."

"We must let go," he whispered. "Nothing good can come of this."

He was right. Nothing good, only pain. Wulf was always right. Her handfasting to Anton ranked the same as marriage in the eyes of the Church. Few people below the rank of kings were ever granted a divorce, and about the only excuse for that was consanguinity. Even if she could prove that she and Anton shared ancestors a few generations back, then Wulf must be just as closely related to her.

If they ran away to cohabit out of wedlock, they would be in a state of sin all their lives. Friends and families would spurn them. Their children would be scorned and despised as bastards. Their daughters would never make a decent marriage; their sons could not enter a craft guild or a profession. Nor could a man marry his brother's widow. She must not even think about that possibility.

"You're right," she said. "Mother will be tearing the walls down. If she isn't, my . . . your brother will be. I must go."

He released her carefully and stepped back, holding her hands as if unable to break the contact completely. There were tears in those golden wolf eyes. Men never wept; it must be the wind.

"Angel lady," he said, staring at her.

"Hero." She smiled. "We have an illustrated *Morte D'Arthur* on the bookshelf. You look just like Lancelot. But handsomer."

He frowned. "And does Anton look like Arthur?"

Oh. She should not have said that. "Not in the least. . . . Um . . . Er . . . What happens now?"

"Mm?" He was smiling at her, apparently not listening.

"I mean the Wends lost a lot of men. That was a big defeat. Will they try again tomorrow?"

He shrugged. "They were trying to distract us while they bring in the Dragon. It was probably just a sop to the hotheads who wanted to do it the old-fashioned, manly way. By tomorrow or Monday their guns will smash the gates to kindling."

So today. . . . "Can you stop them?"

"Us, you mean? Or just me?"

She tugged him close and whispered, "Just you."

His eyes twinkled. "Do you want me to?"

"Yes, please."

"Ask nicely."

"Please, Wulfgang darling, don't let the wicked Wends take the castle."

"Then, just for you, I won't."

They shared a smile at this childish humor, but it faded like a flower in frost. Reality returned. He released her and stepped back.

"Go with God," he murmured, and disappeared into nowhere.

She sighed and gathered her wits. Back to the infirmary.

CHAPTER 9

The vineyard at Avlona was deserted and breathtakingly hot. Wulf threw down his cloak, thought about going around to the door, and decided to sit where he was for a few minutes. Justina probably knew he was there. He'd had a busy morning and needed some time to dream about Madlenka. Who loved him. Who thought his kisses were better than Anton's! That was incredible. Anton knew everything there could be to know about pleasing women. Ever since he was fourteen, Anton had driven Father Czcibor to distraction with his lechery. The old man had even refused him communion once, and there had been a stupendous family row. But lust was a trivial sin; how would the priest weep for Wulfgang, who had just slain a hundred men with a single act of diabolical witchcraft?

Sybilla came sauntering around the corner with her lithesome hips and sultry eyes and those worrisome bulges in her blouse. Alarm bells clanged. Wulf thought hard about Father Czcibor.

"God be with you," he said, doubting it very much. "Is Justina here?"

Sybilla sighed. "No." She bent over to put her hands and elbows on the stone table, so she could look him in the eye

85

and he could peer in the top of her blouse. "She's gone to Elysium. Are you hungry?"

"I would like something to eat, yes. Thank you." It must be noon and time for dinner.

She did not move. "Would you like to kiss me like you kissed that skinny girl?"

"You were spying on us?" Wulf barked, outraged.

Sybilla smiled dreamily. "Of course. Speakers always spy on people. You can Look in on me any time you want. In this weather I sleep without a cover."

"I'm not interested."

She shrugged. That *was* interesting. "Well, except a man, sometimes."

About to ask what she meant, he guessed in time, then veered away from the subject. "Tell me about Rome."

She oozed into a new position, sitting on a corner of the table, with her skirt pulled tight over the thigh nearest him. "It's dirty and hot and smelly and even men don't dare go out at night. There are bodies floating in the Tiber every morning and the pope holds orgies."

"Do you often attend the pope's orgies?"

"Father won't let me go."

"Who is your Father?"

"Cardinal d'Estouteville. He's dean of the College of Cardinals, you know."

"A cardinal, and he's your father?"

"He calls me his niece, but everyone knows."

"Of course." Wulf wondered if there might be some truth in all this.

"Begone!" Justina snapped, materializing beside them. "Go and tidy your room! Or muck out a stable somewhere, if you'd rather."

Sybilla pulled a face and vanished like a bubble.

"Come indoors, squire. I am sorry about the wench. Subtlety is not in Sybilla. If she were a workaday, I'd thrash her backside raw, but you can't thrash a Speaker."

Wulf took up his cloak and went with his hostess. "I find her stories entertaining," he said, being more polite than truthful.

"They're rarely true, but not always lies. If I don't get her jessed soon she'll drive me out of my mind, I swear."

"Jessed?"

"Oh. . . . Never mind. Married and pregnant."

No, that was not what it meant. Jesses were the tethers applied to a bird's legs in falconry. He had just been given another hint, which made no more sense than the others.

"Is Rome really as bad as she says?" He wondered how Anton would react to Sybilla.

"Worse, probably. Please sit. What did she say?"

The kitchen was dim and blessedly cool, with its windows shuttered against the noon heat. Pans and shelves bearing pots or jars of spices festooned the walls; hams and strings of onions dangled from low ceiling beams. Only a soft buzz of flies disturbed the silence. A solid table large enough to seat eight or so was already laden with bread, cheese, grapes, and wine.

"Does the pope hold orgies?" he asked, sitting down.

"Not this one. Or if he does, he just invites boys." Justina handed him a large earthenware bowl, which he balanced on his lap.

"No! Not the pope!"

Smiling at his horror, she brought an ewer and poured water over his hands. "So they say, but Rome eats and breathes rumors. He does have a basketful of nephews and he heaps riches and offices on them. We all know the Church is corrupt, squire. Do you doubt that Bishop Ugne bought his diocese with gifts to the archbishop and Cardinal Zdenek? Probably to the pope, also. Bishop Starsi the same. That's simony: it's a major sin, and it goes on all the time. They all keep mistresses. Oh, there are some good holy men, but the others outnumber them."

"Our chaplain at Dobkov was one of the good ones."

"I think I could have guessed that. Lucky you." She thumped a pot of soup on to the table, then clattered a pewter bowl and spoon down in front of him. "Eat all you want. Speakers never need go hungry."

He ladled some of the soup into his bowl and peered at it suspiciously. Vegetables he recognized, but the bulk of it seemed to be little rings of something.

"This is Friday."

"It's fish," she assured him. "A sort of fish, calamari."

He was hungry and the calamari was tasty, if chewier than any fish he had ever tasted before, other than salt cod, of course.

Justina sat opposite and cut the bread. She gave him a slice, took one for herself, and dipped it in oil. But it was several minutes before she spoke, and he sensed a darkening of her mood since their earlier meeting. When she did speak, however, it was to praise him.

"That was good work you did this morning, squire. With the ladder, I mean."

"Good for a haggard?"

"Good for a fledged Speaker with fifty years' experience. Simple but effective. Most important, it went unnoticed, unless the Wends had Speakers watching the battle and saw you. You're a very skilled Speaker already."

The praise pleased and disgusted him at the same time. "What is the penance for killing a hundred men by witchcraft?"

She shrugged and dismissed that topic with a wave of her aged hand. "They were Orthodox, not Catholic. The pope will absolve you. The Dominican's death is the real problem."

"Not for me." Azuolas had been a Speaker and a very unscrupulous one, in Wulf's opinion.

"For others, though." She chewed her lip for a moment, seeming much older than before. "I'm allowed to give you advice. I had to argue for even that much, and I'm not to give you any more help than that."

He stared at her in shock. "The Spider?" What sort of betrayal was this?

"No, not Zdenek. He can't know about the deaths yet, not unless he has one of his hirelings spying on us."

"Hirelings?"

"His Speaker flunkies. I'm on loan to Zdenek, as a sort of mutual favor, but we don't want to get mixed up in anything as messy as priest killings."

"Who's 'we' in this situation?"

She shook her head and dipped the last piece of crust in oil. Sybilla had said that Justina was in, or had been to, somewhere she had called Elysium.

He asked, "Did you spy on the parley also?"

She nodded.

"Is it honorable to use talent at a parley?"

"Of course not. That Alojz scares me. He doesn't look old enough to have his talent under control. Mind you," she conceded, munching bread, "he slipped a neat stroke by you when he tweaked the bishop. That was deft."

"I wasn't fast enough! How far can you twist a man's mind?"

"Well, there's a limit. If you try to make a man believe he's a horse, you'll drive him crazy. Tweaking only works properly if it's used to make people change their minds when they already want to. If he wants to be brave, you could tweak him into thinking he was brave, at least for a day or two. Your Bishop Ugne would much rather believe he was deceived by an apparition than that he saw what he really saw. So young Alojz nudged him the way he secretly wanted to go."

"Is that within the rules?"

"Not the Saints' rules, but it gets done often enough. I'd say that if you meddle with a man's free will, then God may lay all his future sins on *your* shoulders, not his. But yon Alojz boy would contend that he was striving to uphold the first commandment, concealing a public display of talent—which he was—and that excuses a lot. None of us want the workadays all upturned and shrieking about Satanism, and a sending is less threatening than a materialization. From what you tell me, that display that Havel and Vilhelmas put on in Gallant last night was shocking by any standard. I wish I knew why they did it."

This was the sort of teaching he needed, and it confirmed much of what he had been thinking. She was stretching her orders to drop hints, and he mustn't appear ungrateful. Yet questions whirled in his mind like midges. He forced himself to keep both his eating and his conversation slow and casual.

"Can you tell me what Havel really wants? Whose side he's on?"

"His own, I'd ween. You're sure you saw him with Wends at Long Valley last night?"

Wulf helped himself to more of the fish soup. "Absolutely certain."

Justina shrugged and nibbled a dainty piece of cheese as if she were just eating to keep him company. "That I don't understand. He's definitely in the know. You said he had three Speakers, all related to him?"

"Vilhelmas was a distant cousin, the moronic Leonas is his son, and he presented Alojz as a nephew. His family seems to breed even more of them than mine does."

"They breed more workadays, too. You think he had one of them murder the old count and his son?"

"Yes. I thought it was Vilhelmas, but it could have been Leonas."

"Doesn't matter now. Then he tried to take over the defense against the Wends, so he could claim the earldom as Castle Gallant's savior? I can eat that. But it doesn't explain what he was doing consorting with the Wends."

"If they really were Wends," Wulf said glumly. "I don't know a Wend from a wood dove. Perhaps the whole war is a Havel invention, and he has men at both gates? Duke Wartislaw may not even know what's being done in his name."

"Huh?" Justina was surprised. "By Our Lady, you're as sly as a fox, Squire Magnus! But how many men attacked the north gate this morning?"

"I was too busy to make an exact count. More than a thousand. And I think I saw that many camped down at High Meadows. Enough tents, anyway."

"You think the bombard may be real enough, but still be back in Pomerania? I suppose it's possible." She sighed. Her age seemed to vary all the time, from motherly to ancient and back again. "But if Vranov's really feinting at both gates, I don't know how he can possibly hope to keep his treachery secret for very long. Faith, if there's no real Wends peering over the hills at you, then I'm sure you can handle Havel Vranov and his family Speakers. When he got rid of the old count, he did not expect to run into you and your pack of brothers."

Wulf ate in silence for a moment, relishing a sense of achievement and the old woman's praise. He had certainly done his part. Without him Anton might have been tweaked into inviting the Pelrelmians in, or the Wends might have taken the north barbican and thrown open the gates. Terrified refugees fleeing south would have run into Havel Vranov and been slaughtered. Wulfgang Magnus had done well.

And if the "Wend" attack was a fake staged by the Hound of the Hills, then the war was over. Duke Wartislaw might absorb this morning's losses, but a mere count certainly could not. His troops would melt away after such a mauling.

So now what? "Build on success," Father had always said. Otto said so too.

"We'd better assume the Dragon exists until we are sure it doesn't," Wulf decided. "When I've finished this excellent meal, it might be time for me to go and look for it."

He had not seen her truly startled before. "Gramercy! Now? In daylight?"

"Better in daylight while everyone's busy than at night when it's quiet and they have guards posted and I can walk into trees."

She chuckled uneasily. "Sooth, you're the soldier, young squire, not me. You'll just look, though? Don't meddle. They'll have Speakers, and a halo shows up as bright by day as in the gloam."

Somehow the thought of what he was planning had dispatched the rest of his appetite. Abandoning the idea of a third helping, he moved the bowl away from him. Without touching it.

"I can lift that," he said. "Could I lift the bombard? Roll it over the cliff?"

"No. You'd outblaze the sun, and very likely damage yourself, but nothing else would happen. And you shouldn't be talking about it, if you think that Alojz Zauber is in league with the Wends."

Hellfire! "I forgot that. Well, I'll need to wear something . . ." He shivered as he realized where he would have to look for suitable clothes. "I'll come back here to change, if that's all right?"

This time he wasn't going to ask Anton's permission. *Anton was in the solar with Vlad and Otto. Radim, the secretary, and old seneschal Jurbarkas had been allowed to sit in the other two chairs. Dali Notivova was standing by the window. They were all listening to Vlad, who was spouting a seemingly endless list of things that had to be done, with occasional prompts from Otto. Radim was frantically writing notes.* So the military end of things was being attended to.

"I'll help you." Sybilla slunk in seductively from nowhere.

"What do you want?" Wulf demanded.

"Well, I'll help you change if you want that, but I really meant that I'd like to come with you when you go to spy on the Wends. This place is as boring as shelling peas."

"Can you ride?"

She tossed her head. "Of course. I'm a Speaker. You think a dumb brute could throw me off?"

"She rides," Justina said, frowning.

"Then come and be welcome," Wulf said. He didn't care what happened to the little flibbertigibbet. Only Madlenka mattered.

She was leaning over a blood-soaked table, steadying a wounded man, her hands caked in dried blood. The patient was little more than a boy, but he had taken a longbow arrow in the upper part of his chest. Descending steeply, it had probably lodged against his shoulder blade, for otherwise it would either have gone right through him or she would have tried to push it through. The burly young surgeon had cut off the excess arrow and was inserting a set of tongs, like two pointed spoons on a pivot, hoping to grip the arrowhead and crush the barbs so he could pull it out. The patient, thanks be to God, was unconscious. If his lung had been damaged or was about to be, he would probably never wake up.

Wulf could go there and heal him with a touch. But the first commandment would not allow that, nor let him heal any of the many other injured likely to die within the week. There must be quite enough whispers already about the mysterious squire who had cured Anton, who came and went so inexplicably.

He had never imagined Madlenka calmly assisting in such butchery. Her courage must be as solid as the castle walls. Although he loved her to distraction, he really did not know her very well. In fact, he did not know women very well.

Sybilla was still smirking.

He told her, "I'll come back here. If you want to come to Long Valley with me, you'd better make yourself less conspicuous."

And then he opened a gate into limbo.

CHAPTER 10

He went back to the little bartizan, trusting that it would be unoccupied, and that from there he would have a clear view of the northern approach. The first thing he saw was Madlenka's footprints. The thin snow on the floor had been trampled and had mostly melted, but only her prints showed on the steps outside. He gazed at them sadly. Anton's wife!

But there was a war to fight. Who knew what prize the winner might claim?

He had come to the bartizan to view the Silver Road north of the castle. At the far end, where it turned the corner into the gorge, the Wends had put up blindings to hide what they were doing, but it wasn't hard to guess that they were excavating a gun emplacement for the bombard, a nest for the Dragon.

A party of eight or ten horsemen was heading down to the castle, with a herald in front—obviously a flag of truce seeking leave to recover their dead, plus their wounded, if any had not been killed by the victorious defenders. Wulf could see scores of bodies all over the road, and even then his view of the area directly in front of the gate was blocked by the corner of the barbican. That was where the building stones had been dropped, so corpses would be lying in

heaps there. The attackers had been sent in across a well-designed killing ground, and even the undermanned garrison had managed to put it
to good use.

The truce would be granted, of course, because otherwise the Cardicians would have to dispose of the carrion themselves. The Wends' main
task would be to identify the nobly born among their fallen, which would
not be easy after the Castle Gallant scavengers had stripped the corpses.
The missing nobles would be tallied by now, and close aides sent along
to identify them. A few more bodies might be selected on the basis of
calluses on the inside of the knee from riding, better nourishment, old
wounds, and so on. Those might be taken back to the Pomeranian camp
in the hope that some friend or relative would recognize and name them.
The commoners would be tossed over the edge while a priest chanted a
prayer and sprinkled holy water. Ravens or the Ruzena River could do
the rest. Naked we enter the world, and equal we shall stand before the
Throne at the last day.

It was the charnel ground at the bottom of the cliff that interested
Wulf. The rocky shelf on which Gallant stood jutted out from the side of
the Hogback at a sharp angle, and the corner was cut off by the bend of
the Ruzena. In places the softer rock below the shelf had even been under-
cut, but that corner sheltered a triangle of dead ground, like an armpit, a
rocky slope sheltered from the wind and inaccessible to firewood hunters, so that vegetation had survived.

The ladders had snapped when they fell, with the top parts taking their
burdens over the cliff. The ghouls would not have had time, and probably
not much inclination, to scavenge down there. Wulf chose a large, fairly
flat boulder close to the water and opened a gate to it.

No one would see him appear out of nowhere, because branches
shielded him from the castle above. Behind him the river swirled, fast
and dark and deadly, speckled with flecks of rabid foam. Much of the rock
must have fallen as waste when the road was carved out and the town site
leveled, for it was a jagged nightmare, nothing like a river's tidy shingle.
From where he stood, he saw no bodies; hunting through that nightmare
of shattered rock and thorns and spindly conifers was going to be a slow
and dangerous process. Then he spotted a weathered skull grinning at
him from among the rocks and realized that today's Wends would not

be the first dead to be abandoned here. It was an evil place, a backdoor to hell.

He used talent to move to another perch, and then another, heading up the slope. He found his first fresh body, a gruesome heap of steel and cloth and dried blood, with birds and insects already at work on it. Perhaps he had miscalculated, and all the corpses would be so mangled by their fall that none of them would serve his purpose.

For what felt like a dangerously long time he hunted without success. Bodies were hard to find among the jagged boulders, even after he had located the remains of the ladders, and those he did find were too damaged for his purpose. Their clothes were ripped and bloody, their armor bent out of shape. His time was short, for the Wends would not be as hesitant to investigate this area as the scavengers had been. The dead down here would have been the men near the tops of the ladders, and the odds were good that many of those would have been hotheaded esquires, the young Magnuses of Pomerania, all eager to find fame by being first to surmount the battlements of Castle Gallant. Here, not having been looted and stripped, they could be identified by their finery and their bodies retrieved for reward, or just out of loyalty.

He heard a shout and caught a glimpse of a man descending the cliff, walking backward on the end of a rope. Because the distraction had made him look upward, Wulf also saw a red cloak caught in a tree. He found the owner at its roots, eyes staring glassily as flies walked on them. An absence of blood suggested that the tree had broken his fall enough to save him from being pulped inside his armor, but not enough to save his life. His helmet lay beside him, and it was a nobleman's casque, vizorless and bearing a crest of two stags. The same emblem showed on his surcoat. He was of higher rank than Wulf had hoped for, but he would have to do. He even had blond hair, although not as pale as Wulf's, and had been little older. At a distance, the imposture might pass.

The Pomeranian surcoat was what he really wanted, but the armor looked as if it would fit him well enough, so he might as well take it also. Murmuring a prayer for the dead man's soul, Wulf retrieved the cloak from the tree and spread it out. He laid the helmet on it. Then he stripped vambraces and rerebraces from the man's arms—he wore no gauntlets, perhaps because they would make ladder climbing too tricky. More shouts indicated that more Wends were coming down the cliff. He unbuckled the dead man's cuirass and added it to the loot. He would need a sword, but there was none in sight, and it might take hours to find one here. Whispering another prayer for the man he had slain and now plundered, he gathered up the bundle and took it back to the little vineyard at Avlona.

His brothers had finished dinner and were still at table, reminiscing over child-hood memories. Madlenka was still in the infirmary. Havel was urging on a team of men and oxen hauling guns up the hill from High Meadows. So the Hound was going to make a serious assault on Castle Gallant? Damn. . . . No, Wulf decided not to damn him, because he didn't know what his curses might do now, even at a distance.

He spread out the cloak on the stone table and surveyed his loot. Yes, to be convincing he must get another sword to replace the one he had left on the barbican roof. Not surprisingly, Sybilla appeared. She would have been watching him all this time.

"Robbing the dead?"

"Disguise," he said. "You're going to be conspicuous."

She had changed into a long riding skirt and a scarlet cloak with a matching hat that sported a tall plume. She looked more respectable, but was respectability needed? Every army included a lesser army of loose women, and he had been expecting her to dress more like one of those. But nobles and captains brought along their highborn wives; he should have guessed that Sybilla's ideas would run more to gentry.

"And you won't be? In that helmet? You're a lord, I'm your lady. You *want* me to be conspicuous. You want other men to lust after me. Don't you?"

There was a double meaning in that question, which he ignored, but he did risk a smile of surrender. Sybilla was no delicate damsel in need of coddling. She could look after herself better than he could.

"Well, in the absence of my squire, you can assist me in donning my mail, my lady." He tried on the helmet with the twin-stag crest. Even with the padding still inside it, it was tight on his ears, but it would suffice. He put it down and inspected the cuirass. The back plate had suffered some dents where it had hit some tree branches, but was still wearable. He hoisted the breastplate into place. It was a snug fit.

Sybilla slunk around the table to him. He wondered if her hints of availability were all pretense, all tease, and if that was what he was supposed to wonder. She had guessed his shyness at first glance. She would have tied him in tangles instantly if he had not been armored by his love for Madlenka.

"You're serious about letting that hussy accompany you?" Justina asked, appearing in the place Sybilla had just vacated. She was spinning, and her spindle did not miss a twirl.

"Could I stop her?" he asked. "Pull it tighter, please. . . . I can barely tell night from day in that sallet, so I need her to look out for Speakers. And she can probably vanish faster than I can. She's had more practice. Tighter!"

"I'm better at undressing men than dressing them," Sybilla said.

"If she is," Justina sniffed, "then she doesn't stay around to let them return the favor. Remember I'll be watching you. And remember that this is a matter of life and death, young miss, not an exercise."

Whose death? And what sort of exercise? If Sybilla had been given Speaking lessons to develop her talent, then why must Wulf not have them?

He told her, "You'll need a warmer cloak. There's snow on the ground there and more snow threatening."

She pouted and disappeared.

"I hope she doesn't do that where workadays can see her," he said.

"She won't. She's got more wits than she chooses to show." Justina was suddenly closer to proud grandmother than crabby governess. "This is a good trial for her. Just what are you planning to do?"

"Go to Long Valley and look for the Dragon. I may find the whole force moving out, of course, if they're really Havel's men. If they're Wends and I can find the bombard, I don't suppose I'll be able to get near it. But if there's a bridge I can curse before it tries to cross it, that would help, wouldn't it?"

"If it doesn't get blessed later, to remove your curse."

"Havel Vranov had three Speakers, but all related to him. How many does Duke Wartislaw have?"

"Don't know," the old woman said crossly, watching her spindle twirl ever closer to the paving. "But most rulers keep one or two in the

shadows, even if they don't know it themselves. Warty's been very successful at clawing his way up. If he does have hirelings, they'll certainly be
there, guarding his precious cannon, so keep your eyes open for halos."

Wulf tried on the helmet again. Keeping his eyes open in that was not
much of an advantage over having them closed. He took it off and tucked
it under his left arm, which is what its owner would have done when he
didn't have a squire handy to carry it. The crest would still show. That,
his surcoat, and the scarlet cloak dangling down his back proclaimed that
he was a nobleman. He might run into one of Two Stags's personal friends,
who knew that he was listed among the missing. Wulf must gamble that
the Long Valley camp was in a state of busy anarchy as the army absorbed
its costly defeat and prepared another assault.

Sybilla reappeared in a garish cloak and hat of cloth of gold, the sort of
garments a queen might wear. Admittedly, it set off her nimbus splendidly. Wulf glanced at Justina and met mockery in her eyes, so he did not
comment. Certainly no one was going to notice him with that vision riding alongside him. Which meant that Wulfgang Magnus, esquire, was
about to venture onto a field of battle sheltering behind a woman's skirts,
was he? He couldn't do that!

But he had gone this far, hoping perhaps that Justina would forbid her
ward to accompany him, and now it seemed that she supported the idea.
He reminded his tattered honor that he needed Sybilla to help watch out
for other Speakers, and she would be at no more risk than he would be.
Less, in fact, because even if she did not use talent, men would be much
less likely to shoot a woman out of hand and any man who tried to molest
a Speaker would be very surprised by the results. Also, he realized, a
Pomeranian Speaker would know the *two's company* rule and would hesitate to challenge a party of two Speakers.

He must just hope Vlad never heard about this.

"I need a sword," he said. "And there are horses at Gallant. Join me
when I move to Long Valley, all right?"

Sybilla sat down on the bench, adjusting her cloak. "Don't be too long.
I'm not accustomed to being kept waiting."

CHAPTER 11

Tap . . . tap . . . tap . . . Turn. Tap . . . tap . . . tap . . . Turn.

Anton was pacing the solar—fireplace to window, window to fireplace—and the jerky view was unsettling. Otto was there, too, slumped in a chair and watching the mindless parade. He wished he knew where Wulf had gone. Neither man was speaking, but Anton's thunderous expression threatened hellfire.

He paced. Otto waited wearily for the next outburst.

Vlad had gone off to lead a sally from the south gate, in the faint hope of being able to reach the first bridge and destroy it. Otto and Anton were in the salon, where the war had been forgotten.

Otto had appointed himself Anton's warden. If the situation had not been tragic and potentially disastrous, it might have been funny. Anton was even more casual about women than Vlad. He would fornicate like a billy goat whenever he had the chance, changing partners in a bedroom as readily as in a ballroom. But now he was effectively married, so he was suddenly steaming fury and vengeance against Wulfgang for seducing his wife. Girls were pleasure; wives were property. All he could talk about was what he would do when he caught him, ignoring the fact that Wulf was a Speaker and untouchable.

Once upon a time, Otto had been able to miss a night's sleep and barely notice, but not now; he was getting too old for a military life. He was also deathly worried by the siege. Unless the family Speaker could provide a few more miracles, Castle Gallant was going to fall. As soon as Wartislaw had the bombard emplaced, he would demand that Anton surrender the castle. No Magnus had ever done such a thing, but this situation looked so hopeless that Otto seriously thought he may have to suggest it. The only alternative was sack, and then he might never see Branka and the children again. What would happen to Dobkov while his sons were too young to defend it?

Anton mumbled something.

"What?"

"I said I will kill him! Adultery is low treason!"

"You won't kill him. You need him. Slacken off, Anton!" To remind him of what had happened when Wulf lost his temper yesterday would not help matters at all. True, Anton had been taken by surprise. In a properly staged fistfight, his huge advantage in reach would count, but why should Wulf stick to fists? He was the better man in wrestling or swordplay, and he could work miracles.

Then Wulf was there, although the door had not opened. He was clad in half-armor, carrying a crested helmet under his arm, and sporting a surcoat whose insignia Otto did not recognize. His expression was as grim as his brother's.

Anton wheeled around a chair to confront him, hand reaching for his dagger. Otto struggled to his feet, fatigue forgotten, preparing for trouble.

"What have you been doing with my wife?" the count roared.

Wulf blinked. "What am I supposed to have done with her?"

"You were seen kissing her."

Wulf stared up at him for a long moment before saying, "Does she say so?"

Anton was almost purple, glaring down at him. "Answer my question!"

"No."

"You didn't kiss her, or you won't answer?"

"I won't answer."

Otto tried to get between them. "Brothers, please! We can't afford a family fight at this stage." He was ignored, and his efforts to push them apart met with no success at all.

"Do I have to beat it out of her?"

That did it. Wulf's face turned chalky white. He slammed forward, ramming Anton back with his breastplate. "Don't even dream of it! You touch her, and—"

"Brothers!" Putting all his strength into it, Otto managed to get them apart, but it was Anton who gave the most ground. *"Wulf, you must not lose your temper!"*

Telling a man on the verge of losing his temper that he must not lose his temper was usually the fastest way to make him do so, but Wulf took a couple of deep breaths and then nodded.

Otto sighed with relief. "Now stop it, both of you! So there was a kiss? Wulf, will you give Anton your sacred word that there has been nothing more between you and Madlenka than a kiss?"

"I saw her in the bartizan. I went there and I kissed her. It was my fault." Wulf showed his teeth for a moment, and then muttered, "Sorry." He certainly didn't mean that.

"And your oath that you will never touch her again!" Anton demanded.

There was a pause, and then Wulf raised his right hand. "I, Wulfgang Magnus, do solemnly swear, as I hope for salvation, that if I hear that you have struck Madlenka, or mistreated her in any way . . . Just one slap, do y'hear? Just one slap . . . then I will immediately take her away from here and you will never see either of us again. And if you beat her, I will kill you. *So help me God!*"

He stepped around Otto and went to a chair. The boy Otto had known was being tempered into manhood with fire and water, hammer and anvil. Otto followed him.

Anton just stood where he was, glaring.

The room fell still, like a summer evening just before a thunderstorm.

"Getting back to the Wends," Wulf said, his normally affable face still bleak as death. "The squire that Vranov brought to the parley this morning, Alojz Zauber, was another Speaker. He tweaked Bishop Ugne—changed his mind so he agreed that Havel and his friends were only an illusion last night. Had I not come along to that parley, Brother, he would have tweaked you too. You might have handed Havel Vranov the keys to the castle and invited him and his army to come in and make themselves at home."

Anton didn't react. He might not have heard a word.

Otto felt invisible insects crawling on his skin.

Wulf's bitter expression thawed for a moment into a pale imitation of his old boyish grin. "Or perhaps he wouldn't have gotten that far with you. You are a stubborn pig, as I well know. But he might have done! So listen. This situation is absurd and it is all the fault of Havel Vranov. Speakers never meddle openly like this. They are timid as mice, and stay well out of sight. Havel began it by using Satanism to murder Count Bukovany and his son. I suspect he had Leonas curse them, and the boy wouldn't understand what he was doing. Vilhelmas may have started it all by tweaking Havel's loyalty from Jorgary to Pomerania, but that's a minor use of talent compared to malediction. Cardinal Zdenek countered by hiring me, but I was untrained, and I blundered horribly."

He sounded much more sure of himself than he had this morning. "That Justina woman has been tutoring you?" Otto asked.

"Dropping hints."

"Blundered how?" Anton said.

"Well, first I went storming into the monastery at Koupel and involved the Church, which no sane lay Speaker would ever do."

"I thought your Voices told you to do that? Are they really evil? Is that what you're saying—your Voices are demons, not saints?"

"In that case, they were the voice of inexperience," Wulf snapped. "My next mistake was using open violence. Speakers don't do that, either. We leave brawling to you brawny types. First against the Dominican, then against Vilhelmas. Not knowing the rules, I broke every one of them. So now the whole thing has gone crazy. . . . Also, I should have made this clearer to all of you sooner, but Speakers can spy on anyone they know personally. That means that dear Alojz could have been listening in on everything you were saying here earlier, when you had Dali and the others with you."

Otto wondered if the world had really gone mad or if Wulf was just opening his eyes to the way it had been all along. Thirty-six wasn't really old, not for a noble. A peasant or a laborer might be worn out by then, and few of them reached forty, but the rich aged more slowly. Still, it was close to ten years since Ottokar Magnus had ridden into battle. Now, seeing how these two youngsters flamed around, he felt that he had somehow grown ancient. He didn't know when. His father and grandfather had grumbled about firearms ruining warfare, and now he found himself thinking much the same about this Satanism, although it had probably been around much longer.

"Just what were you saying to my wife on the curtain wall?" Anton said.

"Stop!" Otto snapped. "Don't answer that, Wulf. Anton, we have discussed that, and the matter is closed. I have absolute faith that you have no reason to distrust—"

"I told her," Wulf said softly, "that I love her with all my heart, which she already knew, and we both agreed that there could never be anything between us because neither of us would betray you and her marriage. She is a good and faithful wife to you. So far. Try and be worthy of her, if you can. Can't you think of anything else?"

Anton fumed in silence.

Otto said, "Why are you in that armor? What are you planning?"

Wulf smiled, sort of. "I came to borrow a sword."

Otto rose to unbuckle his sword belt. "Who are you supposed to be in that outfit, and what are you up to?"

"I don't know who I am." Wulf's smile was fleeting. "I robbed a dead man. What I am doing I should rather not say, just in case."

He must be on his way to take a look at the Dragon and try to bollix it up. Otto looked to Anton and wondered if he realized that Wulf was his only hope of living to see another Friday. If he surrendered Gallant, Zdenek would chop his head off.

"Anything we can do to help?" Otto asked.

"Just lend me this." Wulf took the sword. "I can see it's too long for me, but I only need it for show."

"God be with you, then."

"God or someone else." For a moment he stared at the wall. "Havel's men are attacking. Looks like Vlad's withdrawing. Lord save us, but the big fellow can move when he needs to! He could outrun crossbow bolts."

"Withdrawal was in the plan," Otto said. "We want no unnecessary losses."

"There's been some. The Hound is making war on his own king's flag."

"Sorry to hear it. I hoped he wouldn't."

"He's there in person. Alojz Zauber is . . . somewhere else. Indoors. Not sure where. Madlenka is still tending the wounded."

Otto said, "Thanks for that information. Good luck, Wulf."

The family's sole surviving Speaker smiled ruefully. "Don't expect miracles. I may manage to weaken a bridge or break an axel on a wagon, but I won't be able to damage the Dragon itself." He looked to Anton. "All I can do is buy you some time."

"Really?" Anton snapped. "When the Wends' ladders collapsed this morning—that was very suspicious. Very convenient for us, but not natural, more like a miracle. Did you have anything to do with that?"

Wulf smiled but did not answer. He took a step forward and disappeared.

Otto sank back on his chair and rubbed his temples. His head felt as if it were lead-plated. "You mustn't ask that sort of question."

"Why not? Tell me why not! I know the answer. What do you think it is?"

"I don't know. I just don't, and I don't want to. I do know he's fighting, too, but his is a different sort of war, Anton. The whole thing is disgusting, but we didn't start it. And Wulf's power doesn't make him immortal. Remember that three Speakers died yesterday. He's a brave lad, and he's on our side."

Anton drew himself up to his full height and glared down at him, his water-buffalo mustache bristling.

"Well, I know those Wends on the ladders were our enemies, but I think they were all brave men, too. And honorable men, trying to fight an honest battle with muscle and courage and swords, as men have always fought. And I think the devil gathered them up and took them straight to hell, and he did it because Wulf asked him to."

Otto did not try to argue.

CHAPTER 12

Castle Gallant's stables were far smaller than Dobkov's and now they were almost deserted, for half the Gallant herd had been taken prisoner when the Wends captured the Long Valley outpost. Wulf stepped out of an empty stall. He had hoped that there would be no hands present, but two young boys were busily shoveling. They looked up in surprise as he approached.

"I'm Squire Wulfgang," he said. "The count's brother. Saddle up Copper and Balaam for me. Right away."

They would never argue with a nobleman, and were too young to ask where he thought he was going when both gates were besieged. Happy to be useful while forced to miss out on the war, they ran to do his bidding.

Copper was glad to see him, assuming that Wulf had come to rescue him from the noisome cell and take him out to run over the hills. Balaam, Otto's old courser, had disliked Wulf ever since an afternoon seven years ago when Wulf had ridden him on a bet, much to Balaam's disgust and Otto's astonishment. That feat had won him the first florin he ever owned, and the years since had been kinder on the boy than the steed. Now Balaam was practically dog food and Wulf was . . . Wulfgang was whatever Wulfgang was now. Even yesterday he had worried about controlling more than one horse on a trip through limbo. Now he knew better. As Sybilla had implied, anything was possible to a Speaker.

—*Calm*, he told Balaam. *Be happy!* The old warrior raised his ears and put away his teeth. Wulf patted his neck and didn't lose a finger. He had achieved his first tweak! He ought to take his own advice, though, because his heart was thumping much faster than a Magnus heart was supposed to thump. For the first time in his life he was going forth to meet a foe.

When all was ready, he vaulted onto Copper's back and accepted Balaam's reins. He dropped a coin into an eager hand. "That's the only one I've got on me," he said. "Share it, half each."

He rode off with shrill thanks ringing in his ears. The bailey was almost deserted, but not quite, and it was overlooked by many windows. He rode across to the dark tunnel that led out to the street.

Except in his case. He made it lead out to Long Valley, emerging in an icy blast of wind in the pinewood where he had stood when Marek shot down Vilhelmas—was that only last night? It felt like weeks ago. The log wall of the barracks building was behind him, windowless on this side. The horses whinnied and he calmed them with a thought as he reined in. There was no one near to observe, no smoke emerging from the chimney. The air smelled less of pine sap than it had in the night, more of mud and animals. Peace had given way to the squeal of axles and familiar torrents of abuse from teamsters driving ornery beasts over rough ground.

The scenery beyond the pine grove had changed since last night, too. Tents and pavilions had gone. Now steady processions of oxcarts and horse-drawn wagons were creaking by on either side of the trees, heading north. About as many empties were going south, suggesting that the Wends were still ferrying in men and supplies over the lake. And they must be Wends. Count Pelrelm could never raise an army of this size. He might be in league with them, but they were not his own men. Wipe one theory off the slate.

Sybilla materialized alongside Balaam and pouted down in disgust at the needle-filled mud under her pretty shoes. The old horse barely flickered an ear. Before Wulf could dismount to help her, she slid a foot into the stirrup and swung up into the saddle in a flaming whirl of cloth of gold and a flash of her halo. She shot Wulf a smile of triumph and expertly adjusted the stirrup leathers. Suitably impressed by the cardinal's daughter, he passed her the reins.

"Your brothers think you're in league with the devil," she said, smirking.

Of course they did. He had seen the fear in their eyes. Even Otto hadn't been able to hide it. They thought they were putting their own souls in peril by accepting his aid and failing to denounce him. They were probably right.

"Am I?" he asked. "Are you?"

She laughed and tried a coquettish leer on him. "If you were, what would you do with me?"

"Chain you to a rock and send a sea monster for you." He nudged Copper into motion and rode around the back of the building, just in case there were pickets guarding the door at the front. The barracks might be deserted now, for all he knew, but as the only permanent structure available, it might also be Duke Wartislaw's temporary palace, if His Grace was leading his army in person.

The casque's original owner must also have been able to see well enough in it, but Wulf could not, so he removed it and propped it against the upright burr-plate on the front of his saddle. That way he was still an obvious nobleman, but less easily recognized as an imposter. His greatest danger, after other Speakers, were Two Stags's surviving followers.

In a few minutes the intruders came to the edge of the pine knoll, where the land sloped gently down into marshy ground, which Dali Notivova had described in graphic terms. Scabby patches of snow did little to improve its appearance, while the passage of an army had churned the rest of it into ponds and black mud. Although the many small groves of trees had not yet shed their leaves, being aspens, they were managing to shake off most of the snow. Their spindly but densely packed trunks blocked sight lines so well that it was impossible to see more than twenty or thirty yards in any direction, a blessing for a man trying to avoid attention while wearing a nimbus. Having the choice of a dozen new trails, Wulf chose one at random.

Dali had mentioned snowy peaks, but now a leaden lid of cloud lay low on the valley. The wind tugged at Wulf's tattered red cloak and drove flurries of snow in his face. He saw two troops of archers plodding along, a disorganized rabble of women and children with handcarts, many wagons piled high with hay, others laden with more women and children. Although the mob as a whole was heading north, its parts veered this way and that between the little lakes and the aspen groves, with disputes over precedence breaking out wherever two streams joined or tried to cross. Those on foot made way for the mounted nobleman and his lady, but they in turn had to find their own path around the cumbersome wagons. The fighting part of the army was presumably farther ahead, setting up a long-term camp.

"You should be paying attention to me," Sybilla announced, riding at his side. "Not gawking around like a village idiot."

He glanced at her incredulously. "You ought to be gawking, too. If a Wendish Speaker spots our halos, he's going to load up his crossbow and pull the trigger faster than you can flutter an eyelash. And he won't miss." That was one experiment in Satanism that Wulf had allowed himself years ago—directing an arrow. Blessing it, he would call it now.

"Well, he can only fire one bolt at a time, and you'll get the first one."

"That's why I'm gawking."

Sybilla sniggered nervously, and he reminded himself that she was only a kid who liked to play at being a seductress. Since Speakers were both rare and reclusive, he might well be the first one close to her own age she had ever met, and he must seem more intriguing than an elderly Roman cardinal or his friends. Perhaps his lack of real interest in her was just encouraging her to taunt him.

Progress was slow, and he would probably have to go all the way to the front before he would have much chance of finding the Dragon. Meanwhile, there was plenty to look at, but nothing especially useful or meaningful. Likewise, Sybilla's taunting and teasing was even less interesting than her prattling about Rome and Paris. Snow began to fall in earnest. He wondered how much daylight remained in this weather and these mountains.

He wondered who had seen him kissing Madlenka and tattled about it to Anton. Probably nobody he had even heard of, but the juicy gossip would have spread like wildfire through the castle and town.

Vlad had made it safely back to the south barbican and was standing out-side the sally port, gazing back down the trail as the Pelrelmians dismantled the breastwork at the bend. So far they were not daring to come any closer. Otto's thoughts were full of nonsensical shapes and colors, which meant he was asleep; that seemed surprising at first, but made sense on second thoughts because he had not been to bed last night and would be a logical choice to take the night watch tonight. *Anton, even more surprisingly, was visiting the wounded in the infirmary in the company of Dowager Countess Edita.* Who had put him up to that little demonstration of concern and gratitude? If he could concentrate on ceremonial duties, he might be recovering from his obsessive jealousy.

Sybilla said, "What's that?"

Wulf returned his attention to Long Valley. She was pointing to her left, indicating a dray that had become thoroughly lodged in the mire, despite having a team of sixteen oxen to haul it. Men were standing around, arguing and cursing. Other wagons were detouring around it, churning up weeds, turning the snow into great puddles. The division of the road into a tangle of many braids was an advantage for a spy, in that no one could keep track of anyone else in all the confusion. It was also a hindrance, in that Wulf was quite likely to miss his objective: Dragon, the bombard. But the dray Sybilla had noticed might be it.

"Let's go and see." Wulf directed Copper in that direction. "Mayhap we grand folks can tender some unhelpful suggestions."

It did occur to him that he might be growing overconfident.

Drays were low-set, flatbed wagons used for especially heavy or awkward loads, and the giant bombard would certainly qualify as that. He soon saw that the dray ahead was not the one he sought. Its deck had been divided by balks of timber into a dozen compartments, each of which held a stone ball about a cubit across. This shot was so huge it could only belong to the Dragon itself. Unlike other loads, this one had been left uncovered, for snow would not hurt stone. He tried not to imagine the Dragon's fiery roar hurling those cannonballs half a mile into the north barbican, shattering the ashlar walls to rubble.

The loud dispute faded as the participants noted his approach. Now he could not ride by without intervening. His remark about offering unhelpful suggestions had been made in jest, but he must stay in character.

Be Anton!

Worse, be Vlad.

"Make way there!" he bellowed, bulling Copper forward into the crowd. "What're you lazy slobs doing standing there picking lice out of your asses when you've got work to do?"

A gnarled bear of a man saluted. "She's sunk axle deep, my lord!"

"I can see that, cretin! There's an army moving past you! Commandeer another team and add it on. Two more teams! And move smartly or the duke'll have your hide for bowstrings!"

He urged Copper forward again, scattering more men and confident that Sybilla was capable of keeping up with him. He listened with amusement to a wake of obscene suggestions following her. Once he was through the mob and she pulled level with him again, he was pleased to see that her face was flushed crimson.

"A little different from Cardinal Whatshisname's friends?"

"Guillaume Cardinal d'Estouteville," she said. "No. Just cruder. And smellier. Same intentions. Was that an unhelpful idea?"

"As unhelpful as I could come up with on the spur of the moment. They'll be jamming up the traffic on that part of the road until dark. With luck, they'll pull the wagon to bits."

"And a helpful one would be . . . ?"

"Unload half the cargo and come back for it tomorrow. The Dragon will need days to shoot all those balls, if it ever does." Of course, unloaded balls might have sunk out of sight in the swamp, so perhaps that would have been a better suggestion for him to make. But even half the load might be enough to demolish the barbican.

A moment later he saw another dray creeping along ahead, with the same cargo. When one had made it through the bad spot, the second driver had thought he could follow, not allowing for the damage the first vehicle had caused. Or he might be less skilled. And there was yet another team farther ahead. If Wartislaw thought he needed three dozen cannonballs, then either he distrusted the Dragon's efficacy, or he expected to besiege more castles during his conquest of Jorgary.

Those ammunition drays had been easy to identify, but most of the other loads were anonymous. Many wagons were painted in their owners' colors and escorted by men-at-arms in matching livery, now mostly obscured by mud. Wulf could guess that those would be bringing in the silken tents, fine rugs, silver dishes, and other luxuries that great lords required and took along on campaign. And of course the army would include valets, tailors, surgeons, farriers, armorers, bowyers, cooks, paymasters, chaplains, harlots, clerks, heralds, carpenters, coopers, and at least one astrologer. Small wonder that the snow swirling in the air seemed infected by a sense of urgency. Duke Wartislaw could not keep this multitude packed into a mountain valley for very long.

Traffic was becoming thicker as the river on the left drew closer to the mountain face on the right. There were fewer tracks now, and soon they would all merge into one and become the road through the gorge. The snow was growing heavier and the light fainter as the invisible sun lost its battle with the coming storm.

"My lord! My lord! Count Szczecin!" someone was shouting behind them.

"You've been recognized," Sybilla said shrilly.

Hooves made mushy noises in the mud.

"*Do not* look around!" Wulf said. "You are ravishingly gorgeous and I am utterly in your spell, oblivious to anything else. What the hell do we do now?" He could put on his helmet to help conceal his face, but it would be a very odd thing to do.

She gulped and nodded. "Wait until he gets close. He's only a workaday, so we can tweak him. You lead and I'll back you up."

That would fine, if only he knew how to tweak. He had no time to ask for a lesson before the horseman came alongside him.

"My lord, you're alive!" He was a man-at-arms of middle years with a weather-beaten, mustachioed face, and a surcoat displaying twin stags. "His Grace has been desolate since the . . . You're not Count Szczecin!"

Wulf turned to stare at him. He thought, *I am not the man you thought I was; you made a mistake,* but the man's suspicious frown only darkened.

"That's Count Szczecin's casque!"

Wulf wished he was close enough to reach out and touch him. Alojz had tweaked the bishop at a greater range than this, but the bishop had been happy to have his mind changed, as Justina had explained. This man had thought he had found his lord alive after he had been reported dead, and would be chagrined to learn that he was mistaken. Wulf might have been wiser to pretend to be Count Sneeze, whatever complications that might have produced.

Then Sybilla joined in. "Fool! *You are blind as well as stupid!* How dare you insult His Lordship like this? Consider yourself lucky if he does not have you flogged." Her nimbus flashed.

The man's face fell. "My lord, I am deeply sorry! I mistook you for someone else!" He glanced at the bogus surcoat and his voice trailed away into bewildered silence.

"It has happened before. Our blazonries are not unalike." Wulf turned back to his companion to continue his conversation.

The man-at-arms reined in, and no doubt sat on his horse for a while, staring in confusion as the mysterious doppelgänger continued on his journey.

Lesson learned: to tweak people you must speak aloud. Wulf's hands were shaking, much to his annoyance. Yet that had been a damnably near miss, for there were more than enough men-at-arms within hailing distance to rally to a hue and cry. He and Sybilla could have escaped into limbo, of course, but the resulting public outcry would have violated the first commandment and alerted the Pomeranians to his snooping. He was both relieved and ashamed to see that Sybilla looked shaken also. But she was also staring at him.

"Thanks for the help," he said in what he meant to be a comforting tone of voice. "That was quite a close one."

"Idiot!" she said. "Imbecile! Half-wit! Why didn't you tweak him right away? The longer you give him to think, the firmer his thoughts set. Have you any idea of the trouble you might have caused? You expect the Saints to protect you when you run around like a drunken porter, creating scenes, performing miracles? Maybe they'll overlook all those murders and things you did yesterday—although I wouldn't count on that if I were you—but now that Justina's told you the rules, you've got to obey them, or they'll wash their hands of you and let the Church have you."

"They will? Who's 'they'?" *Which saints? Helena and Victorinus?*

"The Saints, of course! You realize they may even blame me if you create a disturbance, for not stopping you? You may have ruined my contract! Stupid cretin!"

"What contract?" Wulf asked. "Marriage contract?" *And which saints?*

Sybilla had gone from pale to brick-red and was almost spitting her words. "*Marriage?* You think that's all a woman's good for, don't you, you stupid, ignorant man! No, I do not mean a marriage contract! The dean of the College of Cardinals does not waste his time with trivia like marriage contracts. You are as dull as a workaday, really you are!"

She wheeled the astonished Balaam, kicking furiously. The old horse lumbered into a run and carried her off toward the river until they both vanished into the driving snow. Wulf made no effort to stop her. She could look after herself, and Justina was probably keeping an eye on her anyway. He hoped she would take care of the courser. Otto would be furious if anything happened to his old battlefield comrade.

Meanwhile Wulf was now free to complete his spying mission. He wasn't going to be able to take it much farther. The road had left the main valley and entered a smaller one, which was rapidly becoming even narrower. The river was close now, and this was undoubtedly the start of the gorge. Traffic had come to a complete stop and men—and some women—were milling about, shouting and complaining. Distant sounds of chopping and hammering indicated that the army was pitching camp not very far away, probably because there would not be enough room to do so in the gorge itself. Without doubt the Dragon would be somewhere in that mêlée, perhaps even beyond it.

To plunge into such congestion would be foolish, if it were even possible to get very far at the moment. There would be more men to recognize Count Szczecin's heraldry, and if the duke had brought any Speakers at all with him, there would be at least one of them chaperoning the Dragon. The Wends must know as well as the Jorgarians did that the bombard was the queen on the chessboard. Wulf had achieved all he could hope to do here and now. Perhaps after dark, if the snow continued, he might return on foot.

Before turning back, he rose in his stirrups to study the view. What had especially caught his eye was a line of three wagons not very far ahead, coming to a halt at the near end of the traffic jam. There might even be more than three, for the flying snow was thick now. They were very heavily guarded, with a troop of ducal cavalry at their rear and a line of hussars along each side; certainly there would be another squad out in front. What cargo could be so valuable that it needed such an escort in the middle of the Pomeranian army? Whatever it was, the loads were heavily draped in canvas or leather, painted red. He thought he could make out the shapes of barrels underneath, but it would be impossible to get close enough to pry. The duke's personal effects? His wine stock? Why were they red?

He had done all he could for now. It was time to turn Copper around and retrace his hoofprints to some unobserved spot, then to Castle Gallant.

CHAPTER 13

Justina had settled in her favorite place, the yard outside her cottage in Avlona. The situation was too dire for wine; she had brought out a bottle of genuine cognac, not bothering with a glass.

Her life had not been one long parade of triumphs, although she had chalked up enough of them to have gained a mythic reputation within the Saints. "Let Justina try" had been a popular motto twenty or thirty years ago. Failures had been rare, but this time everything had gone wrong.

She should never have let Lady Umbral talk her into this mad Castle Gallant venture. She was too old for fieldwork. She was too old even to offer advice, and when she had officially retired five years ago, she had sworn never to leave Avlona again, no matter how grave the shortage of reliable Speakers became. But she soon discovered that she was not yet old enough to sink into the prying dotage that claimed so many Speakers, who often wound up mummifying in cobwebby corners, alternately dozing and spying on everyone they knew.

Then Sybilla, Umbral's daughter by d'Estouteville, had started hearing Voices, and Justina had let herself be talked into taking the girl on as a brancher. It had been a great compliment to her skills as a handler, honed on almost a dozen kids since the start of the century. Sybilla had turned out to be quite a handful, but good company for an ancient hermitess, and there was a cautious streak behind her wildness, which Justina had done all she could to encourage. A handler's duties were not hard: a few lectures, a lot of language lessons, and firsthand experience of all the important cities of Europe. Now the job was done, and well done, for in a few days a new Speaker would be formally fledged and royally jessed.

Swallows and storks were long gone, and a honking V of geese was heading southward overhead. It must be about time for this falcon to go too, to turn in her broomstick, as the Saints said. About time to learn if a Speaker could find salvation. Justina took a long swig from the bottle and gave herself a coughing fit. Her hacking angered her, for it ruined her mood of genteel melancholy.

Wulfgang and Sybilla had split up, each riding alone in the snowstorm. Judging by the way Sybilla kept peering around her, she was preparing to open a gate the moment she was sure of being unobserved. Wulfgang was still interested in the traffic, seeking people out, rather than trying to avoid them.

Tragedy! The boy had so much promise, and it was all to be wasted. Without the Saints' help he was doomed, and Umbral was steadfast in her refusal to take up his cause. Why hadn't Zdenek called for the Saints' help just one day earlier, so this appalling mess could have been avoided?

Although Umbral and Justina were distantly related, the relationship was by marriage, so Sybilla's talent had not come from the Magnus line. The Magnus line was in serious trouble now.

Sybilla stepped out of limbo, shedding snow and her damp cloak. "Oo, that nephew of yours!" she said. "If the devil came for Wulf, he would kick him in the balls. Yummy! Will I find men like him in Paris?"

Justina pulled herself together enough to smile. "If you search a very long time you may, but don't count on it."

"Did you talk with Mother?"

"I mostly listened."

Justina's brancher gave her a long, hard look. "What's wrong?"

Why did good news and bad news so often come hand in hand? Why must joy tarnish like silver? Sybilla's triumph was totally ruined for Justina by Wulfgang's disaster.

"Nothing's wrong, dear. Umbral said to tell you that it's all signed and sealed. Your cadger will receive instruction tomorrow, and you will probably be jessed next Sunday. Congratulations, my dear!"

Sybilla clapped her hands, just once. Her face wore the sort of expression that goes with tasting a delicious mouthful of some favorite treat. Only a few months ago she would have shrieked with joy and behaved like a child. The jessing negotiations had dragged on for nerve-racking weeks, so almost any display of pleasure would be justified. But now she came around the table to sit beside Justina and give her a fond hug. "It is all your doing, my lady! I am more grateful than I can possibly tell you."

"It was a pleasure, and you did all the work."

"Nonsense. Now, what's wrong, grandmother?"

"I am not your grandmother."

"You're a *great* grandmother!"

That little exchange was a joke from their first days together, but they had not used it for years. It was a sign that Sybilla looked forward to their parting with regret as well as joy, and that she was a lot more mature and perceptive than she usually pretended. Now she put a firm young hand over the old one on the table.

"So, what's wrong?"

"Wulfgang."

"Oh!" She understood instantly. "Mother's being difficult?"

That was hardly the word for Lady Umbral when she refused something.

"She has no choice, my dear. Wulfgang killed a Dominican priest and helped kill an Orthodox one. Vilhelmas's death might be excused because he was leading an armed invasion and he's a schismatic anyway. But not Azuolas's. Neither pope nor Inquisition will forgive that. The Inquisition will come for Wulfgang in its own good time, but come for him it will. There's nowhere he can hide."

Sybilla pulled a face. She reached her other hand through limbo and brought it back holding a glass, which she set on the table. Justina poured brandy into it.

"Should I talk to Mother?"

"No. She can't defy the Church when it has really set its mind on something. That would put the whole of the Saints at risk."

Sybilla used a vulgar expression she must have picked up from a workaday. She sniffed at the brandy and tried a cautious sip, then laid the glass down hastily. "I'd better not. I have to get ready for the ball. Wulf is not a murderer!"

"Yes he is. In the eyes of the Church he is. He saw his brother being assaulted and broke into the fight to help him. He was outnumbered, because Marek had obviously been overpowered already, so he shot the bolt first to even the odds. A secular judge would acquit him. If the dead man hadn't been a priest, the Church would absolve him with a massive penance and be willing to accept a big bag of gold in lieu of it. But facts is facts."

"Father, then? Could he help?"

"Why should he?" Justina said sadly. "Quid pro quo? How can the Magnuses ever scratch his back enough for him to scratch Wulfgang off the Inquisition's most-wanted list? What is really damnable is that I was five years too late in finding the boy, and if I'd been even one day sooner I could have prevented all this!"

"Don't worry, we'll think of something!" Sybilla rose and bent to kiss Justina's ancient cheek. Then she stepped into limbo and was gone.

Justina took up the glass of brandy and drained it.

After all these years of success, her career was ending in total disaster. She had failed . . . and failed her own flesh and blood, too!

CHAPTER 14

Snow was falling just as hard in Castle Gallant as it was on the other side of the Hogback. Wulf had planned to return from Long Valley to the same bailey entrance tunnel that he had used to leave, but he materialized in the alley outside, about two house lengths away. His arrival was unobserved, because there was no one close, and the snow was thick enough to hide him from anyone watching through windows, yet the deviation startled him, a reminder that he was still very ignorant of the workings of talent. As he rode along to the arch, a troop of men-at-arms came marching out, proving that his intended destination would have been a very poor choice at that time. He had certainly not known this before-hand, so he must assume that Saints Helena and Victorinus were still looking after him, even if they did not speak to him anymore.

He found Balaam standing in the bailey with his reins looped around the burr-plate. He looked abandoned and bewildered, but was happy to follow Copper into the stable, where the same two boys as before came running to give both horses rubdowns. Fortunately, horses could not gossip about where they had been, or explain the mud on their legs.

Vlad and Anton were in the solar.

Wulf went next to the armory to turn in Count Szczecin's armor as a contribution to the stores. To the victor go the spoils. He detoured to the kitchens to borrow a bed warmer, which he carried on his shoulder like a pike as he went on up to the solar. The few people he passed gave him puzzled looks, but did not question.

The shabby little room felt hot as an oven after the wintery day outside. Vlad was slumped on a chair with a wine bottle, yawning. Anton was pacing to and fro, and jumped like a frog when Wulf walked in.

Wulf lifted the bottle from Vlad's hand and took a long swig. "How's the war going?"

He laid down the contraption he had brought from the kitchen, and took another long swig. Dutch courage, they called that.

"All quiet at the moment," Vlad said. "We can't see the end of our noses out there. I think both sides are bringing up guns. They'll start work on our gates as soon as the snow stops. Gallant will fall on Tuesday or Wednesday."

"You planning some hay time?" Anton demanded, looking at the bed warmer. He sat down also, but he was as taut as a bowstring.

"No." It would be a very good idea, though. Lack of sleep was making Wulf's eyes gritty and his head droop. "How do you transport gunpowder, Sir Vladislav?" He stretched across to return the wine bottle.

The big man reached a very long arm to take it. "In the best barrels. You keep it dry and away from fires."

"Do you mark it as dangerous?"

"Sometimes," the big man said cautiously. "I've seen barrels painted red."

"I've just seen whole wagons painted red. The covers, I mean, but they were over barrels, I'm certain."

All three men looked at the object on the hearth, the usual flat brass pan with a flat lid and a wooden handle about four feet long. Servants used such pans to warm the sheets on milady's bed, or even milord's bed, if milady wasn't already warming it for him.

"Would it work?" Wulf asked, hoping that the answer was no.

"No," Vlad said. "If you mean, would it blow everything sky high, no. At least . . . I don't think it would. Powder's funny stuff, unpredictable.

You have to shut powder up tight to make it go bang. Loose powder just burns."

"A whole wagonload just burns?"

"Yes. Christmas, would it burn, though! Whoosh!"

After a thoughtful silence, Vlad added, "I don't *think* it would blow everything sky high. Might if you fired a gun at it. Or made a bomb. We got some powder downstairs, so if we packed it tight in a metal shell with a long fuse . . . but we don't have one of those, that I know of." He took a drink and wiped his mouth with the back of his hand, which was almost as hairy. "We do got a couple of arquebuses."

Too dangerous. Wulf glanced at the snow-packed casement. "If I was close enough to be sure of hitting it in this, I might go flying with the eagles."

"Very like."

"My way's worth trying, then?" Wulf said unhappily. He could make fire with talent, he was sure, but again he wouldn't get away fast enough.

"If you've got the balls for it."

Did he? He thought about it. Justina had told him his talent couldn't damage the Dragon itself. This felt like a good chance at the next best thing. It must be done now, while the snow would hide what he was doing, so he did not break the first commandment. Set one powder wagon on fire and men would flee in terror rather than try to save the others. A bombard without powder was useless junk, and it might take weeks to bring in fresh supplies, time that Duke Wartislaw did not have. The pass would close soon. Even if Wulf did not save Castle Gallant, he might cripple the subsequent invasion of lowland Jorgary.

Too good a chance to pass up, he decided. *Omnia audere.* He would not be the first Magnus to die before reaching legal adulthood.

"I have them now," he said. "I hope I can keep them."

Vlad muttered blasphemy under his breath. "You'll have to go faster than a farting bat, lad. There'll be powder dust on everything under the covers. One spark can do it, you know."

Wulf knew that much. He knelt down, opened the lid of the warmer, and began picking hot coals out of the fire with the fire tongs. His brothers watched in appalled silence.

The door swung open and Otto walked in, then stopped to stare at what was going on. He had probably noticed Wulf's guilty start.

"Going to hit a mattress?"

"No. Bolt that door, please." Wulf went back to work.

Otto obeyed, raising inquiring baronial eyebrows at Anton, who was officially in charge of anything that happened in Castle Gallant.

"He's located the duke's powder wagons."

"Virgin save us!" Otto went to a chair. "Are you sure you know what you're doing, Wolfcub?"

That was Vlad's name for him, but Otto would mean it as a term of affection.

"Oh, yes. I'm not sure what the powder will do afterward, though." Wulf tossed down the tongs and closed the lid. That job was done. Now he must move on to the next. Which was . . . ?

Which was to go to a moving target. He hadn't tried that before. He could go to people he knew, so he should be able to find a wagon he knew, and it couldn't have moved very far from where he had seen it, if at all.

He hoped that the snow was still falling as heavily over there as it was here.

He was forbidden to use his talent in front of witnesses, but his brothers all knew about it already, so no more harm could be done.

Recalling the wagons, he decided that the gunpowder casks must be much smaller than wine barrels, barely more than large kegs. They had been stacked four across, with a second layer on top, three across. That would explain the shape of the covers and ropes, and would make a reasonable load for a team of four horses on rough ground. Not that he knew how much gunpowder weighed, compared with, say, wine or nails, but an army wouldn't risk too much of its total supply on a single wagon.

The wind seemed stronger than ever, at least in Gallant, and falling off the wagon would not be a good idea. He removed his cloak, which might get in his way. Anton took it for him.

He was procrastinating. Scared, in other words.

Still balanced on one foot and one knee, he turned his back on the warming pan and the hearth. He looked up at three agony-filled faces and was touched by their obvious concern.

He checked that his dagger moved freely in its sheath. The dagger had been Otto's birthday and farewell gift to him when he and Anton had left Dobkov, not much more than a month ago. He caught Otto's eye and they shared a smile.

"Our Lady be with you, Wolfcub."

Anton said, "Amen!"

"And all the saints," Vlad rumbled. "I'd come with you if I could, Cub, but thank sweet Jesus I can't."

That was it, then. Time to go.

Wulf went back to Long Valley.

He was very nearly blown clean off the wagon by the storm. He threw himself flat on the snowy surface and grabbed at a rope, but it was too tightly bound to give him a good grip. He found another he could hold on to, then took stock of his surroundings.

About three feet in front of his head, the carter and a pikeman were huddled together on the bench, swathed in their cloaks in an effort to keep the blizzard from running down their necks. So far they must be unaware of their passenger. The wagon was not moving, and the horses were understandably fretting, stamping hooves and tossing heads. Another wagon directly ahead was similarly stalled. The snow was too dense for Wulf to see much farther, but he could hear a lot of angry shouting as too much army tried to move along too little road.

A row of helmets on his right, almost level with him, was close enough to touch. Fortunately, the men-at-arms wearing them all had their backs to him, cowering away from the wind in the lee of the wagon. They, too, were stamping and grumbling. Beyond them was a cliff of rock and scrub, not quite a wall, but too steep to walk up.

The escort on his left should have been facing in his direction and ramming pikes into him already, but another red-painted wagon had pulled level and extremely close, so the guards had doubled up on the far side of it. Apparently none of them had noticed him—yet.

He rolled over and slid off his perch, down between the two wagons, crouching to make himself inconspicuous. He was already soaked and shivering, and he had banged a knee on the side of the first wagon. At the moment he was safe, but the gap was so narrow that if either wagon started to move, he would be crushed by its rear wheel. There was a fourth wagon right behind these two, and its driver might see him at any moment.

Out came the dagger, and he set to work on the covering of the wagon he had just left, attacking the slope from the top of the upper layer of barrels down to the sides of the lower layer. There must be a hollow under there which he could put to good use. Despite his frantic efforts, the leather was hard as iron and put up a stiff resistance, but his luck was holding so far. Indeed, it was going at full gallop, because he was in the middle of at least four powder wagons. If he could set one ablaze, there was a good chance of the fire spreading to others, seriously depleting the Wends' supply.

But the leather was going to defeat him. His dagger seemed to be losing its edge. Oh, of course! The covering had been blessed. So it could be cursed. *Yield! You are as soft as wet paper.* Rip! There was a second cover underneath the first, so he cursed that also. It gave way, and he opened a rent down to the lower layer of barrels. A quick sideways slash opened a gap wide enough to put the bed-warmer pan through.

His brothers released a yelp of joy when he reappeared. He grabbed up the pan and went back to his place between the wagons.

The adjacent wagon had started to move. Its rear wheel was about to grind him against the front wheel of the wagon he was attacking, like grain in a mill. The driver waiting on the fourth wagon, the one behind, was watching its progress and saw him.

He roared in a voice like a July thunderstorm. "You! Who're you? Guards, *guards*! What's that man doing?"

For a moment, Wulf nearly fled in sheer panic. More men saw him and bellowed in fury. Orders were shouted. Two pikes narrowly missed his head and buried themselves in the covering he had cursed. Fortunately, men started coming over the wagons at him from both sides. For a moment they needed both hands for climbing and their comrades could not use their pikes.

With seconds to spare before he was crushed, Wulf thrust the bed warmer into the gap he had made, and gave it a half-turn to tip the coals out on the lid of the barrel below. *Burn hot, my babies!*

Then he went back to Castle Gallant.

Three men—all of them bigger than he—mobbed him, hugging him, thumping his back. He struggled free angrily, aware that he was shaking as if he had tertian fever.

"You did it, Cub?" Vlad demanded.

"I have no idea. Give me a drink. Let me sit down. Don't suppose I'll ever know if I did it—I mean, whether it worked." Suddenly nauseous, he flopped onto a chair, the chair in which Marek had died. He had been seen. He had broken the first commandment yet again, and he could no longer plead ignorance. He should not have tried it. Justina was going to rip him to strips, and he was fairly sure now that her help and approval were vital to any faint hope he might have of escaping the Church's vengeance for the death of Brother Azuolas.

"What exactly did you do?" Otto asked. "Tell us, dammit!"

Wulf told them, stuttering as reaction dug in like icicles. He had not slept for so long it felt like months. Tomorrow he would be needed again. He must report back to Justina, and he must sleep.

"Go and change," Otto said. "You're soaked!"

"If it blew up, would we have heard it?" Anton asked Vlad.

The big man shook his head. "In this snow? Other side of a mountain? No, but hot coals and powder don't mix, so I'm sure he destroyed one wagon. One won't save us. Nobody's going to stay around and put the fire out, though, so the other wagons may go up as well. Very likely, in fact. And if they all go, then Wartislaw will almost certainly not have the means to breach our defenses. He still outnumbers us hugely, but the boy may have won us enough time for the king's men to arrive. That's as much as—"

The castle trembled as if kicked by a giant. Wine bottles rattled on the table, the candlesticks danced on the mantel, and hot embers collapsed on the hearth.

"Satan's balls!" Anton yelled. "What was that?"

Vlad gave a great roar and charged the nearest window like a mad bull. He flung the casement open, admitting a gale and filling the room with flying snowflakes. It was still daylight out there, but it was barely possible to see across the bailey.

"What in the pit are you doing?" Anton roared.

His brother turned to show a ragged row of big white teeth in his forest of beard. "Waiting for the thunder. It's like mining under a castle wall. You feel the thump before you hear the—"

A long rolling rumble echoed off the mountains, and re-echoed faintly from farther away.

"You ever heard thunder in a snowstorm?" Vlad shouted, waving his fists in the air.

Otto said, "Yes, but it's very—" He was drowned out.

"You did it, Wolfcub, you did it! I was wrong."

Wulf felt a jolt of triumph and leapt to his feet, fatigue forgotten. "One wagon or all of them?"

"Every last one of them, surely!" Vlad slammed the casement.

"Bravo!" Otto clapped Wulf on the back hard enough to jar his teeth, then hugged him.

Anton screamed in joy and waved his fists in the air.

"Devil take 'em!" Vlad bellowed. "Half the shitty Wend army must be plastered all over the forest! What are we waiting for? To arms!" He charged to the door, wrestled briefly with the latch, and then vanished out into the corridor, still bellowing.

Otto said, "Heavenly Father, we humbly thank you for this great mercy that you have . . ." He concluded with a prayer for the souls of the dead. Three brothers said amen and made the sign of the cross.

Wulf had not broken the first commandment after all, because all the workaday witnesses must be dead. But his jubilation soon lost out to shame. And fear too. What had he done? Shaken the mountains? How many dead?

"You lost your dagger," Otto said. "Take this one, you've earned it." He held out his own, an heirloom with an amber handle in the shape of a man's forearm with the fist in a clenched gauntlet making the pommel.

Wulf recoiled. "No, no! I can't wear that."

"You can and you will," his brother said firmly. "It doesn't belong to the reigning baron. The fifth baron had it made for his youngest son. For two hundred years it has been worn by the Magnus most worthy. I didn't earn it, I just inherited it. I brought it along this time because I was planning to give it to Anton if he could hold on to his earldom. But by God, you're the hero now! Wear it till you die. Tell your sons to send it back to Dobkov."

"But—"

"Take it!" Otto roared.

Reluctantly Wulf obeyed and stared in disbelief at the treasured Magnus Dagger. As a small child he had dreamed of wearing it. He hadn't been very old when he realized how slim his chances were, with four brothers ahead of him. "This should be a reward for prowess at arms, not witchcraft."

"It's a reward for courage. Hang it on your belt or stick it in my chest. That's the only way I'll take it back."

"I agree," Anton said thinly.

In disbelief, Wulf hung the heirloom at his right thigh. Today, what was left of it, he would wear the Magnus Dagger. Tomorrow he would give it back to Otto to keep safe for him. Otherwise the Inquisition would steal it.

"Come, Count," Otto said. "Vlad is right. We must strike while we can. Let's go throw the fiendish bombard into the river." He strode out the door.

Wulf shivered. "I need dry clothes first."

"Wait!" Anton shut the door and blocked it, arms defiantly folded. "Wulf, you have done everything we could have hoped for. You have defeated the Wends and saved Castle Gallant and we are all very grateful, but the Inquisition will soon come looking for you. You said so yourself. I realize that you got into the trouble you are in now by helping me, and I promised you any reward I could give you. Name it, take it, and then go. You must flee."

Wulf looked up at his brother and saw a lot more jealousy than gratitude. He felt his temper twitch again. He shivered again as the cold bit deeper. "Pretty speech! The trouble is, the only reward I want, you cannot give me. And fleeing is no answer. Let's see how things are back in Dobkov. . . . Branka is currently reading a bedtime story to our nephews. Old Father Czcibor is teaching a confirmation class. Understand? I can see them and I could go to them. The same applies to the Inquisition's Speakers. I can't hide from them, no matter where I go."

"But you don't need to draw their attention to the rest of us!"

Fury! "Oh, listen, you long streak of stupidity. The Scarlet Spider fooled you, haven't you seen that yet? When Zdenek offered to exalt you from a nothing to a lord of the northern marches, he knew that you couldn't claim the reward without using Satanism. He knew the Magnuses produced both swordsmen and sorcerers. You knew that too, and knew you could twist my arm until I agreed to help, so you accepted. When you twisted, I yielded. I was just as guilty and just as deceived."

Anton unfolded his arms, but one hand sought out his sword hilt and the other went to steady his scabbard. He was probably too mad to listen to reason. "Deceived how?"

"Because if we've won the war, we've won it for that old sinner, not for us. Maybe I've destroyed Wartislaw's powder and Vlad and Otto can do the rest. But the way the Church sees it, I begged help from Satan and you accepted it, too. We are up to our necks in Satanism, *all of us*. The cardinal won't lift a finger to save us, not a pinkie! Once he's sure that Castle Gallant is safe, he'll throw the Magnuses to the dogs and put some dandy courtier in your place. We're all doomed. Understand? Now get out of my way."

Anton's face was fiery, and for a moment Wulf thought he was actually going to draw. Glaring, he stepped aside, and Wulf left.

CHAPTER 15

Wartislaw of Griffin had not won his duchy by being nice to anyone, even his nominal overlord, the Holy Roman Emperor. His entire court was terrified of him. So were his generals, because he liked to boast that none of them ever lost more than one battle. But he had rarely been in such a rage as he was now.

Even his falcons feared him, because they were prevented by their jessing oaths from defending themselves from his rages. He had been known to withhold their powers for weeks on end, and even have them beaten when they especially displeased him. He flew three falcons, who had speeded his climb to power up a ladder of mysterious deaths.

At present, two of them were escorting the Dragon as it was laboriously hauled through this hellhole of a gorge in this hell-sent blizzard. One was riding on the wagon, supposedly keeping watch for enemy Speakers, although at the moment nobody could see anything in this Satanic blizzard. A second was busily blessing the gravel of the road, the fords and bridges, and even strengthening the team of sixteen oxen that hauled the monster.

The third Speaker was supposedly supervising and enabling the digging of the emplacement at the point where the road emerged from the gorge and turned the corner. There the gun would have a clear shot at the gates of Castle Gallant, which would begin a historic first storming of that castle. What not one of the damned-for-eternity military idiots had thought to tell His Grace was that the road there was carved out of living rock. Worse, they had not considered the narrowness of the ledge between cliff-up and cliff-down. Now the sappers had hacked out a trench about three feet wide and two feet deep—not yet deep enough for the bombard, but wide enough to block passage of any vehicle larger than a cart. How did they think the gunners were going to get the Dragon into that hole? The dray was too wide to pull up alongside it. Did they imagine a team of sixteen oxen could *back up?* And if it could, that would leave the bombard pointing the *wrong way!*

Even in the blinding snow, Wartislaw himself saw the problem at a glance. His roar of fury caused the Speaker to vanish, and half his escort moved off, into the fog. The duke wheeled his horse, drew his sword, and prepared to behead the captain in charge. The man screamed in terror, backed away too far, and vanished over the edge of the cliff. Good riddance. Wartislaw ordered one of his mounted escort to remain and take charge—and finish the excavation by morning, or else. Then he bellowed for the rest to follow him, and spurred his horse back into the gorge.

By the time he reached Thunder Falls, he had still not solved the emplacement puzzle. The answer would probably involve ropes, which he had, and dozens of pulleys, which he did not. His falcons could fetch them from Pomerania, but it might take weeks to find enough, while his men starved and froze in this mountain hell.

Perdition!

He had to slow his horse to a walk as the escort attempted to clear a way for him along the mass confusion of the trail, carts bringing forward tools, weapons, and ammunition, and men-at-arms standing by to repel any sortie from Gallant. *There just was not enough room here to fight a war!* Even the rumble of the falls could not drown out the cursing and bellowing of orders, clumping hooves, squealing axles, lowing oxen, clattering shingles. The sides of the gorge varied from sheer rock to almost-sheer moss and scrub. Even above the falls, where the canyon became slightly wider, the extra space was taken up by rocks and tree stumps.

And out of the gloom and the swirling snow emerged an incompetence worse than any yet. He had left strict orders that his pavilion was to be situated as close to the gun battery as possible, so that he could watch the bombardment when it began. But the fools were assembling it on a shingle bank only a third of the size it needed, so half of it would be in the river, and the rest strung through the boulders like a ribbon of colored silk.

"Idiots!" he roared. "What do you think you're doing?"

An elderly servant—Wartislaw never bothered to remember menials' names—looked up at him in terror. "Erecting your tent, Your Grace. You told—"

Wartislaw slashed him across the face with his quirt. "Pig-brained nincompoop! I'll have you all flogged. Where is—"

Huh? Horses staggered, then reared in terror, even his own courser, until he hauled on the reins and beat it into submission. Several men had fallen over, and were scrambling to their feet again. Rocks clattered down the hillside.

"What was that?" he muttered, but nobody answered.

Thunder rolled and echoed. All heads had turned to stare back along the trail, the way they had come. Not thunder; a mine! He had never heard one that big, but the delay between shock and sound meant that it had been at least a mile away. So it must have originated within his baggage train. The train had still been working its way forward while the men were setting up camp. Had one of those cretinous wagoners driven too close to a campfire? Or was this more Jorgarian Satanism like that suspiciously defective ladder this morning? If a powder wagon had exploded in the middle of the column, Wartislaw might have to add two or three hundred casualties to the toll from this morning's fiasco.

He spurred forward again, yelling for men to get out of his way. He must inspect the damage and get the bodies out of sight as soon as possible, or those superstitious churls . . .

And what was *that?* The roar of the falls was growing louder. Except that the sound was not coming from behind him, where the falls were. In front of him? *Above* him?

And then he was flying, horse and all.

CHAPTER 16

Vlad ran down the stairs to the armory, roaring orders to anyone he met on the way. He had divided Anton's forces into three "battles," naming them after city churches. Currently St. Andrej's had the watch, St. Petr's was on standby, and St. Sebastijan's was off duty. By the time he reached the armory, the tocsin was clanging and St. Petr's men were already running in to report for duty.

Dali Notivova arrived at his heels, bare to the waist, with shaving oil on one side of his face and two days' beard on the other.

"Cute whiskers," Vlad said. "Latest Italian style?" He peered around and located Sir Teodor looking for orders. He was a local rancher, well into his forties and too old for real roughhousing, but he'd fought for the Hungarians against the Turks and could handle men. Vlad had made him captain of St. Petr's Battle.

"Muster," he ordered, "and prepare to sortie out the north gate. Dali, muster the cavalry." All twelve horses. "Take every horse we've got, but save the biggest for me."

All around him jaws dropped, eyes widened.

Vlad raised his voice to address them all. "You felt that thump a little while ago? And heard thunder a little later?

I've met that before, when a mine went off. I tell you now the Wends' powder store was struck by lightning! If I'm wrong I'll eat my own balls. Our Blessed Lord smote the evildoers for us! He blew half of them to hell. Now we'll go and finish off the rest."

They cheered like lunatics. Any action was better than being trapped in a cage while an enemy prepared to break in and kill you. Having God fighting on your side was good too. They would have to be lunatics to join a charge up that road in a howling blizzard, but he would lead them, and they would follow. He found the armor he had chosen for himself, the biggest in the castle but still damnably tight on him. Excited boys came running to help him.

Vlad felt no guilt about taking the Lord's name in vain. Every action he had ever fought in—too many to count by now—had begun with someone assuring him—or him assuring others—that God was on their side. The Church, if it ever learned about young Wulf's exploit with the bed warmer, would certainly claim that he had been helped by the devil, but that was just jealousy, because he could work miracles and they couldn't. What a kid! Made a man proud to be his brother.

"No horse armor," he told Dali. "No bows, just pikes and swords. Can't see to shoot." The snow was wet enough to soak bowstrings, and pike handles would make useful pry bars if they found the bombard where it might be rolled off the road. "You stay here and untie any knots."

He was saluted by Sir Karel, who led St. Andrej's Battle. Another local, Karel was younger than Teodor, with less experience and much less sense. "All quiet on north and south roads, my lord. Quiet as mice. Course, we can't see anything in this snow."

"I don't think they'll be crazy enough to attack in this weather," Vlad said, arms spread as a boy struggled to strap his cuirass around him.

"No, my lord."

"We are, but they're not." He leered.

Unwilling to seem less brave, Karel leered back.

Vlad said, "Don't let your guard down on the south gate, but we'll need men to work the north gates for us. We can go out by the sally port, but after we've gone and know it's safe, you should open the outer gate to head height in case we need to make a fast return. Hey, Sir Teodor?"

The knight shouted acknowledgment through the mob, being half-way into armor and unable to move.

"See that you bring four men with shovels and two carrying spikes and mallets." Shovels in case they needed to clear the road, spikes in case they were able to reach the great bombard. One spike hammered into the Dragon's touchhole would make it scrap metal.

It took longer than Vlad wished but less time than he had feared to get the sally organized. The infantry were ready first, and marched off through the streets toward the barbican before he rode out with Jachym at his side and another ten horsemen at their backs, comprising the fearsome Castle Gallant cavalry. He thought the snow seemed less heavy than it had been. Word of the explosion had spread, and crowds cheered the forces. Out into the Quarantine canyon they rode, then through the inner gate into the barbican.

"Follow as quick as you can," Vlad told Karel, "but you may have to clear some drifts. You must be ready for a very fast retreat if we run into a wolf pack. One other thing: don't march your men over the edge of the cliff. It's a long way down."

"Aye, my lord. I mean, no, my lord."

Vlad urged his mount over to the sally port. Men swung it open, snow swirled, in and he was shocked to see that the drift out there was thigh deep. His horse was even more discouraged. Seeing that it would take too long to get everyone out that way, he roared for the main gate to be opened. The men stationed up there must have been listening through the murder holes, because chains and wheels began to clank and squeak at once. If the enemy had crept close under cover of the snow, there would have to be a fight.

The instant there was enough clearance, Vladislav Magnus ducked his head under the steel base plate and rode out to war. He spoke the prayer that Father had taught him for that moment. For centuries it had served the warriors in the family well. It had not shielded all of them, but enough had survived to carry on the family line.

The drifts were patchy, and in places there was no snow at all. Already he had snow inside his helmet, up his nose, sticking to his eyelashes;

and yet, the accursed stuff was certainly not coming down as fast as it had just a few minutes ago. He hoped that this might be just a lull between flurries, but soon he could see halfway to the bend where the road entered the gorge. The sun had gone behind the mountains, the wintery twilight was fading, and the flat light made it hard to judge the drifts or where the edge of the cliff was.

Still, no sniper was taking potshots at him, and once he had made a trail the rest could follow more easily. Pressing his spurs against his horse's flanks, he rode up the Silver Road. As a mercenary, he'd come this way four years ago, but that had been in summer. He'd not been senior enough to meet the count, and all he had seen had been the Quarantine Road, nothing of the town or castle.

Long before he reached the corner, the snow had stopped and the way ahead was clear. Still, he saw no Wends. Poor lads had given up and gone home to bed? The blindings they had set up at the bend had blown over, leaving no cover for snipers.

The post seemed to have been abandoned: not a soul in sight. He found that almost creepy. The bombard wasn't there yet. He paused to inspect the work and let the rest of his cavalry catch up with him. Progress had been slow, but the size of the trench they were planning was impressive. He revised his estimate of the time the enemy would need to emplace the big gun. On the other hand, recoil usually shifted the seating after a few shots, but once the Dragon was nested in the bedrock, it should be able to fire indefinitely without adjustment.

Vlad looked back and saw that the hundred or so men of St. Petr's Battle were making much harder work of the snowy road than the horses had. Whatever happened, the Wends would have to wait a few days for the thaw before they could attack. And before they could hope to move the Dragon.

Even if they still had powder to use it. Yea, Wulfgang!

The rough side of this situation, of course, was that if a company of Wend archers did break cover now, the Cardicians would be trying to flee back home through all that snow with a hail of arrows following them the whole way. So the cavalry had better advance smartly and flush the whoresons out.

He glanced at Jachym and realized that he felt as cold as the man looked. He waved his arm as a signal to follow him, and urged his horse forward again, past the litter of snow and timber the Wends had left, and around the bend.

He had taken part in some mad escapades in the last dozen years, but never anything quite this mad. The air and the ground were all white, even the rocky wall to his left. The corner was abrupt, taking him suddenly into the gorge, but the crossbow bolts he half expected failed to arrive. No sentries leaped to their feet in alarm; no trumpets blew. The footing became treacherous, covered with scattered spars and shorter timbers, collapsed tents, a few barrels, shovels and axes. No people at all.

Vlad's horse balked, understandably, so he dismounted and tied the reins to a heavy beam. Drawing his sword, he set off to pick his way through this appalling clutter, hearing Jachym shouting orders behind him. The going improved as he left the work site. He walked along the road unchallenged until he came upon a couple of empty carts with their oxen still yoked, but no carters. He glanced at Master Sergeant Jachym, who was one step back on his left. "You think the devil came and took them all to hell?"

The old warrior's nervy grin barely showed under his helmet. "My guess, sir, would be that they heard the devil taking a lot of them, and the rest ran back to help the wounded."

That sounded logical.

The snow had stopped, but the light was fading fast under the trees. To walk until nightfall would be ridiculous, asking for trouble. But still there was nobody! Still, no quarrels came hissing out from the quiet.

Where were all the Wends?

CHAPTER 17

Last night Wulf had been assigned a cubbyhole called the Blue Room, just large enough to hold a bed and a wicker hamper. He had not had a chance to sleep there yet, but he had asked a housekeeper to find him some clothes, and she had apparently succeeded, for the basket was almost full.

As he stripped, he reflected that he had killed men by the hundreds that morning and by thousands in the afternoon. He couldn't do penance for such Satanism if he went back and forth between Jerusalem and Santiago de Compostela on his knees for the rest of his life.

Bed beckoned, for he had not slept at all last night and very little the two nights before that; but he had an appointment with Justina to discuss what might be done about the Dragon bombard. He had almost certainly solved that problem by himself, and she might refuse to give him any more help than she already had, but he enjoyed talking with her. He had just pulled on his trunk hose and was reaching for a shirt when the light of a nimbus flared up behind him. He whirled around to face the intruder.

For a moment he did not recognize the demure young lady who stood there in a billowing silken ball gown.

"Pretty," Sybilla said. "Nice muscles."

He stuffed his arms into the shirt he was holding and hauled the rest of it over his head. "Why don't you go to hell and drive the devil crazy? Why pick on me?"

She leaned against a bedpost like a cat rubbing itself against a friend's leg. "Oo! Do I drive you crazy?"

"Not crazy the way you're crazy. What do you want?"

"You for a pet, but I can't have you. I came to say goodbye. Dearest Wulfgang, this is farewell! We can never meet again!" She sighed and clasped her hands in an Our Lady of Sorrows pose.

"I am overcome with indescribable emotion."

That was not the right answer, because she pouted. "I am about to be jessed!"

"Congratulations," he said, as jessing was obviously something worth bragging about. Justina had dropped hints about jessing. And she had used other falconry terms: cadger, haggard, brancher. If he wasn't so tired, he could probably work out how a bird could be a stand-in for a Speaker. "Who's the lucky man?"

"Not a man! A lady."

She had not answered with scorn, so a man would have been possible. If Wulf baited his hooks carefully, he might even start to learn something about the mysterious Saints.

"Ah, you mean your cadger?"

"Of course!"

"Anyone I know?"

That was again the right question, because she flashed a perfect set of pearl-white teeth at him. If her appearance was at all real, Sybilla truly was as beautiful as she thought she was.

"Certainly not, but you must have heard of her: Anne of France!"

"Sorry. I'm just a backwoods esquire with aspirations."

The scorn returned. He had been expected to swoon.

"Anne of Beaujeu, then? Sister of King Louis, wife of Peter of Bourbon. She is fourteen. I am to be her mistress of jewels! I shall live at court. Probably never far from her side."

"Wonderful! Congratulations. What will your duties be, apart from minding the lady's jewels?"

"Oh . . ." Sybilla's shrugs involved much more than just shoulders, and her smile could freeze blood. "Whatever she wants. Within reason, that is."

"This was your father's doing, I take it?"

Anne of Beaujeu's pet witch strolled over to the little mirror to admire herself. "Well, the dean of the College of Cardinals does have influence, you know!"

A hand to wash and be washed by any other, no question. Wulf wondered what the other half of this arrangement was—how much the king of France had paid, in gold or political favors, to obtain a sorcerous fixer-bodyguard for his sister.

"And of course my mother is Lady Umbral," she added.

"I am not familiar with—"

"Prelate of the Saints." From the way she glanced at him in the mirror, she was dropping hints. She had mentioned the Saints before in a way that suggested a non-standard meaning.

"But the Lady Anne is not another Speaker?"

"Of course not." Sybilla did not turn.

She had been disappointed to hear him ask such a stupid question. Which was what he had expected. He was beginning to understand now.

At last.

"Well, I must go," she said. "I have other friends who will be eager to hear my good news."

"I am very happy for you, and I am sorry for any rude things I said. I am sure you will serve your lady well, and Anne of France is fortunate to have acquired such a promising, er, Speaker?"

Sybilla gave him a contemptuous sidelong glance. "Falcon."

"Of course. Saints be with you."

She disappeared into empty air.

He chuckled and laced up his doublet. He thought that Sybilla would make a better guard dog than a falcon, but Anne of Beaujeu should have no trouble keeping her court in line from now on. How soon would she find her tame Speaker flying her, instead of the other way about? The Speakers' fondness for falconry terms verged on the absurd, but it was an obvious defense against dangerous talk that might be overheard. Falcons were also the fastest-moving creatures in God's creation, which was probably no coincidence.

He reached for his cloak.

Justina was sitting in the vineyard, apparently just staring at the vines, but possibly Looking through Wulf's eyes, which suggested the infinite regress of a pair of mirrors.

He stepped through limbo. Near to setting, the sun still shone on golden leaves, and once again the softness of the air took Wulf's breath away. Justina greeted him with a look of sour dislike, but a bottle of wine and three glasses adorned the table, and she pushed the bottle over to his side. Taking that as an invitation, he sat down.

"You've been busy," she said.

"Very." Wulf wearily filled one glass and passed it to her. The evening alone was wine, compared to the weather in Cardice, and if he drank another drop of the real stuff he would fall asleep. His eyelids were heavy as boots.

"When you went spying on the Wends, did you learn anything of value?"

"Not much." Enough to do them a world of damage, but he was too ashamed of the carnage to brag about it. "You weren't watching?"

"You cannot hope to keep a secret around Speakers," Justina said impatiently, as if he were being stupid, "but sometimes secrets keep themselves. We cannot be in more than two places at once—one place in body and another in mind. You cannot watch someone every minute of every day. I know you took a stupid risk in going there, and for no real gain. Let that be a lesson to you."

She pulled a face and drank wine as if rinsing away a bad taste. She had been upset enough by Azuolas's death, and the Long Valley blast must have killed thousands. If she was not aware of that, why did she seem so distressed now?

Snow had stopped falling at Castle Gallant. Anton and Otto were on the roof of the north barbican, inspecting a completed trebuchet. Anton was even congratulating the workers, a courtesy that Otto undoubtedly must have suggested to him, for he would never have thought of it by himself.

Vlad was on foot—which seemed very odd and dangerous—working his way through a litter of broken pine branches that had almost buried the road. He must be in the gorge, where there was no snow falling and not very much light, either. He had a dozen or so men with him, and they were all fighting for every step. What was the big lunk up to? Where were the Wends?

"I agree. Tell me about Elysium." He waited to see if Justina would answer.

She took a sip of wine. "It's wherever Lady Umbral happens to be."

"And Lady Umbral rules the Saints?"

"That brat jabbers far too much. Lady Umbral is our prelate. The pope rules the Church; the voivode rules the Agioi; and Umbral the Saints. People come and go, the names remain."

"The Saints are a guild of free Speakers, like free masons, bound to no lord?" And the Agioi must be the Greek Orthodox equivalent.

"More or less. The Church captures most Speakers as adolescents; rulers also collect them when they can find them. We survive because we do not raid or proselytize to others. We obey the commandments, and the Church lets us be."

"But you do favors for rulers, like helping Zdenek out with Castle Gallant."

"Sometimes," she admitted.

He suspected that answer fell considerably short of the truth. Helping out kings in trouble would be a highly profitable business.

"So am I to be allowed to join the Saints?"

Justina sighed and refilled her own glass. "No. Your execution of Father Vilhelmas was rank murder. The death of Father Azuolas was another. I have spoken twice with Lady Umbral, and she insists that we cannot shelter a murderer."

"I see." Wulf contemplated his future and saw only darkness. No life with Madlenka; no life without her either. How did a man hide from pursuers who could come to him at any time, no matter where he was?

Anton and Otto were still on the roof of the north barbican, staring up the deserted road, waiting for Vlad's return. The entire sortie party had disappeared into the gorge.

Vlad. . . . Vlad had stopped trying to force his way through the nightmare of deadfall, and was watching a peculiar struggle going on just ahead of him. It looked as if the sortie had finally made contact with one of the Pomeranians, who had tried to run from them. Three of the Cardicians had gone in pursuit over the obstacle course.

Justina said, "I wish I'd gotten to you before you started killing people."

"My bite has always been faster than my bark," Wulf said. "But I'm not making excuses. I am sprung of a warrior line. Magnuses kill men and brag about it over dinner. I saw Marek in danger, so I pulled the trigger. I would do it again. If I must pay the price, I won't whine about it."

Justina shook her head, staring at him, but with more pity than disapproval. "You had reasons for both killings. You did not start the aggression. A completely impartial court might levy a lesser penalty than death on you." She was repeating arguments that Lady Umbral must have already rejected. "The Church is not impartial. You killed two priests. We cannot help you escape from that."

"Would Zdenek get me a royal pardon, if I saved his castle?"

"He might save you from being hanged, if you'd rather be burned. Royal pardons don't help if the Church convicts you of heresy or witchcraft. And Zdenek will certainly not admit to employing witchcraft. You're nothing to do with him, my boy. As of today, he'd never even heard of you."

Which was exactly what Wulf himself had told Anton.

Stars were wakening in an indigo east. Wulf rose, stretched. He was weary, aching through to the marrow. "Excuse me. I think the war's over for today."

She nodded. "I wish I could give you better news, squire."

"Not your fault, mine. Is this goodbye?"

"I'm afraid it must be."

He walked around the table and stooped to kiss her cheek.

"What's that for?"

"It's faint, but there's still a trace of Dobkov in your voice. Thanks for doing what you did, Auntie. I know you'd have helped more if you had been allowed to."

CHAPTER 18

Wulf went back to the Blue Room. It was cold and almost dark, because it was on an outside wall lit by only a narrow, unglazed loophole. Many hours had passed since he ate Justina's strange fish soup, but he was too weary to go in search of food.

Anton and Otto still lingered on the barbican roof. They must be really worried about Vlad's sortie, wondering what was keeping it. Vlad himself. . . . *His men had caught their fleeing Wend and were bringing him in, not gently. There was a lot of guttural shouting in several languages.*

Curiosity jabbed Wulf and told him he couldn't possibly go to bed before he discovered what was going on up there in the gorge. Conscience retorted that to materialize in the middle of a group of workaday men-at-arms would violate the first commandment. But wait . . . when Wulf himself had returned from Long Valley a few hours ago, he and Copper had not emerged exactly where he had aimed, but nearby. Somehow his Voices protected him from accidentally exposing his powers.

He opened a peephole through limbo some distance away from Vlad and his men, back along the track they had cleared. They all seemed to be engrossed in the prisoner;

the light was bad, and the piles of tumbled deadfall were almost head high. Confident that his arrival would be unseen, Wulf enlarged the gap, stepped through, and began picking his way between the heaps of wreckage to join the conference. Soon he was noticed, but attracted no special interest. If the count had sent his squire to check up on them, that was not their concern.

The prisoner, who was being addressed as Lech, was a grubby, heavy-set bear of a man. He looked unprepossessing and none too smart. He was far from happy, but everyone else was grinning and chuckling, so the news must be good. Vlad was firing questions, one of the men-at-arms was translating them, and the prisoner's answers were making the same laborious journey back. By the time Wulf was close enough to make out what was being said, Lech's presence there was being explained. He was a carter, and he had been at the mouth of the gorge when "the wind came."

"Says he was sent back to get the oxen, sir. He's to unyoke them and try to drive them back to the bivouac."

"He'll never get them through this muck," Vlad growled. "Who owns them?"

The question was translated and answered, the answer translated: "He thinks Duke Wartislaw does, sir. He says they're not his."

"He's even more of a fool than he looks. If he'd said they were his I might have let him keep them. Tell him we're taking him and all that steak back to Gallant." Vlad glanced around. "We can't do more here than get ourselves killed. Let's—" He jumped, rattling his armor, as he discovered Wulf at his elbow. "Where in flames did you come from?"

"Came to see what was keeping you," Wulf said cheerily. "What's up?"

"Much what we thought. Back home, everyone. No fight tonight. Go and make your wives happy. And tell Sir Teodor to turn his troop around." He waved for his men to leave without him. "Come and look at this." He led Wulf in the opposite direction. "See the trees?"

"Er . . . no." Against the last traces of daylight in the western sky, there were no trees. The steep hillsides had been stripped bare. The trees were down here, in the gorge. In pieces. Wulf had only a rough grasp of the lay of the land, but he was sure the wagon he had fired had been at the far end of the gorge, two or three miles from here. The blast couldn't have stripped hills that far away, surely?

But he couldn't ask Vlad, because the big man was plowing through the branches and debris, evidently returning to some particular place. He was big and clad in steel, heaving debris out of his way like some great impatient bear. Even following in his tracks, Wulf could not go as fast. When Vlad stopped, he had to wait for him to catch up. "Can you hear the waterfall?"

Wulf listened. He heard a million syncopated dripping noises, nothing more. . . . Possibly voices a long way off. "No."

"Thunder Falls. Should be right here, Jachym says, and the others agree. The river's not running."

"That's ridiculous! What can stop a river running?"

"You can. Look down here." What he had brought Wulf to see was under deadfall, almost invisible in the gloom.

Wulf squatted down, then stood up hastily. "Bodies!"

"About three of them, we thought. That's if you put them back together, they'd make three or a bit more. A horse and a half on top of them, roughly, and then trees on top of that."

"No!" Wulf said, appalled. "The explosion couldn't have done this! The powder wagons were miles away." This was destruction on a scale he could barely imagine. Men torn to pieces?

"The explosion rattled Castle Gallant!" Vlad said with a chuckle. "But you're right. The gunpowder went up very close to their camp, the man says. Lech is his name, Polish. The blast did terrible slaughter, he thinks, but all he truly knows is what happened here. One or two men have gotten across, but there's still about a thousand men bivouacking on this side tonight, so let's you and me just creep quietly away and not provoke any nasty reprisals."

He started to move. Wulf grabbed his steel-plated arm. "This side of *what*?"

Vlad chuckled. "Of the avalanche. The blast you set off shook the mountains and started an avalanche. The valley's totally blocked with snow above the falls. A couple of hundred feet high, Lech said, but we caught a glimpse of it and I think he may be short a bit. Who knows? Avalanches start terrible winds, laddie, and this one came crashing down into the gorge. Its wind smashed everything on this side and probably on the other side, too. The debris has dammed the Ruzena."

It had surely damned Wulfgang Magnus. "Then the lake will rise? And . . ."

"Not much, we decided. It's a big lake, the men tell me. But the low point is where the river drains out, so the area just beyond the snow pile is going to fill up. The gorge will become a smaller lake, until the snow melts next summer. If the Dragon isn't under the snow, or gone over the cliff, it's going to be underwater, and when the dam breaks it may even get swept away. Don't make no difference now."

"We won?" Wulf said, unable to comprehend the scale of this disaster.

Vlad gave him a buffet on the shoulder that almost knocked him over. Luckily the giant was wearing leather gloves, not gauntlets.

"It was you who won, sonny! Duke Wartislaw is either dead or beaten. Wulfgang Magnus, you are the greatest of us all. I couldn't believe you were going to do what you said you would do with that bed warmer. You've got more stomach than a herd of cows. Maybe you were just ignorant and lucky, but that's true of lots of heroes. You single-handedly stopped thirty thousand men and lifted the siege of Castle Gallant. I'm so proud of you I want to scream your fame to the skies, and I know I mustn't do that. I tell you, Father would have wept with pride."

Just a few days ago, Wulf would have burst his heart to earn such words from Vlad. Now they made him feel ill. He was doing the devil's work.

CHAPTER 19

How many Speakers eavesdropped on that exchange could never be known. As Justina had said, Speakers could not spend all day and night Looking, no matter how interesting the subject, and they were limited to exploiting the points of view of people they knew. Very few had ever met Wulfgang, and although Vlad's reputation as a warrior had spread all over Christendom, Speakers had little interest in soldiers. Duke Wartislaw undoubtedly had some Speakers with his army, and one or more might have survived the disaster. Cardinal Zdenek's hirelings were certainly watching events, and the Church's huge workforce of Speakers would be keeping watch on Wulf, amassing evidence of his Satanism for future action. Justina was well known among the Saints, and news that the old bird had taken on another hire would have aroused their curiosity. However the news got out, it spread across the continent faster than fire in a powder wagon.

Justina herself was drunk, drunker than she had been in thirty years, still slumped on the bench outside her cottage, trying to get up enough energy to put herself to bed. What a disaster! Those astonishing Magnus brothers, her great-nephews. *Ottokar and Anton were still shivering on the roof of the north barbican. Vladislav was apparently interrogating a prisoner in a collapsed forest . . . and Wulfgang was there with him! Twenty minutes ago the kid had been chalky white and ready to fall over, but he must have found some more energy from somewhere.* Ah, youth!

But then her curiosity was aroused by the devastation. In a life of nigh on a hundred years, she had never seen anything quite like that. She watched as the two brothers went off to inspect something. In a few moments she sobered herself with a flash of talent and sat up straight. She heard every word of Vlad's lecture.

God be praised!

She hurried indoors and changed into a finer cloak and bonnet. She opened a gate through limbo, emerging on a small balcony that seemed to be suspended directly below the stars. Blind until her eyes adjusted to the darkness, she fumbled her way to the solitary high-backed oak chair. She stretched out a hand to find the bell rope and tug it to announce her arrival.

Despite what she had told Wulfgang, Elysium was a real place, the former monastery of St. Pantaleimon, at Meteora, in Thessaly. Although this was not generally known, the original monks had been wiped out by pestilence more than a hundred years earlier, and the Saints had moved in. Like many other religious houses in the area, St. Pantaleimon's was perched on a sheer rock pillar hundreds of feet high, completely inaccessible to workadays. Food and other supplies had to be hauled up on ropes. Speakers, of course, could enter and leave by way of limbo, bringing most of their food with them.

Vlad was still making his way back to the castle. Wulf was already on the barbican tower with Otto and Anton, reporting what he had seen.

Justina leaned back in the chair, keeping her eyes closed. Darkness or closed eyes made it much harder, although not totally impossible, for would-be eavesdroppers to locate her. Besides, there was nothing out there to see except sky. By daylight, this balcony looked out on the great Thessaly Plain, and some rooms had views of other monasteries on other pillars, but no nosy neighbors were close enough to realize that any dark-clad figure glimpsed at a window or on a terrace might be a woman.

The little hatch behind her slid open. Someone coughed.

"Kristina," she said. "Greenwood. Nor angels nor principalities." Her original name, the code word assigned by Cardinal Zdenek, and a Saints password that would fetch Lady Umbral instantly, even if she were dancing with her current beau, King Edward of England.

The hatch closed.

Justina made her old bones as comfortable as possible against the oaken back and contemplated her astonishing day. She could not recall one like it in the eighty years since she was jessed.

Now she had a chance to analyze what she had just heard from Vladislav. Perhaps young Wulfgang had worked his miracle with the help of a lot of luck, but the Saints appreciated luck. Some people knew how to use luck and some did not. Luck rubbed off. He had completely changed the game.

Eventually she began to worry. She had used the "angels and principalities" code only twice before in her long service to the Saints, and Lady Umbral had always responded much faster than this. Was Justina being put in her place as a stupid, dithering, sentimental old woman? Worse, was that what she had become? Today was the first time she had ever returned to the prelate to ask for a decision to be reversed, and here she was back yet again. Voices had been raised at their meeting earlier. Had she slid into senility without realizing?

Then she was addressed from the small grille in the wall to her left. "I hope you realize," said the familiar, faintly mocking voice, "that I was on my way to sup with the pope?"

"I hope I won't spoil your appetite, my lady. The situation has changed."

"I made my views quite clear, I think."

"You did, but I do think you will change them now."

"I doubt that," Lady Umbral said impatiently.

Justina wished she could watch the lady's expression, but a drape hung over the grille on the far side, and Lady Umbral would be sitting in darkness. Elysium had been made as snoop-proof as possible.

"Wulfgang has done what was needed. He went into the Wends' camp and blew up their powder wagons with hot coals from a bed warmer. We don't know yet what damage that did directly, but it brought down an avalanche that plugged the pass. He's dammed the Ruzena River and closed the Silver Road for months or years. The Pomeranian invasion is over."

"Mother of God!"

In the reigns of three prelates, Justina had never before heard an Umbral blaspheme.

"Wartislaw is totally defeated and may be dead. He must have lost thousands of men, plus his camp and complete artillery train. It's a rout."

Umbral laughed. "I grovel! I abase myself! I genuflect to your paramount wisdom. Enlist him! Grab that Magnus boy before Zdenek hears of this. Or the Church."

The game had changed. The fact was that too many Speakers were half mad, like Leonas, or twisters like Vilhelmas. Honest, effective Speakers were rare and very precious. Justina had been one in her day, and Wulfgang was clearly another. Even the Church might prefer to turn him than burn him now. Negotiation might be possible.

"Rome is the biggest problem, my lady. Is that why His Holiness has invited you? Has he heard this yet, do you know?"

"I'm fairly sure he wants to talk about Azuolas's death. Even if he's still thinking of bonfires at the moment, he may change his mind when he hears this news."

Justina felt an enormous sense of reprieve. Wulfgang was not going to burn! On the other hand, he might not be totally enamored of the alternative.

"The girl, Madlenka Bukovany, who was supposed to marry Anton— she and Wulfgang go fish-eyed every time they look at each other. I don't think they've had a chance to make the two-backed monster yet, but I give them two days at the most before they crack."

"He won't want to take an oath of celibacy, you mean?" Umbral said impatiently. "Nobody takes that seriously anymore."

Wulfgang would.

"No, the Church might let him marry and remain a layman, as long as he was jessed by a cleric. The trouble is that Count Anton guessed which way the tide was turning and bullied the girl into a handfasting, which he consummated with dispatch. The pope can annul that and you cannot. They're both the type to want Church blessing."

Lady Umbral muttered, "'Sblood!" under her breath.

"And if Zdenek gets his pitch in, he can play on the boy's loyalty. The

Magnuses pride themselves on having served the kings of Jorgary for centuries, with never a waver."

"No offense to your homeland, but he would be wasted serving such a pipsqueak kingdom."

Justina did not fancy telling the boy that. "And we must fend off the Agioi. Wulfgang and Marek assassinated their Father Vilhelmas, so they may start calling for justice."

"From what you told me earlier, he got justice. Our first priority must be to jess your Wulfgang wonder before anyone else gets him." The lady was starting to sound curt, impatient to return to her supper with the Vicar of Christ. "Offer him protection and we'll settle the deaths somehow. It won't be the first time I've bought a pope, or even the patriarch."

"There's more, I'm afraid."

Lady Umbral sighed. "I should have known there would be. You've never panicked before. Go on, then."

Justina did not consider that she'd panicked now. She had recognized a crisis that required more than her own authority, that was all.

"A woman in the town may have died of plague a few days ago."

"Ignore that," Lady Umbral said firmly. "The Good Lord never asks my permission before He visits pestilence on people, and we can heal our own, as long as we're discreet. Anything more?"

Wasn't that enough? Justina was feeling too old for so much excitement. "I think I've covered the main points."

"Then go back there and enlist Wulfgang Magnus. Do anything at all, but get him jessed by someone in the Saints! I'll happily jess him myself, if he agrees. I'll be available right after this snack with Sixtus. Bring him here, if you can, to Elysium."

"Thank you, my lady. Bon appétit!"

She heard a low growl from behind the curtain and then silence. Justina opened her eyes to glimpse a few stars and one single, lonely light somewhere down on the plain.

Time to go. Wulfgang was still not in bed. In fact, he was talking to . . .

Oh, no!

CHAPTER 20

Arturas Synovec was twenty-three years old, the count's herald, a native of Gallant, betrothed to the most beautiful girl he had ever met, and a bastard. His mother had been housekeeper to the bishop-two-back, and such things happened. He and his brothers had received an education out of the situation, and in their cases not much else. Arturas, though, having displayed some talent with pen and brush, and lacking the brawn for physical work or warfare, had become a clerk in the count's service, then apprentice to Klement, the old herald, and eventually his successor. Life had been simple but penurious, with little hope that he could ever earn enough money to take on family responsibilities. Then Count Bukovany and his son had died suddenly and Count Magnus had appeared even more suddenly. Arturas felt as if he had barely slept since.

If the castle survived the Wends and the Pelrelmians, he could realistically hope to receive a bonus from the victorious count, perhaps even a raise, and thus the means to afford marriage. If the castle fell . . . He tried not to think about that. Gallant sat between two armies like a nut in a nutcracker, and the people prayed as they had not prayed in a century.

Near sunset, rumors of a miracle began to circulate. The count's brother, Sir Vladislav, was reported to be leading a sortie out the north gate, which ought to be suicide. The snow showed signs of ending, but darkness was falling, so perhaps he could still hope to escape detection long enough to damage whatever the enemy had been doing up at the mouth of the gorge.

Then word was passed for Arturas Synovec to attend His Lordship on the roof of the north barbican. Raise or bonus would depend on diligence, so he ran the whole way, arriving almost too breathless to speak. The bitter wind was still howling up there, and the three men standing by the battlements were all muffled like hibernating bears. He could recognize the count by his height, and he was fairly certain that the one in armor was Constable Dali Notivova.

His footsteps were muffled, but they heard him puffing and turned to face him.

"Herald," the count said, "have you heard about the river?"

That was about the most unexpected question he had ever been asked.

"No, my"—gasp—"lord."

"Constable, tell him."

"It's stopped flowing," Notivova said. "Just a trickle here and there. Never seen anything like it."

And what did they expect Arturas Synovec to do about it? He said nothing, which was usually a wise choice for a herald, or so Klement had taught him.

"We heard thunder a while ago," the count said, "and the ground shook. We think a landslide must have blocked the gorge. Nothing else could plug up the river. If the Ruzena can't flow, the gorge will flood. The Wends won't be able to get at us. They'll have to go home. They may all be buried under the slide—my brother's gone to see. The Lord has spoken."

Arturas found breath enough to shout, "God be praised!"

"Amen. But Havel and his Pelrelmians may not know this. I want you to go down there—"

The third man coughed, thereby revealing that he was Baron Magnus, the eldest brother.

"Um, yes," said the count. "I'm *asking* you if you are willing to go down there with a flag of truce to tell them that the war may be over. We don't want any nasty accidents or unnecessary assaults. But you're not a man-at-arms, and this could be dangerous, so I'm *asking*, not ordering."

"It's my job, my lord. Of course I'll go." There! He was quite proud to hear himself say it. Surprised, too.

"Then the sooner the better," the count said. "Try to get to see Count Pelrelm himself, or at least Sir Marijus, his son. Tell him we want a truce until noon. By then we should know exactly what's happened, and if necessary we'll let him send observers to confirm our reports. You may also tell him that, if they abandon their aggression and go home now, we shan't report this morning's skirmish to the king. That was just a case of misunderstood orders."

"Tell him that last bit only if you are pressed," the baron added. "Don't sound as if we're afraid of a fight. They're the ones sleeping in the snow, not us. The constable will see you out the postern. You'll need a flag, of course, and a clean-burning torch."

"Aye, my lord."

"And a clean rag," the baron said. "They may want to blindfold you, so take a clean rag with you."

CHAPTER 21

Wulf narrowly avoided losing his left eye on a branch. Away from the avalanche area, where trees still stood, the gorge was almost totally dark.

"You go ahead," he said to Vlad. "I have snow in my shoes and pine needles down my neck. I am going to strip naked and fall into bed."

"You've earned it." Vlad heaved half a cedar out of their way. "Don't suppose anyone will miss you here."

No. By the time Vlad caught up with his cavalrymen, they would have reached their horses and mingled with Sir Teodor's men coming in. In the darkness and confusion, the squire's absence would not be noticed.

Wulf opened a gate to the roof of the north barbican and stepped through it. "All is well," he said. His brothers jumped like frogs.

Otto crossed himself. "I wish you'd warn me when you're going to do that!"

"Vlad's all right?" Anton demanded. "What happened to the river? Why's it stopped running? A landslide?"

"Just an avalanche, they think; ought to melt in the summer. The war is over. We won. I helped, but it was a genuine miracle. You'd better tell the bishop to organize a Te Deum."

Wulf would attend and give thanks. The full import of what had happened was just starting to sink in.

"The Lord helps those who help themselves," Otto said. "It's a pity you can't get the public credit."

"No matter." Wulf yawned as if he would never stop. He had been running on excitement for too long, and was almost asleep on his feet.

"Anton's planning to knight you tomorrow."

Wulf nodded. "Thanks." He would try and talk them out of that, though. It was not a good idea—knight him for what? Knighthood should be recognition of prowess at arms, not Satanism. "I'm going off watch, my lords. If you need me, sit on it till morning."

Otto thumped him on the shoulder. "Come to the solar and let us drink a toast to Wulfgang the Great."

Anton said, "Yes, please. Let's do that."

However weary, Wulf could not refuse such a plea. "Just a quick nightcap, then." The solar was in the castle, on the far side of town. He opened a gate to it and led the way through. After a couple of muttered oaths, or possibly prayers, his brothers followed.

Tonight someone had thought to order a fire and candles, so the little room was cozy and bright after the snowy fall night. The furniture had been shifted around; Wulf slumped into a chair. Anton played host, fussing with a decanter and goblets of fine Venetian glass. He and Otto drank their toast to the boy wonder, although they were too polite to call him that to his face.

"Thanks," Wulf murmured as they sat down. He raised his own glass without summoning the effort needed to stand. *"Omnia audere!"*

They chorused the motto back at him and all three drank.

"And to the Magnuses of Cardice," Wulf added, directing a smile to Anton, but thinking sadly of Madlenka, matriarch of the future line. Tomorrow he was leaving Castle Gallant forever, pestilence or no pestilence. Perhaps in time the pain would end. "May they prosper for a hundred generations!"

Then it was Otto's turn. One more toast ought to dispose of the rest of the wine, so Wulf could go to bed. But Otto said nothing, just watched Anton, who was leaning his forearms on his knees and staring down into his goblet, studying the wine as he swilled it around. Eventually: "Um, Wulf?"

"Yes, Anton?"

"You love Madlenka?"

"Yes. I told you and I wouldn't lie about—"

"And she loves you?"

Wulf drew a deep breath. His heart began to thump insanely. "Yes."

"Then . . . Oh, I like her. She'd be a good, honorable wife, but . . . I want her to be happy, not miserable. And you too. You've earned . . . I know she doesn't love me. To be honest, given the choice, Giedre's the one I would go for."

Wulf glanced at Otto, who was now staring innocently at the fire. So that long talk on the barbican roof had not been just about what could be keeping Vlad occupied.

"That's incredibly kind of you, Brother. I'd leap at the chance and I'm sure she would if . . . Well, it's too late, isn't it? You're handfasted."

The Church was the problem. Cardinal Zdenek wouldn't care who married the countess now that his frontier was safe again, but the Church would not part a couple whom God had joined together.

Anton drained his glass. "Bishop Ugne keeps dropping hints that his palace is too small."

Annulment? *Choirs of angels!* He was offering to have the handfasting *annulled*? Of course a count might manage that. Ugne would take a bribe if it was big enough, and Anton was a hugely wealthy man now. He might need a couple of years' work to repair the Silver Road before he could collect any tolls on it, but he wouldn't have thought of that yet, being Anton, and Otto could not have mentioned it to him.

"You're serious? You think he'll give you an annulment?"

"Of course he will," Otto said. "And if he balks, we'll get Zdenek to beat on him. He knows who saved his bacon, or soon will know, and it won't cost him anything to reward you this way." He grinned. "She may be all you get, of course."

"She is all I could possibly want. How soon . . . ?"

"I'll find somewhere else to sleep." Anton spoke more firmly than before, now that he was committed. "Starting tonight, I suppose."

He meant it, bless him, but it was still too late. Wulf sighed. "I love you, Brother, and even more for this, but I have no future. The Church will never forgive me. You may buy a bishop, but you can't buy the—"

A newcomer entered the room through a wall and the men leaped to their feet with cries of alarm. She was lovely, as blond as Madlenka and certainly no older, but shorter and . . . Buxom. Bosomy. Voluptuous. Her dress was a miracle of spreading azure satin, and the lace bodice advertised gorgeous things such as Wulf had not seen since he was weaned. She glittered all over with gems, but her nimbus was brighter than sunlight. She dropped a full curtsey—to Wulf. Of course she could see his nimbus as well as he could see hers.

"Lord Wulfgang! I am honored to meet the hero of Jorgary's deliverance."

He tore his eyes away from the lace long enough to manage a courtly bow. "Lady Umbral, I presume?" Who else could she be? "M-m-may I present my brothers. Count Anton . . ."

"Marquessa!" Anton said, stepping forward to bow with more grace than Wulf would ever achieve. "It is indeed a joy and an honor to welcome such beauty to Castle Gallant."

The newcomer's smile faded a tone or two. "Count Magnus? The lancer who bollixed the crown prince's hunt last week!"

"Marquessa Darina." He kissed her fingers. "You were pointed out to me at the St. Matous's Day ball. May I present my brother Ottokar, Baron Magnus of Dobkov? Marquessa Darina is a friend of His Highness Crown Prince Konrad." As she and Otto exchanged bow and curtsey, Anton twirled up his mustache and shot Wulf a pregnant look of warning—so pregnant that it ought to drop triplets instantly, but Wulf had no idea what species they would belong to.

What could the man be hinting at? That the crown prince was friends with a Speaker? Was he the marquessa's cadger or her client? Anton could know nothing of that, and Wulf was still not certain what the difference was anyway. No, more likely Anton was just reminding him that the old king was likely to die any day now. His son would succeed and all bets would be off: the crown prince was known to be no friend of Cardinal Zdenek. The stench of court politics had come to Cardice.

The marquessa declined both a chair and a glass of wine.

"I cannot stay. I came to fetch Lord Wulfgang. His Highness is waiting."

"My lady . . ." Was that how one addressed a marquessa? "I fear you are misinformed. I am merely an esquire, no lord."

Her smile could have melted snow all the way to Pomerania. "But that is why I came! His Highness is very anxious to meet the man who saved his, er . . . future, of course . . . his future kingdom from a disastrous invasion. Public recognition must wait until the public announcement, but he wants to discuss suitable rewards."

Anton was goggle-eyed, Otto frowning. And Marquessa Darina . . . lace. . . . Oh, angels give me strength. . . . Wulf did not feel as tired as he had a few moments ago. He could no more refuse such a lady than he could refuse the crown prince.

"I am hardly dressed to meet my future king, ma'am." He had mud on his shoes and pine needles all over him. He badly needed a bath and a shave. And he was a lot more scared of her and what she might represent than he had been of the Wends.

Her steel-blue eyes scanned him in leisurely fashion from top to toe and back again. "Dress is very superficial. The man inside is what counts, and you look quite perfect the way you are, my lord, fresh from the battlefield. Come!" She held out a hand as a gateway opened beside her.

Wulf shot a terrified glance at his brothers, inserted his forearm under the marquessa's delicate white fingers, and accompanied her through to a dim corridor, which became even dimmer as the opening closed behind them. The air was warm, muggy, and heavily scented. The carpets swallowed his feet.

"This is the royal palace in Mauvnik," she said, not moving.

They were facing a wide door, gilt-trimmed and paneled, and Wulf had missed his cue. He reached out with his free arm and turned the handle for her.

CHAPTER 22

A thousand miles to the south, in Elysium, Justina dithered. Her first instinct was to break in on that charade in the Castle Gallant solar and boot the "Darina" trollop right back where she came from, or at least scare her away with the *three's dangerous* situation. Then she realized that Wulfgang, not knowing the stakes, would probably stay out if it came to a brawl. Also, if Justina was too old for fieldwork, she was certainly too old for roughhousing. The years were taking their toll and it must be three decades since she had used raw power to settle an argument. That "Darina" hussy might very well make pike bait out of her single-handedly, even if she did not have a backup Speaker watching over her, ready to join in if she ran into trouble.

Fires of hell!

How in Heaven's name had the crown prince learned about Wulfgang's victory over the Wends already? The news could not officially arrive for at least a week, or longer. The old king, a very devout man, had probably never heard a whisper about Satanism or Speaking in his realm; and if he had, he had always been happy to leave such shady proceedings to the Scarlet Spider. His grandson was a first-rate dolt, not one of the Wise. Zdenek would never even tell him what day of the week it was, let alone entrust him with the secrets of talent and Speakers.

"Darina"—her real name was Hedwig Schlutz—was well known as the crown prince's mistress and a she-rat from the wrong side of the gutter, the sort of vindictive pervert who gave Satanism a bad name. Many Saints would be frightened to tangle with her. But need must when the devil drove. She opened a gate and stepped through into the solar, just in time to glimpse Wulfgang leaving with the hellcat on his arm. *Hell's britches!*

Anton and Otto were still on their feet, and swung around open-mouthed to meet this latest invasion.

"Good evening, my lords." Justina sighed. "Pardon my barging in like this. I was hoping to prevent a rape."

"Rape?" Otto repeated furiously.

"Probably not literally, although with that Darina woman you can never be sure." Justina would invade the palace to rescue him if she had to, but it would be a desperate and dangerous move. There could be enormous repercussions. "Your brother is very naïve still, my lord."

Anton was glaring furiously.

But now Ottokar was smiling. "May we offer you a glass of wine, my lady?"

She should have changed back into servants' garb, but even that morning he had suspected. Wulfgang had guessed and Otto was the subtlest of them all.

"You may. And I suppose you had better let Anton in on the secret."

Anton turned, holding a filled wine goblet. "What secret?"

Ottokar waited until the glass was safely passed. "The 'servant' Justina is in fact our Great-aunt Kristina, sister of Grandfather Evzen."

Anton gulped and made a fast recovery. "A much younger sister, obviously!"

"A much older one," she said. "I was Liber's firstborn; Evzen was the fourth child. We Speakers wear well." She sat down with a sigh. "But that doesn't mean we don't wear."

At least Wulfgang still had his clothes on; he had just accepted a glass of wine from the doxy's own fair hand.

"I belong to a secular order known as the Saints." Justina sipped her own wine, which was middling good. "We're a guild of free Speakers, owing allegiance to neither Church nor state, although we help out both on occasion. We try to use our powers for good, and we discipline any member who strays. We also keep an eye on all the talented families, like the Magnuses. When I began to hear Voices, I was recruited before the Church got me—recruited, oddly enough, by my own great-aunt, another Kristina Magnus. In due course, when she retired, I became our family's 'guardian,' as we call it. The last time I came around to visit was just after Marek was born."

Otto nodded, smiling. He had been thirteen, Vlad seven, both already tall.

"But I was becoming too obviously too young for my age, so I assigned the Magnus watch to another. He met with an accident involving burning faggots, and his successor mishandled the files. Marek escaped us, the Church got him."

She smiled at the intent young faces. How insulted they would be if she called them that, and yet she was almost sixty years older than Otto.

"Marek, cleverly for a haggard—that's our term for a self-trained Speaker—managed to misinform the Dominican who arrested him. That man was the same Father Azuolas that Wulfgang shot here last night, a nasty type. Marek lied to him about Wulfgang's age. The Church keeps watch on the families, also, and everyone spies on their records. So the Scarlet Spider and the Saints both missed him too."

"Wulf had seen what happened to Marek," Otto said, "and was always extremely careful not to use his powers."

Until Anton had outed him at the prince's hunt.

"Speakers can be very dangerous people," Justina said. "The Church's denunciation of them is not entirely unjustified, and we have even turned a few of our own over to the Inquisition. The best solution anyone has ever found is what we call 'jessing,' which is to bind a Speaker to a wor . . . to a non-Speaker, somewhat like a man doing homage to a lord. I won't go into details, but you have met Cardinal Zdenek?"

Both brothers nodded.

"Did you even notice a mousy clerk scribbling in a corner, probably dressed as a Franciscan friar? He would be a Speaker hired to guard the cardinal. Zdenek employs five Saint hirelings—two to watch over him, two to do the same for the king, and that so-called marquessa you just met to guard the crown prince. Night and day, in her case."

Anton smirked.

Ottokar frowned. "This is the jessing you mentioned?"

"No. The Speakers in question are jessed by workaday members of the Saints, their cadgers. A cadger is a manager. The cardinal contracts with the cadger for his falcon's services. The cardinal is their client, they are his hirelings." She smiled at the bewildered faces. "We have our own code."

"And how much do the Saints charge for that service?"

"You'd have to ask Lady Umbral, our prelate, but the exchange is often more of favors than gold. And don't think of hirelings as bodyguards, because Speakers don't stoop to killing. Assassins are almost always workadays wielding knives or poison."

"Then what do Speakers guard against?"

"Tweaking, mostly. They can recognize other Speakers on sight. Imagine Wulfgang presenting . . . No, he's too honest. Imagine Vilhelmas presenting a petition to an undefended king or minister. It would be approved instantly! People like Cardinal Zdenek need protection against that. The monastery at Koupel has a Speaker to perform its famous cures: Brother Lodnicka, jessed by Abbot Bohdan. The pope has legions of such falcons, of course."

Wulfgang still hadn't touched his wine, clever lad. Hedwig was describing the crown prince's sex life in disgusting detail. Justina regarded that as a breach of professional ethics.

Ottokar was beaming. "So now Crown Prince Konrad wants to meet the young man who just won a war single-handed, in a major miracle? Our baby dragon is going to be appointed personal retainer to our future king?"

"Not if I can help it!" Justina said grimly.

Ottokar said, "Surely an appointment as . . ." He stopped, puzzled, and glanced from her face to Anton's and back again.

"Crown Prince Konrad is a turd," Anton said quietly.

"You slander the heir apparent!"

"I slander turds. He's a worthless brat. He hunts, jousts, drinks, and holds orgies. He favors handsome young men."

DAVE DUNCAN

Ottokar blanched.

Justina said, "Maybe ten or fifteen years from now he will mellow into an honorable and respectable ruler, but at the moment you don't want to give him Wulfgang."

Appalled, Ottokar shrank down on his chair and muttered, "I suppose not."

"I wish to enlist Wulf in the Saints," she said. "He will still be able to serve the throne of Jorgary if he wishes, but he will not be committed to doing so for the rest of his life, and we will see that he is fairly rewarded. I may be worrying unnecessarily; he may find the crown prince as odious as I do."

"Wulf's not stupid," Otto muttered, "but he's still very innocent."

Anton nodded agreement. "Invite him to an orgy and he'd ask what he should wear."

"That's witty for you," Otto said. "Your coronet must be going to your head."

Justina realized that the brothers were more than a little drunk. They had good reason to be so, since their sentences of imminent death in battle had just been lifted. And she was feeling quite sentimental. It was many years since she had sat down with family like this. Her brother would have burst with pride to see these stalwart grandsons.

Otto took another drink. "I know the Church gets fiery-and-brimstony about it," he said, "but I've fought alongside men who had minority views. They did the loot and pillage part well enough, and had their own ideas about rape, if you follow. Their business! In most cases I would much rather have had them fighting beside me than against me. I'm sure Wulf's thinking is quite orthodox, though."

A narrow arch appeared in the unopened door. Through it stepped a plump, middle-aged man in a gray friar's habit, barefoot and wearing a leather eye patch. His cowl was back, exposing his tonsure, whose highlights reflected the glow of his halo.

He waggled a reproving finger at Justina. "Sister, sister! You were present last night when Lady Umbral agreed that the cardinal would be the one to jess Wulfgang Magnus. And did she not contract to provide your assistance here during the siege in return for a one-third share of his lifetime labors?"

"Wulfgang was not consulted!"

"But Umbral committed the Saints and you are trying to renege on that agreement, aren't you?"

Without waiting for an answer, Brother Daniel bobbed his head in a minimal gesture of respect to Ottokar and Anton. "My lords, His Eminence begs the favor of a word with you both, if you would spare him a moment?" He gestured to the arch leading through to Zdenek's council room.

CHAPTER 23

The awful moment came only too soon. Clad in his herald's tabard, Arturas Synovec ducked out the postern gate and set off down the road to death or glory. He kept reassuring himself that his danger was slight, because the Church's laws of war protected heralds from violence. Even so, he had had to stop in a corner to pee twice before he reached the barbican.

He carried a white flag in one hand and a flaming torch in the other. He stumbled down a badly rutted road made treacherous by the frozen waves of ice across it, a snowy cliff on his right, dark nothing on his left. And silence, except for the wind! He should have been able to hear the Ruzena muttering and complaining below him. The Pelrelmians wouldn't notice the absence.

His eyes watered in the wind. The Pelrelmians had built a wooden screen across the road, what the men-at-arms called a blinding. Fifty paces. Forty. . . . Thirty-five. . . .

"Halt! Who goes there!"

He stopped. So far they were obeying the laws of chivalry.

"Flag of truce, a message for Count Vranov from Count Magnus."

"What?"

He shouted louder.

In a moment a gap was opened in the blinding and a man in mail came out and clanked forward to meet him. He wore a sash that probably meant he was a master sergeant.

"Gimme the message and I'll see he gets it."

"No. It's a verbal message, to the count or Sir Marijus."

"Tell me and then get your sweet little ass back where it belongs before I ram a pike up it."

All very predictable. Arturas had to stand there and argue with a dolt who had been given no authority to deal with a parley and had no imagination. Finally he had to be prompted. Arturas pulled out the cloth. "Here. Blindfold me and send me down to the count."

After some thought, the man agreed.

It wasn't easy walking on that rough ground with a blindfold on, so his guide had to grip his arm. And once through the barricade, he was pulled and pushed until he had no idea which way was which, but he could guess that they had to maneuver him between the guns they had been seen dragging up all afternoon. He heard a lot of different voices, so he was starting to collect information in spite of being blindfolded.

In warfare, knowledge could be dangerous to both the knower and the known.

It was hard to say which was worse: the times when he was being urged on after he had twisted both ankles and was almost weeping from the pain, or the pauses when he was made to stand so close to the cliff that he could feel the wind eddying off it, while hundreds of clanking feet went past on the sudden-drop side.

Even a blind man could understand what the oaths and grumbles and the creak of leather meant. Any village idiot would realize that the Pelrelmians were mustering for a night assault. So where was the Hound of the Hills? He ought to be up at the front, ready to direct his guns and lead his men. He couldn't give orders from High Meadows, a mile away. Why was he sending so many men up when he hadn't even opened fire on the gates? Until he battered them down, his men could do nothing. So the guns were a decoy, and Vranov expected some traitor to open the gates for him. That still didn't explain why he wasn't up at the front.

Nothing lasts forever. Eventually sounds of canvas flapping and odors of wood smoke told Arturas that he was now in the camp. He was made to wait until he thought he might freeze to death. He was not allowed to remove the blindfold. Then his hands were tied behind him, despite his protests that heralds should not be treated like that. He was shoved forward into a tent and the blindfold removed.

He blinked repeatedly in the brilliance of the lamps until his eyes adjusted and told him that the light was really quite dim. The tent was astonishingly hot and stuffy after the blustery cold outside, but it was much more luxurious than he had expected, with fur rugs, braziers, and furniture. The way the walls and roof rippled disconcerted him.

Four men sitting on stools, watching him, all four in armor, but with heads still uncovered, their swords and helmets lying ready at their feet. There might be a couple more behind him, but he did not look around.

Count Vranov he knew, and Sir Marijus, one of his many sons. The others were just men-at-arms.

"Well?" the Hound demanded. "You can have two minutes."

Arturas licked his lips, thought about asking for a drink of water and decided that this might be construed as asking for hospitality. He launched into the speech he had prepared.

The count listened in stony-faced silence, so his men did the same. At the end he took a drink from a pottery beaker he was clutching in his big, hairy hand.

"So you're suggesting that the dam may break and a flood will wash us all away?"

"It may."

"Hate to lose the camp, but my men are safe enough at the moment, aren't they?"

"Are they?" He wasn't going to fall into that obvious trap.

The count laughed, and Arturas realized that he was drunk.

"You know where my army is tonight, little herald. And you think I'm going to send you back up the road so you can check your arithmetic?"

"That means you refuse the truce?"

"I won't refuse it. I just won't answer. And if that gangling strip of pig guts you call a count is too stupid to keep his guard up, that's his lookout. You've probably told him all he wants to know already."

Arturas said, "What?" He was horrified at how close to a squeak that sounded. "How would I have done that?"

"Because his brother the Speaker knows what you're seeing and hearing."

"Speaker? You're accusing one of the Magnus brothers of—"

"Oh, plug your bung. You know who I mean. That yellow-haired, yellow-eyed squire of his. A witch he is, I know for a fact."

There had been whispers. The new count's extraordinarily fast response to the old count's death, his speedy recovery from wounds . . . even the way he had ignored being knocked down in the hall by a younger brother, who should by rights have been taken out and scourged. As for today's miraculous destruction of the Wends—people had been talking miracle while keeping their fingers crossed in case it had been the devil's handiwork.

"I know nothing of witchcraft," Arturas said, "except what I saw in the hall last night. I came in peace and expect—" Oh, sweet Jesus! Vranov came and went by witchcraft last night. He was going to do the same now and open the gates himself!

"What you expect doesn't matter." The count glanced at his son. "What do you think?"

"Tie him up and send him home in the morning."

Havel scratched his stubbled chin. "No. I don't like spies." He looked past Arturas at whoever stood behind him. "Take him outside. Give him two minutes to say his prayers, then cut his throat."

Arturas was screaming as they dragged him out of the tent.

CHAPTER 24

Wulf was in a bedchamber, a very large and luxurious one, but the pink silk paneling and lacy draperies were obviously intended for a lady, not a man. He shot a reproachful glance at the marquessa and went over to the bed itself, to peer inside the curtains. There was no one in there. The heaped pillows and cloudy feather mattress looked very inviting, but he just wanted to sleep, not sleep with. He would make an exception for Madlenka, but that opportunity was not likely to present itself tonight.

"I think there has been a misunderstanding, my lady."

Darina was pouring blood-red wine into crystal goblets. He did not need more wine, either.

"If you're looking for the prince, that door leads to his bedroom. He isn't there at the moment. Look if you want to."

"No." He knew he was naïve, but even he could suspect a trap.

"A lot of people are stupid, you know," she said, placing one goblet on a small marble table alongside one of the chairs. "You sit there. And others are timorous, ignorant, ineffective, or plain useless." Clutching the second glass, she sank gracefully onto another chair, facing the first and about eight feet away. If this was to be a seduction, she was setting it up strangely like a business meeting. "And Speakers are just people."

He sat where she had told him and stared blearily across at her. "Very strange people, my lady."

"No, just greatly blessed. You are being talked about all over Europe. Already! Oh, not generally, but the Wise know, the top people know: Speakers and cadgers and rulers. In Paris and Toledo and Edinburgh and Oslo. . . . You pulled off a military miracle and made it seem like an act of God. The latest rumor is that Duke Wartislaw's head has turned up in a slop bucket and the rest of him is still missing. Lesser folk will marvel and praise God when the news of the Wends' destruction reaches them, but the ones who really matter have heard it already—the pope, the sultan, the queen of Castile, and one or two other kings and queens. And they know who did it, which the others never will."

"And Crown Prince Konrad?" That was whom Wulf had come to meet. A political discussion with the marquessa could wait until another day, lovely as she was. Or as she had seemed. . . . A more careful regard told him she was at least ten years older than he had first supposed, pretty enough, but not the dazzling beauty he had first believed. Or that a workaday would believe, maybe. He still had much to learn about the use of talent.

"Cabbage Head?" she said. "He will never be trusted with Speaker secrets if he lives to be twice the age his grandfather is now. The old king never knew, although he must have suspected. Only the Scarlet Spider and a dozen or so other people in the kingdom." She sipped her wine with lips that were not the ruby Cupid's bows he had thought; just lips.

"So he did not send for me?"

"He has never heard of you and doesn't want to."

Time to go.

"Then, if you will excuse me, my lady—"

"Stay where you are and listen. You are a highly effective, insanely courageous, and possibly even honest Speaker. Any cadger in Christendom would gladly jess you, on any terms. You could be the answer to almost anybody's problems. I didn't think you had realized that, and thought you ought to know."

He nodded stupidly and belatedly said, "Thank you." He distrusted flattery. As long as whatever she wanted of him did not involve the bed, he had better stay and learn.

She smiled. "So let me get my problem in first. My cadger is a respected gentleman, elderly now, a longtime member of the Saints. He flies three or four falcons and is very wealthy because of it, of course. Owns about a third of Tuscany. My present client is Cardinal Zdenek, and my duties are to dance attendance on Cabbage Head. I try to keep him from breaking his neck in the tilting yard and I keep an eye open for other Speakers trying to tweak him. That's the most important part. Any day now he's going to be promoted to king, and then my contract ends. I absolutely refuse to extend it, but my cadger is reluctant to leave a reigning monarch without protection."

The juvenile seductress had totally disappeared now. The woman who remained seemed hard and glittering, reminding him of a bronze morningstar, a weapon that could extract a man's brains without removing his helmet.

"I understood that cadger and falcon were equal partners and had to agree?"

"In theory, yes." The marquessa took a sip of wine while keeping her gaze on Wulf, as if counting every twitch of his eyelashes. "But a cadger has the option of forbidding his falcon to use any power whatsoever. This is especially true when he flies several falcons. All she can do then is try to impale him on a rusty pike, but his other Speakers will defend him. Frankly, I want to marry and have children before I'm too old, and this is not the place to do that."

All of which might be the truth, some of the truth, or nothing like the truth.

"Surely His Majesty has hirelings to protect him. Won't they stay on to defend his successor?"

"Their contracts lapse, too, and they have been working twelve-hour shifts for months, just keeping the old warhorse breathing. Zdenek has a couple of his own, but the same thing applies to them. The new king's first act is likely to be booting Zdenek into the moat, if not arresting him and charging him with treason on any fantastical excuse he can think of.

The result will be no Speaker protecting the king and the king not even aware of his danger."

Wulf was too tired to think straight. "So where do I fit in?"

Darina drained her glass and reached for the carafe. "Last week, during the hunt at Chestnut Hill, your brother jumped a ditch into notoriety. A dozen fools tried to follow him and met with disaster. Two of the prince's closest cronies have since died and more are still in plaster. Then the Spider promoted this Magnus madman to earl of Cardice! Cabbage Head saw that as a deliberate stab in his eye and threw a temper tantrum, but as a result the whole court learned for the first time about the Magnus family and its centuries of loyalty to the House of Jorgar." She smiled cynically. "Stupid, really. If your loyalty is never in doubt, you never need bribing. It's the shaky ones who get wooed by both sides. . . . Never mind that." She clattered the carafe down on the table and lifted her goblet again.

"I was hoping that your loyalty might impel you to take the new king under your wing until such time as someone with some sense takes over the kingdom—a new first minister or a warlike neighbor."

Wulf laughed aloud and tasted the wine. "Last week I was my brother's varlet. Now you want me to run the country?"

"Somebody will have to."

"*Me?*" He grinned at her. "Wouldn't I have to live here, in the palace? Hang around with the king? Attend court? And he blames my brother for his friends' deaths. How do I win his trust and approval?"

He expected her to say that he could tweak his liege lord, which he would certainly never do. But that wasn't what she suggested. "Just smile."

"What?"

She shrugged. "Cabbage Head has a great fondness for handsome young men. When he sees your silver hair and golden eyes he'll melt into the carpet. And those calves will make him swoon."

"*Oh, no!*" Wulf sprang to his feet. "There are many ways to get burned at the stake, my lady, but sodomy is the last one I'll ever try. I thank you for the—"

"Wait!" She rose also. "Before you make up your mind, come and pay your respects to your dying lord. He deserves that much."

Wulf followed her to the door reluctantly, still looking for the trap. Again she expected his arm as they proceeded along a corridor, which was wide and high, floored with tiles of black and white marble, lit by candles in sconces every few feet. The plastered walls bore faded frescoes of battle and tourney.

"I know this may sound incredible in view of his reputation," Darina said, "but the prince is practically sexless. His lechery is all bluff. I'm officially his mistress, but I swear to you that the door between our rooms stays closed. About once a month he'll come calling, always when he's very drunk. He'll have a quick scramble and then go back to his own bed. I complain loudly in public about how demanding he is; that pleases him, but it's all pig manure. As for the young men, I'm not sure he is even aware how he ogles them, although of course everyone else can see. He paws and fondles a little, but that's as far as he ever goes. He seeks his fun in jousting and hunting. Lists and forests are his playrooms, not bedrooms. Beds are for sleeping off drinking bouts. He's a magnificent horseman and swordsman. He loves wrestling. Even granting that most of them would let him win in any case, he is really good, very strong for his age, and very fast."

"Orgies?" Wulf said. "I heard enough wild tales in the stables, when I was Anton's varlet." The prince's mistress was said to be an enthusiastic participant in such parties.

"He likes to watch and cheer them on. His trunk hose will bulge sometimes, but he keeps the laces tied."

"What about his wife, Princess Olga?"

"He packed her off to a convent three weeks after the wedding. Officially because she was frigid, but in fact because she was too demanding."

Wulf's skeptical snort annoyed Marquessa Darina, as it was meant to.

Her tone sharpened. "I was Looking! She was a virgin, so she had no idea what was expected of her, or how to arouse a man. She threw tantrums from sheer frustration, and that shriveled him up even more. Women scare him. Men fascinate him, but he knows they're off-limits."

They turned a corner into another corridor, wider and brighter. About thirty feet away, two men-at-arms in shining armor stood guard outside a doorway. They watched suspiciously as the visitors approached, but the marquessa stopped outside another, smaller door. Wulf opened it for her and followed her through, into a room that was barely more than a cubicle: dim, cramped, and furnished with a couch and a low table. It had no fireplace, and thick drapes hid the window, but a smaller window in a side wall admitted a faint light. And to that she led her guest.

In the bedroom beyond, lit by tall candles, lay the dying king, propped against pillows, with his mouth loosely open and his wispy silver beard neatly combed over a coverlet of royal blue. His hands seemed unnaturally large attachments for the slender wrists protruding from the frilly sleeves of his nightgown. Where was the vibrant warrior Wulf's father had described, haranguing his troops before battles? That Konrad had not been a wasted, prune-faced mummy. Nor was this the royal head on the coinage.

Why didn't they let the poor old man die in peace?

A nurse sat on a chair on the left side of the bed, embroidering. On a cushion on the right knelt a tonsured friar, telling a rosary. He had a nimbus and he sensed the watchers right away, for he turned to look at them, especially Wulf.

"One of Zdenek's hirelings," Darina said. "It's been a long ordeal for them, but it can't be much longer now. Even talent cannot keep him alive forever."

Two's company, three's dangerous. The friar rose, strode across the room, and closed a shutter over the window. If he considered that a dying monarch should not be treated as a peepshow, Wulf could not disagree. He muttered an Ave.

"Amen," the marquessa said. "Now come and see Exhibit Two."

So she had more entertainment planned. As soon as Wulf followed her back out to the corridor, cheerful male voices warned him what was about to happen. Darina halted him at a corner to listen. By then the male voices had stopped and a woman was lecturing.

"In the spring," she said, "it matters how long since it was captured. You have to take a hard look at the condition of its fur and how much fat it has on it. If it's straight out of hibernation, then it may put up a good show, because it'll be mean as shit, but it will soon tire, so you bet on the dogs. If its handlers have fed it for a few weeks, then it has a much better chance. But even so, I almost never bet on the bear in springtime.

"In the fall, now, you know it will have built up a good layer of blubber and thick winter fur, and that's when the dogs have a problem. That's when you look at the dogs—how many of them there are, and what scars do they have to show their experience? Too many wounds make a dog shy, a shitty fighter. Just a few will give it experience and teach it some tricks. So you have to sum up the pack and bet accordingly. Unless there are at least six dogs and they look lean and fit and have never been too badly mauled, then I bet on the bear in fall."

A man asked, "And what about summer, sire?"

Sire? Wulf looked in shock at his companion. They had just come from the king on his deathbed. There was only one person in the kingdom who might usurp the title of "sire." If that was Crown Prince Konrad speaking, he must be a countertenor.

"Summer?" the prince shrilled. "Oh, only fools like you would bet on a bearbaiting in summer, Gus."

Men laughed.

"In summer you have to look at both the bear and the dogs. And remember that sometimes when a bear wins in the spring, it will heal enough to be fought again by summer, but of course it has a very slim chance of winning a second time . . . although I did see a bear that won twice. Must have been almost ten years ago. . . ."

The crown prince babbled on, more nonsense. A womanish voice would be a serious handicap for any leader. Vlad shouting orders sounded like a mountain torrent rolling boulders. No matter what his state of mind, young Konrad would always sound panic-stricken. Wulf stole another look at Darina, who raised a painted eyebrow as if to say, *Now you know why we call him Cabbage Head.*

But even he exhausted the fascinating topic of bearbaiting eventually. "Well," he said, "let's go and inspect King Konrad the Late, shall we? Then we can go back and get on with some serious drinking and buggery."

Around the corner he strode, leading an entourage of about a dozen men—six or seven young, brightly dressed male courtiers plus a squad of men-at-arms bearing silvered pikes.

The younger Konrad was a surprise: firstly because he looked no older than Wulf himself, secondly because he was short and one expected royalty to be tall. His tunic, cape, and hat were superbly tailored, but cut from drab grays and browns, as if in deliberate contrast to the peacock grandeur of his escort. To a man, his multicolored companions were all taller and slimmer, but even the men-at-arms were mere fresh-faced youths. He was a moth among butterflies.

The prince's face was pathetically ugly, lopsided and fleshy, as if it had been ill-favored to start with, and later hideously scarred by small-pox. Short, but immensely wide and thick, he had a neck and shoulders that would flatter an ox, and his fancy tailoring could not conceal the barrel-like bulge of his chest, yet his hips and waist were trim. Darina's praise of his wrestling skills was believable.

She sank into a curtsey. Wulf bowed low, sweeping the tiles with his bonnet, and then stood with his eyes lowered because staring at royalty was forbidden. But the prince's shoes had platform soles to make him seem taller, and staring at those was probably even more discourteous. He raised his gaze to the prince's huge chest, decorated with gem-studded orders and a sash of St. Vaclav like Anton's.

"Checking on the morgue, my dear?" The prince tittered. "Is it true his toes are turning black and . . . Oh, what have we here? Head up, lad. Let's have a look at you."

If he did not melt as his mistress had predicted, Prince Konrad cer-tainly gave Wulf his full attention. Thus might a man study a stud horse.

"Darina's taken up pimping for us," said one of the fops, raising a laugh.

"Rough stuff from the stables," said another, getting another one.

The worst part of having a fair complexion was blushing, and Wulf felt his face turn scarlet from his collarbones to his scalp. He heard some sniggers and murmurs of appreciation as the sycophants waited for their leader's verdict.

"Turn around," said the prince.

Wulf turned his back and folded his arms. He heard a few angry mut-ters.

"All the way," Konrad said. "Yes, very pretty. You must bring him along to the party tonight, my love. We'll get Augustin to try him out. What d'yu say, Gus?"

"Jozef has more experience than me at breaking in wild stock, sire."

The prince sniggered. Even the youths-at-arms in the background were leering. But the mood must be about to change, and Wulf was praying hard that he would be able to keep his slippery temper under control.

"What's your name, boy?"

For the first time Wulf looked his future king straight in the eye. "Wulfgang Magnus, Your Highness."

Now it was the prince's turn to redden. "Another of that Dobkov litter?"

The Magnus temper slipped another notch. "I have the honor to be the count of Cardice's youngest brother, sire."

"So you think it's your turn now? You're so young we'll have to make you a duke!"

The pack bayed with laughter at the royal wit.

Konrad glared at his mistress. "Where did you find this knave?"

Wulf braced himself for more devilry. He was not disappointed.

"In the stables, sire, as Lord Jozef said. He's out of work since his brother left, and the Magnuses are such renowned equestrians that I thought that you might wish to appoint this one master of horse, since that office is currently vacant. Or you might have other uses for him."

"Yes, I might. I'll have him stuffed and mounted." Konrad turned his snarl on Wulf. "Your damned-to-hellfire brother caused the deaths of many good men with his insane showing off. I'll set you up as a memorial to them." He moved as if to leave, but Darina was not done yet.

"Come, sire, it's hardly fair to blame young Wulfie for that. He was telling me just moments ago that he witnessed the accident at Chestnut Hill last week and he doesn't understand what all the fuss is about. It was a very straightforward jump for a good horseman, he says."

The prince's ugly face seemed to swell. He turned his rage back on Wulf. "Straightforward, you say?"

Wulf was exhausted, and his temper had long since escaped and flown far away. He shrugged. "Dead easy. I could do it with my hands behind my back."

This time the silence lasted a dozen heartbeats and it was the one called Augustin who broke it. "A wager, sire?"

Several voices echoed the words.

Konrad liked that idea. He nodded and showed an indifferent set of teeth in a crocodile smile. "You would perform that jump on a bet?"

Wulf tried for an even more insulting shrug. "Whatever pleases Your Highness."

"Tomorrow we shall be hunting not far from Chestnut Hill. Meet us there an hour before sunset and show us. With your hands behind your back?"

"Balance the stakes, sire. My horse is all I own in the world." He would have to steal one of Anton's. "I shall be gambling its life as well as my own. For what?"

"Five gold florins?"

A few onlookers whistled at such reckless betting.

"I may be only an esquire, *sire*, but my name is as old as yours. Magnuses risk their lives for honor, not gold. Make me the master of horse, and yes, you can tie my hands behind my back."

The master of horse was the third-ranking officer of the kingdom. The title was hereditary, so he was asking for the impossible.

"There's a whipping post downstairs, sire," said one of the flunkeys. "May I lay on the first fifty lashes?"

"But I get to brand him," said another.

Wulf was well aware that even an esquire might be flogged for such insolence to royalty, and by this time a commoner would be well on his way to losing his tongue as well. He could escape through limbo if they tried to use violence on him. That would shatter the first commandment, but by now he didn't care a spit.

"The Magnuses do have spirit, sire," Darina said nervously.

"Tomorrow, one hour before sunset," Konrad squeaked, and strode off at pace that was almost a run. His entourage lurched into motion behind him. Wulf noticed several winks and grins being directed at Darina. None seemed to be intended for him, fortunately. He tried some deep breaths to calm his fury.

"Just what was all that in aid of?" he demanded. She had deliberately provoked that confrontation, and he couldn't see why.

"Don't ask me!" she said furiously. "Why did you lip him like that?"

Because the royal turd had called the Magnuses a litter. Wulf didn't answer.

She said, "If you really do let them tie your hands, then there won't be any doubt that you're using talent. You'll be breaking the first commandment to powder."

"You don't imagine I have any intention of turning up? To perform like a juggler for that bunch of daffodils?"

Konrad might be as celibate and virtuous as a saint, but he posed as an effeminate lecher. No real man would serve such an ambiguous jackanapes or be seen within a league of him.

They turned the corner and almost collided with another procession, this time entirely female. The leader was young and soberly dressed in dove gray. She clasped a missal in both hands and kept her eyes sedately lowered, but she wore a tiara, and must be Princess Laima. She was followed by a couple of ladies-in-waiting of about her own age, and three much older nuns.

Darina stepped aside and curtseyed. Wulf repeated his floor-sweeping bow. The princess spared them one very fast glance and then dropped her gaze to the tiles again, pacing on by, no doubt heading for an evening visit to her dying grandfather.

"Friendly little miss," Wulf remarked softly after the parade had safely vanished around the corner. Of course, Darina was a fallen woman and he was dressed like a laborer.

"She's twice the man her brother is."

He laughed, and suddenly the rage drained out of him and he remembered how tired he was. When they reached her door, he opened it for her. "Thank you for a fascinating evening, my lady. But you will have to solve Crown Prince Konrad's problems without me. I must consider my reputation."

He stepped into limbo.

Now what? The pale nothingness of limbo seemed very restful after palace, castle, and battlefield; it might be a good place to indulge in that sleep time he needed so much. No one could disturb him there. Or could they? More than anything else, he needed instruction in the uses of talent. He knew where to go for that.

CHAPTER 25

Two days ago, Otto had waited on Cardinal Zdenek in his office, but in daylight. By night the place seemed airless and more menacing. The luxuries of gilt and mirrors, of rich drapes and crystal chandeliers, all failed to lighten it or soften its vaunting arrogance. The scraggy old man was leaning forward on his throne, glaring furiously, with little red patches of rage glowing on the milky skin above his white beard and long yellow teeth. He held out his ring for them to kiss—earl first, then baron.

And he left them both on their knees. Otto held a title created back in the twelfth century, and Zdenek was the son of a butcher. Anton belonged to the premier chivalric order in the kingdom, but this glorified upstart clerk considered that he had put him there, so he could treat both noblemen like errant schoolboys called before their magister. Worse, he was deliberately humbling them in front of a witness, for when Otto risked a backward glance, he confirmed that the friar was still present, now seated at a desk behind the door.

"What does it take, Count Anton, to win your loyalty?" the old scoundrel raged, snarling down at them, spraying spit. "Five days ago I created you out of nothing. I found you in an old woman's bed, swiving her for money, and I made you

181

one of the wealthiest landowners in the country. I deeded you one of the finest counties in the land. I promoted you from cannon fodder to the highest order of chivalry and gave you the hand of a great and beautiful heiress, whom you have now deflowered and plan to hand down to your juvenile brother so he can have his turn with her. What thanks is that?"

Anton's face was redder than the cardinal's robes. "But I am exceedingly grateful to Your Eminence, and I know of no reason whatever for Your Eminence to accuse me otherwise. It is true that Lady Madlenka has indicated that she loves my—"

"Loves! *Loves?* Romantic childish rubbish! Take a switch to her backside and teach her where her loyalty lies. Three or four good beatings will soon change her heart. Let me hear no idle jabber of love."

Otto, who had the great good fortune to be married to a woman of both spirit and intelligence, reflected sadly that Zdenek's views would be those of most men, including Bishop Ugne. Yet for centuries the noblemen of Europe had made a habit of riding away on crusades and leaving their lands and families in the care of their wives, and the wives had done just as good a job of running them as their menfolk would have done. Otto himself had no fears for Dobkov's management while it was in Branka's hands. Women might know otherwise, but most men still thought that only they could make wise decisions.

The butcher's son had not done. "And if not gratitude, why not a little loyalty, eh? Why are you consorting with traitors, tell me that!"

Anton's flush of fury faded abruptly to pallor. "Traitors? I am a loyal servant of King Konrad and know nothing of traitors, Your Eminence."

"What about Hedwig Schlutz? She likes to be styled Marquessa Darina, but she is no more a marquessa than you are. Even less. You expect me to believe that you are ignorant of the current politics of Jorgary? You must know how things stand between the crown prince and his grandfather."

Otto resisted a strong temptation to purse his lips or even whistle, but Anton needed no prompting to find the correct riposte.

"Your Eminence is accusing Crown Prince Konrad of *treason?* I was certainly not aware that matters had descended to that level. Furthermore," he said quickly, "the woman I knew only as Marquessa Darina is obviously a Speaker, because she materialized in our presence uninvited and without coming through the door. To defy a Speaker would be rank insanity. She informed our brother that the crown prince wished to thank him for defeating the Wend army—news she could have only learned by supernatural means—and she led him away. Wulfgang is guilty only of courtesy to a presumed lady, Your Eminence. That hardly calls for accusations of treason!"

"Brother Daniel?" the cardinal snapped. "Where is Wulfgang Magnus at the moment?" Either he was a very good guesser or the friar had given him a signal.

"He is just approaching the king's quarters, Eminence."

The long yellow teeth appeared again. "For what purpose, I wonder?"

Anton's face shone wetly and his mustache was wilting. Otto decided to carry the load for a while.

"Your Eminence, for more than three centuries our family has never wavered in its loyalty to the House of Jorgar. I am confident that His Majesty has no more faithful subject than our brother Wulfgang. He has today performed legendary service and does not deserve your slurs upon his honor. May I suggest that he is being taken to meet the king because His Majesty has expressed a wish to thank him in person?"

Of course he hadn't. They all knew that the king had been at death's door for weeks.

Zdenek paused for a moment to appraise this new opponent. The old villain must know that Otto would be a tougher foe, for he was almost twice Anton's age, with many more years of experience, and he was not the cardinal's own creation, as Anton was.

"We do not trouble His Majesty with business at this time of night. His convalescence requires extensive bed rest."

Just by raising an eyebrow, Otto said: *Even to bring him the glad news of the greatest victory in the history of Jorgary? It is true that he is in his final coma, then?*

The Spider heard every syllable of that silent look. "His Majesty's health," he said bitingly, "is cause for concern, but he still attends to business. That said, he trusts me to handle all but the most vital affairs for him. No regency has been appointed and we have no expectation of one." *The heir apparent is still only the heir apparent.*

"This is glad news, Your Eminence. We pray daily for His Majesty's speedy recovery and long life." *We're still on your side.*

"And recent events at Cardice will not be discussed in Mauvnik until the count's official report arrives."

Otto now saw Zdenek as a frightened, almost pathetic, old man. His power, his great wealth, even his life's work—all were in jeopardy and likely to vanish the moment the king stopped breathing. His cardinal's hat might save him from the headsman's ax, but he could hardly hope for a lesser penalty than lifetime exile. He would fight viciously, giving no quarter, a boar at bay. Perhaps he had seen a secret weapon in Wulf, a new and powerful weapon, whereas Wulf in the prince's hands would be disaster.

"You Magnuses show your loyalty in strange ways, Baron. Consorting with foreign-based, illegal, secret, Satanic cults like the so-called Saints, for example."

Experienced warrior that he was, Otto wheeled his front to repulse this attack from the flank. "Your Eminence, none of us had heard of these Saints people until an hour ago. The woman Justina represented to us that she had been sent by you to aid Wulfgang. Was this a lie?"

The cardinal leaned back on his throne as if his back was aching and regarded his guests with distaste. "You are fools, both of you. The Church is attracted to Satanism like flies to rotting meat. The Inquisition especially loves rich victims, because when a man is charged with heresy, his property is automatically confiscated. It will be returned only when he is cleared of all charges against him."

Which would be never, of course. Anton turned a look of horror on Otto, who had a brief vision of Branka and the children being driven out of Dobkov into winter snows.

"Oh, yes," Zdenek said wearily. "You are in danger, both of you, not just your Satanist baby brother. Does the future hold a candlelight party, with Magnuses as the candles?"

"What do you recommend we do, Your Eminence?" Otto inquired.

The spanking was over and the bargaining had begun.

"What is the Magnus boy at now, Brother Daniel?"

"He did not enter the royal bedchamber," the friar said softly. "He was apparently returning to the marquessa's quarters, but they have stopped to speak with His Highness."

The butcher's son pulled a face. "Listen to what is said. My lords, I am not without influence with the Church. The boy is three years short of his majority, so one or other of you two must be his legal guardian. If you have any sense, you will explain to him that the fate of your entire family may rest upon his loyalty to the throne. See that he pledges his loyalty to me, His Majesty's first minister, and not to that evil coven of witches. Then I may be able to persuade Archbishop Svaty that his powers are now safely under control, and by destroying the Wend heretics he has served the Church as well as the kingdom. Do I have your words of honor on that, my lords?"

Now would not be a good time to inquire about the one-third share of Wulf that Zdenek had promised to the coven of witches, according to Brother Daniel's comments earlier. Nor to mention the late Fathers Azuolas and Vilhelmas.

Anton left the response to Otto, who said, "You have our word, Your Eminence, that we shall do all in our power to persuade our brother to comply with your wishes, in the certain knowledge that they are also His Majesty's wishes."

Wulf was a Speaker. How did you rule Speakers? Moreover, ever since early childhood, Wulf had made mules seem biddable as sheepdogs. Even Father had rarely managed to bully him into doing anything he did not want to do. Now, with love in his heart and a spectacular military victory under his belt, he would certainly go his own way, quietly, politely, and implacably.

The butcher's son held out his ring to be kissed. "You have my leave, my lords. Brother Daniel will see you back to Castle Gallant."

CHAPTER 26

The solar was an untidy mess, littered with empty wine bottles and remains of snacks, but Justina had long since learned to ignore surroundings. Settled in the most comfortable chair, she was happy enough, keeping one eye on what Wulf was doing with the Darina slut and Zdenek with the count and baron. Once in a while she would spare a glance for Umbral and Sixtus IV, but more than two conversations were hard to follow.

Suddenly Wulf was there, peering around in the candlelight and looking almost asleep on his feet. "What happened to Joan of Arc?"

She did not even blink at this curious query. "She was condemned to death for heresy by a panel of French bishops and the English burned her. Sit down."

"No," he said. "How? Why could she save France and not herself? How could she defeat armies and not escape from a jail?"

"It's a long story."

"*Make it short!*" he roared. "I haven't got time for more of your stupid games. Tell me!" Menace normally meant nothing to Speakers, but he was a killer and as powerful as any.

Justina folded her hands calmly. He was wearing the

Magnus dagger, so she addressed her remarks to that, not wanting to strain her neck. Otto must have bestowed it on him. Well earned, of course.

"Speakers must be controlled. Even Speakers agree on that. Our talent is too dangerous otherwise, as you have demonstrated. You have a hair-trigger temper and kill men on impulse. So we submit to jessing. Each of us has sworn an oath to a workaday, our cadger, never to use our talent without our cadger's permission. That's all, quite simple. I am jessed by Lady Umbral, head of our order. That Darina slut was jessed by a man in Italy, who has contracted out her services to Cardinal Zdenek. Both she and her cadger belong to the Saints."

Wulf scowled and blinked some more. "What's to keep you from breaking such an oath?"

"Don't you remember how I warned you to be careful of curses or blessings or oaths? I bound myself with my own talent, so I cannot break my oath without my cadger's prior approval. My cadger can transfer my loyalty to another, but only with my approval."

"Then it's voluntary slavery?"

"No, it's a partnership. Your cadger cannot give you orders, only permission. You can refuse. Two heads are better than one, you see."

Wulf nodded, looking either stupid or stupefied.

"I do wish you would sit down, nephew. I will be seeing Lady Umbral in another hour or so. She will be happy to admit you to the Saints and even jess you herself, which is a great honor. There are several hundred of us, scattered all over Europe, plus maybe a few score cadgers and some dozen branchers in training. We can teach you what you still need to learn. I hope we can also defend you from the Church's wrath."

The way the Sixtus interview was going, that hope was becoming fainter by the minute.

Wulf abruptly sat down and leaned his arms on his knees to shout at her. *"What happened to Joan of Arc?"*

Justina sighed. "She was a haggard, like you; a Speaker without training. She went to see the dauphin. He had a panel of clerics examine her . . ."

"I know all that! Later, why couldn't she escape from the English jail? How could they burn her when she could defeat their armies?"

"Because she didn't have her cadger's permission to escape."

Wulf sighed as if a shutter had just opened in a darkened room. "The dauphin!"

She nodded. "She swore fealty to the dauphin, but neither he nor Joan knew about Speaking. The clerics of his court did, and they made sure that her oath of loyalty was so worded that it jessed her—they did not want a juvenile female Speaker manipulating the future king of France and ruling over their heads. So they deliberately did not instruct the dauphin in the proper precautions. He told Joan to go and lead his armies to victory, nothing more."

"You mean she was not allowed to save herself when she was in danger?" Wulf's face twisted in revulsion. "Swine!"

Justina said, "Quite. But the Saints know how it is done, and we protect our own. The Church does not burn us."

Then honesty compelled her to add, "Or very rarely. I know of a couple of cases where falcons and their cadgers became extremely corrupt and we turned them over to the Church for justice. They deserved it, believe me. The system isn't perfect, but it is the best we have. Even popes have been known to use Speakers for dark purposes."

"Next question, then. Why wouldn't you answer my questions this morning?"

"I am answering them now," she said. "I had to find out how well you had your talent under control, where you rated on the manhood scale, and a few other things."

"And you concluded?"

"You have nerves of steel and balls to match. In the five generations I have seen, the family has produced no finer Magnus. I am proud to be related to you."

He blinked. "Then tell me all the other things you held back."

Justina sighed. "If I told you the moon was blue, would you believe me?"

"No."

"If you saw it blue, would you believe?"

"Yes."

She almost smiled at that, which would have been a mistake. Most people would hesitate, suspecting a trap, or waffle about asking for another opinion. Wulf never had doubts.

"You had no handler. Comfort and counsel are what handlers are for. Talent grows in of its own accord and at its own pace, like adult teeth or body hair. We can do little more than advise and reassure. You were taught that the strange powers you were starting to develop were the work of the devil, and you dared not tell people about them. You suppressed them. You *invented* those Voices."

"I heard them, I tell you! St. Helen and St. Victorinus."

She shook her head. "You imagined them. Did they ever tell you anything you didn't pretty much know already, or could guess? Or that your talent wouldn't reveal to you? Like the pain you felt when you started experimenting in earnest. That came from guilt and fear of hellfire. Once you gained confidence, the pain disappeared."

Wulf pouted disbelievingly and straightened up as if his body weighed tons. "What are the words of the jessing oath?"

"Lady Umbral and I will lead you through them."

He shook his head in exasperation. "Then answer me the most important question of all—where do our powers come from? From God or Satan?"

"You are not ready to know that yet."

Wulf stood up and stepped back into nothingness.

He had vanished, gone nowhere, stayed in limbo. Queen of Heaven, why hadn't she warned him about limbo?

CHAPTER 27

Vlad was not the first man of his troop to return to the castle. Having some misgivings about his current mount's footing, he left the bearer-of-glad-tidings role to a couple of the youngsters, and fortunately neither of them slid over the edge in their race down the road. By the time he reached the gate, a welcome party had assembled to cheer the returning heroes. In fact, none of them had done a piddling thing, but he couldn't give the credit where it was due, and that angered him.

His way to the castle itself led him past the bishop's house, which he couldn't think of as a palace, having seen bigger hawk mews. There he dismounted, hitched his horse, and ran up the stairs to beat a tattoo on the big door. He brushed aside the servant who answered and went in, yelling for the bishop. In a moment Ugne came flustering down from some upper sanctum, from which drifted faint sounds of girlish laughter. He was dangling untied hose laces and the hair around his tonsure stood up like a hedge. His Reverend Lordship looked both alarmed and furious, which did not trouble Vlad.

"Ring your bells, my lord bishop!" he bellowed in his loudest battlefield voice. "The Lord has smitten the heretics as he smote the Midianites. God's wrath fell on them as an avalanche, burying hundreds or thousands of them and closing the pass. Gallant is saved and the Wends are crushed. Ring your damned beg-your-pardon bells!"

Then he stomped back out again, while the bishop was still belaboring heaven with his thanks.

Back at the castle, Vlad stripped off his armor, established that His Babyship the count was believed to be in the solar, and ordered some food to be sent there. It was now Saturday, he decreed, since the sun had set, meaning red meat and none of that salt fish sewage.

The rumors had preceded him, so everyone he met wanted to confirm them, and a celebratory riot was already under way in the castle. It did not extend into the solar. Otto and Anton were slumped in chairs, scowling ferociously and clutching wine bottles with the air of men determined to get drunk as fast as possible. The only other person present was a woman he did not know.

"Wulf get back?" he demanded anxiously.

Anton said, "Yes. Hear we won." And took another drink.

Vlad found this morbidity decidedly eerie. He started with the stranger, putting fists on hips and giving her his best bearded-monster glare. "I am Vladislav Magnus."

She held wine, also, but in a glass. She nodded. "The last time I saw you, you were a lot less hairy and about one-third the height. I'm your Great-aunt Kristina."

"And a sor . . . I mean Speaker?" She must be about a hundred years old!

"Of course. My working name is Justina."

He choked back a couple of military expressions and went down on one knee to kiss her hand, the one without the glass. "And since these two drunks are apparently past talking, will you tell me what the problem is?"

"*Their* problem," she said, "is that Cardinal Zdenek called them in and left them on their knees while he gave them a thorough chiding. Their dignity is sorely hurt."

"Called them in—to Mauvnik? *Tonight?* Sata . . . Speaking?"

She nodded again. "In all my days, I have never seen talent being splattered around as wildly as it is here in Castle Gallant just now. If the Inquisition decides to take notice, it will have a feast day."

Otto spoke for the first time. "It wasn't just our dignity. Zdenek is threatening to turn both of us over to the Church unless we give him Wulfgang."

"Give him Wulfgang," Vlad echoed, but the words still made no sense. He stood up.

"Speakers," his aunt said, "are required to be bound—we call it 'jessed'—by a workaday, a non-Speaker. It makes us a little easier to live with and better behaved. The cardinal feels that he needs and deserves a falcon on his wrist, although he already has several he can call on."

Vlad headed to the bottle table. "My youngest brother, Aunt, may not be of the full twenty-one years the law recognizes, but he is a Speaker and, as of today, a battle-hardened warrior whom I admire enormously. Who in the good God's creation is going to order him around, or *give* him to anyone? Gramercy! If I wanted him to pass the salt, I'd ask politely." He glanced around the group. "Where is Wolfcub, anyway?"

"We don't know," she said. "He went into limbo, and I can't trace him until he returns to the world. He's utterly exhausted and I'm frightened he may go to sleep there."

"And if he does . . . ?" He guessed from her expression that he didn't want the answer.

A knock on the door announced a page bringing the long-awaited food. Vlad took the tray himself, telling the boy to close the door and Anton to clear a space on the table.

Provisioned with a cold goose leg and his wine bottle, he made himself as comfortable as possible on the larger of the two available chairs. Otto had snapped out of his uncharacteristic sulk to start explaining about Wolfcub. Not just Zdenek, he said—a coven called the Saints also wanted to "jess" him. Then there was another coven, which Father Vilhelmas had belonged to, and which might want revenge. And there was the Church, which feared all Speakers it did not control. Since Speakers could find a man anywhere, running away would be a mere confession of guilt. By the time Otto had finished his summary, Vlad understood the prevailing mood of gloom. He tossed the bone in the fire and went back to the manger for more hay. "So what are we going to do?"

Silence.

"I'm waiting for the superior of my order," Justina said. "Lady Umbral. She is the best fixer in Christendom, though I wonder if even she can untie this knot."

"Explain 'fixer.'" Well laden, Vlad returned to his seat.

"She's matchmaker to senior nobility, arbitrator of quarrels, advisor to crowned heads. . . . The world would be in a much worse mess if she didn't exist. Only a Speaker can heal a prince who fractures his skull in the tilting yard, or cure a bishop's leprosy. If the Amsterdam merchants hear that a Venetian galley has sunk with a cargo of spices, they can raise their prices. When a king starts mustering his army, his neighbors want to know that right away. Nothing travels faster than falcons. There are never enough of us."

Vlad tried to whistle around a mouthful of blood sausage.

"It's all done in absolute secrecy, of course, and only very rarely for money. If you need your heir cured of smallpox, then you must give up your threat of war on—" The old woman sat up straight. "He's back!"

"Wulf?" three voices said.

Anton added, "Where?"

The Satanist hesitated, then said, "He's talking with your wife."

Anton uttered a sort of bark and shot out of his chair, heading for the door.

Otto cried, "Wait! Anton, you told him that you wouldn't. . . . That you would ask the bishop . . ."

Anton paused with his hand on the door handle and looked back, his face a cockpit of conflicting emotions. "I was only going to tell him that we must speak with him."

"Let him be, lad! He's out on his feet. Even if he sleeps in your bed, I don't think you need have any fear of being cuckolded tonight."

Vlad rather doubted that, remembering the fires of youth with nostalgia. He had no time to comment—he was planning to guard his tongue for once, anyway—before a section of the plastered wall shimmered and faded away. In walked a nonthreatening, almost tubby little man wearing the dark robes and pectoral cross of a priest, under an oily, professional smile. Behind him loomed two much larger and younger men in garish blue and orange livery, each armed with shiny pike, sword, and dagger.

They made the little room very crowded. The gap in the wall healed behind them.

"Anton," the priest said, "I have urgent business with Wulfgang, your brother. Will you take me to him, please?"

Looking as if he'd been clubbed, Anton just nodded.

The priest smiled down at the Speaker. "You promise not to interfere, Justina?"

She sighed. "I promise, Father."

Anton opened the door and led the way.

CHAPTER 28

Countess presumptive Madlenka had never known a worse day. After gathering up wounded in the morning, she had spent the rest of the day in the madhouse of the infirmary. When her mother became both exhausted and distraught by all the horrors she had witnessed, Madlenka took over and sent her off to rest. She was probably the youngest person there, but leadership was what nobility were for. She ordered the blood-splattered floor washed and the unneeded beds tidied away, and she cleared out all but a necessary minimum of medics, sawbones, and priests.

Anyone with a chance to live had already been bandaged and returned to his family. Eight wounded remained. By nightfall, two had died and another had gone home to do so.

She spent most of her time with Radomir. A year younger than she and the son of a palace guard, he had been a childhood friend of Petr, her brother. Now he was a smith's apprentice, a husky, happy young man. He had just carried a building stone up to the roof of the north barbican when a Wend arrow had gone right through him. There was no way to stitch up bowels. He was bleeding inside, and if that didn't kill him soon, fever would later, so he had been given extreme unction. He writhed in agony, but the town was out of poppy, mandrake, mallow root, and all other known painkillers. It was even short of honey for dressing wounds.

He seemed to find Madlenka better company than the muttering priests, so she sat by his bed, held his huge, rough hand—twice the size of hers—and spoke of the golden days of long ago. She helped him sip water and she wiped away his sweat. Now and again he would speak. Sometimes the one remaining doctor or priest would come by to check on him or ask her permission to do something or other. The rest of the time she just talked, and at times she managed to make him smile. News of the Wends' destruction by a thunderbolt from God arrived, and she was passing on the wonderful news to Radomir when she realized that his eyes were no longer moving. She called the doctor over to confirm that he was dead. Then there was nothing to do except wait for the rest of the patients to die, so she left the priest in charge and went to her room to mourn.

After a while she rang for a light supper and water to wash her face. She knew she must try to get some sleep before Anton came, because she might not get much after. She asked for Giedre, but she had gone out celebrating.

Madlenka had just finished eating when Wulf appeared—not close, over by the bed. She gasped and glanced at the door. There was a bolt on it, but what possible reason could she have to lock her husband out of their bedroom? Then she took another look at Wulf.

"What's wrong? You're hurt?"

He forced a smile and held it. "Just tired. No sleep last night and not much for two nights before that. I'm about to fall over and disappear until morning, but I want to ask a favor. . . ." He leaned against the bedpost as if he needed the support. "A big favor."

Her eyes kept sliding back to the door. "Where's Anton?"

"In the solar, with Otto. That's really what I came to tell you. Anton's going to ask the bishop to annul your handfasting."

She leaped off the stool and went to him, gripped his arms. "You're serious?"

"I'm ecstatic, but how do you feel?"

"Ecstaticker! Oh, Wulf, darling! This isn't his idea of a joke?"

"No." The smile had faded. Golden eyes solemn. . . . "You won't be countess."

"I don't want to be countess. I want to be your wife." She decided he wasn't going to kiss her, so she tried to kiss him.

He turned his face away from hers but he did join in the hug, strong arms tight around her. "Wait, please! We can't. I'm doomed. It was me destroyed the Wends' army. I set fire to their powder wagons."

"I wondered if that was your doing. Oh, I'm so happy!"

"I killed thousands of men, maybe even the duke himself."

She thought of Radomir's agony. "I wish you'd killed every last one of the rats."

"I may have come close."

"I don't care. I love you. The war was their fault. You did right."

"But the Church will not say that, even if the men were schismatics. I killed a priest. The Inquisition may take its time to plan its campaign, but it can always find me. There is nowhere I can run."

"You don't believe that! There must be a way out!"

"Well, maybe. But it's a very thin chance. . . ."

Sudden brightness, and they were not in her room anymore. They were in . . . nowhere. Not truly bright, but not dark; all silent and empty, a sort of shining fog. Nothing in sight anywhere. She cried out in fear.

"It's all right." His embrace tightened even more. "You're perfectly safe. This is limbo. It's very hard to spy on us here, that's all. There's a legion of people after me, not just the Church. King Konrad is dying, so Cardinal Zdenek wants me, and I think he's up to no good. Even the Orthodox Church may send Speakers to hunt me down for killing Vilhelmas. Our life together may be very, very brief. There is one, very faint hope."

"Tell me!"

"There's a group of Speakers calling themselves the Saints. They say they're honorable. They say they can protect me from the Church, in return for my loyalty. They even promise a priest who will absolve me of my sins, although I don't know if the pope himself could do that now. Speakers are only human, and the Saints believe that we cannot be trusted not to abuse our talent. I have a wickedly quick temper, as I'm sure Anton has told you."

She chuckled. "Several times! You laid him flat with one punch, I heard."

"Two punches. He deserved both of them, but that was fists, not talent."

"What do you mean by 'talent'?"

He hesitated so long, just looking at her, that she thought he wasn't going to answer at all. Then he whispered, "The ability to speak to the devil and get him to perform evil miracles."

"Wulf! No! You're not that, not a Satanist!"

"I don't know," he said miserably. "I still don't know! I truly think I must be damned, darling. I try to do good but everything I do turns out evil. Trying to rescue my brother, I killed a friar. Helping Marek kill Vilhelmas was wrong! I know now that he didn't kill your father and brother, although he knew who did and didn't stop him. He did lead the raid that killed fourteen men at Long Valley, and yet I still feel as bad about Vilhelmas as I do about destroying the Wend army. I didn't intend to wipe out the army, just its supply of powder, but that blew thousands of men to mush."

"Vilhelmas was a traitor and a killer and you saved Jorgary from an unprovoked war. How can you call those results evil?"

He pulled her head against his, so that they were cheek-to-cheek. "Well, I may do even more terrible things if I'm not controlled. People who know about Speaking insist that a Speaker must be bound to a person who isn't a Speaker. The master is called the cadger and the Speaker the falcon. They're just code words. The cadger can limit what the falcon can do. Not give orders, just permission. It's a partnership. The Saints want me to swear to their leader, Lady Umbral, but I haven't met her. There's only one person in the world I trust enough, and that's you."

"Gladly! If an oath's all it takes, I'll swear to be a dormouse."

"But it would mean that you may share in my guilt."

This gnawing doubt wasn't like him, she knew, but he was visibly exhausted, at the end of his tether. He should be comforted and put to bed to sleep around the clock.

She said, "I'll happily share in your entire life, as long as I have your love. I just want you to live. And my second wish is to live with you."

She felt him draw a deep breath. "I won't swear to the Umbral woman. I don't know her or what her motives are. I could trust Otto, but I'd be tied to him all my life, always the baby brother. I want to swear to you."

"I swear to love you forever. What else do I have to do?"

"Just accept my oath. Now, don't let go of me!" He removed his hug and took hold of her hands instead; then he knelt down on . . . on nothing at all, but she was standing on nothing at all and looking down made her feel dizzy. "Madlenka, I swear by my immortal soul that I will never use my unnatural powers except to do things that you have given me permission to do, and I will never hurt you or threaten you in any way, and I will always defend you and keep you from harm, and I swear to God that I will keep this oath all the days of my life. That's it, and all you have to do is accept my oath, which shall bind us unless and until I agree to let you transfer it to another cadger."

"I so swear, and may God help me keep this oath all the days of my life."

He stood up, still holding her hands. "Do I have your leave to return us to your chamber, cadger?"

"Yes, after one more kiss and . . . Mmmph!"

He was very good at kissing already. But then they were back in her room, in dim, wobbling candlelight.

They kissed again.

Eventually he muttered, "I must go to bed."

He wasn't exhausted beyond all reason. Their embrace was close enough that she could feel the signal.

"Anton may be here any minute."

"He said he won't sleep with you anymore."

Joy! "Then into bed with you! Right over there, and right now. And sleep, my darling." She would bolt the door.

"There's something else we have to do . . ." he said vaguely.

"I'm willing!"

"Didn't mean that."

The door squeaked and Anton peered in. He opened it fully and stepped aside, admitting an ominous little figure in a black cassock and cloak; a jeweled cross hung on his breast. His smile made Madlenka think of melting butter. Behind him came two tall men-at-arms bearing pikes.

"Wulfgang, I must ask you to come with me."

"Where to?"

His only answer was a smile.

Madlenka opened her mouth to scream *"Fly! Go away! Don't do what he says!"* but not a sound emerged. Her tongue lay limp in her mouth.

Wulf glanced at her and shrugged hopelessly. "When I said 'brief,' I didn't expect it to be quite this brief." He did not try to kiss her in front of the priest. Without another word, he walked to the door. The intruders followed him out, and Anton closed it from the other side.

CHAPTER 29

On a dull winter morning, Madlenka could take two hours to complete her toilet. Today, she slipped on a better pair of shoes, coiled up her hair, wrapped it in a turban, pulled her fox fur cloak over her shoulders, and tore out the door, arriving at the solar out of breath but directly behind Anton. He turned in the entrance, frowning at her.

"I don't think this involves you."

"I am sure it does." It was a real pleasure to contradict him.

"It may be dangerous. The Inquisition may draw the wrong conclusions."

"I suspect it does so quite often," she said with an airy confidence she certainly did not feel, "but I assure you that the Wulfgang problem now concerns me more than anyone. Shall we go in?"

She staged as regal an entrance as she could manage, nodding politely to Otto and Vlad and heading for an empty chair. There was a fourth person present, who was presented as Great-aunt Kristina, to be addressed as Justina. She was of advanced years, but well preserved. She wore a fine royal blue robe, which she had opened for comfort in the stuffy room, exposing a dowdy gray servant's dress below it. Evidently the robe was the correct signal, for she did not rise to defer to a countess. In this company, it was a fair guess that Great-aunt Whoever was a Speaker and a member of the Saints guild that Wulf had mentioned.

Vlad rose and brought Madlenka a glass of wine, letting Anton take his chair. The big man would not normally defer to a younger brother like that, but Anton outranked all of them. And the youngest of all was a Speaker. If Vlad now saw himself as the junior brother, the big man's self-esteem must be suffering, but he showed no sign of sulks. There was nothing small about Vlad.

"Wulfgang left with that priest," Anton said glumly. "He put up no resistance. The four of them just walked out into the dressing room and vanished."

The gloom spread as quietly as a stain. "Does anyone know who the priest was?" Madlenka asked. "Was he from the Inquisition?"

"The Inquisition usually sends friars, Dominicans or Franciscans," Justina said, "but it is certainly possible. He was a Speaker."

"Why did he come here first," Otto asked, frowning, "instead of going directly to Wulfgang? Courtesy to Anton, as host?"

Courtesy did not sound like the Inquisition; but what other reason could there be?

"To warn me off, I think," Justina said.

Madlenka suppressed a need to scream at the memory of Wulf's despairing surrender. When no one else spoke, she did. "So what happens now?"

"We are waiting for the prelate of my order, the Saints. She was prepared to jess Wulfgang—bind him, that is. The time for that has passed, if he is in the hands of the Inquisition."

"The time has passed because he is already jessed. To me."

"*What?*" Great-aunt Justina could be very nearly as loud as Great-nephew Vlad. "Who told you the words of the jessing oath?"

"He did."

Justina gave Madlenka a look that suggested a desire to burn her at the stake. "Did he include anything about transferring your authority over him to another by mutual consent?"

"Not that I recall." Madlenka didn't see why she shouldn't lie if everyone else could. If she told the truth, they would just insist that she transfer his oath to someone else, which would be a betrayal of his trust.

Justina muttered something barely audible and likely indecent. "And what liberties did you give him?"

"Liberties, Justina?"

"Standard permissions. What did you tell him he could do? Defend himself from attack? Defend you? Look wherever he can? Walk through limbo to escape from jails?"

Madlenka saw the pit yawn before her and mutely shook her head.

Justina emptied her glass in one great gulp. "Then he is as powerless as a workaday. They can rack him, flog him, break him. Just like Joan of Arc, who worried him so much."

"He did say something about defending me. Why don't you tie me to the flogging post and see if he . . . No?"

"How is he to know you need defending, you witless wench? You left him blind and deaf."

Holy Mary forgive me! Was she to be Wulf's Delilah? Madlenka covered her face, unable to bear the reproach in their eyes. Wulf had been almost out on his feet, but she had no such defense. She had let love blind her, or at least bypass her wits.

"Let's tilt at this thing once more," said Otto, ever the peacemaker. "Where is he now, Justina?"

She bit her lip. "He's asleep, that's all I know. They took him straight to a dark room. I did see that it had a bed in it. He was out cold in seconds. He isn't even dreaming."

Vlad grunted. "Bed is good. Straw in dungeon is not."

"But they may want to try jessing him. They'll try kindness and trust-us first. If he refuses—as now he must—then things will get harder."

"Let's start with the Inquisition, then," Otto said. "They'll have trouble making a public case for the death of Father Azuolas without admitting that he was a Speaker himself. How did he come to Cardice? What was he doing in the bedroom with the two monks when Wulf shot him?"

"They don't have to go public," Justina said. "All they need is Wulfgang's signed confession. They'll leave him enough of a hand to hold a pen."

Madlenka was confident that her stubborn beloved was as capable of resisting torture as any man, but all men could be broken eventually. She said, "Can we be absolutely certain that the Inquisition will try to make him confess? Won't they try to enlist him in Azuolas's place?"

"He's already jessed by you, and you say your loyalty cannot be transferred. He killed a priest, so he must die, one way or another. He's helpless without your permission to use his talent. If you die, he's a workday forevermore. One thing that seems certain is that you will never be allowed near him again."

Madlenka had not thought of that. Wulf should have known—must have known! But Wulf had been stupefied by lack of sleep and hadn't thought of it in time.

Otto waited. When no one else commented, he said, "Can we rescue him?"

"Can I rescue him, you mean?" Justina said. "No. The Saints do not launch armed assaults on the Inquisition. The Church is leery enough of us already. We exist on its sufferance. Some future pope will launch a crusade and wipe us out."

"Can we bargain, then? Ransom him?"

This time her response was slower and more measured. "Umbral did hint that she might be able to buy the pope, as she put it. But that was when the boy was still a haggard. Now he's jessed, can't be un-jessed, and in the Church's hands already. A novice falcon jessed by a novice cadger is not a promising addition to the Saints. He's unpredictable and ungovernable. She'll wash her hands of him."

So their only ally was leaving the battlefield. More gloom. Madlenka could not help thinking that two days ago there had been five Magnus brothers; so now there might be only three.

Anton asked the next question. "That leaves Zdenek, then? He says he can buy off Archbishop Svaty."

And Otto answered. "Maybe he can. But how does he buy off the Inquisition? Jorgary is a small kingdom. What does he have to offer?"

"What about Crown Prince Konrad, soon to be king?"

Otto said, "I can't see Wulf wanting to serve a man with his reputation. Birds of a feather flock together, snicker, snicker. We aren't certain that it was the Inquisition who took him. Could it be the others—the Agioi?"

"He was dressed as a Catholic," Justina said. "Orthodox priests have beards, and this one was clean-shaven."

No one commented. The meeting seemed to have run out of ideas. The clamor of church bells came and went, only faintly audible through the walls. The castle staff were celebrating around a bonfire down in the bailey, with drums, singing, and trumpets, but despair, not joy, ruled in the solar. The man who had saved the castle, the town, and the kingdom seemed to be doomed to a horrible death which no one could save him from except—just possibly—the mysterious Lady Umbral, whose help he had not wanted. It would, Madlenka decided, be better than nothing, under the circumstances. She was starting to regret her lie about transferring the oath; Wulf should at least be given the chance to decide.

"Let's talk about something cheerful," Vlad said, "like pestilence, maybe?"

Granted that the big man had a very odd sense of humor, plague was nobody's joke.

"What pestilence?" Madlenka demanded, alarmed.

"Fake pestilence, maybe? This mind-changing sorcery, Justina? Could it make someone believe in plague when there wasn't any?"

"You mean one or two cases, or a raging pestilence?"

"Just one case."

Madlenka had thought of Vladislav as being the stupid brother, but no one was laughing.

Anton was actually leering. "Yes! You think that that's how Havel got rid of the *landsknechte*? I knew there was something wrong about that story! When I first met Captain Ekkehardt, in the cathedral, he just wanted more money. When I spoke with him later that evening, no price in the world was going to keep him in Cardice. The change was very sudden! Justina, could that have been witchcr . . . tweaking?"

"Tweaking?" Madlenka thought she must be the most ignorant cadger in the history of Speaking.

"Changing his mind for him," Anton said. "Speakers can do that. Like making women think they're in love with them, for example."

She felt her face flame. Was that what he thought? That Wulf had used his talent to win her love? There was rage in Anton's eyes. He would still be within his legal rights in ordering Madlenka into his bed tonight. If Wulf had gone forever, there would be no annulment.

"Tweaking has limits," Justina said quickly. "It works best when the subject is already inclined that way and just needs a nudge, and it tends to wear off. But certainly, Father Vilhelmas was a very skilled and unscrupulous Speaker. He could have tweaked your *landsknechte* man into believing he'd seen a case of plague."

"Vilhelmas wasn't in town then, though. Bishop Ugne had refused to let Vranov bring an Orthodox priest in with him."

"Oh, really?" Justina said. "A Speaker can go anywhere and not be noticed. Besides, Vranov had another Speaker with him this morning, one you hadn't met before. If Vranov wanted to hobble you by removing your mercenaries, that would be an easy, clever way to do it. Inexpensive, too."

"Could be good news, then." Vlad yawned hugely. "Wolfcub isn't the only one needing to catch up on sleep. The best sleep of all is the one after winning a great battle. Thanks to Wulf, that's what we can all enjoy tonight. Call me early and I'll kill you."

"Good idea," Otto agreed. "But we were waiting for Lady Umbral."

"Don't," said a girl in a sumptuous orange and black ball gown and a hat like two great wings. Her jewels sparkled like sunlight on fresh snow and her teeth flashed even brighter. The men all lurched to their feet.

"This is Sybilla," Justina said in long-suffering tones, "my brancher. I really have the worst luck."

"About to be jessed!" Sybilla snapped. "So you won't have anyone to nag and bully."

"About to be jessed, may God in His Heaven be praised."

The luscious Sybilla favored the room with another lovely smile. "And I am also Lady Umbral's daughter."

Justina's face darkened. "You're not supposed to say that!"

"Oh, dear, I forgot! Anyway, Mother sent me to tell you, my lords and ladies, that the Wulfgang situation is out of her hands, so don't wait up for her."

When no one else spoke, Madlenka said, "What does she mean by 'out of her hands'?"

Sybilla sighed. "She didn't explain exactly, but she was supping with the pope tonight and I was Looking—not all the time, just now and again—and it was quite obvious that His Holiness was refusing to bargain. He regards Wulfgang Magnus as a dangerous homicidal Satanist, and will see him burn if he has to light the pyre himself. Now, if you will excuse me, I will return to the ball. Royalty must not be kept waiting, you know."

She turned away and vanished like a maltreated soap bubble.

No one was looking at anyone else. This was the end. The Church had Wulf and the pope had decided. Abandon hope.

Eventually Madlenka said, "Can we believe her?"

"Sometimes," Justina said. "And in this case, yes, because I also Looked in on the pope's little supper party a couple of times and that was how the conversation was going. Sixtus the Fourth is a very determined man, very inflexible. All popes are, but he's the hallmark. He has far more falcons at his beck and call than anyone else, so he really doesn't need another, no matter how effective. He won't want anyone else to have him, either." She heaved herself to her feet as if the hour had suddenly grown heavy on her shoulders. "This has been a great day for some, and very bad for many. A pleasure to meet you, my lady." Giving Madlenka a nod that conveyed no clear message at all, Justina disappeared.

"That concludes the fun," Vlad said. "Now the business begins, Count. You and I must go and inspect the troops."

"What business?" Anton stood up, almost as wearily as his great-aunt had.

"Can't you hear the bells out there, the bands? You have a victory to celebrate. The town and the castle will expect you to turn up everywhere, making speeches and leading extempore prayers. Not to mention decreeing public holidays and thanksgiving. And your report to the Spider must leave at dawn, even if you do know that he knows already."

"I suppose so." Anton looked doubtfully at Madlenka. Was she or wasn't she his wife now?

"Go without me," she said. "I must check on Mother, and on the infirmary, and it has not been an easy day for me, either." She was going to bolt the bedroom door.

He probably knew that, but he nodded. "And I have work to do. Good night, my lady."

"Personally," Otto said, "I am going to spend some time in the chapel first. This was Wulfgang's day. He destroyed the Wends and he pulled the Hound's teeth. The fact that Gallant is celebrating tonight is entirely due to him. I intend to give thanks to the Almighty and beg Him to extend mercy to a boy who may have made mistakes, but means no evil. I will beseech Him to soften the heart of His servant the Pope, so that he will grant Wulf absolution."

"I will pray also," Madlenka said. It was her fault that Wulf had been taken by his enemies when he was helpless to save himself. But she was exhausted, and must sleep. Perhaps tomorrow she would think of some way she could find him and give him back his magic.

Like Vlad said, nothing was going to happen before morning.

CHAPTER 30

Madlenka set off toward the great hall, meaning to check on the last of the wounded, but before she reached the door, she realized that it was no longer being used as the infirmary. Beds and priests had gone and the castle staff were celebrating. A band with more enthusiasm than style was banging, blowing, and scraping away. She beat a fast retreat before someone tried to drag her into the frenzy.

She went in search of her mother. Dowager Countess Edita was having a private celebration in her very restricted new quarters, entertaining her closest cronies, Noemi and Ivana. She looked up with disapproval at her daughter's somewhat haphazard attire and offered a lukewarm invitation to join them, which Madlenka politely declined.

Carrying a lantern, she entered her dressing room and closed the door. She had taken two steps when the bolt clicked behind her. She swung around, and the door was indeed now bolted. *Wulf? Could it be Wulf returned?* Trembling with a strange mixture of fear and excitement, she raised her lantern high. There was no one else in the dressing room. A light was burning in her bedroom. She hastened there.

On the stool sat Sybilla, still dressed in grandeur. "You took your time," she said.

Madlenka's feet wanted her to spin around and flee. "What are you doing here? What do you want?"

"To rescue Wulfgang, of course. He's cute and he's valuable."

"You? You think you can rescue him from the Inquisition?"

It seemed absurd, and yet the daughter of Lady Umbral might be a much more powerful person than her years suggested.

"The Inquisition doesn't have him," Sybilla said, in the sort of tone used with a very slow child. "So far. But we must act quickly, before he wakes up and other Speakers can locate him."

"You know where he is?" A wisp of hope quivered like an early snow-drop in a wintery blast. Sybilla could be trusted to tell the truth some-times, her cadger had said.

The girl smirked. "Of course I know where he is! I opened the gate for Father Giulio and his musclemen. Wasn't that tall one a dream? Now get dressed in the best you have."

"Where is he?"

"Hidden right under the Inquisition's nose. Move! You have work to do. First you need to meet someone. He's at the ball, so we must go there."

"Me? What can I do? Aren't you Wulf's cadger? That makes you man-ager of one of the most valuable properties in Christendom right now. Have you any idea . . . ? No, of course you don't. You can ask the earth for him. So get dressed, and I'll help."

"Wulf is not for sale!"

Sybilla sighed deeply at such stupidity. "His talent is! Speakers serve other people, very rich, important, powerful people. For that they are greatly rewarded, and they are protected. A Speaker on his own would be like a mad dog, dangerous and out of control, responsible to no one. Now get dressed!"

Madlenka turned and headed back to her dressing room, but her head continued to whirl. Was this a dangerous trap, or just a stupid prank? Or could it be real? Most valuable property in Christendom?

"How long is this going to take?"

"Ten minutes? Have you more important things to do than rescue your lover from the worst death imaginable?"

Of course not. "What's in it for you?"

Sybilla had followed her and laughed joyfully. "Now you're starting to talk sense! Always ask that question, even if just to yourself. The man you are about to meet is my brother, who has a problem. Wulf can help him. And he can help Wulf. These things are always quid pro quo. Heaven bless us, is *that* the best you've got? It looks like Justina's wedding dress from eighty years ago."

Impudent brat!

Madlenka dropped the offending garment and reached for another, simpler one. "It takes hours to pin me into that," she agreed. "I'll wear this one." And she wouldn't try to compete with all the other Sybillas at the ball. She was a backwoods nymph, and could never hope to score in that sort of contest.

Her companion looked doubtful. "You'll look as if you just escaped from a nunnery kitchen. But you're probably right. Businesslike, not frivolous. After all, you're not going to be presented to the king. Now, let me see what shoes you've got here. . . ."

"Where is this ball?" Madlenka asked in sudden alarm.

"In the Louvre Palace."

"In Paris?"

"That's where it was when I left it. To celebrate the Eve of St. Michael the Archangel. . . . Listen!" Sybilla abandoned the shoe basket. "I'll go back there so people won't start wondering where I've gone, and I'll cut Louis out of the pack and arrange a rendezvous somewhere private. You do the best you can and I'll come back for you in, what? Twenty minutes?"

"Twenty minutes," Madlenka agreed, now talking to empty air.

She was adjusting her hat in the mirror and wondering if she had gone crazy or was having an especially wicked nightmare when Sybilla appeared behind her.

"Mm. . . . I suppose that will have to do. The Grand Promenade is due to start in half an hour and we must complete our negotiations before that. Ready?"

"No." Madlenka spoke firmly. "Who is this brother and what is his problem and how can Wulf—"

"Gramercy! All right. Fair questions." Sybilla sat on the bed, perching on the extreme edge to show that she was not planning to stay. "You know that yesterday the baron went to see Cardinal Zdenek? Well . . ."

"No. Otto did?"

"Yes, Otto did. Listen to me! He reported that Wulf had moved Anton to Gallant and Anton had established himself as count, but he pointed out that the Wends were known to have at least one Speaker on their side and probably others, so Wulf was going to need help. Zdenek agreed. He sent one of his hirelings to a secret place he knows of, to deliver a message. And late last night, or very early this morning, Lady Umbral and Justina went to Mauvnik to meet with him."

Madlenka nodded. "That was the meeting that the priest mentioned?" So far it made sense, if one could adjust to a world of magic.

"Yes." Sybilla babbled on, like a pebbly brook. "Lady Umbral agreed to let Justina help Wulf for a few days, but she and the Spider disagreed on the price. For months now Zdenek has been hawking Princess Laima around the aristocracy of Europe, wanting to see her betrothed while he can still control the terms and take his cut. Lady Umbral wanted her for my brother. My half-brother, not her son. He's Louis of Rouen and he will impress you. Zdenek refused, saying that the contract had already been initialed. They settled on dividing Wulf one-third-two-thirds between them."

"Oh, did they?"

Sybilla grinned, looking even younger than usual. "I'm sure neither intended to keep their word, and Mother soon learned that no contract had been signed yet, so Zdenek was lying and the game was still on. Understand?"

Madlenka understood some of it, but this was not her world and she was going to have to learn very fast. Baron Otto would be the one to consult. And Wulf himself, of course.

"How do you split a Speaker?"

"*Never* use that word! Why do you think we have all these codes? He's your falcon. When he's under contract, he's a client's hireling. Zdenek employs five hirelings and flies no falcons of his own, so far as I know. He wanted to be Wulf's cadger and let Lady Umbral be his client for four months of the year. Now come along and meet Louis."

* * *

The room was a bedchamber, bright with many candles, their light glittering on gilt and crystal and fine enamel. The only occupant was a youngish man sitting on a chair, the only chair. The window drapes were purple velvet; the carpet was thick and soft. A huge crystal mirror above the dressing shelf made the place seem less cramped than it really was. The door stood ajar, admitting sounds of distant music.

The man sprang up and bowed. Sybilla made introductions. Madlenka curtseyed; he kissed her fingers.

Yes, he impressed. For some reason she had expected an effete courtly fop, although she had never met such a creature, for there were none in the hills of Cardice. Louis was not that. He was not unlike Wulf, in fact, although a little older—broad, deep-chested, and muscular, as evidenced by the calves filling his hose. His face was more craggy than handsome, and certainly not soft or feminine, but he had a wonderful smile that flaunted a complete set of white teeth. He was clean-shaven of course, bronzed and of fair complexion, although not flaxen like Wulf. His eyes were gray, not golden, and his clothes had cost a coach and four.

Yes, so far he impressed.

He gestured at the other chair. "Do please sit here, ma'am." His Latin was much better than hers, and her French was too despicable to try. "Sister, you will have to settle for the bed, I fear."

He dropped on one knee and leaned his forearms on the other. It was the attitude of a humble petitioner, and made him seem eager and attentive. Sybilla closed the door and sat as directed.

"Ma'am, will you pardon my atrocious manners if I come straight to the point? My sister and I must soon return to the ball and the longer we talk, the more people are likely to start spying on us."

"Please do, m'sieur."

He nodded graciously. He did have a wonderful smile, and knew how to use it.

"I am a suitor for the hand of your beautiful princess. Yes, I have seen her, although we live at opposite ends of Christendom, but I would not admit that if I had not been assured that you are one of the Wise." He shot a twinkling glance at his Speaker sister. "Laima has beauty to make fire flow in the veins of any man. Her wit and grace are well known. I concede that I am far from her only suitor, and very far from the greatest."

Madlenka must say something. "But not the least favored, I am certain."

"You flatter, ma'am. Here in France I am the youngest son of a marquis, which is better than being a schoolmaster, but in Jorgary, I would be a prince. My offer to your sovereign, King Konrad, included a pledge that I would reside in your country and learn to speak your vernacular tongue, whereas most other suitors would expect the lovely Laima to go and live with them in their homelands. I am sure that difference would matter to her, but I doubt if her opinions are of importance, alas, or even known. I am not rich; my estates bring in a few thousand livres a month, but that is penury by royal standards. I cannot increase my original offer to your esteemed Cardinal Zdenek, which was one-half of whatever dowry the princess brings to the marriage."

One-half...? Madlenka must have let her outrage show, because he shrugged. Graciously, of course.

"Alas, it is to be expected. That is how 'arrangements' are made, and others will have offered him more. Because of my own circumstances, more than one-half would be unfair to my bride, exposing our poverty to the shame of all."

Then Louis paused to let her comment. Her mind spun frantically. She was not accustomed to managing the most valuable livestock in Christendom, or whatever Sybilla had called Wulf. But, of course, there was something very obviously missing.

"You want me to contract my, um, falcon's services to Cardinal Zdenek, so he will agree to accept you as Princess Laima's husband?" She took his nod as acceptance. She thought he was hiding his amusement at her fumbling attempts at negotiation. "And what are you offering me, as his cadger?"

That smile again. . . .

"I have an uncle who stands very high in the Church. He will do all he can to further my suit. He could provide your falcon with a papal absolution for any past misdeeds. Sybilla has established that your handfasting to Anton was highly irregular and not properly explained to you in advance. You were subjected to unseemly pressure. A papal order to your bishop to annul it would be included."

Stars danced and birds sang. Then clouds of doubt swept in. "According to a reliable source, His Holiness has already prejudged the case and found my, um, falcon, guilty of Satanism." Madlenka looked to Sybilla for confirmation, since she was the source in question.

Sybilla nodded impatiently.

Louis said, "I expect that His Holiness was merely establishing a bargaining position."

"Oh, was he? Is your uncle higher than the pope?"

Brother and sister exchanged glances of amusement.

Louis said, "Not quite, although he came close to being elected pope by the conclave of 1458. He is bishop of several places, including Rouen and Ostia, and he is dean of the College of Cardinals. If my uncle asks for the documents I have mentioned, the Holy Father will sign them as a personal favor to him."

A churchman's "nephews" were often his illegitimate sons, but did this apply even to the dean of the College of Cardinals? Madlenka had certainly soared to new heights. Vertigo was a clear and present danger. She nodded while thoughts whirled in her head like snowflakes.

Cardice was not all mountain, and its lower slopes nurtured herds of wild horses, which local ranchers would round up and sell to traders traveling the Silver Road. Madlenka Bukovany had spent a significant part of her childhood watching horse trading.

"So you offer me my falcon's life and liberty. You offer Cardinal Zdenek the same bribe he has already rejected, but presume that this time he agrees and gives you the hand of the princess. You must raise your bid, m'sieur."

Louis smiled with all those wonderful teeth again and glanced at Sybilla, who was starting to fidget.

"I told you," she said, speaking as fast as a drumroll, "the Scarlet Spider has five hirelings. That is a remarkable collection when even the king of France has only six. Zdenek has two of them guarding him, one watching over the crown prince, and two keeping old Konrad alive. Those two are exhausted, working day and night. He is sorely in need of more, especially to tend the king, for if one of the attendants nods off, the patient will die. If he spares one of his own bodyguards, he may be kidnapped or tweaked. He saw Wulfgang as a gift from the gods even before he did anything. Now that he has slaughtered the Wends single-handed, he is beyond price."

"So how long would my falcon be required to serve him?"

Louis had the grace to look shamefaced. If he wasn't genuine, his duplicity was impressive. "That is up to you to negotiate, ma'am. You are his cadger. Zdenek is a very old man and may not last long. He cannot ask for more than a lifetime contract, or until he is dismissed as first minister."

"Which will be no more than fifteen minutes after the old king dies," Sybilla said tartly. "Young Konrad detests him."

Louis spread a hand, palm up. "In return, I am offering to save your falcon from the Inquisition, to snatch him out of the torture chamber and the pyre. His only alternative now would be to swear fidelity to the pope, a transfer of allegiance that would require your compliance. The pope may not even want him, as he has many falcons already and sees Wulf-gang as a priest killer. Surely two or three years' service to a high state officer is a better price to pay than being burned? And you might die with him."

So Madlenka was now expected to go and bargain with the Scarlet Spider? If that prospect was more attractive than being burned at the stake, the difference was slight. As Zdenek had a reputation for working far into the night, she had no excuse to put off the ordeal until morning.

Sybilla stood up. "The music has stopped. The Promenade will be lining up. You go, Louis. And you, ma'am? You want me to send you back to Cardice?"

Madlenka rose also. "Yes, please. No, wait. . . . If I have to negotiate with the cardinal . . ." How could she travel to Mauvnik and back? Justina? No, she would sell out to Lady Umbral. "I need my falcon."

"You can't have him. At the moment I doubt if you could wake him with a clap of thunder in both ears."

"Then you will have to move me to the cardinal's presence."

"I will do no such thing!" Sybilla said. "His current hireling watchdog would flatten us. Besides, I have never been in his office or met him, so I can't go there." She grinned. "But one rainy afternoon, Justina took me around a dozen of the best palaces of Christendom, so if I can just re-member which is which, I—"

"Don't be cruel, Sybilla!" Louis said from the door. "Do as she asks."

Sybilla pouted. "I've seen the door to Zdenek's antechamber. I'll put you there and you can ask for an audience."

"And, please . . . In case he does not send me home again, will you look in on me later and see how I am doing?"

CHAPTER 31

When he was eight years old, Herkus had lied about his age and won a job as a stableboy for the bishop. At fourteen he had been doubling as waiter and bouncer in a tavern. One night he broke up a four-way fight single-handed—wielding, it must be admitted, a stout ax handle—and thus caught the eye of Sir Karolis Kavarskas, who was then the constable. Kavarskas promptly enrolled him in the palace guard.

Since there was already one Herkus in the guard, the two were at first distinguished as Young Herkus and Old Herkus. But Old Herkus was the smallest man in the company, while Young Herkus was already one of the largest and still growing almost visibly, so they rapidly became Big Herkus and Little Herkus, respectively. Any man who mixed them up had to buy the drinks.

Now Little Herkus was twenty-two and had been enjoying life heartily until the previous day. He had a wife, a child, and another on the way, plus a very cuddlesome mistress, a woman of boundless bounce and enthusiasm. The war had provided even more excitement, with Herkus managing to kill a Pelrelmian brute during the south gate skirmish this afternoon. Sir Vladislav had congratulated him personally. Herkus really ought to be in there celebrating that victory tonight. Everyone else was celebrating. But Herkus was on sentry duty at the upper door.

The upper door, on the third floor of the keep, was connected by a drawbridge to the walkway atop the city wall. In peacetime the bridge stayed down and the door was locked at night, guarded by day. After the new count put the castle on war footing, the drawbridge had been raised every night. No need to do that tonight, Master Sergeant Jachym had declared, but the gate should be guarded, and man-at-arms Little Herkus was just the two men to do it. All alone, and apparently all night. Jachym promised he would come around, personally and very often, to make sure he was still there. If he wasn't, then it would be fifty lashes and a dishonorable discharge. Or possibly the new count would hang him, like he'd hanged Kavarskas.

By midnight, Jachym was still coming around, still sober, and the penalty had gone up to a hundred lashes and discharge. Unfortunately, yesterday Jachym had somehow learned the identity of his wife's lover. Herkus, he said, was going to stay there until his rammer froze and fell off.

That began to seem quite likely. Herkus was frozen through to the core. Snow came and went, but the wind never stopped, and the porch where he had to stand was steadily drifting in. He had no gloves, and his boots were thin. Meanwhile, the town roared: bells, trumpets, drunken singing. There was a huge party going on inside the keep itself, tantalizingly audible to Herkus even through the six-inch oaken door. Every now and again men would come out to relieve themselves over the edge of the bridge in the hope of scoring on someone walking on the road below, but no one was out in the streets tonight. They all laughed at the snowman sentry.

Fortunately, a couple of the other men-at-arms took pity on him when he showed them how his fingers had turned white, threatening frostbite. They went and brought out a brazier, so at least he could warm his hands. Jachym was sure to remove it on his next visit, so Herkus leaned his pike against the wall and held both hands close above the coals. He could barely feel the heat.

Thus he had his back to the drawbridge and was bent over when a steel-clad arm across his face dragged his head up. The knife at his throat was cold as ice and burned like fire. He had barely time to realize what was happening, or why the brazier was suddenly spluttering and steaming, before sentry and brazier toppled over together, into the scarlet snow.

CHAPTER 32

Madlenka found herself in a dark corridor, just outside an open door. The hall beyond it was dim, but three lamps did burn at the far end, and there were people there. Assuming that they marked her destination, she squared her shoulders and began to walk, her feet making little tapping sounds on the floor. Reflections shone off big chandeliers overhead, off crystal mirrors and gold-framed pictures on the walls, and even in the polished marble underfoot. She went by a group of a dozen or so silk-upholstered couches, occupied by a total of five people. The way they were spaced suggested that no two of them were together. The four men stared curiously at her as she passed; but the fifth, a dowdily dressed woman, appeared to be asleep. Or perhaps she had died of old age while waiting to be admitted to the inner sanctum, the center of the Spider's web.

The small and unobtrusive door at that end of the big room was guarded by an elderly tonsured man at a large desk, reading a document. A simple wooden bench nearby held three boys writing on slates. All four looked up as she arrived. The man was a Franciscan friar, which was no surprise, for almost all clerks were clerics. His face bore no expression whatsoever, but his desk was littered with books, folders, and papers in heaps and bundles. She wondered if he was a Speaker.

"I wish . . . I need to see Cardinal Zdenek."

The chancellor frowned and consulted a list. "You have an appointment?"

"No, but—"

He smiled wearily. "I can add your name to Thursday's provisional list."

"Pray tell His Eminence that Countess Madlenka of Cardice is here. I believe he will be anxious to see me much sooner than Thursday."

The friar's frown deepened, but he reached for a pen and dipped it in his inkpot. "On what matter?"

"Wulfgang Magnus."

That brought a reaction. He looked up sharply. "Magnus, you said?"

"Count Magnus's brother."

He replaced the pen. "If it would please you to take a seat, my lady, I will advise his secretary that you are here."

Madlenka withdrew to one of the couches, placing herself as far from the other petitioners as possible. Silence returned. Once in a while one of the boys' slates would squeak. No one was paying her any heed, so she was free to gawk around as well as she could in the gloom. Now she understood why Petr had raved about Mauvnik when he returned from his visit in the summer. It was all very impressive, and grander than anything she knew in Cardice, although even thinking so made her feel disloyal. Yet even this hall could not stand up against the one room she had seen a little while ago in the Louvre. This decor tried too hard. It was crude. The bedroom in Paris had taste. This tried to overawe you. The room in Paris just *was*, and left you to draw your own humiliated conclusions.

She wondered how many hours or days the other people had been waiting there. She wondered what she would do if she was sent away unheard. And supposing that flibbertigibbet Sybilla forgot to come looking for her? She would be stranded alone in a city she did not know, without money or friends and no admissible explanation for how she got there.

Suddenly delayed shock struck her as if she'd been dropped into icy water. She was alone in a strange city. In a *city*! The little country girl who had dreamed of visiting Paris or Rome was suddenly alone in the first real city she had ever seen. In her dreams she had traveled with her handsome-prince husband. She had no husband here. She might have no husband at all, if Anton followed through on his offer to have their handfasting annulled. No Anton, no Wulf. . . . Thoughts of Wulf calmed her. Wulf was probably safe, if Sybilla had not lied about that, and she was doing this for Wulf. Marry Louis of Rouen to Princess Laima. . . . Madlenka Bukovany, matchmaker to the House of Jorgar! She felt an urge to giggle and beat it down.

Then came despair. This expedition was absurd. Zdenek had already spoken to Otto and Anton that evening, and would refuse to waste any more of his time seeing their juvenile sister-in-law. Even if she was granted a hearing, she had as much chance of winning a bargaining match with the Scarlet Spider as she had of throwing and pinning an ox.

After twenty interminable minutes or so, a very grandly dressed man with ostrich plumes in his hat strolled along the hall and spoke to the friar. The words exchanged were inaudible, but he was clearly refused. He walked all the way back out again, his feathers seeming to droop lower than they had on the way in.

Another fifteen or twenty minutes and the door opened a crack. The friar rose and went to speak with whoever was on the other side. Then he turned and tried to beckon the dozing woman. When she ignored him, he gestured to one of the novices, who hurried over on bare white feet and spoke to her. She jumped up and went inside, then the door closed and everyone else went back to doing what they had been doing before.

Madlenka Bukovany was being given a lesson in humility.

The woman's interview was apparently very brief, for soon the door opened again, and this time the friar looked to Madlenka. She nodded her thanks as she went by him. Beyond that first door lay a very short corridor to a second, which was being held open for her by yet another friar, a fussy little man with an eye patch.

Beyond the second door was Cardinal Zdenek's study, brilliantly lit by four great crystal chandeliers. There was gilt everywhere—on paneling, furniture, picture frames. What wasn't gold seemed to be scarlet—cushions, brocade draperies, and, not least, the cardinal's rich robes and broad hat. His chair was almost a throne, flanked by a table and a writing stand. Unusually for the times, he wore a beard, a long white one, and when he looked at Madlenka, the light caught his eyeglasses, so all she could see through them was fire. He held out a hand bearing his ring.

She knelt to kiss it.

"A seat for the lady, Brother Daniel."

She rose and held her polite smile, hoping it had not frozen into a grimace, and fighting down a desire to babble like a baby. After a delay that seemed too long not to be deliberate, the chair was clattered down on the marble behind her. She sat and folded her hands on her lap. That was the signal to begin.

"Why you?" the Spider snapped. "Where is he?"

"Sleeping. He hasn't slept for days. Er, nights."

"Well, why not send one of his bovine brothers? Or the chief witch herself? Why you?"

"Because I am now his cadger."

"*Ha!*" The cardinal's guffaw startled her, as it was meant to. "An unfledged falcon and an unhatched cadger? Did you come here to back me into a corner with your vicious negotiating tactics?"

He sounded just like her mother, and Madlenka had long ago learned that the best defense against browbeating was defiance.

"I am reliably informed that you are in a corner already, Your Eminence."

"You are insolent!"

"You are very ungrateful. I think that what Squire Wulfgang achieved this day hardly justifies describing him as unfledged. You do not wish to negotiate for his future services?"

He leaned back, fiery eyes studying her. "So?" he murmured at last. "State your terms, my lady." As a surrender, that rang as false as a stone bell.

"I offer my falcon's exclusive services for the next year, with extensions thereafter by mutual consent."

"Or until the Inquisition burns him, or his brother has to hang him for murder?"

"No criminal charge could be proved in court, and I have been assured that a papal pardon and absolution can be obtained for any suspicion of past sins."

The old man chuckled. "I see. Provided I marry off Princess Laima to Louis of Rouen, of course? That Umbral strumpet never gives up."

Madlenka felt as if her horse had just balked at a jump and she was about to land in a ditch. The old scoundrel was so far ahead of her at this sort of wrangle that he was almost certainly just playing with her. He probably meant her to think that.

"I have never met nor spoken with Lady Umbral."

"How about Cardinal d'Estouteville?"

"No. Is he Sieur Louis's uncle?"

Zdenek shook his head mockingly, as one might at a child showing off. "That is what he calls himself. Twenty years ago, just after he was appointed bishop of Rouen, Guillaume seduced the governor's wife. The sweet little product of their happiness was the cause of much merriment in the town, but the ancient marquis was so flattered at being thought capable of siring a child that he made no complaint. So, while young Louis claims to be related to the king of France, he is in fact naught but a priest's bastard. His true father is anxious to advance him, of course. Had Louis shown any talent for the church, he would be at least a bishop by now, probably holding several benefices. He isn't a warrior, either; just a bit of a scholar, apparently, and a good musician, but there's no money in those. Now d'Estouteville sees a way to catapult his by-blow into royalty at no cost to himself. But why should he pick a faraway and insignificant country like Jorgary to bless with his offspring? Have you worked that out yet, Countess?"

"There aren't many marriageable princesses around?"

"There are many. So many, in fact, that you have the question reversed. Ask rather why d'Estouteville should bother pursuing our dear Laima for his bastard?" Zdenek shrugged his scarlet shoulders and abruptly changed the subject.

"I agree that your falcon achieved an outstanding success today, but I have absolutely no interest in being his client. Not for a year, nor for life. His cadger, yes. Then I would be interested. If he—and you also—would agree to transfer his jessing to me, then I would be willing to discuss the matter further. I insist on negotiating with *him*, though, not you. Now I have work to do. Have you means of returning to Castle Gallant, Countess?"

"No." There was nothing left to say. She didn't understand why her offer had been declined so emphatically, only that there must be deeper currents that she had not seen and perhaps never would or could. Her first attempt to help Wulf as his cadger had failed totally, and tomorrow might bring even worse disaster.

She rose, knelt to kiss the cardinal's ring without meeting his eye, and then turned to Brother Daniel.

He, surprisingly, smiled at her, as if to compensate for his client's rudeness. A narrow darkness appeared beside him.

"The only part of Castle Gallant I know," he said.

She hesitated until she realized that she was looking into the solar, lit only by the embers in the hearth.

"My thanks, Brother," she said, and stepped through.

The room grew even darker as the gateway closed behind her. She waited until her eyes had adjusted, then found a candle and lit it.

She opened a window a crack and heard partying still continuing. What did she do now? Where did she go? The door to her rooms would still be bolted on the inside.

The solar was a mess of uneaten food, empty bottles, and dirty dishes. It reeked of wine. The candles and firewood had all gone, and the fire itself was burned down to embers. She huddled close to it and fought with problems as uncountable as a plague of roaches. Sybilla had promised to look in on her later, so if Sybilla could be trusted, she would eventually be rescued and returned to her room. *If* Sybilla could be trusted.

Could Lady Umbral be trusted? If Cardinal d'Estouteville was father to both Sybilla and Louis, then Louis was nothing to Lady Umbral, and Sybilla was acting on her own in offering to rescue Wulf.

And what about Great-aunt Justina-Kristina? Whose side was she on? Was even Anton loyal to Wulf now? Love had driven a wedge between brothers. She needed Wulf! It was his life in peril, and he knew much more about his strange talent than she did.

Why had Zdenek rejected her offer so contemptuously? Was that just bargaining? Or had he obtained another falcon from somewhere to help him through his crisis, so he no longer needed Wulf? If Sybilla forgot her promise or decided that Wulf's services were no longer available to buy the princess for her brother, then Madlenka might find herself still locked out of her room in the morning, when the castle awoke.

The celebration sounded louder than ever: much shouting and less singing, perhaps, but the clamor had spread even to this, the private area of the keep. Her father would not have allowed that. She could even hear gunshots, and he would certainly have disapproved of wasting ammunition like that.

She needed to speak with Wulf, but *they*—whichever *they* had him— would never allow that. Half a dozen words from her and Samson would have his hair back. Idiot! Moron! Why had she not given Wulf permission to use his talent any way he saw fit? Half a dozen words. Probably Sybilla had spied on her conference with the cardinal. If she knew the Wulf gambit wasn't going to win the princess's hand for Louis, she would wash her hands of Wulf and Madlenka.

"How did it go?" Sybilla asked.

Madlenka jumped a yard in the air and choked back a scream. "You startled me!"

"You get used to it." Sybilla sounded slightly slurred. "People appearing and disappearing, I mean. I think you're in danger."

"Me?"

"You told the Spider you're Wulf's cadger. Other people spy on him and may have heard you. Come with me. . . ." A hole appeared in midair, showing a narrow corridor lit by a flickering sconce: walls of bare plaster, flagstone floor.

Madlenka rose and eyed the prospect uneasily.

"Go on!" Sybilla said impatiently.

Madlenka stepped though and then stopped. The air smelled old and dank.

"No! Where is this?" She spun around, but the gate had vanished, and she was facing another bare plaster wall.

CHAPTER 33

Wulf became aware that he was studying a paneled ceiling that had been badly stained and warped by leakage. He must, therefore, be alive and awake. He had never seen that ceiling before. He had never slept in this bed before. He must find a commode very soon. He surged upright.

He saw a small, sparse room with a very large crucifix on the wall, a compromise between a private bedroom and a monk's cell. Some light and—he now registered—raised voices drifted in through chinks in an ill-fitting shutter, and he had certainly slept well into Saturday. He had vague memories that he had been kissing Madlenka when that little priest arrived with the men-at-arms, and then he was moved, and saw a bed right in front of him. He must have been told he could sleep there, because he had started dropping his clothes where he stood. He certainly wasn't wearing them now. He didn't see them lying on the floor, either, but what appeared to be neatly folded clothes lay on a little chest near the door. That other box was almost certainly the commode.

Neither luxurious nor squalid, this accommodation did not match what he would expect of the Inquisition.

He padded over bare boards in bare feet and found the

relief he needed. He Looked for Madlenka and saw nothing. Anton? Otto? Nobody. Gallant, Dobkov . . . nothing. He was a workaday again. However much he despised his inhuman powers, to be deprived of them was to be struck blind and impotent. A small mirror on the wall told him he still had a nimbus, which could only make things worse. He was defenseless, yet any other Speaker would see him as a threat.

Closing the commode lid, he stalked across to the window and opened the shutter, confident that the sill was high enough to defend him against charges of indecent exposure. He was three stories up, looking out at a gray, drizzly day and what had once been a garden but was now a building site, a wasteland of rubble, stone blocks, and timbers. At least a hundred laborers were hard at work on a scaffolded monster that looked as if it might grow up to become a church. Beyond that . . . Just as he had recognized Castle Gallant when Anton showed him a lithograph of it, so he knew Castello San Angelo looming over the rooftops. And the very long building with the pointed bell tower out front looked much like drawings of St. Peter's. So he was in Rome, and it was raining.

Chilled, he went to inspect the clothes. The only item that he recognized was the Magnus dagger, neatly laid on top. The undergarments were linen, but as soft as silk, clean and almost certainly brand new, finer than any he had ever worn. Those he could manage, but the trunk hose had one blue leg and one mulberry. Worries about being in the grip of the Inquisition faded even more, unless it had taken to torturing its victims by ridicule—he could not begin to imagine what Vlad would say if he ever saw a Magnus wearing anything like this. Still, it was a perfect fit and of much better quality than any garment he had ever owned. *Never look a gift hose in the mouth.* The shirt was at least white, and of equal fineness. He had barely started lacing the two together when there came a tap on the door. Whoever was spying on him didn't mind his knowing it.

When in Rome . . . *"Intrā!"*

An elderly manservant entered, carrying a steaming ewer, which he laid on the chest beside the empty washbasin. He smiled politely and turned on his heel.

Wulf said, "Wait!" unable to find the Latin equivalent soon enough.

He got another smile but that was all. The door closed. Although no bolt clicked, Wulf would bet there was a troop of pikemen out there.

Hot water, razor, soap, oil, comb. A steaming hot bath would have been better, but one can't have everything. Feeling much refreshed and readier to face the world, he returned to dealing with the appalling apparel. The next garment was a thigh-length doublet of forest green with the forearms slit to show the shirt underneath, and over that went a heavier, fur-lined, pleated coat of mulberry to match his left leg. Its sleeves were slit to the elbow, so the lower halves just dangled. Saints preserve!

The floppy liripipe hat was blue and hung down to his shoulder. The left shoulder, he decided, trying to adjust it in the tiny mirror. This was not Jorgarian wilderness; this was Rome, the center of the world, but if Madlenka saw him dolled up as a clown like this, her love would be greatly tested.

He was still adjusting his liripipe when the same servant brought in a tray, whose mingled odors caught Wulf's attention like honey caught ants. He pulled over the stool and set to work on fish, pasta, eggs, and fresh figs. Meanwhile the man attended to the wash water and the commode, even making the bed. And then he departed, having spoken not a word.

People suspected of heresy could be shut up in dark stone boxes on dry straw for thirty years before the Inquisition even thought to interrogate them, and might never hear the charges against them. So this was not the Inquisition, not yet anyway. If Wulf had to guess the name of his host, he would bet on Sybilla's father, the shadowy Guillaume Cardinal d'Estouteville. Whoever he was, he would want to cajole Wulf into accepting a new cadger. And if being nice didn't work, he would have other methods to try.

He ate, and the empty dishes remained uncollected. The next hour or so felt like a good part of that thirty year sentence. Bells clanged from a score of campaniles, but he had no idea which canonical hour they were calling, for the clouds hid the sun. He addressed a few appropriate prayers to the crucifix. Eventually he did try the door, but merely confirmed that it was locked.

He had been a total fool last night! He could remember Father's frequent warnings of the need for adequate sleep. Fatigue was not restricted to sissies, he would insist. One of his favorite stories had been of a commander who had led his army on four ten-hour days of forced march, and marched every pace with them to prove how tough he was. When the enemy sprang the ambush, the men were still alert enough to fight, but their leader was too exhausted to think.

Wulf had let himself get into that state last night. Exhaustion and pride. He had behaved as if the Wends' destruction had really been his doing and not a divine miracle. He had grossly insulted his future king and spurned Lady Umbral, who had been willing to put him under her protection. Choosing Madlenka as his cadger had been a triumph of love-sick folly over common sense, for she could not provide the guidance that an experienced cadger could give him. That had been another of his crazy impulses, like shooting Father Azuolas. Worse, because he had put the woman he loved into terrible danger. Now she held the only key to his powers, so his enemies could torture her to make him do their bidding. Fool! Idiot! Moron! Cretin! Dolt!

The next hour felt even longer.

It was interesting, though, how his strike against the Wends had changed everything. Before it he had been a murderer, despised even by Great-aunt Justina, and after a heroic warrior. Modesty aside—no Magnus was ever much hampered by modesty—he had done remarkably well. The Speakers he had met so far had been an unimpressive collection. Justina might have been good in her time, but young Leonas was an imbecile, Father Vilhelmas and his brancher, Alojz Zauber, were unscrupulous. Inquisitor Azuolas and Brother Lodnicka had bungled their attempt to return Marek to the monastery at Koupel. Sybilla was a flighty, immature girl completely bedazzled by her own importance and her destiny as the king of France's sister's hireling.

But what of Marquessa Darina? Yes, she was probably competent, in a cold-blooded, mercenary way. Dangerous, certainly. And a liar. She denied being a leading performer in Konrad's notorious orgies. She had given no credible explanation for sweeping Wulf off to the palace last night and letting him spy on the dying king. Or for contriving his meeting with dear Cabbage Head. What was she up to?

Even last night, deadened by fatigue, Wulf had suspected that there must be a conspiracy afoot, dirty work directed at the younger Konrad; as his imprisonment dragged on into the afternoon, he became more and more convinced of it. Zdenek would be at the heart of it, just because he was at the heart of everything. He was certainly the main axle of the government, but there had to be wheels as well: jurists, financiers, generals, ministers of this and that. Cardinal and prince were reputed to detest each other. On whose side was the royal mistress? Had the Scarlet Spider been behind that strange visit to Cardice and the even stranger encounter between Wulf and the prince?

None of which should concern a penniless workaday esquire trapped in a locked room a thousand miles away.

But if he wasn't somehow important, why was he here?

CHAPTER 34

Wulf's ordeal was ended by a polite tap on the door. The visitor was the same dumpy little priest who had brought him to Rome—the same black cassock, jeweled pectoral cross, and Speaker's halo shining bright. And the same oily little smile.

"Good day to you, Wulfgang. You slept well?"

"I did, thank you, Father." He could have slept on sharp rocks, but he would not sleep as well again until he received some answers. He was encouraged to note that the man had left the door open behind him.

"I apologize for leaving you here so long. Your host is a very busy man, as you can understand." He was taunting.

"I do not know the name of my host, or yours. Or why I am here."

Again the smile. "I am unimportant, but my name is Giulio. Come and meet His Eminence. He will be happy to answer all your questions."

Maybe he would or maybe he wouldn't, but he would be Guillaume Cardinal d'Estouteville without a doubt. Wulf nodded acceptance and followed his guide out to a simple, plain corridor, then down a narrow, plain, and quite steep staircase to a more majestic corridor, with paneled walls and tiled floor, and then down grander stairs. And eventually to a large, high chamber.

It was the room of a scholar, with books everywhere, covering two walls, stacked in corners, heaped among the litter of papers on a large table in the middle. Despite its size, it was cozy, with a fire crackling in a marble fireplace, thick Flemish carpet underfoot, a few battered fragments of classical statuary scattered around, and heavy velvet drapes hanging ready to hide the watery wintery afternoon that lurked beyond the mullioned windows. The man in the big chair by the fire was elderly, the hair around his red skullcap silver, and his scarlet robes buttoned up under his chin to hide his neck. His face had once been fleshy, even sensual, but now it sagged in pleats. His nose was long and prominent. He was a workaday, of course, not a Speaker. Speakers lurked in shadowy corners, not on thrones.

He extended an age-spotted hand to let Wulf kiss his ring. His smile was too mechanical to seem sincere. How well did those filmy eyes see?

"Wulfgang! I am honored to meet a man who has achieved so much in so little time. You almost restore our faith in youth. Rise, rise! Sit there, my son." He indicated a chair as large and heavy as his own, on the far side of the fire. Beside it stood an inlaid table bearing a carafe and a goblet of cut crystal. "Help yourself to some wine, please. I cannot join you, I'm afraid, because my doctors regard all pleasures as unhealthy." He shrugged. "Your glorious victory over the schismatics yesterday bears the stamp of a holy miracle."

"Indeed it does, Your Eminence." Wulf made himself comfortable and poured out one mouthful of wine. "No one knows that better than I. All I did was try to burn a wagon I thought carried gunpowder. Everything that followed was the Lord's work."

D'Estouteville nodded approval. The odor of hypocrisy grew stronger. "And now what? The Lord has granted you great powers, so to what purposes will you put them?"

Trap? "I have heard it said, Your Eminence, that powers such as you attribute to me are sent by the Father of Lies." Wulf thought he had worded that rather well.

Evidently his host did also, for his next smile seemed more genuine. "I would not be entertaining you at my fireside if I believed so, my son."

Wulf blurted, "Then they are sent by God?"

A penniless, juvenile esquire should be much more respectful to one of the senior figures in all Christendom. He should let the older man guide the conversation and not bark out impertinent questions like that. Yet d'Estouteville merely smiled that mechanical smile again.

"You are a healthy young man, Wulfgang, are you not?"

Wulf nodded, then remembered that the old man might not see well. "Yes, Your Eminence."

"And a strong one?"

"Yes."

"And where did you get your health and strength?"

"From God?"

The cardinal nodded. "You have flaxen hair. I am told you have golden eyes. Where did you get that coloring?"

"The hair from my father, Your Eminence. I never knew my mother. I am told I had an uncle with yellow eyes."

"All these are gifts from God, and yet black sheep bear black lambs, white sheep white lambs. Talent runs in your family, does it not?"

"So they say." Wulf thought of Whitetail, the canine companion of his childhood, and the time he and Anton had thought it humorous to lift him over the gate into the compound where the hound bitches were confined when they came into heat. Whitetail had enjoyed his visit much more than his human accomplices had enjoyed their subsequent beatings, but ever since then the Dobkov hunting pack had sported a high proportion of white tails.

He realized that the silence was aging. "But what *is* talent, Your Eminence?"

"It is just a talent, my son. Some people sing well, others have quick wits. Some have good looks, some are ugly. Gifts from God. Sometimes He seems capricious, but He has His own purposes that we cannot know. Your talent is an ability to make your wishes come true, that is all. Whatever you want, within limits, comes to pass. Like strength or beauty or any other talent at all, it is a gift from God that should be used to His glory and purpose. Yes, you can do the devil's work if you wish, just as you can kill men with crossbows or seduce girls with good looks and a glib tongue, but you can also use all your attributes to serve Christ."

Wulf wondered if he dared ask for a written testimonial to that effect but decided it would be a waste of time. The Church's official position could be denied only in private. *Your wishes come true!* It described his powers exactly, the powers he had now given to Madlenka for safekeeping. D'Estouteville must know about that, though, for Wulf could not have been confined in a servants' bedroom otherwise. And obviously the conversation was reaching the point where he would be "invited" to put his abilities at the disposal of the Church.

"Your hospitality and shelter are very welcome, Eminence, but you must have summoned me for some purpose. How may I demonstrate my gratitude for your hospitality?"

"You have not met Cardinal Zdenek, I understand?"

"I have not had that honor."

A flick of the cardinal's eyebrows implied that Wulf had suffered no great loss. "But you are aware that your noble king will shortly go to meet his Creator, as we all must in time. He will be succeeded by his grandson, whose heir presumptive will be his sister, Princess Laima. To put the matter in a nutshell, Zdenek has been peddling her around the courts of Christendom. He has been offering a dowry comprising estates that he values at three hundred thousand florins, plus a further two hundred thousand florins' worth of gold and jewels."

Wulfgang pursed his lips. All Dobkov would not be that much.

The age-dulled eyes studied him for a long moment. "The unwritten part of the offer is that the dowry goes back to the cardinal."

Deep breath. *"All of it?"* When money changed hands, some of it always stuck to fingers, but not usually that much.

"All of it, so it is probably worth much more than he admits. We offered the gems and the gold, while retaining the estates, and our offer was rejected out of hand."

"'We,' Your Eminence?"

"Agents negotiating on behalf of my nephew, Louis of Rouen. Louis is a fine young man, a year or two older than you, cultured, personable, and related to the king of France. He is well qualified to be consort to a princess, and will even consent to live in Jorgary."

"I do not doubt his merits, my lord, but how . . ." Wulf was currently feeling very stupid, but not stupid enough not to guess where this was going.

"But how does it concern you? When your brother the baron warned the cardinal that you would need support in your dealings with the Wends, Zdenek appealed to the woman known as Umbral, who runs an international coven of witches. No offense intended. She saw the chance to gain my favor and set the Louis-Laima match as her price. Zdenek absolutely refused. He claimed the marriage contract was already signed, but that was a lie. He is still dealing with at least three rival parties. That was our third refusal, in effect."

So now Wulf's life, freedom, and service were going to be offered in a fourth attempt?

"Last night," d'Estouteville said with a faint smile, "while you were sound asleep upstairs, your cadger, Countess Madlenka, went to call on Cardinal Zdenek."

"*She did?*" Wulf damned himself to the pit for ever having involved Madlenka in this.

"She did. I am told she acquitted herself amazingly well."

Half the Speakers in Christendom were watching every move in this game, no doubt. Listening even now and laughing at him.

"She is a determined lady," Wulf murmured. He remembered the first time they met and how she had climbed up on his bed to help him sit up, gripping his bare arm. For an unmarried noblewoman, that had been a stunning breach of decorum. Madlenka refused to be bound by convention and let nothing faze her; that was why he loved her. He forced the memory away to concentrate on what d'Estouteville was saying.

"... offered you as a hireling for at least one year. Zdenek rejected the offer without hesitation. But he did make one interesting concession." The ensuing pause was carefully calculated as only a preacher would know how. "He said he would be willing to take you as his falcon, but he would negotiate only with you personally. What do you suppose the Spider had in mind there, mm?"

D'Estouteville was an old hand at these snaky games and Wulf an absolute tyro. He wet his lips with the wine to gain a moment's thought.

"Why he wants me as his falcon, not his hireling?"

"Yes, why should that make a difference?"

Trickier . . .

"I am a beginner at this, Your Eminence, but I would guess that His Eminence may foresee a need to have a Speaker perform some unsavory tasks for him. He does not wish a third person to be able to intervene and override his orders."

The old man nodded. "That is my conclusion. You, I believe, are an honorable young man, who would not be easily led into serious crimes."

Wulf could counter that with some of his own agenda. "I have a great need to confess major sins at the moment, Your Eminence." No mere parish priest would have authority to absolve Satanism and mass murder, but a cardinal could.

"I would hear your confession, my son, but at present we have other matters to discuss."

Absolution but not yet. And when the Inquisition arrested him in Jorgary? Would it accept his word that his sins had been forgiven? It might take long enough to refer the question back to Rome and for d'Estouteville to respond; the old man might die in the meantime or insist that all confessions were secret.

As if guessing Wulf's doubts, the cardinal said, "Francesco della Rovere and I have been friends for a great many years."

Who? Oh, yes, the pope, Sixtus IV.

"Yes, Your Eminence?"

"Were I to ask His Holiness to issue a decretal absolving you of any blame in the death of the late Brother Azuolas of the Dominican Order and stating that you are under no suspicion of dabbling in Satanism, I am confident that he would sign it, as a personal favor to me. And of course we should be well disposed toward helping with any lesser problems you might wish to discuss."

Now the threats and bribery were piling up. In fact, the air was so thick with hints, nuances, and subtleties that Wulf could hardly breathe. Any promise by Zdenek to bring pressure to bear on Archbishop Svaty could be discarded as worthless; the Vatican would overrule it. An annulment of Madlenka's handfasting would be available if Wulf cooperated, but if he didn't he would be in the Inquisition's cells by nightfall. The

Inquisition would be eager to avenge one of its own, and would soon have him begging them to take him out and burn him.

Just why was it so important to marry Laima of Jorgary to Louis of Rouen? Was this just the cardinal's pique at being thwarted in his efforts to place his son in a royal family, however inconsequential? Never mind what Zdenek was up to—what was d'Estouteville up to? "May I ask, Your Eminence, who the three rival candidates are?"

The old man's shaggy eyebrows shot up. His surprise might be either a compliment or a warning. "I forget their names, but one is a middle-aged blind Italian with the coughing sickness, one a twelve-year-old Catalan, and the third a Polish nobleman who is also a congenital idiot. Why do you ask, Wulfgang?" The question was accompanied by a very foxy smile.

"Sieur Louis must feel quite insulted at being ranked behind those three."

"Oh, he is. But why did you ask?"

When in doubt, be as truthful as possible. "Because my father was both a warrior and a diplomat, and he taught us that more wars were won across a table than on a battlefield. He also said that the first thing one should know was what the other side really wanted."

"Indeed? And what do you think Cardinal Zdenek really wants?"

"I think he is definitely up to no good, Your Eminence. As a loyal subject of King Konrad the Fifth, and our future Konrad the Sixth, I think he must be stopped."

That was clearly the right answer, but if d'Estouteville asked what Wulf thought *he* was up to, then some very creative lying would be required. He didn't.

"Are you willing to stop him, my son?"

Wulf drained the mouthful of wine in his glass. "I am willing to try, Your Eminence." What choice did he have?

"Excellent! Then you have until vespers tomorrow."

"Tomorrow?" Wulf straightened up in alarm. "With respect, Your—"

The old man's face was suddenly as hard as baked brick. "You will return to this room before sunset tomorrow. If you have real progress to report, we may extend you some additional time, but if you have not succeeded by then, I doubt that you will succeed at all. Speakers are re-nowned as fast workers. That is why you are known as falcons."

"I am a very inexperienced Speaker, Your Eminence. I had no han-dler to train me, and my cadger knows much less than I do."

D'Estouteville shrugged. "All you need is your cadger's permission. She has agreed to provide it, but for this limited time only."

They had Madlenka! Of course they would hold her as hostage for his good behavior. That was undoubtedly one of a cadger's purposes. Wulf should have seen that last night.

Now he had no choice at all. "Then I shall return here before sunset tomorrow." And if he didn't return voluntarily, he could be fetched. "You will, I am sure, monitor my actions while I am gone."

"Many people will, I expect." The cardinal's brown-splotched hand lifted a small handbell and jingled it. The door opened so promptly that the newcomer might have been waiting right outside. Or he might have been waiting in the land of Prester John, because he bore a shining nim-bus. He was a gaunt man of about thirty, with a hard, ascetic face; he wore the white habit and black cloak of a Dominican friar.

"This is Brother Luigi," d'Estouteville said, "prior of the Roman In-quisition. Bring in the countess, if you please, Brother."

Brother Luigi acknowledged the order with a nod, but then did nothing at all except stand there and stare intently at Wulfgang, whose mind madly chased its own tail and caught nothing. Any attempt to snatch Madlenka and carry her off to freedom would be absolutely useless. He could fly with her to the realm of the Great Mogul, but the Inquisition would follow.

A gate opened in the bookshelves, wide enough to reveal two women standing there. One of them was Madlenka, who smiled with relief at the sight of Wulf as he sprang to his feet. The other had a nimbus. *Three's dangerous.* For a moment he thought the second girl was a nun, for her black gown was sexless and shapeless, and her wimple hid her hair, ex-posing only her face. Then he recognized Sybilla, whose involvement in promoting family affairs was only to be expected. Her own jessing hav-ing been arranged, her half-brother's marriage was now the business of the day. She, too, smiled at him, but his attention was on Madlenka.

Obviously she had been rehearsed and had consented to follow the playbook. She raised a paper and carefully read off the words: "Wulfgang

Magnus, I freely and voluntarily give you my permission to use your talent in any way you please from now until sunset tomorrow, except that you may not spy on me or try to locate me or communicate with me in any way. You will not break the first commandment under any circumstances."

Wulf said, "Wait—"

Brother Luigi stepped through the gate in front of the women and it closed behind him.

Wulf's talent was back, though. *Otto was standing at a window, staring out at the bailey in Castle Gallant, watching men clearing snow. Vlad was striding along the battlements.*

"Well, you must be on your way," d'Estouteville said wearily. "Forgive me for not rising to see you out, Wulfgang. About the only consolation of old age is that it lets us pander to native laziness." He held out his ring to be kissed. "May the Lord go with you and aid you."

"Amen to that, Your Eminence."

As Wulf straightened up, he decided that the key to his problems must be Marquessa Darina. Justina first, though. *Justina was in the kitchen of her cottage at Avlona.* He opened a gate to go there.

CHAPTER 35

Except that he did not arrive in the kitchen, but in the vineyard outside. That was what happened when workadays
were present to witness. He must ask Justina to explain how
this worked.

*Justina was standing at the big table, chopping cheese into tiny
fragments, but she was talking to someone in a tongue Wulf did
not know.*

He leaned against the stone table in the warm sunshine
that always seemed to permeate Avlona and thought about
all the things he must do, and in what order. When time was
so short, it must not be wasted chasing false scents. It wasn't
sunset tomorrow that was his most urgent deadline, it was
sunset today. Here in Greece the day was obviously closer
to ending than it felt under Italy's cloudy skies. Last night
he had made an appointment with Crown Prince Konrad, a
date he had never meant to keep, but now obviously must,
even if it killed him, as it well might.

There were more discarded golden vine leaves lying under the trellises than there had been yesterday, so even at
Avlona fall must come. Otto's advice would be vital. *Otto
was still brooding at that same window.* Why? *Vlad was dog-
gedly wading through the snow on the battlements, his shadow*

going ahead of him. Neither man seemed to be talking to anyone. Anton . . . *All he could detect from Anton was a shadowy fog, vague images forming and dissolving.* Wulf had learned enough about talent now to know that this meant sleep. No doubt Anton had been interviewing candidates for the position of count's chief concubine.

Otto, then. Wulf stepped through into the room and coughed politely.

Otto spun around. His face registered fright, then relief. The brothers took one pace apiece and crashed together in an embrace. They hugged like bears and thumped backs.

"We were so worried about you!"

Wulf laughed. "Not as worried as I was. And I'm not out of the swamp yet."

"Then you haven't been hired as the pope's court jester?"

"Um . . . It does look like that, doesn't it?" From Otto's grin, Wulf knew he must be blushing. "Latest Italian style. You rustics can't appreciate fashion. Seriously, I am frantically short of time and I need counsel. You're the family expert on law."

Otto faked a glare. "Are you looking for a fight?"

"No. Give me your hand and don't let go." Wulf gripped Otto's wrist and pulled him into limbo. Otto yelped. "Don't let go!" Wulf repeated. "You're quite safe otherwise. This is limbo."

"Where unbaptized babies go?"

"Haven't seen any around. We can't be spied on here, so please listen, because this is vital. The king is very close to death. The prince has yet to father an heir. Suppose he meets with an accident right after he succeeds?"

Otto's eyes narrowed. "That is not a comfortable speculation, and could be a dangerous one to make in public. Are you hinting that he is *likely* to meet with an accident?"

"Let's keep this on a just-suppose level," Wulf said, with a smile meaning, *Yes.* "Next in line is his sister. A woman can reign, can't she?"

"I expect so. Roman law doesn't apply here. Jorgary has never had a queen regnant but many countries have: Sweden, Poland, Hungary, Bosnia. But—"

"But she is only sixteen and unmarried."

"That does get tricky," Otto admitted, rubbing his chin with his free hand. "Back in Dobkov we've never worried overmuch about palace politics. When the king calls, we go to war, and that's that. A few kings have succeeded at that age or younger, but a woman . . . I imagine she would, but she'd get married off very quickly."

"Who would choose the lucky bridegroom?"

"Even trickier. I'd think the Assembly of Nobles. Or a civil war."

"But if she were already married to a personable, popular young man of royal blood with no especial enemies?"

Otto took his time responding, probably wondering what his kid brother had fallen into now. Yesterday lifting a siege, today settling the political future of the country? Whatever would he get up to tomorrow?

"Then her husband would probably be granted the crown matrimonial. In other words, be made king. Officially appointed by his wife, no doubt, but in reality by the Assembly of Nobles."

Of which Anton Count Magnus must now be a member, while a mere baron would not. That was ironic, but Wulf did not mention it. "But what if she were married to someone totally unsuitable? Say a blind old invalid, or a boy much younger than herself, or a congenital idiot?"

Otto looked even more unhappy, appalled at where this was obviously leading. "Then I doubt if she would be allowed to rule at all. She might be allowed to wear the crown, but a Council of Regency would wield the power. With a civil war always looming on the horizon. She'd become a pawn. . . . Very nasty. Does that answer your question?"

Wulf nodded glumly. "It's what I expected."

"So which do we have to look forward to? The personable foreign prince, or one of the horrors?"

"That will depend."

"On what?"

Wulf shrugged. "Possibly on me."

"And which side is planning to have the new king meet with an accident?"

"Both of them."

"Then you must tell Cardinal Zdenek as soon as—" Otto stopped when he saw Wulf's bitter smile.

Wulf said, "What was the name of those rocks that would clash together to crush the Argonauts when they tried to sail between them?"

"The Symplegades."

"That's where I am, except I'm between two clashing cardinals. One wants to marry Laima to his nephew, who may not be too bad but isn't what he claims to be. The other plans to marry her off to an impossible king so he will be left alone to run the country for the Assembly. I am almost certain that both sides intend to dispose of the young king before he can louse up the country too badly."

"Is he really as bad as they say he is?"

Not knowing the answer, Wulf shrugged. "I remember Father saying that kings were like babies: you just have to take what you get."

Aghast, Otto said, "And it's up to *you* to stop them?"

"Me and Madlenka. I was a criminal idiot to involve her! Pray that she'll come out of this safely. Now you're up to date, and you've confirmed what I feared. I must go before the sun sets."

"Wait!"

"What?"

Then Otto seemed to think the better of whatever he had been about to say. He shrugged and smiled wanly. "It doesn't matter now. When will we see you again?"

"Tomorrow, I hope. The day after more likely. If not then, then likely never."

Wulf opened a gate into the Unicorn Room. Vlad had returned and was standing at the window, staring out, so he did not notice his brothers' arrival. Otto stepped through and Wulf went back to Avlona.

CHAPTER 36

Justina was alone now, laying out bowls of food. A trencher of stale bread and a spoon lay ready, and there were mouth-watering scents in the air. She smiled at him.

"I know you must be hungry. Sit down."

"I don't have time. You heard me getting my orders?"

"You must make time, boy! No man can operate without food and sleep, so you must always make time for them."

He sat. "Just because you're my Great-aunt Kristina, I have to do as you say?"

She smiled happily. "Of course!" She pushed an empty bowl over the table to him and raised a pitcher of water.

He held out his hands to be rinsed. And when that ritual was over, he began loading the trencher with lamb and goose and rice and savory sauces.

Prince Konrad's hunt had brought a stag to bay. The hounds were all around it, in their usual frenzy, and the huntsmen were trying to drive them off so they could close in and administer the mort. It was at least an eight-pointer, so His Highness should be in a good mood. Marquessa Darina was not at the hunt. Nor had she been at Chestnut Hill last week when Anton had pulled off his death-defying jump, or Wulf might have noticed her nimbus. That had been the start of all this madness. *No, the fair Darina was in bed, watching a man dressing and making jokes about his hairy chest.*

Wulf brought his attention back to Avlona as a wine bottle and beaker were set in front of him. "Who's that with Marquessa Darina, do you know?"

Justina's eyes went blank for a moment and her lip curled. "One of today's lucky courtiers. No one I know."

"Is she really so promiscuous?"

"If it's held to pee, she'll take it."

"Tell me about her."

"Born Hedwig Schlutz, daughter of a Viennese notary. She managed to keep her Voices secret until she was close to fledging age, but one day she saw a Speaker in the street and by then she could detect his nimbus. He noticed her staring and introduced himself. He took her to the Saints."

"Who's her cadger?"

"Don't know. We don't discuss things like that."

Well, of course! Wulf should have worked that out. The workaday cadgers would be much more vulnerable than their falcons.

Justina laid a loaf and knife in front of him, and went on producing food: hot fish, cheese, olives, and grapes.

"How did Darina get to be the crown prince's hireling?"

Justina sniffed. Obviously her opinion of the former Hedwig Schlutz could not be lower. "She's Zdenek's hireling, not Konrad's. Young Konrad is not one of the Wise, and I don't think he will ever be. Hedwig wanted to be a great lady at court somewhere. Mauvnik is peasant country compared to Paris or Vienna, but it was the best her cadger could find for her. The courtiers saw through her fancy airs right away, and they despise her. She's the prince's official mistress, but she keeps the gardeners and stableboys happy, too. He doesn't seem to care."

"What do the courtiers think of him?" Wulf asked with his mouth full.

A shrug. "He's pathetic. Hunting, fishing, parties, orgies, banquets, military parades. Likes fancy uniforms, although he has no military skills at all. The mind of a child in the body of an ape."

She sat down opposite and began to chatter about five or six generations of Magnus family. Wulf listened with half an ear, nodded politely, gulped down food as fast as he could, and analyzed strategy, all at the same time.

Obviously there were at least three factions involved in the current plot, two led by cardinals and one by Crown Prince Konrad, although his party might not have any members except himself. A man must be loyal to king and country, but which took precedence?

However elliptical Cardinal d'Estouteville's way of talking, he had made it quite clear that Wulf's only chance of staying out of the Inquisition's dungeons was to arrange the betrothal of Princess Laima to Louis of Rouen, a match which only Cardinal Zdenek could approve, but utterly opposed.

If Wulf failed in his mission, he would probably drag Madlenka and his brothers into the darkness with him. Everything now depended on the betrothal of a young man Wulf had never met to the princess he had glimpsed for a few moments last night. Was she involved in the plotting? Probably nobody had thought to wonder what she wanted. If the Scarlet Spider was really planning treason, as both Wulf and Cardinal d'Estouteville believed, then the fate of the country also rested on Wulf's shoulders, and he had about twenty-six hours to find a solution.

How? He had been forbidden to break the first commandment. He tried to Look in on Madlenka and couldn't find her. That was forbidden too, so his jessing worked as it was supposed to. No public miracles! He interrupted Justina's reminiscences.

"You Looked in on my talk with His Eminence." Not a question.

"Some of it."

"Did you hear the eminent gentleman tell me that talent is just a God-given ability to have your wishes come true?"

"I did. I tend to agree, but I was surprised to hear him say so, because it's not the Church's official story. But it is as reasonable a guess as anyone's ever come up with."

"What is the Church's official explanation, if not that Speakers' powers come from the devil?"

"That's the public one. For the churchmen who are Speakers, it is that they are especially holy men, and the Lord answers their prayers."

"And which theory do you believe?"

Justina smiled and nodded. "Most of the time I agree with the cardinal. I have trouble believing that the Lord approves of some of the work being done in his name."

Wulf reached for the cheese again. "A little while ago I tried to come here and the gate opened into the vineyard instead. You had someone with you. The same sort of thing has happened before. How does that work?"

"It works because you don't want to break the first commandment by appearing in front of workadays. That's part of your wish, even if you haven't realized it. Your lungs breathe all night, even if you're not telling them to. You release a bowstring without deliberately warning it not to cut your left thumb off, don't you? Are these things done by your guardian angel? Or is it just you? If I faked a punch at your eye, your eye would close before you told it to."

"Don't. My fist might bounce you off the wall before I told it not to. But why Voices?"

"You were a haggard, all alone. You didn't dare talk with anyone about it, so you imagined holy friends who could advise you. Lonely small children invent imaginary friends. Lonely Speakers invent angelic Voices. A handler would have smoothed the path for you."

That made little sense, although Wulf recalled Father saying that expectation had strange effects on people. Warriors who went into battle expecting to live through it—as they had done the last time or several times before—had a much better chance of surviving than beginners who lacked that confidence. Wulf couldn't take the time to think about it now. He might have months of leisure in a dungeon ahead of him.

"Can you give me a piece of paper, please?" he said. "And a pen?"

Without a word she went to the shelves and fetched the paper and pen, plus an inkwell and a dish of sand. Wulf folded a small strip at the bottom of the paper and sliced it off with the Magnus dagger. He pinned it flat between the thumb and middle finger of his left hand. "Now close your eyes in case someone's Looking."

Then, with his own eyes shut so that even he couldn't see what he was writing, he scribbled seven words. Hoping they were legible, he kept the paper covered with his hand until the ink dried, then quickly folded it and tucked into his pouch, all without glimpsing what was on it. "You can open your eyes now."

DAVE DUNCAN

She was watching with an amused expression. "Where'd you learn that trick?"

"Just thought it up." He washed down his last bite with a draft of wine and stood up. "Thanks for the food and the information. I must fly, as we witches say."

Justina smiled sadly. "Glad I can be of help. If you need more, let me know."

"Thanks . . . Auntie." Wulf walked around the table to give her a kiss. "I'm going to visit the former Hedwig Schlutz, as soon as I can get her alone. Would you please keep an eye on her after I leave? I'd like to know if she reports to somebody."

Justina pulled a face. "You can do that for yourself."

"Oh, no! I'm much too innocent."

He opened a gate into Darina's bedroom.

His timing was unfortunate, or fortunate, depending on viewpoint, and he had a very good viewpoint. Darina, née Schlutz, had just thrown back the cover and sat up, preparatory to getting out of bed. She looked at him with no sign of embarrassment.

"How dare you enter my room like that? Take off those clothes at once."

Wulf had been intending to take a very stern line with her, but the unexpected humor threw him off. He very nearly laughed aloud, but he was aware that he was blushing scarlet and she was not. She had the halo of a saint and the body of a succubus.

"I did not come for pleasure, my lady. Strictly business."

"I'll accept money if it makes you feel better." She swung her legs down and continued to sit on the edge of the bed in full view. "I might even offer it. How much?"

"You need my brother Anton for that, not me." He turned away, pretending to admire the room.

"I like the rags. Italian? But I still think you'd look better without them. "

"Not today, thank you."

"Then what else can I do for you, Sir Wulfgang? There isn't a perversion I haven't watched at the prince's parties."

"It's him we must talk about." Wulf forced himself to face her again, trying not to stare at the scarlet nipples or the dark wisps at groin and armpits that contradicted her blond tresses. "What's your real reason for wanting to leave court as soon as the old king dies and your contract lapses? I frankly don't believe your story of wanting to marry and have children."

She put her head back and laughed, making her breasts bounce. "I'm not the type, am I?" Then she scowled. "You really want the truth?"

"I always want the truth."

"You'll grow out of that pretty fast, sonny. The real reason? Because this place is a cesspool—everybody trying to seem what they're not, everybody waiting for the king to die, everybody sponging off the prince, the prince himself pretending to be a perverted hedonist when he's just a juvenile drunkard, terrified of sex with men or women. I'm no saint . . . well, my cadger and I belong to the Saints, but the Church won't beatify me anytime soon. I enjoy men. I don't like what goes on at the prince's parties. They sicken even me. The whole place sickens me. Satisfied now?"

"Thank you. Last night you listed your duties for me, but you did not mention blocking assassination attempts."

Surely nobody else could shrug so seductively. "I don't have to. Even supposing anyone wanted to kill the dolt, who would try it here in the palace? He's always with a group of other boys, and usually some of them are armed. He eats out of the same pots, drinks from the same bottles. Even if someone tried, I would hear of it and reverse it, unless it was a very fast death."

"He isn't in the palace now, he's out hunting, and that's exactly where most assassinations are tried. There are weapons, and lots of cover. Why don't you go with him on the hunts?"

She shuddered, another very widespread movement. "Don't be stupid. Any riding I do is done right here, in bed. Fending off assassination attempts is not included in my list of duties."

"Has that always been the case, or has the list recently been changed?"

She fluttered eyelashes at him again. "Whatever do you mean?"

He could not threaten her; she was a Speaker and would simply disappear. "When you came to collect me last night, who put you up to it? It wasn't Crown Prince Konrad who sent you, as you said. Who was it?"

Darina slid off the bed and walked straight at him. He stepped aside hastily and she continued on to a closet to find a wrap. Golden hair flowed down her back to her hips.

She said over her shoulder, "Two nights after your brother slaughtered the hunt at Chestnut Hill, he was pointed out to me at a ball. Next day I heard Cabbage Head screaming that the Magnus madman had been made a count, so I Looked in on him. He was obviously already in Castle Gallant, ten days' ride away. He has no nimbus. It didn't take me long to find you." She headed for the fireplace.

"Who's planning to kill him, Darina?"

Smiling mockingly at him, she took hold of the bell rope and tugged. "That's not my problem."

"Then your cadger forbade you to defend him?"

She smiled and said, "Can't say," offhandedly. "I just thought the famous Magnus loyalty might be interested."

"So that was why you came and fetched me from Gallant last night?"

Shrug. "Can't say."

"You're on the prince's side, then?"

She seemed surprised by the question. "I suppose I am. He's a moron, but not usually malicious. He's bored crazy, because Zdenek won't let him do anything."

"Why does he pretend to be such a pervert if he isn't?" Wulf realized that he was desperate to hear that there was something there worth saving.

Darina turned to stare at him appraisingly. "You've been thinking about this a lot, haven't you? I don't know, because he was doing it when I was assigned to him. He was barely shaving then."

"Guess for me. You know him."

"He may have started it to get back at his grandfather for ignoring him. He got the whole court seething with scandal. Now everyone's surfeited and lost interest, but he can't stop."

"What will he do when he becomes king?"

That was easier. "Whatever it is will be a disaster."

"The Bavarian war really was his idea, then?"

"Before my time," Darina said. "I haven't been here quite two years yet, but that's what I was told: he talked his grandfather into it. The old man was senile already, but he could still speak then, after a fashion. It was Cabbage Head's war, though."

Wulf's worst fears were confirmed. He knew now what he was going to have to do, and the wraiths of a dozen generations of Magnuses moaned in the shadows.

"I am very grateful for your help," he said. "I hope I can return the favor sometime. Meanwhile, I don't know my way around the palace yet. Could you put me where I could get in to see Cardinal Zdenek?"

Darina cocked an eyebrow at him. "If he feels like it, he'll make you wait a week."

"I haven't got a week." Less than an hour.

Knuckles tapped on the door.

"That's my maid," she said, "to help me get ready for a gentleman visitor. I'll show you Zdenek's exit door. Petitioners go in through the anteroom and out this way. The moment he's alone, barge in, if you have the courage."

It wasn't hard to smile at such a lovely face. "No courage, just desperation. Thank you for your help."

The marquessa opened a gate for him.

CHAPTER 37

Wulf found himself standing on a small landing at the top of a long staircase. A single door presumably led into the cardinal's office. No, there was no handle on this side, so it only led out. There was nowhere to sit except the steps themselves, but the window offered a fine view over the rooftops of the capital—where he had once spent three weeks, about a hundred years ago.

He had a problem, the sort of problem workadays had all the time but a Speaker should be able to overcome. He needed to know what Zdenek was doing, but could not Look through his eyes because he had never met him. A couple of hours ago he would have been baffled, but now he tried what d'Estouteville had suggested: he simply wished that he could see through that particular door. The massive enameled and gilded oak became like smoky glass for him.

The Scarlet Spider was seated on a chair as grand as a throne, scowling down at a pudgy, rubicund man of middle years, seriously overdressed, like a burgomaster anxious to display his wealth. He had been left on his knees to plead his case, which could not be doing his fancy silken hose much good. His complaints about too much tax being collected in his city seemed to be falling on deaf ears.

Wulf leaned back against the wall and thought about tweaking. When he had first learned of it, he had been disgusted. It was forbidden by the second commandment, but its use must be impossible to prove unless another Speaker was present to witness it happening. Wulf had seen Marek tweak a guard and Alojz Zauber tweak the bishops, and in each case there had been a flash visible to other Speakers. Even if he were to tweak some workaday when there was no other Speaker present, he could never be certain that one was not Looking from afar. Yet now it seemed that duty, personal survival, and his hopes of marrying Madlenka were all going to require him to use tweaking. Father Czcibor had taught him that the devil could always show people how to justify their sins.

Wulf had not been joking when he told Otto he was between the clashing rocks. Both cardinals employed Speakers to defend themselves against tweaking, so he could not manipulate either of them that way. But unless he could change Zdenek's mind about the Louis-Laima betrothal, d'Estouteville would let Brother Luigi have him. Which brought him back to the Inquisition and a full realization of how terrified he was. Terror was the inquisitors' business. Whole families could vanish into the darkness. Acquittal in the secret trials was almost unknown, and anyone who did emerge into daylight again was scarred, impoverished, and universally shunned.

Dark as a thundercloud, and escorted by a Franciscan friar with a nimbus, the burgomaster came stumping over to the door. Wulf caught it as it swung open. The fat man jumped in alarm, but Wulf just smiled and begged his pardon. Then he stepped into Zdenek's office.

The friar spun around in a swirl of robe and his nimbus flamed bright. Wulf ran into a perfectly transparent wall that felt hard as steel. He thought, *I wish this wasn't here*, and the wall disappeared. The friar was tall, with reddish hair and an eye patch. He was quite young, but when Wulf made no offensive move, he did not retaliate; just stood there, watching him warily.

"Wulfgang Magnus, Your Eminence. You want to see me, I understand?"

The old man glared. Red patches flamed above his beard and he bared yellow teeth in anger. "Go and give your name to the chancellor! You cannot barge in on me unannounced."

DAVE DUNCAN

"I already did." Wulf stepped around the friar and walked over to the throne. He knelt. "I have urgent business that I must attend to or I will be delivered to the Inquisition." He waited for the ring to be offered.

"An excellent idea. What do you want?"

"It is more a matter of what you want, Your Eminence." Seeing that he would not be offered the ring, Wulf stood up. A workaday guilty of such disrespect would be heading for the dungeons already, but one furious cardinal was a benevolent and almost pathetic old man compared with the overweening nightmare of the Inquisition. "You told my cadger you wished to speak with me in person."

"Cadger?" Zdenek snorted. "That chit of a girl? I'll give you two minutes, no more, and even that was only because of what you accomplished yesterday. That was impressive, I admit, although you were undoubtedly aided by the hand of the Lord, may His name be praised. All I have in mind is this. It is no secret that our beloved monarch must soon pass to his reward, and Crown Prince Konrad will accede to the throne of his ancestors. A king needs protection, and the Speaker who currently looks after his safety leaves much to be desired. His Highness is anxious to replace her. Having proved your loyalty and skill, you would be the natural successor. You would be well rewarded with income and a suitable title."

He smiled mockingly. "But the idea of a falcon here in Mauvnik being flown by a juvenile cadger ten days' journey away in Cardice is ludicrous. I would insist that she transfer your jessing to me."

Rubbish! Cardice was a mere blink away for a Speaker. Moreover, a cadger of Zdenek's age was liable to drop dead without warning, and then he would take his falcon's talents with him.

Zdenek was just confirming the suspicion that Wulf had shared with d'Estouteville and with Otto, that he was up to no good. Marquessa Darina had hinted that she was not permitted to defend Cabbage Head against soft-footed gentlemen with stilettos. Even Speaker bodyguards were useless if their cadgers were in league with the assassins. Crown Prince Konrad was not among the Wise, and unlikely ever to be admitted.

To throw all this back in the old man's face would be pointless. Wulf said, "The first Baron Magnus helped put the House of Jorgar on the throne, and his descendants have served it faithfully for centuries. At least two have served as royal bodyguards, and I can imagine no greater honor. However, I currently have certain problems involving the Inquisition, Your Eminence."

The cardinal waved a hand as if to banish a mosquito. "I shall have a word with Archbishop Svaty."

"Unfortunately, that will not suffice. Whatever his decision, he can be overruled by the Vatican. I have been ordered to return to Cardinal d'Estouteville by tomorrow evening with a contract of betrothal between Princess Laima and his nephew, Louis of Rouen. In return, I will be provided with a papal decree declaring my innocence in the relevant matters."

Give him his due, the tough old rascal barely swayed. "Then I can offer only my deepest sympathy, Wulfgang." He held out his ring as a sign of dismissal.

Wulf ignored it. "You haven't told me what you want, Your Eminence, not what—you—really—want."

The cardinal's eyes narrowed. Regarding his visitor steadily, and probably taking him a little more seriously than before, he withdrew his hand and entwined it with the other on his lap. "And what do you think I want, young man?"

Now for it: *Ready, Aim, Fire!*

Wulf said, "I think you have served this land of ours since before I was born, with all your heart, loyally and diligently, winter and summer, day and night. Its caring governance has been your lifework. I think you cannot bear the thought of seeing it being ridden over a cliff by a lazy, incompetent, dimwit, drunken rakehell."

That might be slandering the crown prince, but was probably a good description of what Zdenek thought of him.

The low sun flashed red on the cardinal's eyeglasses. "Such talk is seditious, squire."

"Then we shall not repeat it. As a true patriot, loyal to the House of Jorgar, I would dearly love to see you continue to handle its affairs while you train your new young master—and your own successor, whoever he may be."

Zdenek sneered. "You, perhaps?"

"Heavens, no! I am warrior-bred. I can't count above ten. You could find a thousand older men better suited than I. But I could make a good bodyguard, whether official or unofficial."

Silence. The old man glanced over at his Franciscan guardian, as if judging his reaction. Wulf Looked through the cardinal's eyes and saw the friar nod. Confirming that what was being hinted at was possible? Or that Wulf was sincere?

"Tweaking?" the cardinal murmured. "They call that tweaking, I believe, and even the Speakers condemn it as a sin against the Lord's will."

"Call it counseling," Wulf murmured back. "Talent must be used for good."

"As I recall, unwelcome tweaking fades rapidly and must be renewed every few days."

"By someone close to the subject."

Then the mood broke. The old man leaned back and laughed. "A fiendish suggestion! I could never trust you to keep your word."

"Yes, you could," Wulf said irritably. "When I wait upon the Eminent Cardinal d'Estouteville tomorrow to deliver the marriage contract, I will receive from him the document that absolves me from the taint of witchcraft and certain other allegations. Your secretary must accompany me to oversee any final details, Your Eminence."

This time the pause was longer. Wulf could almost imagine the cardinal's mind turning like a millstone as he ground out the risks of trusting this juvenile sorcerer's good faith and compared them with the horrors of murdering or even just deposing his sovereign lord. Wulf had no doubt now that this was what the old devil was planning, but surely he must see it as a last resort, after a lifetime of faithful service? The English deposed kings all the time, but other nations regarded them as sacrosanct, anointed by God.

Zdenek nodded thoughtfully. "You met His Highness last night." The unasked question was whether Wulf could possibly endure the thought of serving the dolt.

"I did have that honor. In fact, His Highness and I made a wager. I am due to meet him very shortly to demonstrate my horsemanship."

The Spider was openly startled. He whispered, "Saints preserve us! I heard about that nonsense. You were serious?"

"Of course I was serious!" He was now, anyway. Whatever would Madlenka say if she knew?

"Nobody believed you. I doubt very much that Crown Prince Konrad will turn up for your rendezvous. Even he remembers his dignity sometimes."

"Let us hope he at least sends a trusted witness," Wulf said, trying to hide how much that suggestion dismayed him. If his bragging had been dismissed as mere insolence and nobody came to watch, then his chances of winning the prince's trust would drop to much less than zero, tweaking or no tweaking.

The Scarlet Spider was regarding him with much more interest now. "What do you hope to win?"

"Just His Highness's favor. He is an equestrian of note himself, I understand."

For the first time, the old man smiled. "Yes, he is. That much we all concede. Well, maybe he will be fool enough to show. Tomorrow you said?"

"Yes, Your Eminence."

"I shall attend Mass in the morning, of course, but I expect to be here after dinner. If you have some progress to show me by then, you may come and do so."

Wulf sank to his knees.

Zdenek extended his skeleton hand. "His Highness must at least accept your service, though that alone will not persuade me."

"Of course not, Eminence." As Wulf kissed the ring, he slid a small wad of paper into the old man's fingers. The cardinal's complete lack of visible reaction suggested that people passed him secret notes that way all the time.

CHAPTER 38

A horse, a horse. . . .

Wulf went to an empty stall in the Castle Gallant stable. He had never jumped Copper, so the horse he needed was Anton's Morningstar. Morningstar had cleared the lethal brook at Chestnut Hill for Anton and would remember it. As usual the stable was dim, warm, and musty, full of the inevitable munching sounds and gentle clink of iron on flagstones, but there was a strange lack of voices. A quick look around confirmed that there were no people present, which was a surprise, but a welcome one. Wulf located Morningstar, who knew his voice and was pleased by the prospect of exercise. He made no complaint at being saddled.

Crown Prince Konrad was sitting on a fallen tree within a group of hunt companions, lecturing as usual. "The most I ever won at a single game of Nine Men's Morris was two hundred florins, as I recall. You were there, weren't you, Pavel? The night when that Italian bet a night with his mistress and lost?"

"Yes, sire. And the Greek mercenary who won her demanded his valet instead?"

His audience cackled like crows. Wulf recognized several faces from last night's encounter. They were all fidgeting, impatient to be on their way.

They were almost certainly already at the rendezvous, but Konrad was paying no heed to the scenery, so the secret watcher could not be sure. They must be tired after a day's hunt and anxious to head home, but none of them would be brave enough to tell Cabbage Head that he was wasting his time waiting around for the braggart Magnus brat to show up. They would rather let him make a fool of himself.

To ride out of nowhere at Chestnut Hill itself would be disastrous if the hunt was already there, so Wulf recalled a wooded hollow where the approach road dipped through a marshy area—not the sort of place people would linger. He arrived there safely, but then ran into an unexpected problem.

It had only been a week since Anton had tricked him into exerting his talent for the first time, but that week had turned the royal forest to red and gold. Trees had changed shape, also, as they shed their burdens of leaves, so that Wulf's memories of the scenery were no longer accurate and he wound up far from where he meant to be. He needed more practice as a Speaker! Morningstar ran happily enough, enjoying this lush country after days in Gallant's stable, but Wulf began to panic. He was already late, and now the sun was very close to the skyline. He was an hour's workaday ride from the rendezvous, and everything would be lost if he failed to show up for his audience. Assuming that there would still be an audience.

Furthermore, he had ridden Morningstar often enough but never jumped him. This did not bother him, but it might bother Morningstar. A horse could not see past his own long nose to view the landing, so jumping was a great test of how much he trusted his rider. Morningstar had made the impossible double leap once, so perhaps his simple horsey mind would assume that he must be able to do it again. Or he might have been having nightmares about it ever since.

At long last a grassy slope reminded Wulf of one near Chestnut Hill itself. Forgetting about the beech wood on its crest, he concentrated on the grassland he wanted and suddenly saw it through a gateway straight ahead. Morningstar shied slightly at the change of terrain when his hooves hit softer ground, but Wulf kept his head down. Soon they were pounding along the edge of the beeches, with the trees on their left and the green slope down to the stream on their right, gradually becoming steeper as they came around the hill.

But there was no one in sight.

As Zdenek had predicted, Crown Prince Konrad had reneged on their wager. No one would question his right to snub an insolent esquire. Even to send a witness would be an astonishing concession, and to waste his own time on such an absurd scam would make him look ridiculous. Of course the insolent puppy would not have been serious.

And truly, Wulf had not been serious. He had never intended to follow through. Events had forced his hand. Now his noble plan had collapsed in ruins all about him.

Then he saw them, the whole hunt. There were almost twice as many people as last week, so word of his bravado must have spread. Instead of assembling at the top of the slope, as he had expected, they had gathered down by the stream, to have a better view of his dramatic suicide. Already the prince had given up on him and the entire party was moving out. Konrad and his entourage were in the lead, recognizable by their fine garb and grand horses. There were a lot more men-at-arms than last week, too. Princes should not announce their travel plans in advance, and somebody in his guard had been smart enough to see the opportunities for ambush.

Wulf pulled off his hat to wave, then saw that he had been seen. Faint shouts drifted in on the wind. The column broke formation as everyone started heading back to the killing ground.

Suddenly that label seemed very appropriate. He had forgotten just how appallingly long and steep that slope was—grassy, but very nearly a cliff. The stream at the base was hidden within a double line of shrubbery and willows, and recent rain might have raised its level. Wulf's blessing had undoubtedly saved Anton's life. Doing it for himself probably required a different sort of witchcraft entirely. Fortunately he really had no alternative, and breaking his neck would be a kinder death than some. Most Magnus males died young.

Besides, since Anton had risked it, there was nothing left to debate.

Three horsemen stood at the edge of the wood, where his death ride would begin. As he drew nearer, they became distinguishable as a priest, a courtier, and a groom. Closer yet, he recognized the courtier as one of Konrad's favorites, the youth called Augustin. Wulf walked Morningstar up to the group and saluted him.

Augustin held up a scarlet cord. "Hands tied behind your back?"

Wulf felt goose bumps rise on his arms. "Of course, Lord Augustin." He adjusted his bonnet, pulling it down firmly on his head.

The youth smiled sweetly. "Not a lord, just a knight so far. Next month maybe more." Then his friend would be in a position to grant titles. As a prophecy of the king's death, that was probably criminal sedition.

"Your pardon, Sir Augustin."

"But Father Michal wants a word with you first." Augustin rolled his eyes.

The priest rode forward and Wulf went to meet him, hoping to draw out of earshot of the courtier. He saluted the cleric respectfully. He was an elderly, hunched man, whose sour expression suggested a permanent bellyache.

"What you are planning would be a major sin, my son. You are risking the life the Lord gave you to no holy purpose."

"I assure you, Father," Wulf said softly, "that I have a very serious and worthy purpose."

"Suicide is a mortal sin."

"I am taking a risk, yes, but my brother did this a week ago and I am a better horseman than he is."

"Are you in state of grace? How long since you confessed?"

"I spoke with a priest this afternoon, Father. Now please give me your blessing, for I have already kept His Highness waiting long enough." He removed his bonnet, bowed his head.

The priest blessed him grumpily.

Wulf replaced his hat, looped the reins over his head, and turned to Augustin, who had followed him. He put his wrists together behind his back.

The priest barked, "No!"

The youth agreed with a laugh. "No, Father. His Highness forbade it, but said to try and see if he would be crazy enough to submit."

Wulf discovered he was crazy enough to argue. "I don't mind. I did say they could tie my hands."

"I mind!" Father Michal said. "That would add murder to suicide."

"Then we are ready, Squire Wulfgang," Augustin said. "If you are quite sure?"

"Quite sure."

"Go, then. They do say the devil looks after his own!"

Wulf looked at him sharply, but Augustin's pretty face was showing no superstitious dread, just amusement—and possibly even admiration.

He headed Morningstar over to about the place where Anton had commenced his madness, and the courser suddenly balked. He reared, punching the air with both front hooves and whinnying in terror: *Oh, no! Not that again!* Big chump! Even without Speaking, Wulf could have handled that nonsense, and now he merely patted the massively muscled neck and tweaked him into fighting mood. *You have done this before! You can do it! You are the best, the strongest. Show all those mares down there, stallion!*

Then they were off, straight down that impossible cliff. To increase its speed, a horse must lengthen its stride, and soon Morningstar seemed to be flying, feet barely touching the ground. The hedge came rushing at them, and Wulf had only a moment to wish someone could tweak away his own terror before he was fully occupied with getting his horse in position to jump. *Up, over the first hedge. Down into the water. And up over the second hedge.* Had any horse ever jumped quite that high? And managed to land safely?

Which he did, if only just.

Thump, thump, thump, as Morningstar came to a halt, whinnying in terror. Wulf patted him and calmed him. Otherwise, silence. Not a cheer. Maybe they didn't believe their own eyes. Did they have Speakers present, who would have seen Wulf blaze like a comet as he came over that second hedge? Morningstar was shaking like an aspen tree. His rider wasn't much better, waiting for screams of "Satanist!" Wulf slid from the saddle and gave the reins to a wide-eyed groom.

He walked stiffly over to where Crown Prince Konrad was standing, hands on hips and face thrust forward in a massive glower. He looked even uglier in daylight than he had under the lamps last night. His riding cap hid his batwing ears, but the all-over smallpox scars were even more obvious. His teeth were as crooked as a heron's nest. The only parts of him that a man might envy were the oversized chest and shoulders, but they cruelly emphasized how puny and bowed his legs were. Poor Konrad! He was no older than Wulf and already looked dissipated.

Around him stood his sycophants like a grove of lilies in their hunting clothes of Lincoln green. They cleared a path for the hero, but all faces were staying blank until they saw how their leader responded. The correct reaction would be to praise Wulf's courage and horsemanship, but was Konrad man enough to do that? He might feel that he had been made to look a fool, although then he would be confessing that he had come to witness a spectacular suicide.

Before Wulf could drop to his knees, one of the courtiers whipped off his cloak and spread it on the mud for him. Several applauded, others scowled because they hadn't thought of it first. It was a showy gesture, but Wulf's Italian hose might be worth as much as the cloak. He knelt.

"Incredible!" the prince squeaked. That childish voice was surely the cruelest of all the tricks that malicious Nature had played on him.

The onlookers cheered and shouted agreement.

Wulf said, "I humbly apologize for keeping Your Highness waiting. I confess I lost my way."

"It was well worth the wait. You have not been knighted yet?"

"No, sire."

"We must put that to rights. Jozef, give me your sword." He took it and tapped Wulf on the shoulders. "In recognition of your incredible courage and horsemanship, I dub you Sir Wulfgang Magnus and welcome you to the Christian fellowship of knighthood."

Again the audience cheered.

About to rise, Wulf realized that he had not yet been told to do so, and remained where he was.

Konrad glanced around the audience to judge its mood. "I cannot make him the king's master of horse. Yet. But I could appoint him master of mine."

"It was inexcusably—"

"I have not finished, Sir Wulfgang."

Wulf gulped into silence.

"After all," the prince continued, "since my own master of horse died while trying to do what Magnus has just achieved, this stripling is obviously a better rider. You accept the appointment, Sir Wulfgang?"

"It was unpardonably impudent of me to mention that possibility last night, sire. And on hearing now how it touched on the death of Your

Highness's friend, I am doubly ashamed. I shall be rewarded far more than I deserve just to receive Your Highness's pardon for my crudity. But if Your Highness is serious, then no honor would please me more."

That was about the truest thing Wulf had said for hours. He had gained the access to Cabbage Head that he would need to keep him tweaked in the right direction. Even years of groveling servitude would be a small price to pay for survival and marriage to Madlenka.

"Then you are appointed and must swear the oath. Where'd our marshal go? Ah, Jozef, give him the words."

Wulf put his hands within the prince's and swore in the ancient way to be his man. So now he was on staff! If he hadn't yet caught up with Anton, he had at least confirmed that the younger Magnuses were rising fast. He stood up and glanced at the faces around him. Their expressions seemed to alternate between narrowed suspicion and fixed rictus smiles. He was an interloper in the hive.

"Time to go, or we'll be benighted," Konrad announced, and the chorus murmured the inevitable agreement. He turned to regard Wulf again.

"Where are you living now, Sir Wulfgang?"

"At the Bacchus, sire."

"We'll find you quarters in the palace. Speak to Lubos. He's my chamberlain—the skinny one with buck teeth and the longest cock in the kingdom."

"Has he met my brother Anton, sire?"

"Oh, was that why Zdenek made him a count?" The future king bellowed with laughter at his own wit, and his future court joined it.

CHAPTER 39

The prince rode a showy black stallion. It was real horseflesh, though, willing to try a little resistance even at the end of a hard day. He brought it under control with no visible effort. Of course he rode in the van, and of course he wanted Wulf at his side. He would naturally be curious about this mysterious adventurer who had sprung out of nowhere. They had not gone twenty yards before the questions started.

"You are warrior-trained?"

"I am, sire."

"So you joust?"

"Some, sire, although my brother the baron puts more emphasis on firearms and infantry training."

"And you wrestle, of course?"

"I do." Wulf had seen that coming. There were few men in Dobkov who could throw him now. Anton wasn't one of them, but Vlad would likely still take him—although maybe not, because he would be slower now. Did Crown Prince Konrad allow others to beat him? Who could prevail against those shoulders?

"Excellent! So do I. Best of three throws tomorrow morning. Tell me more about yourself."

Wulf recited some Magnus history. He decided that the

other riders could not eavesdrop over the beat of two hundred hooves, and even Speakers must have trouble spying on a moving target, so this would be a good place to start his new career. "Your Highness is aware that we Magnuses pride ourselves on our unwavering loyalty to your noble house?"

"So I heard." Konrad was unimpressed. Who would brag of family disloyalty?

"I am determined never to betray those three centuries of tradition. In short, sire, *you can trust me.*" That was a tweak, he hoped. His cadger had forbidden him to break the first commandment, but the second had not been mentioned.

Crown Prince Konrad blinked and then nodded. "After watching that jump, I would trust you to ride into hell and steal the devil's codpiece. I shall need men I can trust when my grandsire finally gets around to dying."

"You can always count on me, sire." Tweak again. Was this to be his life from now on?

The sun had set. The moon was new and would give no light. Thanks to Wulf's tardiness, the hunt could not possibly reach the palace before true darkness, but its destination had probably always been the hunting lodge at Kastan. Meanwhile, the prince was setting a fierce pace, and conversation became impossible whenever the road grew rough or the forest closed in on it. The rest of the time it progressed in fits and starts.

"Describe Dobkov."

"An ancient but minor baronetcy near the Moravian border, known for its horses and its wine."

"When will that brother of yours reach Cardice?"

"Knowing Anton, I am certain he is there already, sire."

"How did he rate his chances against the Wends?"

"He will prevail or die trying. It is our way."

"You will dine at our table tonight."

A new liege lord could not be refused. "That will be both an honor and a pleasure."

"Now tell us what you were up to with Marquessa Darina. In detail."

"Nothing carnal, sire, alas. She accosted me, as she said. I confess that I saw an opportunity to be presented to Your Highness. The encounter turned out badly, as you know, and right afterwards the lady and I parted on unfriendly terms. By God's Grace, the ending may yet be more profitable than the beginning." Wulf wasn't quite lying, but he was closer to it than he liked to be.

"Indeed? I noticed some of my friends regarding you with interest just now. Quite understandably so, of course."

His leer made Wulf squirm. Loyalty did have its limits, and he doubted that his would stretch that far. Sex, in his opinion, was a private matter, no matter who was involved, and his choice of partner would be conventional. He prayed fervently that Darina had not lied when she said that Konrad's debauchery was mostly pretense.

"You flatter me, sire, and many of your companions are remarkably handsome young men." Why did such an eyesore surround himself with male beauties—was he proud of his ill looks? "The truth is," the utterly trustworthy servant lied, "that I am newly married and cannot imagine betraying my wife. Not yet, anyway. In a year or two I may slip back into old habits."

"What's her name?"

"M . . . Magdalena, sire." Madlenka was an unusual pet name for Marie. The Magnuses were in the public eye now, and to have two of the brothers marry Madlenkas in a week might raise questions about how many husbands she needed. Wulf had foreseen the need to tweak the prince, but not all this disgusting mealymouth lying.

The heir apparent snorted. "I don't believe it. I don't believe what you said about that slut Darina. You can't expect me to trust you if you lie to me. I grant you your horsemanship—I could barely believe my own eyes when I saw what your brother did last week, and I truly expected you to break your insolent young neck today. But I don't believe Darina picked you up in the palace stable. And she set up our encounter last night, not you; I want to know why."

Either Konrad had been primed by some perceptive crony, or he was smarter than he pretended. That was encouraging.

"I'm not at all sure you do, sire."

"Do what?"

"Want to know. It's very bad news. I mean, I am a loyal subject of the House of Jorgar, and I began picking up worrisome rumors. I stress that I have no hard evidence and I am not completely sure of my facts, but it felt like my duty to—"

"Evidence of what?" The prince hadn't slackened his pace at all, and yet he was giving all his attention to Wulf. He must have remarkable faith in his horse and his own horsemanship.

How to convince him? Konrad was not among the Wise. Told that Wulf was a Speaker, he would either flee in terror or scream for the Church. And even sorcery had given Wulf no hard facts.

His father had always said that truth was safer than lies because it was easier to remember. "Treason, sire. The brewing of a plot to depose you very soon after your grandfather's passing."

Konrad's sudden pallor showed through its coating of dust and a long day's sun- and windburn. Deposed monarchs had the life expectancies of mayflies. Everyone knew that, even stupid princes. But he did not scoff, so he must have at least considered the possibility.

"I will have their heads! Who are they? Give me names!"

"Names I do not have. It may reach up to the Assembly of Nobles."

The prince's muttered blasphemy suddenly changed to a shout of annoyance as the cavalcade came to a ford. The stream was flowing rapidly, and several minutes were needed to cross. Then he dug in his spurs, yelling for Wulf to close up again. Other courtiers were looking disgruntled at this blatant favoritism.

"Talk!"

"Yes, sire." First lay a foundation of truth. "You know my brother was serving in the cavalry. I was his varlet and had much time on my hands." Now build an edifice of lies. "I overheard some nasty jokes about 'King Konrad the Brief.' I accompanied my brother for a couple of days on his way north, and then doubled back to join my wife. Being known in the stable, I could prowl around, and I made it my business to do so. What the marquessa told me last night confirmed my suspicions. There is a plot forming in the shadows. Of course I may be worrying unnecessarily, and nothing may come of it."

"That slime Zdenek is behind it, I'll wager. I swear that the first thing I will do when I succeed is throw him in a dungeon."

"And who will replace him?"

"I will. I intend to rule, not just reign."

Heaven preserve Jorgary! "A very noble sacrifice, sire."

The horses had slowed to a walk for a stony hill. The prince scowled at Wulf, suspecting mockery. "What does that mean?"

"Just that the old man works all day and half the night. No more hunting for you, sire. No grand balls or late parties. No wrestling, no jousting. Just reading all those reports would keep a team of clerks working from dawn to dusk. *Your life will be nothing but drudgery.*"

Konrad's scowl became a glare at such impertinent back talk. But he had to believe what Wulf was saying. "I'll find some senior underlings for the routine. Maybe two or three good ministers to do the rough work, and I'll supervise."

"An excellent idea, sire. Of course they will have to be trained."

Probably no one had dared question any of the lummox's harebrained declarations since he was shoulder-high. He shot Wulf another suspicious glance. "Now what are you getting at?"

"If Your Highness is really asking my opinion, I would suggest you tell the Scarlet Spider to start training his successor."

"I can't tell him a damned thing! Nothing! He just nods very solemnly and then ignores everything I say."

Wulf just smiled until the pause was obvious, then said, "I could suggest some orders he would accept from you already, sire. Sadly, we all know that your accession is only a matter of days away. So there are certain instructions he would have to take now, without waiting for your grandfather to die. I don't know for a fact that His Eminence is involved in the plot against you, but I am sure the plotters will want to enlist him as soon as possible. Of course, the Assembly of Nobles—if that is who is behind this, as I suspect—are a quarrelsome bunch." No one had ever told him so, but any collection of nobles was certain to be a quarrelsome bunch. "So it seems likely that their plan will be to keep Zdenek on, running the country for them and their puppet king."

"What puppet king?"

"Whoever they choose to receive the crown matrimonial." That was what Otto had called it.

Konrad practically screamed. *"Laima? Laima wouldn't do that!"*

"They may leave her no choice, sire."

The pallor had faded, but now it returned. They had stopped discussing deposition and moved on to assassination.

Fifteen minutes and three tweaks later, the hunt arrived at Kastan Lodge, a minor timber palace on the shore of a small lake. Wulf had seen it a week ago, when the water had been jade green, reflecting the forest around it, but now it was silver below the darkening sky. The sun had set and he had less than twenty-four hours to betroth Princess Laima to Louis of Rouen.

A haze of wood smoke greeted the visitors as they dismounted, grumbling about stiff muscles and saddle sores. Between the escort and the lodge staff, there must have been two hundred servants fussing around a royal party of thirty or so. The hounds had long gone back to Mauvnik; grooms led away the horses and the hunters climbed four steps to the front door.

They passed directly into a large hall, open to the rafters and lit by four great chandeliers of a hundred candles each. This was new to Wulf, for last week he had not been allowed indoors. A staircase led up to a gallery flanking three sides of the hall and giving access to bedrooms. He wondered uneasily if it also served as an observation gallery for orgies staged on the main floor, because the furniture there consisted of well-padded divans and thick rugs, not the spare, rustic seating he would have expected in a hunting lodge. Did new boys get hazed, and if so, in what ways? Half a dozen girls were there to greet the hunt—either well-dressed street girls or informally dressed court ladies, who could tell? They squealed with childish delight at being reunited with old friends, kissing the men with more fervor than discrimination. Darina was not among them.

Darina was dining with a grandfatherly, well-dressed gentleman, just the two of them. Most likely he was her cadger, and she was reporting the results of her meddling.

Pretty servant girls were proffering silver cups of wine. Manservants were emerging from an upstairs door to carry steaming water buckets along the gallery. The courtiers, now entangled in twos or threes, were congregating at the foot of the stairs, while an elongated young noble stood a few steps up, vainly calling for silence. His buck teeth identified him as Lubos, the prince's chamberlain.

"Pavel Chlebicek of Podpazi," announced a slender youth, blocking Wulf's path. He was dusty and windburned, but last night he had been a true dandy. "Wherever did you get those *exquisite* duds, my dear Wulfie?"

"These, Pav?" Wulf's finery was well used now, much in need of a wash, and reeking of horse. "They were a wedding present from my wife. I can only pray that she came by them honestly."

Pavel uttered a shrill titter, but his eyes remained icy. The onlookers' laughter seemed more genuine.

Lubos jangled a bunch of keys overhead until he was allowed a hearing. "Your Highness, we are short a room. Where do you wish me to billet Sir Wulfgang?"

Predictable vulgarity broke out all around.

This problem had been worrying Wulf since they arrived. When the hunt had overnighted at Kastan last week, he had found a place in the hay barn with the rest of the lowlife. Now he would feel safer under a bush in the forest.

Konrad smiled as if he, too, had been waiting for this. "It's my fault for inviting him to join us, so he can double up with me."

That produced an outburst of ribaldry ranging from the racy to the openly obscene. Wulf blushed furiously—he could Look through others' eyes and see his own face, redder than holly berries. Although that definitely did not help his mood, it seemed to improve everyone else's.

As long as they were laughing at him, they did not suspect Satanism.

CHAPTER 40

Lubos started handing out tagged keys. Konrad had his own. He led Wulf upstairs and along the gallery to the royal chamber. It was large and luxurious enough to have a separate privy. The bed was also large and luxurious, but there was only one of it, which was to be expected. A bowl of water steamed on a marble-topped table.

The prince began hauling off his clothes. "You told me your preferences," he said gruffly. "And, frankly, I'm too tired for games tonight." His childish sneer showed for a moment. "I hope you aren't worried about your reputation?"

"I have no reputation to worry about, sire." Now Wulf could start to credit Darina's claim that the royal debauchery was all pretense, but he wouldn't let down his guard.

The door opened briefly to admit a young manservant, who hastened over to help the prince. No surprise that he was blessed with cherubic good looks.

"Ah, Nenad! I can manage. See if you can find anything to fit Sir Wulfgang."

Nenad changed direction. He walked around Wulf, eyed him for height and scanned him from front, side, and back. Then, instead of heading for one of the cedar chests, which must hold clothes, he went out again, having not spoken a word and hardly even slowing down.

Stripped to the waist, Konrad went to the wash water. Eyeing his massive back and shoulders, Wulf decided that only sorcery would let him escape humiliation and possibly injury during tomorrow's wrestling. By the time it was his turn at the basin, Nenad had returned with an armful of clothes, presumably looted from other guests. He had brought two or three of everything, and at least one of everything fit Wulf perfectly. The service at Kastan was impressive, a hint that Konrad's judgment was more than skin deep. If he didn't choose the menials himself, he had delegated the job to an aide who did it well.

When they went downstairs again, six tables in two rows of three were being loaded with food, and wine was flowing. Under the great chandeliers, Sir Wulfgang was meeting everyone, being told their names, bowing, bowing, bowing. His reenactment of Anton's miraculous jump was described in detail, over and over. Mouthwatering odors left him relatively unmoved after his late dinner at Avlona, but it promoted salivation among hungry hunters, and very soon the party moved to the tables, where he found himself seated at the prince's right hand. By then he was feeling thoroughly ashamed of himself. What should be a great honor was tasteless when it had been won by cheating.

During the meal, the hunt was described for the benefit of the ladies, and the prince pontificated on Julius Caesar, Bohemian dancing, and viniculture. Wulf knew enough about grapes to know that Konrad was talking nonsense there, and he suspected that Julius Caesar had never conquered Russia. No one commented, though. Servants kept bringing more food.

Sir Augustin Vila, who sat on the prince's left and appeared to be a special crony, rose to propose a toast to the new master of horse, provoking loud cries for a speech. Wulf stood up, said a terse thank-you, and toasted the prince. A whiff of sorcery had made his wine much less potent than anyone else's, but even so his head was starting to buzz. No one proposed the king's health, but that would have been hypocritical. They all expected the old man's death to bring them prosperity.

He took note of the men who seemed especially resentful of his sudden rise, and also the smiley ones, who might be more dangerous. He tried to analyze expressions—resentful, wistful, disgusted, envious, and so on—except that they kept changing.

If Konrad truly was a fraud as an orgiast, then at least some of these people must know it, so why were there no secret smirks to suggest that the new boy had a big disappointment coming? How many knew and were loyal enough to keep the secret? Could this be some sort of test? A leader normally expected his cronies to keep his shortcomings confidential. Konrad seemed to be running a reverse deception.

Whatever the rules, the path to acceptance was to pretend to enjoy the game.

Eventually the servants were chased away and the doors locked. Quickly the rugs were heaped into one thick pile and all the seats and couches rearranged in a circle around it. Foreplay began almost immediately. Konrad settled on a sofa to watch, and Wulf sat next him, hoping that this was the safest place to be.

Soon a half-naked Pavel set off up the stairs carrying a wholly naked girl, who squealed and struggled and giggled. The onlookers jeered and shouted "Shy!" as they vanished into a bedroom. Several couples were down on the rugs.

The prince rose and stretched. "I am fatigued," he announced. "You will excuse me if I retire early?"

Wulf leaped up eagerly. "So am I, sire!" he declared. "Absolutely exhausted. I'll come with you so I don't waken you later."

He glanced swiftly around the faces, but again learned nothing—courtiers made a living out of being inscrutable. He followed the prince upstairs. The others carried on with what they were doing.

Wulf bolted the door. In the light of only four candles and the fire, the big room was dim, but warm. The bed had been turned down on both sides and two silk nightshirts laid out. An ankle-length nightshirt seemed an odd choice of garment if there was seduction planned. Wulf had never worn one, but he certainly intended to do so now.

Konrad chose one side, Wulf went to the other. Last week he had

been a varlet sharing a bed with his brother in a garret in Lower Mauvnik, tonight he would sleep beside next month's king in a bed eight
times the size.

"None of my randy friends appeal to you?" the prince remarked as he
undressed.

"They might have done a month ago, sire. Or maybe next year. Not
while my heart is pledged."

The candles were extinguished, bed curtains drawn. Wulf lay on his
back and waited to find out what would come next. He suspected that
Konrad, having been tweaked to trust his new friend, was ready to make
confession, and would feel happier doing so in pitch darkness. The room
was not quite silent. The fire crackled, and the wildlife downstairs peri-
odically booed, cheered, or chorused, "Shy! Shy!"

"How many brothers?"

"Four. I am the youngest of five."

"You were lucky. I had two brothers, but only Laima and I survived."

"There were times when four brothers felt like four too many, but
now I do agree with you. I was lucky."

"Only Laima," Konrad murmured.

Wulf felt guilty that he had never wondered how the prince and princess felt about each other. Were they close or did they fight? Did he want
her to be happy or to remain a permanent spinster? Live close or move
far away? Did he see her as only a political bargaining chip, as so many
royal families saw daughters, or did he love her?

Silence. . . . Then, "Why? Tell me why they want to depose me? Is it
this? These parties?"

"I expect that's some of it, sire."

Konrad snorted. "I know it is. It's meant to be! I groped a girl when I
was fifteen. She tattled and Grandsire ripped me to shreds. He made me
promise to stay away from girls, so I started chasing boys instead." Snig-
ger. "He went utterly rabid! It sort of grew from there."

And so did his confession. Once started, he seemed unable to stop.
He told what it had been like to survive the smallpox that had wiped out
the entire royal family, other than the king himself and two infant grand-
children; what it was like to grow up despised for being scarred and ugly

when the beautiful sons had died; how he had been reared by a procession of nuns and priests who tried to twist him to suit their own political ends. Courtiers were self-seeking, as were their children, who should have been his friends. Obviously he had never found anyone to look up to, and never had there been anyone he could completely trust—until now. Having found a truly reliable confidant, he poured out all his woes until he was almost sobbing.

Wulf had got what he wanted and hated it. He knew his work had barely begun, and he must stay around for years to keep the puppet dancing on his string. It had been far too easy! Officially it was Darina's job to stop this sort of treachery. By rights, she should take note of any new friends he acquired, especially any with haloes, and even any sudden changes in his opinions. She should report problems to the Saints. If the Saints were anything like a workadays' guild, they would aid their own. Lady Umbral would see to the matter.

But Konrad was not Darina's client, Zdenek was. In Wulf's case, Darina had set up the treason herself. So would Zdenek allow the "education" to continue, or would he stop it? Wulf was still sailing between the clashing rocks, for he must outwit and deceive one of the cardinals, either Zdenek or d'Estouteville.

"So what do I do?" the prince whimpered.

Last night Wulf had joked about running the country and already he was veering close to that precipice. "It is not up to me to advise you, sire."

"Yes it is. No one else dares speak plainly to me. Counsel me, Master of Horse."

The simplest advice would be: *Make some allies, idiot! You have antagonized everyone in the realm.* A prince should have learned that much at his mother's knee, but Konrad had been a third son, so no one had bothered, until it was too late and there was no one to teach him except a distant and embittered grandfather.

"I suggest you start by getting the Church on your side. As soon as your honored grandfather is called to his reward, announce an enormous endowment in his name—a cathedral or monastery, perhaps. The bishops will keep you in power until it's finished! Promise more to come. Ban all festivities during official mourning. Include your own parties and make sure everyone knows that. If the clergy support you, the nobles will be much more hesitant to oppose you. Moreover, if you will excuse my presumption even farther, your position would be a lot stronger if you produced an heir to put the evil talk to rest. *Call Princess Olga back to court.*" Tweak!

"Bah! She's cold as an icicle."

Not according to Darina, but only fools would believe everything she said.

"That won't stop her conceiving." With a silent prayer for forgiveness, Wulf put it in terms the prince might understand: "Work her hard every night! She'll soon learn to enjoy it. When you've gone a full month without being turned down, you'll know that you have gotten her with child." So Anton had told him once.

"And that's it? That's the only reason they hate me?"

He sounded like a hugely overgrown child, bewildered by grown-ups.

"You also get blamed for the Boundary Stone War. People whisper that you talked your grandfather into it."

"So I did, but if he'd let me lead it as I wanted to, then it wouldn't have been such a disaster!"

That sounded like absurd childish dreaming, but the letters Vlad had written from captivity had described incredible incompetence among the Jorgarian leaders, most of whom had shown just enough sense to die in battle instead of coming home to be put on trial. Perhaps the prince would have done no worse, although it was hard to imagine that boyish treble shouting orders. At least he would not have to defend his kingdom from a Pomeranian attack any time soon, thanks to Wulf.

"Laima?" Konrad said. "You seem to have a ready opinion on everything. You really think she's part of this plot you suspect?"

"I have no idea what her views are. But if things go as far as assassination, then she will be your heir and have no choice in the matter. Is she likely to support such a conspiracy?"

"Never! We're very close. She disapproves of a lot of my friends, but she would never, never, never want to see me killed!"

"That's good." Wulf hoped it was also true. Konrad might believe anything he wanted to believe—which would make Wulf's own job easier as long as he could keep the prince's ear. "Then let's worry about deposition. If you were to be set aside, whether by palace coup or armed rebellion, then your brother-in-law would have a strong claim to the crown matrimonial. He would have to win the trust of the nobility. So your choice of a husband for your sister may carry a lot of weight in deciding your own future."

At last they were getting close to Wulf's problem. A burst of cheering from downstairs was more likely related to the progress of the orgy.

"If you mean," Konrad growled with unexpected vehemence, "that I should marry Laima off to some misshapen dwarf who slobbers when he talks, then you can go jump your horse off another cliff. I've heard rumors about the toads Zdenek has been dredging out of the swamps. Not that he ever talks to me. Or listens to me. I think he's going to fake Grandsire's name on a marriage contract so I don't even have a say."

He was right, but Wulf was not supposed to know that.

"Unless he acts very quickly, the choice will be yours. Choose some healthy young nobleman. Someone she will like and will come to love, and who will love her as she deserves. But not a prince! You don't want your kingdom entangled in foreign alliances. Best of all, someone who lives far away won't get caught up in local conspiracies." Someone like Louis of Rouen, for example, except that Louis was offering to move to Jorgary instead of having his wife move to France.

Rhythmic clapping from downstairs must mean that someone was putting on a superior performance.

"I'll sleep on it." The bed roiled as the prince turned over.

Wulf murmured agreement. That had certainly been the hardest negotiating session of his life so far, and he was glad his liege lord had chosen to conduct it in the dark.

He had never met anyone like Konrad—built like a bull, born to the purple, raised on royal jelly, yet still only a child. His sense of humor belonged in privies and bawdy houses. All his life people had agreed with his opinions, laughed at his jokes, and allowed him to choose the games to be played, the topics to be discussed. No one ever dared contradict him. Very soon now he would inherit one of the oldest thrones in Christendom.

Yet Wulf had caught glimpses of something more. There was hope.

CHAPTER 41

Before dawn, Wulf was wakened by a hard kick in the back
and a command to fetch Nenad. He fought his way out of
the billowy feather mattress and sweet dreams of Madlenka,
with no help at all from the entangling silk nightgown.

"Where do I find him, sire?"

"Outside, of course."

Yes, the cherubic valet lay snoring on a pallet right outside
the door. The hall below was littered with discarded clothes,
but there were no bodies in sight. Already fully dressed but
understandably rumpled and bleary-eyed, Nenad attended
his master and was told to produce hot water, wine, and the
two drumsticks he had been ordered to save from last night's
roast geese; horses to be ready at the door in fifteen minutes.
Wrestling was not on the agenda, apparently. Immediate return to Mauvnik was.

The valet's efficiency was incredible. In moments he
was shaving the prince and had returned Wulf's Italian finery, washed and ironed and smelling pleasantly of wood
smoke from the fire that had dried it. Meanwhile the lodge
resounded with bellows of anger as the guests fought to find
their own clothes and take turns with the chamber pots.

Princes wait on no man. It was very little more than

fifteen minutes before Konrad ran down the long stair and out into the
first flat light from a sky the color of duck eggs. He was freshly shaved,
fed, and dressed in finely laundered hunter's green. Nobody else was. He
had enjoyed a full night's sleep, too.

He caught Wulf's arm as their horses were being led forward. "We can
talk more back in Mauvnik. I've made you unpopular enough already.
Watch your back from now on." Then louder: "Pavel! You ride with me.
And Juraj, you great pervert. I want to hear who was doing what to whom
last night. Which girl was screaming?"

Wulf found himself alone, wondering how literally Konrad had meant
the warning. Were any of these baby-faced parasites capable of sticking
a knife in him?

"May I ride with you, Sir Wulfgang?" inquired the buck-toothed
Lubos.

"I would be honored, my lord."

As the cavalcade streamed off down the road with half the riders still
dressing, Lubos opened the interrogation. "I trust you slept well, Sir
Wulfgang?"

"Eventually, yes."

"Eventually?"

"His Highness talked a lot."

"Ah." Lubos smiled cryptically at his horse's ears. "How do you fancy
your chances on the mat with him?"

"Those shoulders terrify me."

That began about three hours of conversation, none of which made
any sense. Wulf was partnered with a dozen different people in turn,
even a couple of the very few women whose palfreys were capable of
matching the prince's frantic pace. Half the guests dropped out. At one
point the new master of horse had to ride forward to warn Konrad that he
was damaging some of his guards' mounts. Konrad pouted, but did rein
in the black super-horse he was riding. By the time the hunt thundered
through the palace gates, the courtiers knew everything there was to
be known about Wulfgang Magnus, which was effectively nothing, and
he had learned more about them than they had guessed or he had ever
wanted to know.

As they entered the palace, Konrad grasped his arm in an oversized fist. "To the mat! I want to see how far I can throw you. After that—hot bath, dinner, and then we'll beard the Spider in his web, mm?" He stormed along the hall at a pace Wulf's longer legs could barely match.

How many hours left until Cardinal d'Estouteville's deadline? Wulf's impatience was scratching like a hair shirt. *Zdenek was already in his office. He had a pile of papers on his lap and was discussing them with Brother Daniel,* a different Brother Daniel.

"Now might be a good time to catch His Eminence before the crowds . . . I mean, a good time to catch him, sire." Even the cardinal would not make the crown prince cool his heels in the anteroom.

Wulf had not made his remark a tweak, at least not deliberately, so he was surprised when the prince agreed. Perhaps he was trained like a hound already, eager to obey his master's wishes.

"Let's go and see." Konrad took the grand staircase at a run, with his cronies trailing behind him. Servants and courtiers hastily cleared out of his path and bowed after he had already gone by. Wulf did not suggest that more royal decorum would be in order. He had tweaked and nagged far too much already, and a show of youthful energy might be just what Jorgary needed after Konrad V's long decline.

Even on a Sunday, the cardinal's big anteroom held a couple of dozen petitioners. The friar guarding the door looked up in astonishment at the army of green-clad hunters bearing down on him. Then he recognized the leader and sprang to his feet.

"I shall inform His Eminence of your arrival immediately, sire."

"Or sooner," Konrad remarked cheerfully, but he did come to a halt. His train caught up with him and gathered around, grinning and, in some cases, puffing.

In his office, Zdenek looked up from his papers with the start of an angry protest, but then nodded and laid his work aside.

"Your Highness, His Eminence will receive you now. . . ."

Konrad took one step before his nerve failed him, and he gestured for Wulf to accompany him. Wulf did, aware that every one of the dozen men he was leaving was mentally measuring him for a coffin. He had stolen the sun from their sky, cut the ground from under their fancy shoes. They must assume that he was now Konrad's lover. There was no other possible explanation—except the truth, which would be much worse to have them believing.

By the time he entered the now-familiar office, the prince had already kissed the cardinal's ring and was making polite apologies for not warning of his coming. The cardinal returned to his throne. The friar in attendance—an older, tubbier one than yesterday—fetched a chair for the prince, exchanging a nod of respect with Wulf, each acknowledging the other's halo. Wulf had not expected to be presented, but he was.

"Sir Wulfgang Magnus, Eminence. He's a brother of that exhibitionist clown you made count of Cardice."

Zdenek nodded as if mildly surprised and extended his ring. He murmured, "Sir Wulfgang," as a man might in the circumstances, but there was enough fire in his eyes to warn that he was displeased about something. He said, "Your honored grandfather made that appointment, not I, Highness. I heard that Sir Wulfgang accosted you a couple of nights ago and offered to repeat his brother's jump with his hands tied behind his back."

Konrad uttered his high-pitched titter. "We didn't tie his hands, but he did repeat it. Quite amazing. He used the same horse. I'm going to steal it off him."

Wulf, standing at the prince's side, said not a word. If his new liege continued to perform throughout this meeting as well as he had started, then he would have earned Morningstar. He was bearding the lion for the first time. The interview was probably costing him as much cold sweat as the jump had cost Wulf.

"Quite right, too." Zdenek's faint smile somehow conveyed the message that he had greatly enjoyed this little chat but now he had work to do.

"To business." The prince raised a thumb. "First, I want you to send an escort for my wife and bring her back to the palace as soon as possible."

"I am delighted to—"

"And issue a proclamation along the lines of needing her love and support during the trying times ahead."

Brother Daniel was scribbling notes.

The cardinal frowned. "That would be an admission that His Majesty

284

is dying. It is customary for monarchs to remain in excellent health until they are actually dead."

"Everyone knows it's coming," Konrad snapped. He raised his index finger. "I think we have had too many Konrads already. I mean, I feel unworthy to fill the shoes of et cetera, et cetera. No one will argue with you on that. When the time comes, have me proclaimed by my second name, Krystof. King Krystof the Second? *Christoforos Secundus Rex.* Has a nice ring to it."

The cardinal did not quite close his eyes and shudder, but Wulf did expect him to protest that hundreds of documents had already been prepared with the other name on it, awaiting only a date. He didn't, but it must have cost him.

"Should have asked me," the prince murmured anyway. He raised his middle finger. "I wish to be briefed on the funeral plans. Tomorrow morning?"

"Certainly, Your Highness. I will have the lord herald wait upon you." A faint flush had appeared in the cardinal's normally ivory cheeks. His fists were clenched. As Wulf had predicted, he could not now refuse such instructions.

But the prince had the bit between his teeth. For the first time he was tasting power, and sweet it was. Wulf waited to hear what was coming next. He wondered what his lectures and gentle tweaks might have created, or at least allowed to hatch. No doubt Zdenek was even more apprehensive.

"And I want the official mourning for my dear grandsire to be both strictly defined and stringently observed. No unseemly partying or jollity during the entire . . . how long?"

"Two years."

"*Jesus!* Really? The entire two years. Lastly—and most important—we must plan for the transfer of power, mustn't we? Several members of my grandfather's council are well past their allotted span and should be replaced before they crumble to dust. We can scrape the moss off a few others and allow them to remain for the nonce, provided they start training successors. Some lists of names, if you please, as soon as possible. You . . ." Smile. Teasing pause. . . . "But you, Your Eminence, are irreplaceable. I count on . . . Nay, I *insist* on your remaining my first minister, or whatever your formal title is, my principal advisor, for as long as your health allows, and may the Lord make that many years."

This time the old man did blink. Yet still he did not look in Wulf's direction, which showed remarkable self-control. "This is indeed an honor, sire. I am most gratified to learn that I have Your Highness's confidence."

"Who else could I trust? You are the government, and have been for years. And one other thing. . . . A husband for my sister. Will this be the last decision of this reign or the first of the next?"

Again the cardinal was careful not to look at Wulf, but he must have made his decision right there, without an instant's hesitation. Wulf had delivered tenure, and now he must follow through with his side of the bargain.

"It is an extraordinary coincidence that you should ask this today, Your Highness. Just this morning, His Majesty made his decision. He is well aware, of course, that a betrothal ought not be announced during the official mourning following his death, and feels it would be unfair of him to delay any longer. He agreed to accept the noble Sieur Louis of Rouen as his future grandson-in-law. His Majesty will sign the documents within the hour, and they will be conveyed to the Medici Bank for delivery by their couriers, who are the fastest in Christendom. I was just about to send the good news along to Her Highness. Brother Daniel, the Rouen file, if you please."

The cardinal opened the package. "This is a miniature of Sieur Louis. And here is the final draft of the contract we have drawn up."

Konrad looked briefly at the miniature, which depicted a smiling, handsome young man, no doubt to his advantage. He handed the document up to Wulf, standing respectfully at his side. "Tell me the highlights."

The contract was a sizable sheet of vellum covered with crabbed minuscule script. A nobleman should both speak and read Latin, but an extempore translation of legal prose would test an expert.

"Hmm. Your Highness would not prefer to have me jump a horse backward somewhere . . . ? Contract of betrothal. . . . Names. . . ."

Fortunately Wulf could guess at the gist of each clause from a key word or two. He especially hunted for any mention of where the happy couple would reside after their marriage. The contract must be based on d'Estouteville's offer, which would have stipulated that they would dwell in Jorgary, while the note that Wulf had passed to the cardinal the previous day had said merely: *France is a fine place to live.* The farther Laima could be kept away from the fester of Jorgarian politics, the less danger she would present to her brother. If Zdenek had specified a home in the text, then the cardinal's clerks would spot the difference right away, d'Estouteville might reject the offer, and the Inquisition would get its chance for revenge. He saw no sign of *habitaculum* or *domicilium* as he skimmed through the document. The French might not miss its absence, especially if the cardinal had thought to change the order of the various clauses. He must have done so; the old fox was still the wiliest around. With a little luck, Wulf thought as he quoted highlights, this draft should be accepted.

"Then space to sign, seal, and witness. Did I pass, Your Eminence?"

Zdenek actually smiled. It was a thin smile, but it was a smile. "You are wasted on horses, young man."

"No, he isn't," Konrad squeaked. "Keep your hands off of him. Why don't I take this material and show it to my sister? So I can be the one to share the *good* news." Merciful heavens, was the lunk learning sarcasm now?

"No reason at all, Your Highness. Please give her my congratulations. His Majesty certainly considered her happiness when he chose the fairest and most personable of the many candidates for her hand."

In sarcasm, the cardinal was still the expert.

Konrad stood up. "One more thing: I have appointed Sir Wulfgang my master of horse. Have that proclaimed. I may let him serve me in that capacity when I succeed."

The moment of camaraderie ended abruptly. The cardinal looked shocked. "Sire, that post is hereditary in the House of—"

"But the present marquis is twelve years old. Until he comes of age, we need someone to keep the seat warm. Or the saddle warm, mm? If necessary, Sir Wulfgang can be deputy master or acting master. Meanwhile, he needs somewhere to live, he and his wife. Are any of the grace-and-favor quarters currently available?"

"I believe so." The cardinal was sulking as he offered his ring. The prince kissed it, and Wulf was about to when the old man said, "Wait. If

Sir Wulfgang could tarry a moment, sire, Brother Daniel can take notes on what size of household he will be setting up, and so on."

"Of course." Triumph flamed in the prince's mangled features. "Have a nice chat. Supper tonight, Sir Wulfgang. And bring your wife." He snatched the Rouen file, spun around in a swirl of his short riding cloak, and headed for the anteroom door.

Zdenek had let the cat out of the bag.

CHAPTER 42

The moment the door closed, Wulf sat down unbidden on the chair the prince had vacated. He glared at the cardinal. "Now he knows that you and I are in cahoots."

Zdenek bristled at his insolence. "What matter? The boy is a fool. You handle him as well as you handle your horse."

"No longer." Without turning, Wulf said, "Brother Daniel, I am a haggard and need your wisdom. Tweaking the prince will be much harder if he has reason to believe I am conspiring against him, will it not?"

"Very much so, Sir Wulfgang," said a quiet voice behind him. "And also dangerous. You may drive him crazy."

"He's insane already," the cardinal said.

"I don't think he is," Wulf countered. "Darina, come here a moment."

The marquessa stepped out of nothing and bobbed a mocking curtsey to the outraged cardinal.

Wulf stood up, noting that Brother Daniel had disappeared: *two's company, three's dangerous.* "Do you consider the prince a fool, my lady?"

She tilted her head and put a finger to her lips in an affected gesture. "Not really. He is limited in many ways, but his lechery is a pose. I'd call him sly. He's a fox that no one has bothered to housebreak."

Wulf said, "Thank you," politely.

"You're welcome."

"There's something you could do to help the prince: give Princess Olga lessons in, um, her duties."

The marquessa drew a breath. "Olga? Olga is in a *nunnery*! You expect me to just walk in there? Taking along a male accomplice for demonstration purposes, I suppose?"

"I am sure you'll find a way."

"No, I won't! I told you: she's hotter than an alley cat. He's the one who needs lessons, and that's your job. The moment this gig ends I'll be out of here. I've got my eye on a little port in Sicily. Oh, those Sicilian fishermen!" Darina rolled her eyes and disappeared.

Brother Daniel returned.

Zdenek was livid with fury at such incriminating antics being performed in his office. They could put him in peril of investigation by the Inquisition, and were a reminder of how vulnerable a workaday like him was to Speakers in general. His hireling guardian Daniel had abandoned him the moment he felt outnumbered.

"Trollop!"

"She's no saint," Wulf said, "but I think she's actually quite fond of the prince." And possibly more loyal than certain other people.

"Forget the idiot for the moment, Wulfgang. Explain to me why the Pomeranian flag is flying over Castle Gallant."

"The what?" Wulf opened a gate to the battlements and shut it after one glimpse of the standards flying above the keep. An eagle had replaced Jorgary's bear, and a Vranov hound the Magnus mailed fist. Appalled, he slumped back down on the chair. *Otto and Vlad were sitting on the bed in the Unicorn Room, playing chess. Anton . . .* He could not find Anton. *He could not find Anton!* Yesterday Anton had been asleep in the middle of the afternoon. But Otto had said nothing about . . . Otto had said, "Wait!" as Wulf was about to leave, and then, "It doesn't matter now." Vlad and Otto were prisoners—on parole maybe, but prisoners. And where was Anton?

"I can't find my brother," he whispered.

"I am truly sorry," Brother Daniel said, sounding sincere. "We thought you would know. Count Magnus died of wounds in the night. He is at peace with the Lord."

But when had this disaster happened? Obviously the night before last. Wulf had been asleep in Rome, and yesterday he had been denied the use of his talent until Cardinal d'Estouteville sent him off on his quest. Ever since the jump at Chestnut Hill, he had not had a moment alone. Before that he had gone to consult Otto, and Otto had kept the news from him, seeing that he had major troubles of his own. He had thought Anton was asleep then, but he must have been either unconscious or drugged. Wulf could have healed him! Why had Otto not told him?

Marek dead. Anton dead. Wulf himself in the shadow of the Inquisition. Vlad and Otto both hostages.

Rescue them? But he couldn't. The fact that they were under room arrest and not chained in a dungeon showed that they must have given their paroles, so they would refuse to leave.

"This is sorcery! No workaday could take Castle Gallant away from my brothers! What happened? Pomeranians? Revenge for what I did to their powder wagons?"

"Havel Vranov," the cardinal said. "As you say, he must have used sorcery to bypass the defenses."

Vranov! Wulf stood up. "Excuse me for a few moments, Your Eminence. I have a traitor's head to bring . . ."

"*Wait!*" shouted the friar. "Vranov's fate is not for you to decide. His case will be considered this evening."

"By whom?" Wulf demanded furiously. "A man must avenge a brother's murder!"

The friar hesitated, glancing uneasily at the workaday Zdenek. "The Saints are deeply concerned about the Agioi's meddling in Catholic territory, and the Agioi have brought countercharges regarding the death of Duke Wartislaw. There is to be a conference this evening. Lady Umbral hopes you will be able to attend, but the invitation does not include a safe conduct."

Of course not. Obviously Castle Gallant would have to wait.

Wulf turned again to face the cardinal's glittering eyeglasses. "First I must satisfy Cardinal d'Estouteville, or by this evening I may be tied to a ladder in the dungeons of the Inquisition. Will you please attach the royal seal to the contract and let me complete that business?"

The cardinal stood up. "For me, as for anyone else, to forge our sovereign's signature would be high treason. You may accompany me, so that you can testify that you watched His Majesty sign. Brother Daniel?"

The friar placed the betrothal contract in a bulky document bag, tied it securely, and then ushered his client through the two successive doors to the anteroom. Wulf followed. Konrad and his cronies had gone, but dozens of waiting blue bloods raised their heads hopefully, then sprang to their feet in surprise as the great man himself emerged. Hands tucked in sleeves, he trod a dignified pace toward the distant doorway, passing through their midst like a scarlet swan among mallards, acknowledging their exaggerated bows and curtseys with the merest twitch of spiky white eyebrows.

Whatever they might be making at that moment of the flaxen-haired young man in the bizarre foreign outfit who followed him so humbly, Wulf knew that they would not rest until they had identified him. The prince's coterie would supply both his name and his lofty new rank as the prince's master of horse. They would also report that the bonny lad gained his title by horsing around in the royal bed. Already the court must be agog at the news that Konrad had paid a visit to the Scarlet Spider and seemed to be reconciled with him—and now here was the prince's new favorite in close attendance on His Eminence! These momentous events would be debated for days.

Wulf regarded his new fame with dread, feeling the teeth of doom closing around him. A second untried Magnus being raised to high office in less than a week would drag the family history out into full sunlight. Historians, archivists, and genealogists would recall that the Magnuses of Dobkov had for centuries been famous for their swordsmen and infamous for their sorcerers. Miracle promotions, wondrous-fast journeys, and military catastrophes of biblical proportions would combine in a witches' brew of suspicion that the Church could not possibly overlook, no matter how much the eminent Cardinal d'Estouteville might want it to. And perhaps that reverend gentleman wouldn't care, once he had squeezed everything he needed from the youthful Satanist.

So Sir Wulfgang Magnus left the hall in the company of the king's first minister. Brother Daniel might as well have been invisible, and so might the three young novices dispatched by the chancellor to scamper along the sides of the hall and vanish out the door before His Eminence was halfway there. They would be carrying word of his coming and summoning helpers he might need. Zdenek had his staff well trained.

Once out into the corridor, he gestured for Wulf to come forward and walk at his side.

"Assuming the Eminent Cardinal d'Estouteville does not consign you to the flames, what will you do about Castle Gallant?"

The audacity of the man! Was Wulf now expected to solve every single problem in the kingdom? Single-handed? Of course Zdenek's predicament was obvious and totally beyond his workaday control. He certainly did not want King Krystof II marching his army north to lay siege to Gallant. Within days the news would be out, and instead of the stunning triumph of the Wends' defeat, he would be announcing that a traitor had seized the king's strongest fortress. Zdenek was at the mercy of the Saints, and Lady Umbral might set a price beyond nightmares of avarice.

Wulf would have terms of his own, which he need not mention now.

"Assuming I can satisfy Cardinal d'Estouteville and escape the Inquisition, Your Eminence, then my duty to His Highness will certainly include seeing that Cardice is returned to its loyalty. Disposing of the traitor Vranov will also be a personal pleasure, of course."

The heralds would have an interesting problem of succession to settle. As Anton's younger brother, Wulf would normally inherit his title, but he had taken on other duties. Otto would want to retain his barony. Vlad, currently unemployed, could supply the military skill to modernize Castle Gallant's defenses: guns, redoubts, and so on. Yes, Vlad it would have to be.

Zdenek waited for more and then shot him a suspicious glance. Neither spoke. Theirs was going to be an interesting partnership.

The decor began to look familiar; soon Wulf heard a familiar flute-like voice spouting forth the wisdom of the ages regarding the natural superiority of man over woman. Once around the corner, he saw that Crown Prince Konrad had brought only three male companions and two of his pretty boys-at-arms. Princess Laima was there with a pair of her dragon-slayer nuns. The crown prince could have chosen a more tactful subject on which to harangue his sister.

He broke off with a leer of ill-sorted teeth. "Ah, Your Eminence! My sister is delighted with your . . . I mean, she wishes to thank our grandsire for choosing such a fitting husband for her." The leer became a smirk. "And I thought that, under the circumstances, it might be appropriate for me to be one of the witnesses."

"Indeed it will be, Your Highness," the cardinal said smoothly. "I cannot imagine why I did not think to suggest it." He glanced at the others. "Lord Pavel . . . Sir Augustin . . . Sir Lubos . . . You brought your seals, I trust? And I asked a couple of other noble lords to attend. I am sure they will be along expeditiously. Do you wish to present your new master of horse to Her Highness?"

For a moment Konrad hesitated, regarding the cardinal as if wondering what lay behind the question. That pause was more confirmation that, while he was certainly stupid, he might not be as stupid as he pretended.

"Sir Wulfgang Magnus, my dear."

Seeing Laima in daylight for the first time, Wulf decided that their mother must have saved up all the beauty she could bestow until she gave birth to a daughter. Her brother was a gargoyle. She was a nymph, with eyes of jet, matching curls showing decorously under the edge of her bonnet, and a skin as smooth as new snow.

Wulf bowed. "An honor to cherish always."

Black as jet, Laima's eyes assessed the unfamiliar Italian style of his clothes and finally his face. And then, as if the three of them had practiced for weeks, she and the two nuns simultaneously crossed themselves. Had the tocsin sounded a great warning clang right overhead, the message could not have been clearer: the Magnus reputation for sorcery had emerged.

Had Zdenek planned this? Had Konrad planted the necessary seed? His cronies were looking startled, so probably not. And if the cardinal had expected that response, what was he playing at?

He, of course, showed no reaction. "Shall we wait upon His Majesty?"

The grouping parted to let him lead the way. The guards on the royal sickroom presented arms and Wulf opened the door. The chamber was much larger than he had realized from his previous glimpse of it. The bed itself was big enough that the dozen or so visitors could line up around it to view the dying occupant. The prince and his cronies went to the king's left, the princess and her companions to his right, and Wulf found himself at the foot, beside the cardinal.

For a long moment there was silence. Another friar with a nimbus had been in attendance on the patient, so now there were three Speakers present, but Wulf was confident that one of the other two must be fully occupied keeping the king alive.

If he was alive. The bedcover had changed from blue to red, but otherwise the old man lay exactly as Wulf had seen him two days ago, a shrunken image of the great warrior-king of times now half forgotten: eyes closed, death-mask face carved from white candle wax, wisps of hair spread on the pillow like combed gossamer. His hands still seemed too large—indeed, they seemed unreal, just models resting on the coverlet at the end of white silk sleeves too flat to contain a warrior's arms. His colorless lips were slightly parted, but the straggly mustache hairs overlapping them did not move to indicate that he still breathed.

"Well?" young Konrad inquired. "Do we start the necromancy now or wait until midnight?"

"Your Majesty," Zdenek announced. "His Highness is here."

Very slowly, the ancient head on the pillow tilted in the prince's direction. In a moment it returned to its previous position. The eyes had not opened.

"And Her Highness also."

The same thing happened, except that this time the king's lips shaped a faint smile.

"Don't get him too excited," the prince muttered, surprised and disappointed by even that small response. He had not come to witness a betrothal contract, but a death certificate.

Princess Laima's eyes glistened with tears. Her nuns were glowering at Wulf, as if he were responsible for desecrating a corpse, but it was the nimbus on the friar who had been attending the king that was glowing brighter than before.

"Your Majesty," the princess said. It was the first time Wulf had heard her voice. It was tuneful and pitched much lower than her brother's.

"Dear Grandsire, I am very happy to hear of the wonderful husband you have chosen for me."

The smile might have widened a fraction. The king certainly nodded. The movement was slight, but it was a nod. He returned to his previous cadaver pose.

Two well-dressed men of middle years came hurrying in. The witnesses were all present and business could proceed.

"We have brought the contract for your royal consent," the cardinal announced.

Brother Daniel was already at the king's right hand, with writing equipment laid out on a bedside table. He uncapped his ink bottle, dipped a quill, and reached across to offer it to the king, whose fingers closed around it.

The other friar's nimbus brightened even more. The king's hand rose. His eyelids might have lifted an eyelash width—it was hard to tell. The friar held out the vellum sheet, resting on a writing board, and positioned it so the pen hung over the appropriate space. The king signed. The princess and the nuns crossed themselves. So did Pavel and Augustin, but Lubos and the prince just stared in disbelief.

Displaying no sign that anything untoward had happened, Brother Daniel sprinkled sand on the ink and repeated the process with a second vellum. Then came the rigmarole of wax and candle and attaching the king's seal. The witnesses signed and attached their smaller seals. Peering over shoulders, Wulf could see that the king's signature was firm, *Konradus Rex*. Indeed, it looked steadier than the prince's *Konradus Princeps*. His Highness was definitely shaken. He must be wondering how long Jorgary would be ruled by a corpse.

Nobody asked Wulf to be a witness, which was just as well, because he did not possess as much as a signet ring. He was entitled to wear one now, though. An emblem of a wolf and a sword had been his childhood dream. Now something Satanic might be more appropriate: a wolf howling at a crescent moon, perhaps. A wolf, definitely. He would ask Madlenka.

Their business completed, the visitors bowed their respects and took their leave. The prince stomped out the door in obvious fury. He had come to expose the cardinal's trickery and succeeded only in putting his own seal of approval on it, quite literally. His guards and sycophants hurried after him.

"And what happens now, Your Eminence?" the princess asked eagerly.

The cardinal beamed down at her like a doting grandfather—a doting but triumphant grandfather. "Now we send the agreement off to Rouen by the fastest courier service in Europe. You do understand that the terms are not binding until both parties have signed? I anticipate no last-minute difficulties, but we must not count our dragons until they are hatched, as I once heard your dear mother say. To be honest, I do not foresee that your wedding can be celebrated anytime in the next two years. Not in Jorgary."

She nodded sadly. No one must mention official mourning, but everyone knew it was looming like a thundercloud.

"If your brother permits, Your Highness," the old man continued, benevolent as a bishop addressing a class of postulant nuns, "and if a winter journey would not distress you, you might think on being married in Rouen, or perhaps Paris? Paris in the spring is said to be very fair."

Wulf could only admire the devious gyrations of the old rascal's mind. Now that he had granted the second in line to the throne a fiancé who might someday be seen as a potential king, she must be evicted from her homeland as fast as possible, to somewhere beyond the reach of perfidy. If Krystof II did prove unmanageable, then the Assembly of Nobles must see no option except to leave the government in the hands of the true and trusty Cardinal Zdenek.

Soon everyone had gone except for the Scarlet Spider, Wulf, and the two friars. Plus the undead king.

Wulf's hands itched to clasp those precious sheets of vellum, so vital to his happiness and Madlenka's. "I may now play the fastest courier in Europe, Your Eminence?"

"Shortly," the cardinal said smugly. The ancient eyes missed nothing, not even Wulf's impatience. "We must take note of the witnesses and so on, and I need to make arrangements to spare Brother Daniel, so he may accompany you. That was our agreement."

"It was," Wulf agreed.

"He will find you when we are ready." He offered his ring in the sign of dismissal.

CHAPTER 43

Wulf emerged from limbo in a deserted corner of the palace stables. He demanded his horse, and watched as Morningstar was saddled up. With two or three hours before his sunset deadline, he must now turn his attention to Guillaume Cardinal d'Estouteville. It was make or break time. It felt very much like that breathless moment when the lances were couched, when his horse was pounding along the lists toward the other horse approaching, when the crowd was roaring, and a fearful, jarring impact was about to settle who stayed in the saddle, and who flew over his horse's rump to hit the ground inside sixty pounds of steel. And in this case the stakes could not be higher: the hand of the lady, or the hatch to hell.

As soon as Morningstar was ready, he vaulted into the saddle and rode off through the sleepy Sunday town to the Bacchus. There he tied Morningstar to the hitching rail and ducked through a low doorway into the dim, tiny lobby. Thus his great-great-grandfather must have often come, perhaps even on peaceful Sunday afternoons like this one. The owner he found behind the counter would have been the two-or-three-greats-grandfather of the current one, Master Oldrich, who was standing there now. He was a plump, jovial man, with the oddly babyish appearance that came from a total lack of hair, even eyelashes. He wore an elaborate, old-fashioned red turban that concealed his baldness, and he had painted eyebrows, but the result was still bizarre.

He beamed. "Squire Wulfgang! God bless! Very happy to see you back so . . ." He hesitated, calculating. Wulf and Otto had visited only three days ago, and they had certainly not had time to ride home and return. "Is anything wrong?"

"Nothing at all. Life is wine and music and the joy of youth. You have a room for me and my dear wife, who will be joining me shortly?"

After a flurry of blessings and congratulations, Oldrich enthused that the Horse Room was available, the best room in the house, top floor, very quiet, and for newlyweds he would cut a special rate. It was Magnus family lore that the Bacchus's rates were always special and the best room varied every time; but none of the rooms were really bad, which was what mattered.

"That will do splendidly. Has anyone been asking for me?"

"No, squire."

Wulf had told the prince he was staying here. Evidently Konrad was not yet suspicious enough to think of confirming that.

"If anyone does, then I have been here since Wednesday."

Nodding vigorously, Oldrich reached under the counter for his slate. "I distinctly remember writing that."

"When we leave," Wulf said, "there will be no need to change what you remember writing." He was being very generous, considering that his pouch did not contain one copper mite. "I did not sleep here last night, though. I was off hunting."

"I trust your chase was well rewarded?"

"An eight-point stag. His Highness was well pleased." Wulf hesitated. Esquires were notorious braggarts. Years of denying his Voices had made him unnaturally reticent, but he should stay in character. He must behave like a swordsman, not a sorcerer. "Yesterday His Highness knighted me and appointed me his master of horse."

Oldrich of course responded with a blizzard of congratulations mixed with compliments on the House of Magnus, but Wulf had noticed the momentary twitch of disapproval from the lashless eyelids. Konrad had done such a splendid job of ruining his own reputation that now Wulf would be tarred with the same brush.

With a final "Please have the lads see to Morningstar," he headed for the stairs. He trotted up two steep flights and explored a gloomy, squeaky-floored corridor, passing images of a bell, a fish, and a snail, until he found a door with a horse on it. The room was modest in size and cramped by the presence of a single overlarge bed. *Oh, Madlenka!* But it should be quiet on this side.

Cardinal d'Estouteville was engaged in conversation with a man, probably a young man, from the sound of his voice, but the cardinal's eyesight was so blurred that Wulf could make out no details. Whatever they were speaking, it did not sound like Italian. It might be French, but if it was, and the other man was who he thought he might be, then it was likely Norman French they were using, and that would be very different from the French of Paris. Not that Wulf could understand a word of either.

He stripped, laid out his Italian outfit on the covers, and set to work to ensorcel it. After a few hastily corrected misjudgments, he made the trunk hose a uniform pale gray and the doublet and coat a somber blue of modest cut and sensible sleeves. When he had dressed again, he was a stylish Jorgarian gentleman.

He still could not Look in on Madlenka. *Vlad was stretched out on the bed and staring at the canopy, while Otto gazed fixedly out the window.* He went to them.

Otto spun around. "Thank the Lord! You're safe?"

"So far," Wulf said. "Why didn't you tell me that Gallant had fallen and Anton was wounded?"

His brother sighed and avoided his eyes. "Because there was nothing you could do. Rumors of Satanism are flying, Wulf. People suspect the Vranovs more than us, but the bishop set up a vigil of two priests at all times in Anton's room. You could not have meddled this time. They caught him in the street, without a helmet. He took such a terrible cut to the head. . . . You saved his life twice. You have nothing to repent."

Wulf nodded. It was too late to explain that he had healed Countess Edita in that same room without entering it. Otto's decision made sense, but the failure would haunt Wulf for years. If he had years.

"What's your news, Wolfcub?" Vlad growled.

"Nothing much. I am Sir Wulfgang Magnus, the crown prince's master of horse. I am on my way to Rome to meet with Guillaume Cardinal d'Estouteville, to negotiate the marriage of Princess Laima, and the Scarlet Spider expects me to rescue his castle from Vranov. Tonight there is going to be a Walpurgis Night party of all the best Satanists in Europe, to which I am invited but from which I may never return."

"Glad to hear that one of us is still able to hold his head up," Vlad growled.

"It may be higher yet if it ends on a pike," Wulf said. "How in hell did you lose the most impregnable castle in Christendom?"

"Gross fornicating incompetence!" Vlad roared. "I made the worst mistake in warfare—I counted on the enemy doing what I wanted him to do! Vranov had been told the river had stopped running, and he could confirm that. His allies were beaten and he had nothing to gain by continuing his rebellion. If he was in any sense sane, he would be halfway home to Woda by now. I went to bed. I woke up with a sword at my throat."

"You didn't allow for talent? Sorcery?"

The big man nodded miserably. "I had set guards on the gates, but they must have been as drunk as lords. All the church bells were already ringing, so there was no way to sound the alarm; the whole town was drunk by then. The Satanists brought Vranov's men right into the keep, I think. They beat us from the inside out."

Vlad was obviously crushed by his failure. The first commandment forbade such trickery, but once again Vranov had broken the rules.

"I think we can sort it out. What Speaking has done can be undone by Speaking." Wulf had an appointment to keep. He was also famished. "I must go."

"God be with you, Brother," Otto said formally. He was deliberately avoiding emotional farewells, and probably that was wise.

Back at the inn, yesterday's Brother Daniel, the younger, thinner one, was sitting on the edge of the bed with a document case beside him. His head jerked up as if he had been close to falling asleep.

Wulf's dreams of food faded. "Long hours?"

"Thirty hours a day, eight days a week," the friar said ruefully. "You are doing well, Sir Wulfgang. The Spider is not easily impressed and rarely gives his trust."

"The Greeks said we should not judge a man until we know how he dies."

The friar conceded the point with a sigh. "And that is especially true of Speakers. Open the way, please."

Wulf extended his hand.

Daniel frowned and then gripped his wrist.

Wulf led him into limbo and closed the gate. "How far does this contract differ from the terms of the Frenchman's last offer, do you know?"

"Very little. My brother took the Spider's dictation and wrote the draft for him to edit; I just copied it out in fair. His Eminence altered the order of the clauses, which makes comparison harder. The only change I noticed was omission of a provision that the couple will reside in Jorgary. There's no prohibition against them choosing to do so, though."

Except the cardinal's future displeasure.

"And the dowry kickbacks?"

The friar smiled. "He was quite generous—for him. He rarely settles for less than one hundred per centum. A draft on the Fugger bank for one-quarter of the amount will be supplied as soon as the terms are accepted. The rest will be due on the wedding day, but I am authorized to mention that there may be delays in payments. Likely no one will ever know who pockets what."

So goes the world. "Then let us see if it is acceptable."

"Why should it not be?"

"Because the omission you noticed was deliberate. Cardinal d'Estouteville is anxious that his nephew live in Jorgary. Cardinal Zdenek is anxious that he not. Please do not draw attention to the change and pray fervently that the Roman scribes are less observant than you."

Wulf opened a gate into d'Estouteville's study. There was no one present.

D'Estouteville was asleep somewhere. So there would be no immediate decision. An old man deserved his nap. The fire had been banked and a warm sun shone beyond the windows. Brother Daniel wandered over there to look out at the city. Wulf eyed the books heaped on the big table and wondered if he dare pry.

Before his conscience and curiosity could decide on a winner, the door opened to admit two priests, so mismatched that they might have been chosen for comic relief: one tall and cadaverous, the other short and pudgy. The first was a workaday, as was the servant who followed them in. The plump priest was Father Giulio, the Speaker who had fetched Wulf from Cardice to Rome. He wasted no time on formalities.

"Brother," Giulio said, "we have been sent to examine the documents you bring. We assume that you will wish to be present while we do so." Taking the friar's consent for granted, he turned to Wulf. "And I am told that you, my son, have had no chance to eat yet today. If you go with this man, you will be fed."

Obviously a very detailed watch had been kept over him for the last twenty-four hours, but food was an irresistible offer. He accepted, following the servant out and along a corridor with walls painted in a jarring red above oak wainscot. Their destination was a small, stark room containing only a rectangular table and six chairs. Most likely it was designed for meetings, and it was easy to imagine clerks spreading their exchequer cloth there to tally money. At the moment it was being fitted out as a private dining room, with four men laying out dishes and jabbering among themselves in fast Italian, but never addressing him. He was given water to wash his hands, and offered dishes to accept or refuse. Once his platter was loaded and his goblet filled, the servants departed, leaving him alone with his thoughts and dishes for seconds. The fare was cold and largely unfamiliar: rice and pasta, two fish of unknown species, roast goose, beans, and fruit.

He had eaten little when his appetite was seriously wounded by the arrival of an elongated, skeletal Dominican. He closed the door in silence and came on silent bare feet to the table, taking the place opposite Wulf. He made no sound even as he moved the stool on the tiled floor. Of course he was Brother Luigi, prior of the Roman Inquisition. He rested his forearms on the table and stared across at Wulf with the austere, accusatory face of a dying Christ, even to the glowing nimbus, lacking only the crown of thorns. He was younger than Wulf remembered.

He did not speak.

Such tricks were intended to frighten Wulf into speaking first, so he carried on with his meal, however hard it was to summon up saliva. He could probably magic enough spit to drown a horse, but then his own nimbus would brighten and give him away. He avoided the drier dishes and concentrated on the fish, which was salty and came with sauce.

"You commune with Satan, Wulfgang." Luigi's voice was soft and seductively gentle.

Wulf finished chewing and swallowed. "No I don't."

"Then how did you come here from Jorgary today?"

Another mouthful. Eating did give one time to think between comments.

"The same way you left the cardinal's room yesterday."

"Even if that were true, it would not excuse you, Wulfgang. I have ordered a woman's nipples ripped off with pincers. If you did such a thing, you would be hanged. I did it for the woman's salvation and the glory of God. I did it in the name of, and with the blessing of, Holy Mother Church."

There was no way to argue with such madness. The Church defined good and evil, and to even question its definitions was heresy. Wulf carried on eating, and now his saliva flowed more freely. Anger worked better than fear.

"Tell me about Father Azuolas," Luigi murmured, his voice still sweet as a viol.

Well, Wulf could argue that he had merely come to the aid of Magnus when he was physically assaulted by two men, both much larger than he. He could assert that his shot had only wounded the Dominican, and either he or Brother Lodnicka could have healed him, had Lodnicka not rejected Wulf's protests and insisted on trying to subdue him. By the time the fight was over, Azuolas had been beyond saving.

Such excuses would be admissions of guilt.

He continued eating.

Luigi continued to stare at him with very dark, somber eyes and an expression of deep sorrow. "You have broken the first commandment."

Wulf acknowledged that remark with a frown while he chewed. When he had swallowed, he said, "I do honor the Lord. I try to obey His commandments, yet I sin, like all men."

"I do not mean the first commandment of the ten given to Moses, but the devil's first commandment."

"What's that?"

"That you must use the powers he gives you in secret."

Any response to that would damn a man. Denial was useless when mere suspicion allowed the use of torture, and confessions extracted by torture were accepted as true. Accusation was as good as proof.

Luigi let the silence drag on a long time before he spoke again. "It is possible that the Holy Father will give you absolution today, Wulfgang."

"Bravo il papa!"

"And perhaps even an indulgence, also, to remit your penance. He may not, of course. But even if he does, he will not absolve your future sins. Can you go and sin no more, as Our Lord commanded the woman taken in adultery?"

"Could you?"

"We are discussing the peril to your soul, not mine."

"I see you love your fellow men, Brother. But your love is so overwhelming that it would destroy them rather than tolerate any deviation from perfection. I don't think you understand what love truly is."

Wulf stood up and stepped to the water basin to rinse his hands. He had taken the edge off his hunger and would have to be satisfied by that. What Luigi was hinting, but would never put in words, was that even if the pope absolved him, the Inquisition would not. It would pursue him relentlessly, every day of his life, until it could find cause to charge him with sorcery, and his death for that would avenge Father Azuolas.

The friar rose, fired with a righteousness so intense that it could admit no dissent. "Go and fly, little falcon," he whispered. "Soar and circle as you will, but one day you will stoop, as falcons do, and then our snares will have you. We will catch your jesses then, falcon, and haul you down." He turned and padded to the door.

As soon as it closed behind him, Wulf went back to his seat and resumed his meal.

CHAPTER 44

Father Giulio and Brother Daniel were bent over the table, apparently comparing two documents word by word. There was no sign of the taller priest, or Prior Luigi. Or Madlenka. Cardinal d'Estouteville was slumped in his favorite chair, looking weary, and older than he had yesterday.

Wulf knelt to kiss his ring, then waited in vain for the order to rise.

"You truly are a remarkably effective young man, *Sir* Wulfgang."

"Your Eminence is kind to say so." He was starting to believe it himself.

"We are impressed," the old man mused. "He has obtained almost exactly the betrothal terms we required. He won a knighthood and the trust of his prince, and he persuaded the Scarlet Spider to change his mind for the first time in decades. And all within the time limit we set for him—which, frankly, we did not dream he could meet."

Puzzled, but forced to assume he was still being addressed, Wulf said, "Happy to serve Your Eminence. I am free to go?"

"Oh, no!" The cardinal's voice sharpened. The half-blind eyes looked down at him for the first time. "'Almost exactly' is not exactly 'exactly.' Zdenek's draft proposes sending the girl to France instead of receiving my nephew there. Whose idea was that?"

So the change had been noticed and Wulf had failed. His chances had never been good. "I honestly believe that these are the best terms that—"

"Answer my question!"

Wulf would never see Madlenka again, for she could give Samson back his hair, and Samson in his strength was too *effective* to be trusted. It would be safer for all concerned, Church and state, to dispose of him. Light the faggots! Make him a salutary example of the hazards of Satanism.

Magnuses did not plead for mercy.

"My idea. Granted Crown Prince Konrad is not the most promising clay from which to fashion a great king, but he does have the right to wear the crown of his forefathers. He deserves a chance to try."

"You are saying that the presence of my nephew in Jorgary would imperil your future king? That my nephew would foment revolution to put himself on the throne instead?"

"The temptation would be there."

"Opportunity!" d'Estouteville shouted. "The opportunity would be there. I want Louis to wear a crown, and I am not accustomed to being thwarted by apple-cheeked boys, *Squire* Wulfgang. You want to rule Jorgary yourself. You would make your prince a puppet and manipulate him by sorcery, bring back his wife and tweak the impotent pervert into siring a son—change his name, ban his orgies, make the people cheer, leave the Spider spinning webs into his dotage. God save King Whosis! You dare to pass moral judgment on me?"

Wulf had no defense against those charges. In the absence of defense, attack. "Since you mention morals, by what right did you bring me here? By what right did you abduct Countess Madlenka?"

"By what right do I hold back the Lord's Dogs? Shall I call for Brother Luigi?"

Someone laughed. "That's enough, both of you," said a new voice.

Wulf glanced around and then jumped to his feet. He had not heard the newcomers enter, so they could not have come through the door. There was no doubt who the young man in front was—Wulf had seen his face on a miniature. They bowed to each other.

At the back, beyond the big table, was Sybilla, beaming with glee. . . . And Madlenka, paler than usual but wearing an expression of unspeakable relief. Her eyes met Wulf's and for a moment there was no one else in the world. The temptation to rush to her made him sway on his feet.

"Sir Wulfgang!" Louis of Rouen spoke as if he had said this before and not been heard. He both looked and sounded amused. "You may not have satisfied my uncle, but you have more than satisfied me."

Hope sprang anew, like returning pain in a wound that had gone numb but might not be mortal after all. "You are gracious, my lord."

"And you are dangerously ingenious!" He laughed. "My remorseless uncle there wanted to throw you to the Inquisition. I told him that I was more than happy to accept what you had made possible. Every night I dream of clasping your lovely little princess in my arms. I will ask only one favor."

"If it lies within my power, it is granted."

Louis smiled. Already he had registered as a very personable man. Therein lay his danger, of course. "Don't be so hasty with promises! All I ask is that if your King Krystof does prove impossible—if revolution begins to bubble and you can no longer in good conscience support him—then I ask that you transfer your loyalty to his sister."

If the new king had produced an heir by then, the child would take precedence, but Louis and Laima might very well be the best guardians available. The last few days had taught Wulf to take life as it came. "You have my word on it, my lord."

"Give him his absolution, Uncle."

D'Estouteville grunted, but he was holding back a smile. "Giulio?"

Father Giulio came forward with Brother Daniel at his heels. If those two large rolls under the priest's arm were the betrothal contract, then they had sprouted several more seals since Wulf had last seen them. But first Giulio handed a smaller document to the cardinal.

"This is signed by the Holy Father," d'Estouteville said. "And bears his seal. It absolves Wulfgang Magnus of all sins committed before this date. That would include any involvement in the death of Father Azuolas or any Satanic practices that might be charged against him."

Wulf reached out a hand, but Brother Daniel's was there first.

"I take this," he said.

Wulf nodded. Madlenka stared across at him in horror, but that was the unspoken deal Wulf had made with Zdenek: the cardinal would hold the parchment that stood between Wulf and death, so that he must keep his side of the bargain.

Father Giulio seemed surprised, but did not question. He handed another paper to the cardinal. "The annulment, Your Eminence."

"Ah, yes." The old scoundrel had decided to enjoy himself. He was one of those people who are always on stage, playing roles. He unrolled the scroll and pretended to study it, although he was much too blind to read without a lens. "This is addressed to Bishop Ugne, disallowing the alleged handfasting he approved, on the grounds that a handfasting is only admissible when there is no priest present to perform the sacrament of matrimony and the woman has been properly advised of her rights. Of course the dates are a little unorthodox, since your petition has not yet had time to reach Archbishop Svaty, let alone be referred by him to Rome. And this reply cannot reach Jorgary for weeks yet."

He glanced up and changed his tone to one of professional sympathy. "We have not yet commiserated with you on the death of your brother, Wulfgang, but we now do so, and will remember him in our prayers. You could not marry his widow, but this document effectively removes that obstacle, if such is your wish." He beamed at Madlenka. "Is it?"

"Oh yes, Your Eminence!" She curtseyed, not knowing that she could be no more than a blur in his sight.

"And the betrothal," Father Giulio concluded, holding out the two major rolls.

"Give those to my nephew. When Sybilla returns him to Paris, he can file one copy and send the other off to Mauvnik, after a suitable delay. Daniel, you may assure my eminent brother Zdenek that the terms are acceptable and the contract will shortly be on its way back. You have our leave and our blessing."

Brother Daniel departed.

Now Wulf could hold out a hand to Madlenka. "And we too, Your Eminence?" he asked as she hurried to his side.

D'Estouteville grunted and frowned. "And where do you think you are off to in such a hurry? Heading for a bed, I shouldn't wonder!"

Louis and Sybilla both chuckled, sharing smiles.

"Definitely," Madlenka said.

Ladies were never so outspoken. Everyone stared at her in shock and even Wulf was startled. With Anton not yet buried? "Definitely?"

"Definitely," she repeated. Her smile lit up all Rome.

He was still getting to know this Amazon he loved. Their life ahead would surely have stormy patches when two strong wills collided, but rather a wildcat than a lapdog.

"Definitely," he agreed.

"Mph!" said the cardinal. "We cannot condone such carnality outside holy matrimony. Father Giulio, will you do the necessary, please?"

The priest looked outraged at this roughshod shortcut through proper ritual, but he would not argue with His Eminence.

"Certainly. Wulfgang Magnus, as the Holy Father has specifically ruled that there is no impediment . . ."

CHAPTER 45

Wulf took his bride into the privacy of limbo and kissed her. There was no danger of either letting go. Between kisses they spoke of love and longing; they promised faith and happiness. They spoke also of sorrow and guilt.

"I truly mourn Anton," Madlenka said. "Had there been time, I might have accepted my duty to love him. You would have gone away—I might have managed."

Wulf doubted that he could ever have recovered from the loss, but that did not stop him from mourning his closest brother. "He gave you no cause to love him. And me very little, but I shall miss him terribly. Had I known he was hurt, I could and would have healed him."

"He did give me up, remember? He wanted us both to be happy. He would not stand between us."

When Otto forced him not to. . . . But what she had said was true.

"There is no cure for death, and only time heals wounds. My father told us that when he was dying."

She already knew that Anton was dead and the Pomeranian flag flew over Gallant. He listed what else had happened in the two days they had been apart: that he was now Sir Wulfgang, so she was no longer a countess, but he was

311

the prince's master of horse, so they would live in Mauvnik, and her name was officially Magdalena, and they would have to make up some story about who she was and how they met. And they had to sup at the palace that evening.

She kissed him again. "First things first," she whispered. "Let's find that bed. I can tell that you need it. So do I. And I want there to be no doubt that we are now husband and wife."

An offer he could not refuse. He opened a gate. "Welcome to the Bacchus, in Mauvnik. The Horse Room."

She stepped in and peered around in near-darkness. "Did you say 'room' or 'stall'? Is that bed really big enough for what you have in mind?"

Oh, that smile! Was his face as flushed as hers?

"What I have in—"

"At last!" Justina appeared in a swirl of cold air.

Madlenka jumped in alarm and he tightened his embrace. He peered over her shoulder at the twilit landscape beyond the new gate. "Where is *that*?"

"Elysium. A former monastery and the Saints' meeting place. Lady Umbral is in conference with the Agioi, and we have been waiting for you. Come!"

Reluctantly he unwound himself from Madlenka so they could obey, but they were still holding hands as they stepped through the gate into a tiny paved courtyard, barely more than a passage between two stone buildings. A river of wind rushed through it, billowing his cloak and the women's dresses. Straight ahead was a perilously low parapet, and beyond that, nothing, only air and sky, all the way to far-distant hills, dark against the last glow of sunset. Overhead the stars were wakening.

"You must be careful what you say," Justina said, pushing through the wind to a low doorway. "Weigh every word. And you keep that temper of yours firmly nailed down, Wulfgang. You had better leave all the talking to your cadger."

Madlenka squeaked in alarm.

Wulf squeezed her hand. "She just means you must not let me lose my temper."

"Yours? What about mine? My temper's much worse than yours."

"No, it's not! Mine is a hundred times worse."

"Imagine what ferocious children we will have!"

"How many? Five brothers to teach one another fighting and five sisters to love?"

"Will you two alley cats stop that!" The old lady had managed to wrestle the door open. She ducked under the lintel, but both Wulf and Madlenka had to stoop as they followed, still defiantly holding hands. The wind slammed the door behind them and continued to moan through chinks in the shutters.

The room they had entered was roughly square, packed with a motley crowd of standing men and women. Four brass lanterns dangled on chains from smoke-stained ceiling beams and swung wildly in the draft, providing little light and making shadows dance over rough-plastered walls. Heads turned toward the newcomers, and bodies shuffled aside to open a narrow aisle, along which Justina scampered, with Sir Wulfgang and Lady Madlenka at her heels.

Wulf thought there must be forty or fifty people present, and about half of them sported halos. Assume, then, that this was a meeting of both falcons and their cadgers, prearranged so that the *three's-dangerous* rule did not apply. The participants must have gathered from far and wide, for their dress styles varied hugely, and even the odors that wafted by on drafts were alien: fish, garlic, lavender, horse, cumin, and cinnamon. He squeezed past monks and nuns, men-at-arms, serving women and grand ladies, gentlemen and workers, priests both Catholic and Orthodox, Muslim men in turbans with womenfolk in burkas . . . old and young, fat and thin. He soon worked out that those on his right must be Agioi supporters, and the Saints' contingent was to his left.

He confirmed that guess when Madlenka and he reached the front row and Justina directed them to go and stand next to the left-hand wall. She then disappeared back into the crowd. The room had once been a chapel, for the low dais that stretched across that end would have been the sanctuary and held an altar. Now this was a courtroom, so the judges sat there. To the left, on a high-backed chair just a few feet in front of him, was a lady in white, and he knew at once that she must be the mysterious Lady Umbral. She was slim and probably tall; her gown was finely styled and glittered. But what she herself looked like remained a secret even now, for the chair bore the sort of canopy called a cloth of estate, which shadowed her face. More than dim lighting was at work, though; some sort of sorcery was masking her features even more. If he met her again tomorrow he would not know her. The intent must be that no Speaker could Look through her eyes or open a gate to wherever she might be.

On the right side of the dais, the man cross-legged on a divan was a real surprise, for he was a Turk, and the Agioi were supposedly the Orthodox counterparts of the Catholic Saints. Of course, the Orthodox patriarch still dwelt in Constantinople, and the Ottoman sultan who ruled there now would undoubtedly keep a firm hand on the Speakers in his empire. Not just a Muslim, either, for he was wearing the garishly multicolored uniform of the sultan's janissary warriors—high headdress with a neck cloth, baggy trousers, curved sword, dagger, and all. Personal slaves of the sultan, originally Christian boys taken in tribute and forcibly converted to Islam, janissaries were the most dreaded warriors in the known world. Even without his Speaker nimbus he would have looked dangerous: big, slit-eyed, tough as tempered steel, and very little older than Wulf himself. Unique among Muslim men, janissaries wore mustaches but no beards.

For a few moments only the moan of the wind disturbed the silence, while the shadows swirled and the two judges appraised the newcomers.

Wulf glanced sideways. The front row comprised a monk, two women, one Orthodox priest, and two men in turbans. The priest and the friar had halos. Beyond them, against the far wall, cowered none other than Alojz Zauber, Havel Vranov's squire, in civilian dress. The hunched way he was standing and the wide-eyed look he gave Wulf suggested that he was terrified. At his feet lay Leonas Vranov, only half dressed and curled up like a cat, apparently fast asleep on the cold flagstones.

"I am Umbral," said the woman in white, "prelate of the Saints. We recognize Madlenka Magnus and her falcon, Wulfgang Magnus. Lady Magnus, I appreciate that you have not yet applied for membership in the Saints, but we claim jurisdiction over you. You have the choice of accepting our authority or appealing to the Church instead, which is no choice, really. Sir Wulfgang, you have only recently accepted the woman who is now your wife as your cadger, so you may have to answer alone for any misdeeds of which you are convicted this evening."

Had Wulf jumped out of the Inquisition's fire and into the Saints' frying pan?

"We reserve comment!" Madlenka snapped, her tone more abrasive than Wulf expected or would have dared use.

Lady Umbral did not reply. "Opposite me is Mudar Sokullu Pasha, right hand of the Agioi. We are assembled here this evening to discuss certain trespasses by the Agioi within Saints' territory."

"Alleged trespasses," the Turk growled in a harsh accent. "And trespasses by your falcons in our territory."

"Alleged trespasses both," Umbral agreed. "Are you ready to begin, Pasha? I believe yours is the earliest complaint."

"May the Omniscient, the Bringer of Justice, guide our deliberations. I accuse Magnus and his cadger of being accessories to the murder of the priest Vilhelmas, Speaker of the Agioi, may he find peace."

Before Wulf could decide whether he was expected to reply, Madlenka made a vague gesture that was not quite like a schoolchild raising a hand to attract the teacher's attention, but had the same result.

"If by 'earliest,'" she said, "you mean that it happened first, then I object. The beginning was the murder of my father and brother. They were smitten at the same minute, miles apart. Obviously that could only be—"

"We shall discuss details later," Lady Umbral said, "but I accept your correction. Pasha, the earliest transgressions on the paper will be the cursing of Count Bukovany and Sir Petr Bukovany, which we attribute to your Vilhelmas."

"I was not warned that such an allegation was to be included. I believe it is irrelevant, and neither the man you name nor his client can be here to testify. Alojz Zauber?"

Alojz's teeth actually chattered before he did. He brought them under control. "P-P-Pasha?"

"Speaking only as a witness, maggot, can you shed some light on those deaths?"

"Pasha, my handler denied doing those things. He told me that this boy at my feet, Leonas Vranov, cursed the two victims to please his father the count."

"I assume there is no use questioning the boy himself?" Umbral asked.

The sleeping or unconscious Leonas had not twitched at the sound of his name.

"None," the janissary said. "Let us agree on his guilt, and may the All-Forgiving have mercy on him. The wretch's talons will have to be clipped. Obviously both the curser and his victims were Jorgarian and there was no trespass."

Wulf could only guess what clipping talons meant, but it gave him cold shivers anyway.

Lady Umbral said, "If we accept the brancher's word."

"So we can move on to the matter of Vilhelmas's murder."

"Not yet. Prior to his death, Vilhelmas transported himself and others out of a crowded hall in Castle Gallant. In as much as he was an Agios, he offended by using talent within Saints' territory, and what he did was a flagrant violation of the first commandment."

The janissary yawned, showing a maw full of yellow teeth. "Maybe so. Vilhelmas has gone to the Affirmer of Truth, and is beyond human judgment. So has the man who shot him, the cleric Magnus. But Marek's accessory is here present. He was equally guilty, and that public assassination was certainly both trespass and a violation of the first commandment."

Madlenka squeezed Wulf's hand encouragingly, but did not look at him.

"We can include it on the paper without accepting your interpretation of it."

"More important than that," Mudar Sokullu Pasha said, as if everything so far had been trivial and they were at last getting to the meat of the matter, "the next day that same Wulfgang Magnus destroyed half the Pomeranian army, about sixteen thousand men. This may be the worst sorcerous bloodshed since the days of Tamerlane. That, too, was both trespass and violation of the first commandment!"

Wulf had been thinking of the Inquisition as his greatest danger. He might have been misled by his ignorance.

Umbral said, "We do not yet concede either of those acts to be crimes. Two nights ago, a member of your order, namely Alojz Zauber, transported Havel Vranov and some men inside the defenses of Castle Gallant so that they could overpower the garrison and open the gates. Count Magnus was among the dead. That is a much worse violation of the commandment, for it has no workaday explanation, and it is blatant trespass."

Baring his teeth in a menacing smile, the janissary glanced around the room. "'No workaday explanation'? Have you never heard of simple treachery, woman? Can you produce witnesses who saw who opened the gates? What pig filth! Does that complete the charge sheet? Have you more to add?"

Impossible jumps at Chestnut Hill did not count, Wulf concluded, nor instantaneous trips between Jorgary and Rome. All that mattered in this court were secrecy and territorial boundaries, with killing other Speakers a distant third. And yet the Saints and Agioi gathered here might be the true rulers of Europe, for who could gainsay their decisions?

To his astonishment, Madlenka released his hand and took a step forward. "My lady . . . and Pasha. . . . All his life, Havel Vranov has been the Wends' bitterest enemy. This year he has been supporting them, a traitor to his king. I charge the Agioi with . . . I believe the word is 'tweaking'? . . . tampering with his mind."

Nothing of Lady Umbral's expression could be read, but her tone of voice registered surprise. "A very cogent suggestion! We add it to our complaints. But it must have been the first trespass, and traditionally we now judge the charges in reverse order—the reason being that recent events are more easily examined. Also, once an offender is sentenced to death, his earlier misdeeds no longer matter. Two nights ago, Pasha, an Agioi Speaker, caused a Jorgarian fortress to fall to a traitor, Havel Vranov. That is trespass!"

Astonishingly, the ferocious-seeming janissary laughed. "You think so? Brancher Alojz Zauber, go stand there!"

He pointed to the center of the dais. The squire nervously stepped over the sleeping Leonas and went where he was bid, stooping as if afraid of losing control of his bladder. He seemed unsure of which direction he was supposed to face. "P-P-Pasha?"

"Normally, grunge, since you are not yet fledged, your handler would have to answer for your actions. But since he was murdered, you have taken to using power on your own authority, so you must suffer the consequences." He showed his yellow teeth again. "If any. Understand?"

"Oh yes, Pasha."

"Where were you born, you louse-infested, unclean, eater of pigs?"

As if seized by a sudden revelation, Alojz swung around to face Lady Umbral, and began to gabble. "In Jorgary, my lady, in Pelrelm. I was a shepherd like my father, and baptized a Catholic, but four years ago, about the time I was due to have my first communion, Father Vilhelmas came to see me. I'd never heard of him, but he explained that my mother was an illegitimate child of the count's late brother, so we were both related to the count. He showed me what a Speaker could do and promised me that Speakers never want for anything: riches, comfort, respect. Herders don't live long, you know. Rustlers don't want witnesses, so they cut our throats; even if they just hamstring us to delay pursuit, we may freeze to death or die of wound fever. But Father Vilhelmas promised me long life and health, warm beds, no hunger. He said I would have to confess before my first communion, and if I told a Catholic priest about the Voices he would call me a Satanist. The Catholics would burn me at the stake or lock me up in a—"

Mudar Sokullu broke into the tirade. "Cease, in the name of the Eternal! The infidel priest bribed you and probably tweaked you. You were born in Jorgary, so you're a Jorgarian. And you are still unfledged. So no trespass!" he told Umbral.

"But who told him to help Vranov take the castle?"

"His own idea entirely. Four days ago he brought the priest's body to us at Alba Iulia, as he should. He was told to return to Cardice and wait until we assigned him a new handler." The janissary made a gesture of dismissal, as if throwing away a walnut kernel. "The boy is weak-minded. Whatever he did was his own idea and the voivode did not order it. The wretch is solely to blame. You may have him! Hang him, burn him, stone him, whatever you want."

"You told me to make myself useful!" Alojz shouted, then cowered even lower, clearly terrified of what he might have provoked.

"And how else did you make yourself useful?" Lady Umbral inquired gently. "By ancient custom, we keep no secrets at these conferences."

Staring at the floor, the squire muttered, "I tweaked the bishops at the parley to help cover up Father Vilhelmas's blunder at the banquet. That's a permitted exception to the second commandment! I helped the count's attack on the castle because he told . . . er, asked . . . me to.

I was trying to help my handler's client!" He blinked like a child about to weep and blurted: "I'm only three months short of being fledged. I hoped if I did a good job they would jess me and let me take over the contract!"

Umbral's face remained unreadable, but her chuckle was eloquent. "We are aware that the Agioi, unlike the Saints, let their falcons fly without the restraint of cadgers, answering only to the voivode. So Father Vilhelmas, a member of the Agioi, had a contract with Havel Vranov, a count in the peerage of Jorgary? This is not trespass?"

Mudar Sokullu gave Lady Umbral a glare so toxic that it should have melted her into a puddle of terror, although it might have been directed at Alojz. "There was no contract between Vranov and Father Vilhelmas."

"So on whose behalf was Vilhelmas acting?"

There was a long pause before the janissary answered. "Duke Wartislaw's."

Until then the spectators had been eerily quiet, but at that news Wulf detected a sort of wordless murmur, a shuffle of feet. The wind moaned and the lamps continued their crazy dance.

"Wartislaw," the janissary continued, "flew three falcons of his own. We were not aware until a few days ago that he had also hired Vilhelmas and was using him to meddle in Jorgarian affairs. Vilhelmas should have informed us and obtained our permission. But this sniveling trash is a Jorgarian, and no concern of ours. Take him and clip his talons, or kill him and let us proceed to discussing the massacre of the Pomeranian army."

"I am not sure I want him," Lady Umbral said tartly. "As he indirectly caused the death of Lady Magnus's husband, Sir Wulfgang's brother, we shall let them pronounce sentence in due course. Stand over there, brancher."

She pointed at Wulfgang. Alojz lurched down the step and hurried to his side, giving him a nervous smile, which Wulf did not return. Madlenka sought out Wulf's hand again.

"When," Umbral demanded, "did the Agioi learn of Vilhelmas's trespass, and why did they not act to stop it sooner?"

"Vilhelmas has gone to the Source of Peace. The matter is of no importance."

"It is of importance to me."

And to Wulf. Now he knew how Vilhelmas had turned up at the head of the Wend invaders. Almost certainly he had been watching Anton, the unexpected new count who had arrived to take charge of the defenses. They had not yet met in the flesh, but Vilhelmas would certainly have been Looking in on Vranov's visit to the town that Sunday and seen Anton announce himself in the cathedral. By then Wartislaw must have infiltrated an advance force into Long Valley, and when Anton rode off to inspect the frontier post on Tuesday, Vilhelmas had gone to take charge. *He had gone to commit murder!* When Anton had been wounded, he had mockingly sent him home to bleed out or die of wound fever. Very likely he had cursed him to make sure. Any lingering guilt Wulf felt over the priest's death now evaporated.

The janissary scratched his right armpit vigorously. "As Allah is my judge and witness, the Agioi discovered the situation only a handful of days ago, but we decided it was a personal vendetta and the politics were incidental. Vranov was so convinced that Wartislaw could take Castle Gallant with his bombard that he turned his coat. Half a year ago he wrote to Wartislaw and offered to deliver Castle Gallant to him without a shot being fired, helped by his cousin Vilhelmas, a Speaker. Wartislaw meant to take Gallant by force, but to have Havel Vranov give it to him would have been much cheaper and an exquisite pleasure. Making Havel Vranov pay—pay long and hard—for all his crimes was an old ambition of his, so much so that he had ordered Vilhelmas to contrive the Hound's utter destruction. He was to be branded a traitor and a Satanist, so that both king and Church would turn against him, and his nights would be filled with terror."

"But of course Vilhelmas had tweaked Vranov to turn his coat in the first place, as Lady Magnus suggested?" Umbral's voice oozed scorn.

Madlenka squeezed Wulf's hand.

"Oh, Vilhelmas may have nudged him a little," the janissary growled in his harsh croak, "but you are well aware that tweaking cannot move a man far along a path he does not wish to tread. Havel succumbed because he is a coward and afeared of his sins."

"Then why are you so hard on the brancher? He has completed his handler's work magnificently. Vranov has made war on his own king, is now seen to be in league with the devil, and is trapped in a stolen castle with his would-be ally buried under a mountain of snow. You should be heaping praise on the boy."

Alojz straightened up, leering. He glanced at Wulf as if expecting approval, and promptly shriveled again.

The pasha spat on the floor. "If you think he is so good, you jess him. Let us discuss Magnus's cold-blooded destruction of the Pomeranians."

"By Our Lady, I am surprised to hear a member of the sultan's army worry about bloodshed," Lady Umbral said. "That was a brilliant application of talent, with a tiny effort producing great results. Clearly the powder wagons were ignited by lightning and the explosion brought down an avalanche. It has been accepted all over Christendom as an act of God."

"But not all over Islam. Not in Pomerania. And not by the Agioi. It was trespass!"

"*It was not!*" The shout came from Madlenka. "Those lands belonged to my father . . . er, my . . . to the count of Cardice! It was the Pomeranians trespassing, not Wulf!"

"Lady Magnus is correct, Pasha," Umbral said. "Occupation is not ownership. There had been no surrender or peace treaty. Is there anything more to discuss?"

"Certainly!" The janissary pointed a hairy finger at Wulf. "He murdered Vilhelmas!"

"Sir Wulfgang," said Umbral, "advance to the center."

Wulf strolled to the middle of the room and stepped up onto the dais, where he bowed to Umbral, then turned to bow to the pasha. Madlenka noted admiringly how handsome and brave he seemed, completely calm, and very unlike the cringing Alojz who had stood there a few minutes ago.

"Your brother pulled the trigger to kill the priest," the Turk said. "That was cold-blooded murder!"

Wulf shook his head. "With respect, Pasha, it was justice. Two days previously, that same priest had led an attack on that same building and slaughtered the garrison, offering no preliminary challenge or quarter. The post belonged to my king and my brother the count, who gave us permission to perform the execution. As lord of the march and lord of high justice, he had the legal authority to so."

"You were seen by workadays! That was a violation of the first commandment."

"Marek was seen, true. But less than an hour earlier, Vilhelmas had created a major display of talent in the hall of the keep at Gallant. He tore up the rules first!"

Madlenka heard a few quiet murmurs of amusement and approval behind her.

But Wulf had not finished. "I am grateful to you for revealing his motivation, Pasha, because we have all been puzzled by it. Now that we know that Vilhelmas was working for Wartislaw and not Vranov, it makes complete sense. Vranov lost his temper, which I daresay is not an unusual occurrence, and uttered curses, so then Vilhelmas made him vanish—in a puff of sulfurous smoke, I expect. He was instantly branded an agent of Satan, until Brancher Alojz tweaked the bishops the next day and undid all that good evil, er, I mean good work." He bowed again.

The Turk showed his teeth in a snarl. "Then let us discuss the bloodbath in the Ruzena gorge and the death of Duke Wartislaw. You blew up their powder wagons and slaughtered thousands of innocent men!"

"Do you have eyewitnesses that saw me do this terrible thing?"

"I have witnesses who heard you claiming to have done it!"

"But I am such a liar!" Wulf said sadly.

This time there was open laughter at the way this newly fledged falcon was defying the dreaded hand of the Agioi. The Turk flushed with rage.

"You may withdraw, Sir Wulfgang," Lady Umbral said sharply. "Unless Sokullu Pasha has more questions. Pasha, we have discussed the charges. Shall we ask the jury to find a verdict?"

"May the Giver of Wisdom guide their deliberations."

The six people in the front row joined hands. Led by the monk, they stepped away in a daisy chain and, one by one, vanished into the air. The room erupted in a babble of many tongues.

CHAPTER 46

After the jury left, Lady Umbral beckoned Madlenka. Taking a firmer grip on her husband's strong hand, Madlenka led him forward. She had not expected to find herself treated as the senior partner, but he seemed to accept that strange situation quite happily. He flashed a smile at her and they halted together at the edge of the dais. Madlenka curtseyed; he bowed. Even at close quarters, Umbral's face remained bizarrely indistinct and unfocused.

"I congratulate you both on your so-recent marriage," she said. "And you on your choice of husband, my lady. I know of no falcon ever achieving so much so soon. If you wish to join the Saints, we shall be most glad to welcome you both."

Madlenka glanced at Wulf; he nodded.

She said, "We are honored, my lady. We have much to learn."

"We shall see that you are instructed. Meanwhile, I am confident that the judges will support our case. Despite that ferocious leer the pasha is wearing, he knows that he is about to lose."

They all looked at Mudar Sokullu, who bared his teeth at Madlenka. "But if I win, woman, I will take you home as a gift for my imperial master."

He was joking, wasn't he?

"Over my dead body," Wulf said cheerfully.

"That is understood."

"We are agreed, though," Umbral said, "that the boy Leonas caused the deaths of your father and brother, and Sir Wulfgang's brother. Although he cannot understand how he has sinned, he is more dangerous than a mad dog and must be clipped. It is a brutal process, which will leave him with even fewer wits than he has now. Do either of you disagree?"

"No," Madlenka said sadly. "But then what will happen to him?"

"He is a pretty thing," the janissary said. "I will take him and sell him in the market in Constantinople."

Madlenka looked at Wulf and saw her own horror reflected in his face. "Is there no alternative?" she asked.

"I know a monastery that would take him in," Umbral said, "but he would almost certainly run away, and then he would likely starve. Slaves are fed."

Wulf said, "A dead Magnus should be revenged, but I cannot kill a half-wit boy, and the real criminal is his father. So I do not object."

"We will accept your judgment, my lady," Madlenka said.

"Very well. Take him, Pasha." Lady Umbral raised her voice slightly. "But give whatever you get for him to the poor! Now, what of that Alojz Zauber? He is not short of wits, but his ethics came out of the cesspool. He caused the death of Count Magnus, your former husband. Pronounce sentence, Madlenka."

Madlenka started to protest that Wulf had lost a brother and should get that dubious honor, but he frowned and nodded at her to speak. "Obviously the squire has talent," she said. "Could he be taught to behave himself, while securely bound to a better handler for, say, another year?"

"Probation?" Umbral murmured. "I believe there have been precedents."

Wulf said, "I am sure Justina will be very bored without her present brancher to keep her company."

A couple of eavesdroppers chuckled, but Madlenka did not think either of them was Justina.

Lady Umbral shrugged. "Will you accept probation, brancher, or would you prefer the traitor's death?"

Alojz fell on his knees and was still spewing out his thanks when a gate opened and the judges filed back into the room. The tallest of them, one of the bearded, turbaned Turks, announced their verdict: "We find for the Saints on all counts. Wartislaw was employing a hireling within Catholic territory and the Agioi should have stopped him. The use of talent to invade Castle Gallant was a second trespass, and the brancher obviously regarded himself as subject to the voivode's orders at that time. The Saints may claim compensation. The execution of Father Vilhelmas and destruction of Wartislaw's army were both extreme actions, but justified by the laws of war. No compensation is required."

Nobody cheered or applauded.

The pasha sighed. "The Utterly Just has spoken, but he will remember his children another day."

"Lady Madlenka, Sir Wulfgang," Lady Umbral said, "you may speak for the loss of Castle Gallant and the fate of Havel Vranov and his accomplices. You cannot ask for the return of the dead, but you may suggest any other penalty or compensation."

The castle was a military matter, and Madlenka was not going to meddle in that. "Falcon?" she asked quickly.

Wulf's face was grim. "Count Vranov is a traitor to his king and has treasonously slain my brother Anton and many others. I will attend to him myself."

"You will not," Umbral told him. "You may demand his death, but others will carry out the sentence. This must be justice, not revenge. Remember that he holds your remaining brothers hostage."

Wulf set his jaw defiantly for a moment. "I demand that Havel Vranov suffer a heart attack, and that he survive just long enough to make confession and receive absolution, no more than one hour. His son, Sir Marijus, was obviously an accomplice in his crimes, but if he will at once withdraw his forces and return to Pelrelm, handing over Castle Gallant to my brother Sir Vladislav, then I will see that he receives a royal pardon."

The listeners muttered.

Umbral laughed. "You can guarantee such a pardon, Sir Wulfgang?"

"Yes, I can. If Marijus refuses the offer, then I demand his death also."

Madlenka had married a warrior and must expect him to think like one. She would not argue. But she remembered how Radomir had died while she held his hand. "And we want compensation for all the widows and orphans in Gallant, not just victims of Vranov's attack, but the Wends' assault, too."

"Indeed?" Lady Umbral seemed surprised at such a notion. "About a thousand florins?" She ignored a loud gabble of Turkish from the janissary. "Does any member of the jury consider these penalties excessive?"

None of the six spoke.

"Very well. Pasha, take the boy Leonas and deliver a thousand sequins to Lady Magnus by tomorrow noon. Vranov must be dead by then, and his army must be back home in Woda within a week. That concludes our business."

The janissary sprang nimbly to his feet. "For today, yes. But there will be many tomorrows." He was looking at Wulf as he said it.

Mine Host Oldrich looked around from a heated argument with his wife as the front door of the Bacchus opened to admit Sir Wulfgang Magnus with a striking young lady on his arm. A glance at Lady Magnus's clean gown told him that she must have arrived by coach, although he had not heard one draw up. He bowed low, greeted the guests, and presented his wife.

"Our luggage has been delayed," Sir Wulfgang announced. "I believe we could use a supper, a fairly substantial supper. Right, my dear? What is on the table tonight?"

"Roast boar, honored sir? And partridge pie. Well hung, very delicious. Ham, trout, a fine selection of cheeses."

The prince's latest favorite glanced at his companion and received a smile of acceptance. "That will be excellent. Send up a couple of flagons of your very best wine, right away, and the food as soon as possible. After that, we are not to be disturbed, even if King Konrad himself arrives at the head of the Royal Hussars, understand?"

"Indeed, I do, sir. A linkboy . . ."

"Just give me that lantern and we'll light our own way," young Magnus said, with the impatience of youth.

Oldrich obeyed. "The wine will be ready in an instant!" He sighed as he watched the couple trotting up the stairs, being rewarded for his attention by a glimpse of Lady Magnus's divine ankles. Some men were just born lucky.

"I thought we had to sup with the prince tonight?" Madlenka said as Wulf escorted her along the corridor.

"Plans have changed. Cabbage Head had a harrowing interview with Cardinal Zdenek today. As a result, he has already drunk himself into oblivion. His cronies put him to bed. You will have to wait until tomorrow for the joy of being presented to His Highness, but then the sight of your beauty will at once cure his hangover and arouse him to avid anticipation of reunion with his darling wife, a lustful eagerness second only to my own present state."

"Your fingers are trembling."

"I may need some guidance." He unlocked the door of the Horse Room.

Madlenka went in. "And Otto will be the next count of Cardice, I suppose? He is the eldest."

"Vlad," Wulf said. "Otto won't want it, and no one can do a better job of modernizing Gallant's defenses than Vlad."

"Can you really arrange things like that?"

He closed the door and turned to face her. For a moment the shifting lamplight seemed to shine through a crack in his façade of wedding-night joy and excitement to illuminate the dread inside. "I must!" he said. "It is my duty, plain and simple. For three hundred years the Magnuses of Dobkov have served the House of Jorgar without cavil or stint, and more than half its sons have died in that cause. My service will be different, but to be true to my ancestors, I must do my utmost to keep King Krystof on his throne as long as I have breath in my body. You won't," he added with sudden alarm, "forbid me this, will you, my darling cadger?"

"Of course not," she said. "My family has held the northern gate of the kingdom for even longer, and many a Bukovany has fallen defending it. We'll serve together." Then she couldn't resist adding, "And God save the king!"

Wulf exploded in laughter and pulled her into an embrace.

HISTORICAL NOTE

The corruption in the Church in the Early Renaissance is well documented and was no secret at the time. As an example, Pope Sixtus IV was deeply involved in the "Pazzi Conspiracy," a plot to murder two leading Florentines, Lorenzo ("the Magnificent") de' Medici and his brother Giuliano, planning to replace them with Girolamo Riario, one of his own nephews. The two de' Medici were assaulted in front of the altar of the cathedral during Mass. Lorenzo was wounded, but escaped; his brother died. Sixtus also established the Spanish Inquisition and confirmed the notorious Tomás de Torquemada as its grand inquisitor. He was one of the bad popes. Some of his successors were even worse, and yet it was almost fifty years before Martin Luther launched the Reformation.

GLOSSARY

AGIOI: A guild of Speakers loyal to the Orthodox Church and the Porte. See voivode.

BRANCHER: In falconry, a bird that has left the nest but cannot yet fly; to the Saints, an apprentice Speaker. See *handler*.

CADGER: In falconry, a man who carries birds to the field, in cages or on perches; to the Saints, a workaday who manages one or more falcons.

CLIENT: A workaday who has contracted with a cadger for the services of a falcon.

FALCON: Normally birds of prey used for hunting; a Speaker sworn to a cadger.

FIRST COMMANDMENT: A rule recognized by all Speakers, that talent must be exercised in secret.

FLEDGED: Of birds, having adult plumage; of Speakers, adult, with stable and reliable talent.

HAGGARD: In falconry, a bird taken from the wild as an adult and thus untrained; to the Saints, a self-taught Speaker.

HANDLER: In falconry, a general term for people who work with birds; to the Saints, a brancher's trainer.

HIRELING: A falcon under contract to a client.

JESS (verb): In falconry, to fasten tethers (jesses) on a bird's legs; to the Saints, to bind a Speaker to a cadger by oath.

LOOK (verb): To see through the eyes of other people.

PORTE: The court of the Ottoman sultan in Constantinople.

SPEAKER: In popular usage, a person who can ask the devil to perform magic, a witch; to Speakers themselves, a person with talent.

TALENT: The ability to perform miracles.

TWEAK (verb): To use talent to change a workaday's thinking.

VOIVODE, THE: Leader of the Agioi.

VOICES: Supernatural voices commonly heard by branchers but not by fledged Speakers.

WENDS: People of Slavic descent living in what is now eastern Germany.

WORKADAY: A person without talent.

WISE, THE: A (restricted) group of people who know the truth about Speakers.